Paladins

An Anthology

A Collection of hard-hitting fiction

Featuring

Keith Nixon

Bill Baber

Darren Sant

Cal Marcius

Robert Cowan

Gareth Spark

Graham Wynd

David Jaggers

Jason Beech

Aidan Thorn

Ryan Bracha

Linda Angel

Craig Furchtenicht

Matt Mattila

Christopher Davis

Gabriel Valjan

Copyright © 2016 by Near To The Knuckle

Printed in the United Kingdom

Cover Design by Mark Wilson
Formatting and Design by Craig Douglas
Editing by Aidan Thorn

First Printing, 2016

ISBN 978-1-53014-344-3

Near To The Knuckle
Rugby
Warwickshire, CV22

www.close2thebone.co.uk

Foreword

I have come to realize that heroes often grace our lives when we least expect them, sometimes in the form of complete strangers. The authors of the stories you are about to read are a perfect example of that. Social media has the amazing ability to bring our worlds closer, to offer us the chance to meet those people we would have otherwise never known. We share our shining moments with them along with our darkest days. Eventually the world in which we all live in seems a little less foreign and a whole lot more inviting. We find that no one is truly a stranger and that the heroes have been there all along.

A few years ago I would have never imagined myself writing these words on the night before Christmas 2015. When my oncologist first diagnosed me with Multiple Myeloma in June of 2012 he only gave me 6 months to live. I was already in the last stage of this rare form of blood cancer that attacks the plasma cells found in the bone marrow. At the time of my diagnosis I had seven broken ribs on my left side. He told me that there was no cure for my type of cancer. We could only treat it to the point of remission with high doses of chemotherapy and stem cell transplants. This is when I was first introduced to Dr. Guido Tricot, the finest oncologist that Belgium has ever produced. He has kept me alive, though at times I thought he was trying to kill me in the process.

My husband Craig and I are so fortunate to live very close to the University of Iowa Hospitals and Clinics. In the first year we easily spent more time in that place than we did at home. I underwent two stem cell transplants each consisting of 3 ½ weeks of being quarantined in a hospital unit with nothing but Craig and a puke bucket. Neither of them left my side during the entire ordeal. During the hours that I was in a self-induced trance Craig wrote to keep his sanity. By the end of the second transplant he had finished his first novel. Months later I found it hidden away in a desk drawer. After a bit of wifely persuasion he reluctantly published it.

Because of that book, through one social media site or another, we have both become friends with each of the contributors of this anthology. Fighting cancer was not how I wanted to meet any of these amazing people, but whether they knew it or not they gave me encouragement I needed from a world away. They kept me going when it would have been so much easier to just give up. I saw Ryan and Rebecca Bracha bring their beautiful daughter Delilah into the world, went to Borneo with Robert Cowan and got to wish Aidan Thorn's father a happy birthday. Darren Sant told me what an oatcake was. I saw Matt Mattila go to California, admired Katrina Tia Davies in her wedding dress and watched Keith Nixon move his family across country. I've seen a little girl paint her dad's fingernails and his son holding a "Refugees Welcome" sign in his little red boots. Each one of these writers and so many others have given me the strength and hope that the cancer has tried to take away.

I have read many of the stories written by these authors, including my husband's. Though they are dark and gritty and downright unwholesome, I must laugh when I get over the shock of reading them. I know for a fact that each of them truly has a heart of gold. When Aidan Thorn approached us with the idea of putting a book together to help support the Multiple Myeloma Research Foundation, words could not begin to describe how blessed I felt. So much love for these people that I thought my heart would burst. So enjoy the book and take comfort in knowing that the proceeds will go towards finding a cure someday.

Thank you all for giving me a love for life. Much love to each of you:

Linda Angel, Bill Baber, Jason Beech, Ryan Bracha, Robert Cowan, Christopher Davis, Craig Douglas, Craig Furchtenicht, David Jaggers, Cal Marcius, Matt Mattila, Keith Nixon, Darren Sant, Gareth Spark, Aidan Thorn, Gabriel Valjan, Mark Wilson, Graham Wynd.

Henrietta Furchtenicht
Christmas Eve, 2015

Acknowledgements

This collection wouldn't have been possible without the selfless hard work of a great many people.

My first thank you has to go to Henrietta Furchtenicht, the wonderful lady that inspired me to try and pull this thing together. I'm thankful to writing for so many things, the main one being the great people I get to meet, people like Henri. All of the profits from this book will go straight to the Multiple Myeloma Research Foundation **http://www.themmrf.org/** to support Henri and people like her.

Obviously I have to thank all of the authors, I'm not going to list them all again here. You're about to read their work. They're all good people, who donated a story for a great cause, do them a favour, seek out their work outside this anthology, leave them a review and tell other people about them – you won't be disappointed.

I have to thank the Near to the Knuckle boys. Darren Sant for doing the edit on my story, Strangers in Vegas (I could hardly do my own!) and Craig Douglas who volunteered his time to get this book formatted – a thankless task that comes with little glory, but a hugely important one that I'll be forever grateful to Craig for.

Thanks also to Mark Wilson. Mark is a top author who was unable to contribute a story to this collection, however he's very much part of the team. The book is called Paladins, Mark came up with the name. Mark is also the designer of the incredible cover artwork for this collection – a striking image that I'm so impressed with I'm getting it tattooed onto my body at some point.

Finally, thank you for reading and not only supporting the Multiple Myeloma Research Foundation but also for supporting independent fiction

Aidan Thorn

Paladins

The Paladin is a class of Warrior that is fully devoted to kindness and ridding the Universe of Evil. In combat, a Paladin with a cause is almost impossible to defeat.

Paladins fear nothing, for Evil fears them.

Proceeds from this book will be donated to the Multiple Myeloma Research Foundation

http://www.themmrf.org

Contents

Heir To The Throne

By Keith Nixon

Dedication:*To Grandma Joan, always thinking of you.*

5am, Sunday

The sun pushed over the horizon like a drunk hitching his trousers. Slow. Persistent. Inevitable. The yellow orb's grip was scrawny, the rays insubstantial at this hour. Was it only a day since she went missing?

It felt like eternity.

In comparison the sea was a power. Bitterly cold, an embrace which was steadily sucking the life out of him. The waves caressed his legs, the tide receding as the sun's disc rose in an opposing yaw.

There was a benefit to the chill. Numbness. The pain from the beating dissipating as his blood coloured the waters.

Two pairs of boots stepped into view. He couldn't see above the ankles, his skull was too heavy. He knew who they were though. He'd evaded the twins longer than he'd thought possible. But it was over now. One pair of boots moved closer.

He didn't fight when a hand grabbed his jacket at the shoulders, didn't resist being yanked around. He hit the surf with a shallow splash. The water was only inches deep. It was enough. His mouth and nose were below the surface. The spume coursed through his nostrils, sucked down into his lungs. He coughed, which ultimately allowed more water to enter through his mouth and to where it shouldn't go.

Finally his body fought back, something inside refusing to accept death. He jerked upwards like a rising fish, dragged in a gutter of air.

A heavy foot between the shoulder blades quickly put paid to his resistance. The spark died and soon, so did the man. However, not before Turner remembered where it all went wrong.

The beginning…

5pm, Saturday

"Is this her?"

Detective Sergeant Guy Gregory peeled back the white sheet to reveal an even paler corpse. The body was naked, featureless. Utterly sexless despite the large breasts on full view. Not even a raw autopsy scar from sternum to stomach to add depth and colour.

The room was cold. Gregory's breath fogged as he waited under the tungsten lamps. Their hum filled the space. The other was an out of towner. Northern, by his accent. Short, wiry, gnarled. Booze washed off his breath. Gregory would have guessed very tough, except for the apparent tear in his blue eyes, the jaw clenched in a seeming fear of the unknown. Gregory had seen it all before. Death and its effects.

"Mr Turner?" said Gregory as a prompt. He had to repeat himself, with more force, to get Turner's attention. He felt tired himself. Old before his time. Hairline on the wane. Shopping sized bags under his eyes. Burning the candle solidly at one end. "Sir, is this her? Is this your wife?"

"No, no it isn't." And with Turner's utterance the dread visibly twisted into relief. He sagged, put a hand onto the gurney for support. "Thank God."

Gregory didn't think Turner the religious type. Then again, we'll have faith in any corporeal savior in times of strife.

"Are you all right?"

"I'm fine. Nothing a beer wouldn't sort." Turner affected a weak grin at his weaker joke.

"Okay, we're done," said Gregory.

The mortuary assistant, who'd been hovering in the background like a bad smell, drifted forwards. He pushed at the footboard. The reclining deceased slid silently into the wall space and away from view to rest among the other bodies patiently awaiting postmortem, identification and interment.

Neither man spoke until they were in the corridor. The beige walls were oddly comforting, the muted hue shockingly bright after such an absence of warmth.

Turner hunted down a cigarette packet, made to put the stick in his mouth before Gregory reminded him of the smoking ban. Turner uttered some acerbic comment about do-gooders, but relented anyway.

"What's next?" he asked.

"We keep looking," said Gregory. "Do you have any idea where she might have gone?"

"None. Look, as I said, we were only passing through – this morning's ferry brought us in from Belgium after a few days away in Bruges. She went to the bathroom just before we docked in Ramsgate, never came back. We searched the ship… Nothing." Turner's recollection faded away. He hunched both shoulders, arms out, palms up in a visual query. "Maybe she fell overboard?"

It was a reasonable assumption and why Gregory had shown Turner the corpse. A woman, found in the brine. Although it was summer the muddy North Sea wasn't particularly balmy. It didn't take long for people to get into trouble when out of their depth. For the chill to seep into their muscles. For their consciousness to falter.

"I'll call if we find anything."

"If?"

Gregory didn't answer Turner. How could he?

6pm

Something sounded anomalous, out of place. Konstantin Boryakov paused, cocked an ear, fists poised. The punch bag rocked, momentarily relieved of the pounding it was absorbing.

There it was again. An uneven beat. Recognised now for what it mean. Bad news. Always did. Konstantin thumped the bag once more, just in case the canvas was getting too comfortable. Then went to find out what trouble was coming his way.

Again.

"It's you," said Konstantin when he opened the front door. He dropped the Russian accent, kept to Queen's English. Gregory wasn't aware of Konstantin's true nature and that was how it would stay.

Gregory was leaning nonchalantly against the wall. Konstantin's accommodation was a row of seemingly derelict houses. Like him, everything was on the inside. The cop pointed at Konstantin's thinly bandaged hands. "Cut yourself?"

"No." Konstantin didn't use gloves when he trained. What was the point? He wouldn't be wearing padding in a fight. The skin had to be durable, rough. Shorts and a sweat stained white t-shirt completed the Russian's attire.

"Can I come in?"

"Why?"

"I need your help."

"So?"

"A woman is missing."

"Someone is always missing."

"I'll buy you a beer. If you still say no, I'll walk away."

Gregory knew him too well. Worrying.

"Make it a vodka and I'll listen."

"Done."

"No guarantees."

"Never are."

"I need to change. Wait." He closed the door on the copper.

6.20pm

"Here?" asked Gregory.

A quick nod from Konstantin. "My local."

The pub was called The English Flag, a melting pot of fervent anglophiles and sociopaths, loners and losers on the edge of the Old Town. Down at heel, even for Margate. It was a place where you could always get a drink, where the regulars kept to themselves, unless there was a fight underway. Then everyone was fair game. Or an outsider intruded and a temporary alliance was formed. Mob mentality ruled. Konstantin liked it.

"They'll spot me from a mile away."

"You'll be fine."

"Can we go somewhere else?"

"It's here, or nowhere."

Gregory hesitated still. "If I wind up dead, tell my girlfriend I love her."

"I don't know your girlfriend."

"Neither do I. Still waiting for the right one."

Inside was a faded glory. Rutted carpet. Tacky tables. Wobbly chairs. A slot machine with half the lights out. Morose regulars. In contrast a huge, pristine George Cross flag affixed to the wall behind the bar. The only fixture that really mattered.

Richard was the landlord. A man with ant sized aspirations. Dick to his antagonists (which was everyone) because he was.

"You're back," said Dick. Leant on the faded surface of the bar which might once have been wood. Fatal mistake. Like touching fly paper. The hairs on Dick's arm would peel away nicely when he reversed his position.

"Obviously," said Konstantin.

"Who's the bacon?" Dick nudged his chin at Gregory who was attempting to appear stalwart under the onslaught of suspicious and shrewd stares.

"With me. And that's all you need to know." The Russian met everyone's eye. None looked away. None argued either. "My usual. Lager for him."

"I don't like lager," mumbled Gregory.

"You do now. Whine anymore and you'll get lime too."

The alternative was Dick's home brew bitter. Its noxious properties provided the local hospital, and occasionally the mortuary, with a periodic stream of patients.

Dick stood. Winced as the predicted waxing process occurred on his forearms. Stoic wasn't his middle name. He pulled two pints, meted out a miserly vodka shot.

"Make it a double," said Konstantin. "He's paying." Threw a thumb at the luckless Gregory. He took a table as far from anyone as possible. Everything had ears here. Sat back and watched the negotiation unfold.

"Do you take Visa?" asked Gregory.

Dick paused, tumbler in mid-air, suspended in disbelief. "What's that?"

"Stupid question?"

"Understatement of the year. Look son, this is a proper pub. No women. No jukebox. No credit. No crisps. Just nuts, pork scratchings, good beer and shit company."

A couple of the regulars diverted their attention from

morose contemplation, disbelief at Dick's final two points – one true, the other not. Though nothing was said in response. Conversation was a rarity in The English Flag.

"Right," said Gregory. "One minute." He left Dick, arms folded, at the bar. Crossed over to Konstantin. "Have you got any cash?"

The Russian had a folded tenner already between his fingers. Figured this was coming. Handed it over.

"Thanks."

Gregory procured the booze and the shrapnel, carried everything over, walking as if Konstantin would punch him should the glasses end up on the floor. Which was remarkably astute.

The vodka lasted less than a second. Half the lager tripped along on its heels. Gregory observed in amazement.

"I need the calories," explained Konstantin.

"Oh-kay."

Silence reigned for the remaining semi of alcohol. Konstantin pointed his empty at Gregory's partial, said, "Another?"

"I'm all right, thanks." Mimed driving.

A minute later Konstantin sat with two pints.

"I said I didn't want another," said Gregory.

"They're not for you."

"Oh."

"You mentioned help."

"Yes, well, strictly it's not for me. A member of the public, Philip Turner. His wife disappeared this morning."

"Go on."

So Gregory did. When he was done Konstantin sat back, nursed his urine coloured nectar in contemplation.

"Why me?"

"Something's not right about his story."

"Same question."

"Look, there's places you can go, people you can speak to that I just can't. I checked the guy out with the ferry company. He did travel over on it, with a woman apparently his other half. Both passports seem above board. However, there's a couple of problems.

"The mobile number Turner gave me doesn't work and he's not registered at the hotel he claims to have been staying at. The car belongs to a company, not him. Seemingly it doesn't exist either. Nothing on the internet, nothing at Companies House."

"So a man reports a missing person, then provides false details?"

"Half right. He didn't call it in, that was the ferry operator. And that's not all. Turner went out on his own. Came back with her."

With two fingers Gregory pushed over an image of the missing woman. A copy of the passport photograph. The poor quality scan couldn't hide her drabness. Not much of a looker. Plain, if truth be told. Downturned mouth, an ugly glint to her eye.

"Claire Turner. Although I can't find anything out about her either."

An image of the husband followed, pushed across the table by Gregory's stubby fingers. Konstantin didn't see the man's face, he was staring at the woman. Gregory was wittering away, still attempting inducement, but the Russian wasn't receiving anymore.

Konstantin had spent most of a lifetime in one conflict or another, always at someone else's behest. Margate (of all places) was supposed to be a fresh start. Away from intrigue. Far from it. Since arriving he'd attracted strife like virulent disease to a rampant hooker.

"Yes," said Konstantin.

A frown marred Gregory's forehead. "I hadn't finished

trying to persuade you."

"Well done. The woman's surname is Pigeon. She used to live around here."

"I'll check her out."

"Stay in touch."

6.55pm

It was too early to be open. Not yet properly night. Peak time was about three hours away, marked by the sun plunging beneath the horizon. Then they'd be out. The shambling drinkers, the jerking dancers, the drug dealers peddling to both.

The club itself was well off the beaten track. A dead end, a constricted lane off a narrow road. The entrance was a locked black door recessed a few feet. No sign above.

Konstantin's pounding fist echoed within. An unblinking CCTV lens camera stared down at him. He responded in kind.

It took a full minute for Ken, the club's owner, to open up. He blinked momentarily in the sudden light, threw the door wide in an unspoken invitation and stepped back into the gloom. Konstantin manhandled the door shut, followed the pale, short man with too many tattoos deeper within.

"Want a drink?" said Ken over his shoulder. His tone spoke of cigarettes and hard nights.

"Sure."

A whisky bottle and a couple of tumblers in hand, Ken took a chair at the nearest table. As Konstantin sat a peaty malt wet a good inch of the glass.

The club was neat at this time of day. Usually it looked like a tornado had cut through its centre and relocated glasses and booze from the bar to every conceivable flat surface. The cleaners turned up each morning to restore some sort of order to the interior, ready for the whole process to occur all over again less than twenty four hours later. Must be soul destroying.

"Ice?"

"No, you heathen."

"Haven't seen you around for a while."

"There wasn't a reason to be around."

"Until now?"

Konstantin held out the picture of the woman, Pigeon. Couldn't think of her as Turner. "Look familiar?"

"No. Should she?"

"Not necessarily."

"But you do."

"Yes. She's missing. I thought you could put some feelers out."

"What do you know about her?"

"Not much. She used to live around here. Been gone a while."

Ken swirled the whisky, contemplated the liquid's legs as in an apparent alcoholic equivalent of reading tealeaves. "Not very helpful."

"You're a big boy. I thought your connections may be able to help."

The nightclub owner had a shady background, one Konstantin didn't fully comprehend. He didn't need to. Grey was more than enough for him. All the booze Ken sold came from overseas, so did the cigarettes, smuggled in. He knew everyone the average man on the street would be seen dead with. And that's what Konstantin was relying on.

"This guy's her husband, apparently."

A blow up of Turner passed to Ken who raised his eyebrow at Konstantin's final word.

"Don't know him either," said Ken.

Another couple of generous whisky slugs hit the backs

of their throats while contemplation took centre stage. Eventually Ken spoke. "All I can suggest is asking around."

"That'll do for me. I'd better get going. Call me if anything turns up."

"Sure. I'll see you out."

When Ken opened the door a man was standing on the threshold, his knuckles poised. Turner.

He said, "I understand you can find people."

"Where did you hear that?" asked Ken.

"Who's he?" Turner drooped an eye over Konstantin who returned the favour. Noted the toughness evident in the shorter man's stance, but also the anxiety. It dripped off Turner like a cold sweat.

"A friend," said Ken. "And I asked you a question."

"I made enquiries. Your name kept coming up."

"Lucky me. Unfortunately you were steered wrong."

"I can pay."

"Makes no difference."

"What does?"

"Whether I like you or not."

"Who are you looking for?" asked Konstantin.

"My wife. She's missing. And pregnant."

Konstantin looked at Ken. That was a game changer.

"You'd better come in."

7.15pm

The chair had barely cooled before Konstantin parked his arse again. Ken poured more whisky, none for Turner. The man eyed the alcohol, licked his lips. Maybe he was a drinker, Konstantin considered.

"This is her." Turner passed over his phone. A quick snap of the woman. Not well framed. Definitely Pigeon.

"How long have you been married?" asked Konstantin.

"Why is that relevant?"

"I'm interested."

"Just a few months."

"Where do you live?"

"Up north," said Turner, making it sound as if it was a foreign country, which maybe it was. "Look, we're wasting time here. Can you help or not?"

"Ten grand," said Ken.

Konstantin swore Turner's eyes poked out of his head on stalks then.

"What?"

"Up front."

"I thought you said money makes no difference?"

"No, I said what matters is whether I like you or not. And I don't. Something smells about all of this."

Turner looked like he was going to collapse into a heap. Eventually he said, "Can I get a dram?"

"Sure." Ken took a fresh glass from the bar, dabbed at an optic. One of his imported grains.

"Make it a double."

Turner grabbed the tumbler with both hands, poured the booze down his throat, wiped his mouth with the back of a hairy hand.

"Okay," he said. "Okay. She's not really my wife."

"Go on," said Ken, prompting Turner who seemingly wished to say no more.

"She's having my boss's baby, the heir to his empire. If I don't bring her back, I'm a dead man."

"Who's your boss?" asked Konstantin.

"You won't know them."

"Try me."

"The Stanleys."

"I'm more than familiar with the twins." The memory of their stand-off with the pair, right here in the club, came to mind. When they were seeking a friend of Konstantin's. They ran an empire in a North Eastern industrial town, somewhere near Middlesbrough, wherever that was. Styled themselves on the Krays.

As kids they'd run errands for dealers, learnt the trade at the sharp end. By the time they were teenagers they ran the school. Beat up anyone who got in their way, teachers and pupils alike. Sold drugs, sold girls and boys, traded information. You name it, they were into it.

They were about as non-identical as twins could get. As if they had different fathers, created from different sperm. Which was entirely possible, given their mother was rather a prolific prostitute at the time. One kid had stupidly pointed out this possibility. Which happened to be the last time he spoke. Lost his tongue, rather carelessly. The culprits were never caught, although it was rumoured the muscle was kept in a jar of formaldehyde (stolen from the school labs) in a twin's bedrooms. Nobody knew which one.

Which led to another peculiarity. No one used or could remember the twins' Christian names. Their mother certainly didn't. Too off her face on a cocktail of class A's. No-one asked and they didn't tell.

"High gradenutters," said Ken, seemingly echoing Konstantin's thoughts. "I want nothing to do with them or this."

"They'll come looking for her," said Turner. "Tear the town apart if they have to."

A chirruping phone interrupted the evocations of a small-scale war. "Me," said Konstantin. It was Gregory.

"I've found her," he said.

A nail bitten thumb ended the call. Two pairs of eyes stared at Konstantin, loaded with expectation.

"I've got a lead," he said.

"What?" asked Turner.

"One I'll follow up."

"I'm coming with you."

"No." Konstantin rose, towered over Turner, who appeared out of his depth, a drowning man. "Call here on the hour, every hour."

"Okay."

"I assume that means you're paying the ten grand, then?" said Ken.

Konstantin left them to their negotiations.

7.30pm

In truth, Gregory hadn't really found Pigeon. He'd tracked down an address for her parents. They were deceased, the mother only a few weeks ago.

"Probably a dead end," he'd said, seemingly oblivious to the pun.

"I'll check it out," replied Konstantin. Pigeon could be using the house as a base. He began the hike home. While walking one question he'd failed to ask Turner bubbled up in his mind. Why was the pair in Europe?

A kick of the pedal jerked the Bullet into life. The motorbike's engine warbled, the revs deeper than would be expected, a larger engine under the cowl than it was originally designed with. Hidden depths.

The Bullet cleared the handful of miles between Margate and more genteel Broadstairs in a matter of minutes. The house was on the Western Esplanade, a sea view out to the front. Prime position. Konstantin left the Bullet a street away, walked round the corner. The windows were dark, curtains drawn across them and an estate agent sign loomed over the narrow front garden. It said 'Sold'.

A protesting creak marked the gate's breaching. Konstantin rapped his knuckles on the front door. Of course, it wasn't answered. He glanced up and down the street. Nobody in sight.

Another gate blocked the side alley off from access. Although he hadn't seen a burglar alarm on the wall, Konstantin waited a few seconds after dealing with the simple lock, ear cocked for the bleeping of a tripped contact or running feet.

Nothing.

He headed inside, soles light on the parquet floor.

The search didn't take long because there wasn't much to go through. It looked like the place had been ransacked, heaps of junk everywhere, rooms largely empty. The kitchen and bathroom both showed their age, better days long past. He guessed a partial clearance before the new owners moved in, started a new life between old walls that had seen plenty of people come and go.

In the living room Konstantin riffled his fingers through a sheaf of paperwork. Fuel and water bills, financial statements and tax returns. Old Christmas and birthday cards, letters and some newspaper articles on books to read and walking routes to take. The flotsam and jetsam of an ordinary life.

One document caught Konstantin's eye. It was a rental agreement. For a facility a stone's throw away from the house. A long shot, but something to go on. He locked up and left.

There was still no one on the street.

7.45pm

Above Konstantin's head a gull wheeled, using the thermals from the chalk precipice to glide. He kept a good eye on it as the rats with wings had a tendency to crap all over anything and everything in sight.

After a descent down a switchback road opposite the deceased Pigeon's abode Konstantin reached the esplanade which ran from the main tourist beach east and west to the lesser sands.

The esplanade was a long, cast concrete slab which protected the soft cliff material from the forces of the sea. It was also a convenient location to place beach huts. They were basically glorified sheds in Konstantin's opinion. The British loved them, though.

Even at this time of the evening plenty were still occupied. Doors flung open to reveal twee interiors, one even containing a Welsh dresser and candelabra. Kids played on the beach, men drank beer, women chatted. Konstantin paused for a moment, took in the view. Rolling waves, a couple of sailboats cutting through and beyond the distance marred by a plethora of wind turbines.

Konstantin calculated that number thirty-three would be at the extremity of Stone Bay, popular with the locals, rarely frequented by tourists. He shambled along, hoped he appeared to be a one of the former just out for a walk. Which he sort of was.

It seemed he was in luck. The hut rented by the Pigeons had its doors flung back also, a deck chair in front unoccupied, the brightly coloured material flapping in the light sea breeze.

A female stepped out, a cup in her hand. There was steam rising from it. She was heavily pregnant, the lump protruding an unfeasible distance in front sufficient proof. She carefully eased herself into the deck chair, kept the hot drink at arm's length while she did do.

As she took a sip her eyes fell on Konstantin. She froze, like a doe in a car's bright headlights. But with that stomach she wasn't going anywhere fast.

"Kettle's just boiled," said Claire Pigeon.

8.05pm

The coffee was good. Produced via a French press. No milk, but that was Konstantin's preference.

"How did you find me?" asked Claire.

"It wasn't difficult."

A look of fear flittered across her face, quickly replaced by lassitude. "I'm tired of running."

A sleeping bag attested to the fact that this was where Claire slept. It couldn't have been comfortable, even with the sofa cushions between her body and the rough sawn wood floor.

"Or are you here to take me to him?" she asked.

"Not necessarily."

"That's comforting."

Claire looked to have aged since the last time Konstantin had laid eyes on her and more than with the simple passage of time. Some of the rough edges appeared to have been knocked off also. More quietly spoken, less aggressive, fewer demands. Maybe it was the imminent motherhood.

"What have you been told?" said Claire.

"Not much," said Konstantin, then elaborated, repeating Turner's comments.

Her laugh was loud, short and ironic. "That's half true."

"What half?"

"The bit about me being pregnant by the Stanleys."

"Both of them?"

"I'm not sure which. Kind of their thing, you know?"

"Not really."

"I'm their surrogate."

"Okay."

"Fucking awful is a better way of putting it."

"Why?"

"Same as always, money. I had none and needed some. After, you know, the other stuff, I had nothing. No skills, no options and no work. Even my mother disowned me. It got so bad I even considered going on the game, but who'd pay for this face?"

"There are some strange people out there. I'm sure somebody would have."

Claire glared at him. "It was supposed to be a joke."

"Oh. Sorry."

"Whatever. I'd read about surrogacy and a friend of mine, about the only one I had left, put me onto a few websites. One advert stuck out. It said, money no object. I answered, went up north to meet the father, well, fathers. The choice between ginger or tanned. However they seemed nice, the fee was massive and the rest is history, as they say."

"The Stanleys."

"Yes. I had no idea who they were then."

"How did you end up in Belgium?"

"Once I was up the duff with a boy, I won't go into the details as to how, the Stanleys turned nasty. I was basically held in a fur-lined cell. All they cared about was their heir. I was just a vessel to them. But it wasn't just them. I changed too. This baby, he's *mine*.

"I saw how those two behaved, what they did to people. It was obvious what my son would be moulded into. So to cut a long story short I ran. I reached Brussels before

Turner caught up with me. He was bringing me back to them. He got pissed on the ferry and I managed to hide in a camper van and disembarked before he woke up and realised I was gone."

Which explained Turner's fear. He'd go from superstar to dead duck once the Stanleys found out he'd blown it. Konstantin said as much.

"Very perceptive," said Claire. "Now you've found me, what are you going to do?"

In what appeared to be a developing habit, Konstantin's phone rang at a critical juncture.

"Where are you?" said Ken.

"Catching up with an old friend."

"Lucky you. Any news? Bloody Turner keeps calling."

"Where is he?"

"Out somewhere, looking for the woman."

"Okay, good." Konstantin told Ken his next steps. "Well, there's been another development," said Ken. "The Stanleys are on their way down."

"We need to get you somewhere safe," said Konstantin.

"Tell me something I don't know."

As Claire levered herself up Konstantin figured she'd have difficulty getting on the Bullet.

3am

"They'll be here soon I reckon," said Ken.

"How far is Middlesbrough?" asked Konstantin. A vodka was already waiting for him. He'd yet to go north of London. Hopefully, never would.

"About 300 miles, give or take. Could take them anywhere between five and fifteen hours, depending on the traffic. At this time of night? More like the former than the latter."

Konstantin checked his watch. The other variable was how much time the Stanleys spent on tooling up.

"Of course, it all depends on how much time the Stanleys spend tooling up," said Ken.

"I hadn't thought of that."

"Stick with me and you'll be all right." Ken even tapped the side of his nose.

"I'm lucky to have you."

"No arguments from me there."

The pub door swung back on its hinges. The exterior of the English Flag was the only building in the area lit up like a Christmas tree. Everywhere else was sensibly closed. There were still plenty of regulars at tables and ensconced Dick behind the bar.

Turner stepped inside. He glanced around, said, "Are they here yet?"

"Clearly not," said Ken.

"Is she?"

"No."

Turner's initial relief was slapped away by the calloused hand of dread.

"What do I tell them?"

"The truth."

It wasn't Ken or Konstantin who'd spoken the last words. Turner slowly rotated his head. The Stanleys were framed in the doorway. The one on the left was ginger, pasty and short. The one on the right was tall, perma-tanned and clearly a keep fit nut. A preener. The pair swept the room, heads rotating in opposite directions, seeing everything between them.

"What a dump," said the Preener.

"Where's my son?" said Ginger.

"Our son," corrected the other Stanley.

"Not here," said Konstantin.

"Must be the brain surgeon this one," said Ginger. He seemed to like the sound of his own voice.

"What can I get you?" asked Ken.

"The child, with or without the woman."

"I meant to drink."

"We're not here to socialise."

"I'll have a beer," said Turner. Caught the look on both the Stanleys faces. Mumbled, "If that's okay."

"The bitter's unique," said Konstantin. "And we're not going anywhere soon."

"Why?" asked Ginger.

"Because it's not time."

"For what?"

"You'll see."

"Go on then. A beer for me and the lush."

"Mineral water," said Preener.

Konstantin went to the bar. Placed the order. Dick appeared particularly pleased some out of towners were trying his special bitter. But he was thrown by the aquatic request.

"Water? I don't think anyone's requested that before."

"Have you got a tap?"

"Somewhere."

"That'll do. And when you're done, call Gregory." Konstantin handed over a slip of paper which Dick unfolded and glanced at.

"The cop?"

"Yes."

"Is there going to be trouble?"

"I don't know."

When Konstantin returned to the table with the drinks the Stanleys were seated. The group was stretched out in a long line, no one willing to put their back to the room. It would make talking interesting.

Turner sank a decent chunk of the bitter. "That's

good," he said.

"Where is it?" asked Ginger. "The baby."

"I told you to wait."

"That's not our style."

"It is now."

It took a while for Gregory to arrive. Utter silence reigned. Turner went through a couple of beers in between. When Gregory entered Ginger recognised him for who he was. Turned to Konstantin, said, "What is this?"

"He's friendly. Don't worry."

"We never worry."

Ken pushed out a stool for Gregory. He perched on the rickety furniture.

Gregory pulled a photo out of his inside pocket, unfolded it. "Is this her?"

The Stanleys bent over in unison. Took in the deathly pale face, the closed eyes, the plastered hair. Turner dropped his glass. It shattered on the floor. Nobody took any notice.

"Where?" said Ginger. His face was as white as Claire's.

"Hit and run in Ramsgate. Dead before the ambulance got to her."

Ginger turned to Turner, said, "You've fifteen minutes."

Turner was already half out of his seat. He completed the move and ran.

"Overly generous," said his brother once the door banged shut behind their ex-employee.

"I was lying," said Ginger and stood.

"I hate this place," said the Preener.

The Stanleys departed.

"Bye then," said Ken to thin air. He turned to Konstantin, asked, "What's next?"

"Claire can stay at my place for a couple of days. Then I'll put her on a train to somewhere."

"I'll be off. It's about closing time at the club."

Now it was just Gregory and Konstantin. How it had all started.

"Nice job with the make-up, she looked as pale as a ghost," said Konstantin.

"There's more to this face than meets the eye. Look, I'd better be off too. My shift starts in a couple of hours."

"Thanks," said Konstantin and held out a hand. Gregory took it and shook.

Konstantin sat alone for a few moments. It wasn't over for him, not yet. He had Claire and the baby to look after. He stepped into the night air.

Began the walk home.

Jabs And Uppercuts

By Jason Beech

Dedication: *I dedicate the story to my two grandmothers and my Uncle John, who all suffered through cancer. I don't know Henrietta, but her foreword brings out all her colour and personality as if I did. Here's to her complete recovery.*

Jim is in the mud and the trees, afloat amongst leaves which swirl like helicopters. His face is in the wheels of that car, his disappointed grin rotating like old vinyl, but with the needle stuck. All I, Fred, can hear are birds, wind, the snap of twigs beneath my feet. My breath could put wind in a boat's sails and launch it to the New World, but that's what happens when I don't run for a while. I never thought I'd lose the habit, but ... all I need is a little motivation.

But there's a young fella out on the jog, for crying out loud. For a moment, the blond tuft sat on his head like the horn of a unicorn makes me think he's Jim. He's headed towards me, all Lycra-ed up – his chicken legs an embarrassment. Not Jim, then. I expect this fella's name is Nigel. Whatever, as long as he doesn't engage me. Ah, for God's sake, he's pulling out an earbud. He'll say hello with one ear on some high energy music, one ear for the expected reply from me.

"Hey."

Hey? "Fuck off."

I don't look back as he runs beyond, but I know he'll have craned his neck in surprise. I feel a little ashamed, but these people have to learn to give me a wide berth. That man over there I think looks at me like my old man would at a black man with a white girl on his arm. That woman over there has the right idea. She clocks me. She looks away, quick, as if she wished she hadn't seen me at all.

I get back home before the sun pokes over the horizon, filtered through a fag-ash cloud as always. I rub at my hands, cracked in the cold, all milk-bottle white.

"Hiya."

For God's sake. Another soul out at this time – five-thirty in the morning. What is she thinking?

"Hi." I fiddle with my keys. I can see the one I want. It's distinct, with a cross as its head, but my fingers won't control it.

"We're a right pair, aren't we?"

I control my sigh better than the keys and stare across at her. My smile is as flat as my old car's tires after those little bastards let the air out. My bottom lip flops - a slug in rest above my chin. The skin around my eyes resists the effort to join in with the upper lip. I nod. I hope she realises I'm not made for small talk and communal laughter. She lives four doors down and now she leans against the brick by her front door, in her nightgown, a fag in the air as she holds her elbow. We're definitely not a right pair, but my celibacy has made me agree that her chest holds a right ... I furrow a ploughed field across my forehead to hide my embarrassment.

"Who gets up at this time of day, eh?"

Murderers and the socially inept, that's who. Or the new breed of gym-wanker. "Who knows?"

My fat sausage fingers grip the key at last. I insert it in the lock like a knife into the conversation, and twist. Push in to kill it dead.

"You have a good day." My head has already entered the house as I start my wave, a final salute to our morning meet.

Ugggh, that little social interaction hurt. Hurt more than the left hook from Tommy Ahmed that sent me down in my final fight. And that took a week to get over. Sod that, activity will solve the problem. I do the press-ups I'd promised to do every day, but which I'd not performed for a week or two. I bathe. Slap on shaving cream before the shadow across my face reaches six o'clock, and stroke bare stripes in the scruff until my skin shines like a new-born's. My cropped hair doesn't need a comb, but I pass one through, anyway. I poke my nose to the left, a daily habit, though Ahmed's packed glove had crooked it to the right forever. The cold makes it twitch, a diviner always on alert for Jim.

Rituals done, I sit on the edge of my bed and settle my eyes on the flat grey roofs of neighbours' council houses, and wonder about the lives which live beneath. By eight, the kids pile out their houses for school like they'd been condemned, eyes to the floor, hands in pockets. One kid, I'd seen him round here for a few years, has a broad white face with little black dots for him to see from – tight camera apertures he uses to focus on pissing off his neighbours. The way he kicks stones without care, where some ping off cars and chip paint... How he swings out his bag at each vehicle he passes... There's a boy in need of an old man.

His mum calls out for him to come back and get his packed sarnies. He kicks a last stone, which fires an "oi from some woman I can't see. I crane my neck to look down the street. A young mum pounds the pavement, her pram and bambino thrust out ahead. She jabs a finger at him. The kid, he looks about eleven, smirks. His pin eyes snap her anger beyond annoyed.

The kid's mum comes into view. The woman from this

morning. She has her arms wrapped round her waist, beneath her boobs, as if she points her nuclear warheads for the younger woman. A finger shoots out and jabs the air in front of the youthful mum's face. The kid slouches away from them and heads off to wherever his day will take him, without a care for the sandwiches which dangle from his mum's hand.

I can't decipher much from each of their rants. I turn away.

***

I pull the case from beneath the bottom drawer of my chest-of-drawers. There's only so much daytime telly I can take before my brain cells attempt to clamber from my ears. I run fingers across the case's fake leather and rip the front pocket's zip up and down a couple or so times. I jerk at the main zip. Age and a lot of use have made the track uneven. I huff and puff and dive in. The Queen stares back at me, as pleasant a sight as always, but she's diminished. I handle a wad, turn it over, flick the notes like a pack of cards, and free them from the band. I have maybe a year before the world of work snatches me back into its claws. I rub at my neck as if I'm tied to a rod connected to a wheel in need of perpetual motion. I transfer my hand to heart and make circles to flatten the palpitations. I run a finger up and down my crooked nose and sway from a punch the world aims at me.

There's a dull tick-tock outside my house. Incessant. Like the feet around my head when I lied half-baked on the canvas. The glass wobbles and the frame shakes at how I thrust the window up. He must have heard the commotion, but he sits on my wall as if he's some poet in contemplation of pot holes and the graffiti tags on the lamppost. I swivel to search for something I don't care for. There's not much in my house I give a toss about. I charge from room to room and grab a bottle of body wash.

"Oi."

I throw the bottle out the window. The kid pretends not to hear – or does he wear earbuds like that Nigel ponce from earlier? – and the bottle thuds right into the back of his head. The kid shrinks into his shoulders and I'm a little nervous now. I don't know why he annoyed me so much. I know - the lack of respect. It's only a wall, sure, but it's my wall. My bit of the world.

He turns his head, all slow, like those horror films, where one of the good guys reveals his change through black eyes and red teeth. The kid - the one who kicked the stones about this morning - reveals only his pin-eyes. He's outraged. I've shown disrespect. That's how his scowl makes me feel.

"What d'you do that for, you fucking prick?"

I was a little bastard as a kid, I don't deny it. I nicked from the newsagents, fought for my school's honour against other schools, and caused absolute mayhem for my teachers – when I turned up. But when I got caught, I never spoke to them like that.

"Get off my wall, lad."

"Why, what will you do?"

"You don't want to know."

"That's what they all say. Which is nowt. I'm staying here. I'm not bothering anyone."

I land my palms on the windowsill and almost fall out head first. I scrape at the paint until it curls under my finger nails.

"You just got a taste of what I'll do. Get off my wall before -"

"Before what? Shampoo my hair? Get off with yer, old man. I'm just sitting here minding me own business. Do your fucking worst."

Jesus. I'm a bit lost for words at that. I blaze inside, but

I don't want to be on the front page of the local newspaper as the man who beats kids, no matter how rude they are. Still, the kid needs a firm hand. I take careful steps down the stairs and out the front door. The kid looks over his shoulder at me, like he might at a substitute teacher. I guess those teachers handle him with a leaflet campaign. Tell him he ought to, you know, improve his social skills, then back away all slow to the safety of the staff room.

That's it. I'm done. The sneer on those lips slashes at my patience and shreds it to little bits. He jumps off the wall at my change of speed. He's bent his knees for a change of direction – a shimmy here, a feint there. I see Ahmed and I hesitate. I don't realise my hands are up to my face, ready to parry and counter-jab, until his face brings me back to reality. I let them drop to my side, a little embarrassed.

"You're fucking weird." He spits at my feet. "I don't know who you are. I've lived here forever and I've never seen you. Who are you?"

"I'm somebody you don't piss off. Now stay off my wall."

I turn my back on him, like I should have from the start, and gather the bodywash on my way back inside. I give it a shake. I need to wash myself.

***

I grab a handful of conkers from the bowl next to the telly, slide open the back door and pelt the ginger cat from my garden. It wears a collar, so it should know its territory. I flop into my armchair, the only furniture in my living room, to watch some mindless soap opera, when the doorbell makes me jump back to my feet. I never have visitors. I don't invite them. The only ones allowed over my threshold had official business. The gas man. TV repairman. Policemen.

I peek at the shape I see through the frosted glass. I make out a white coat and dark hair from the porch light. I could pretend I'd gone out, but I reckon she could hear the telly. I unlatch the chain and open the door wide. Let her see my displeasure in widescreen.

She seems my age, with wear around the eyes which told me she had kids. Ah, the mother of that kid. I see.

"What do you want?"

"Can I come in?" She rubs at her arms in battle with the cold.

I scrabble around all the excuses I'd ever used to keep arm's length from people, but I couldn't latch onto one. The house is a mess - seemed feeble. I'm sick - even worse.

"Come in."

She enters head down, before I realise what I'd said. She checks my place out. Takes in the sparsity, the old TV, and the cracked boxing gloves I hang on the rack with the tea towels.

"You hit my son."

I expect a rant, a finger-wag of the sort she gave the young mum this morning. I roll my jaw and shrug my shoulders.

"He said you punched him on the back of the head."

I let the night's cold air inside, my open door an invite to witnesses. I stay put in the hallway as she stands in my living room.

"I threw a bottle of body wash at him from my upstairs window. My aim was poor."

"The bottle hit him."

"As I said, my aim was poor ..."

"So you admit you hit him?"

"Are you recording this chit-chat?"

"No." She curls a hair strand round her finger and pretends to check the décor – as if that would take more than a wasted moment.

"I know my son ... he's a –"

"- disrespectful little shithead."

She laughs. It tinkles with repressed recognition. "You could say that ..."

"I did say that."

My doorway frames a man who upsets my balance more than the woman's intrusion. My space seems to have undergone a full-blown invasion. "Hey." His voice sing-songs like I should know him.

"Who are you?"

"Sorry." She steps into the hallway. Her scent pulls at the strings which hold me down. "This is my boyfriend, Alan."

"Hi." His voice strips my ears. Makes my eyes wander from his head to his toes as if he's a car salesman trying to sell me an old banger with no tyres, or clutch, or engine, as a top-range BMW.

I ignore him and turn back to the woman. "And who are you?"

"God, sorry. I'm Rhiannon. We met this morning."

"So what's going on? Is this about ..." Alan's eyebrows look like sound waves in repeat of what he's probably said about a million times.

"Yes." I doubt you could slip an atom between her lips.

"Again ... What's he done now?"

"What he always does, Alan. He just winds people up and causes us mayhem."

"Your son is a prick, Rhiannon. Sorry, but he's a prick." It's like Alan reached his index finger and thumb into her eye sockets and squeezed out her lights. "So, we've never met." Alan sticks his hand out. "When did you move in?"

I leave his hand in suspense. "Four years ago."

His laugh comes out an octave too high. "Ah, right.

You keep yourself to yourself."

Rhiannon holds herself tight and brushes past me. Her eyes are on the floor and she enters the kitchen instead of exiting the front door.

"It's the best way." What's she doing in my fucking kitchen?

"You have a wife? A girlfriend?"

I shake my head and stare him down, but I think he'd survive a nuclear holocaust, so he carries on, oblivious to how my nose must look like that of a bull after a jab with a Spanish spear or two in its arse.

"Kids?"

"I have no family. At all."

"Wow. That's tough."

I'm about to wrap a hand round his scrawny neck and javelin-throw him out the front door, through the gate, and – if I time it right - into traffic, but –

"You box?"

Rhiannon has lifted my old boxing gloves from the dishtowel rack. She turns them over to read my history in every crack. She runs a finger across the tiny split caused when I almost took Ahmed's head from his shoulders. I shiver and I think she sees it, because she places them where she found them, with care.

"This is what Kieran needs." Her pilot light flickers back to life.

Alan's inside the fucking house, now. They've broken a UN charter somewhere, I'm sure, and I need to fire some warning rockets soon before my night of solitude is ruined.

"Teach Kieran to use his fists? He's already an arsehole - imagine what he'll be like when trained to use his hands properly."

"Alan, I wish you'd stop calling him such names. He is my son."

"Oh, I know he's your son, alright, and he lets me know I'm not his father."

"Well, if you'd treat him with a bit more respect."

"What did he do, anyway? Why are we here?" Alan has his arms in the air, his fingers curled over the door frame, as if ready for a pull-up.

What about they treat me with some respect?

"You know, he has no self-respect, so how can I give him any." He confides in me. I feel dirty. "I run a little fast food franchise. I had him work for me a little bit. He was always in the staff room arsing around."

"He's eleven, Alan."

"Still …"

She moves towards me and gives me Disney eyes. "You could teach him."

"Errr, no, I don't think so." I feel the little urchin's eyes on me, even though he's probably on his backside in front of the telly now, all smiles at the roasting he imagines I'm on the end of. "You don't even know my name."

"What is your name?"

"Fred."

"Like Fred West? Ha." Alan slaps a thigh.

I'm all defensive about the comparison because of the earlier insinuation. This man searches for weakness and then grinds its bones with a blunt needle. No wonder the kid is a ragbag of resentment. I feel a twinge of sentiment and recognition. I ran about wild as a kid, in search of …meaning, I suppose, though I wouldn't have thought about it like that back then.

"I'll teach him."

She puts a hand over her mouth and grabs that scream. Holds it. She might need it later.

"Nobody, and I mean nobody, has ever done anything for my boy. This will make his day."

Alan rolls his eyes and backs out the door. "Good luck, Fred. Good fucking luck."

Maybe I can train the boy to turf this cuckoo out of the nest.

***

Next afternoon I see Rhiannon in a ruck of local kids. She laughs, gives out a few sweets, ruffles a few heads. Part of the community, though I'd never seen any such thing round here. I suppose I never looked - I'm definitely not part of any community.

Kieran knocks on the door, each slow rap full of resentment. The news has made his day, alright. I hesitate before I open the door because I know those narrow eyes he framed and tried to compartmentalise me with yesterday would turn my fists into wrecking balls. I squeeze my fingers and fling the door open. His look is sullen - a result, I'm sure, of an hour's-worth of persuasion from his mother.

I nod an invite inside. He bobs about like a cat in search of danger before it enters a cardboard box, drops his head into his shoulders and steps in my space, my home, my sanctuary. I think of his mother's fella to gather sympathy. It gathers at the same pace as moss. He leans against my hall wall with his hands in his pockets. His face is all "what now?" My fingers twitch as I anticipate that foot of his raising to rest on my wall. It's not a well decorated wall at all. I don't deny it could do with a lick of paint, but if he does what I expect, I'll teach him the first thing about boxing.

He arches his back to push himself off the surface and he eyes my batwing eyebrows. Well, he didn't mark a footprint on my yellowish paint, I'll give him that. He looks around my eyes, never into them. I'm fine with that, though it makes him appear shifty.

This awkward silence won't end itself, so I suggest he runs.

"Run?" He checks himself out for my benefit. He wears jeans and boots. Look like Dockers.

"Your mum told you the reason for coming round here, right?"

"So you could teach me how to punch somebody's lights out."

I pull air into my lungs with the intention its release would slap him round the ears and plant him with some oomph.

"It's an art."

"It's punching. And ducking. And punching. Can I kick?"

"Wrong sport. And kicking is ungentlemanly."

He pulls a chewing a gooseberry and wasp sandwich face. "Kicking is pretty cool, what you on about? Ninjas, Kung Fu, do you know any of that?"

"I know how to duck and weave, jab, hook and cut. I look for those moments of weakness, and try to hide mine."

His eyes dull. I grab the gloves from the rack and hand them to him. He sparks. Bare fists don't match the beauty of these red beasts as they pulse at the end of your arms. He weighs them against the ninja jumps, I reckon.

"Nah." He drops them and they hit the ground all dramatic, like I hit the canvas. I doubt he clocks the little shake of my head. I'm all sullen, now. Nobody watches boxing anymore. Not that I socialize with anyone, so I don't rightly know, but this sort of confirms it for the up and coming generation. He darts out my house and leaves a faint smell of fresh air, like he'd wagged school all day.

***

Rhiannon takes the only chair in my living room, without invite. I can see right down her skimpy top. She shuffles - fiddles about her shirt's neck. I'm invited to ogle, or is that me being a man? I don't know anymore, I'm so out of practice. I lean against the wall and wait for her words.

She bites at her lips, annoyed I don't start the conversation. "So, how did it go?" She strokes a hair strand away and tries to reach inside me. Good luck with that.

"He said, in so many words, that he can't be arsed. He wants to be a ninja. He wants wantswantswants, but I don't reckon he'd settle on any one thing. Sorry."

She rubs imaginary fluff, crumbs, indignity off her above-the-knee skirt, and stands. "Did you try to persuade him into trying it?"

I shrugged my shoulders. What did I care?

"Then he's just like you. And his dad. And … Alan."

She turns her back on me as she stands in the living room's doorway. She swings her look both ways. She tries to make me out from the look of my house. She can see what I am without much detective work.

Empty.

***

"I'm sorry about yesterday, mister."

"Your mum ordered you round?"

He nodded, his eyes all over my face again, without ever latching to mine. Gets right on my nerves now, it does.

I send him round the block and time his run. If he has anything about him, he should make it back here in no more than four minutes. I patter about the front garden. Pretend I'm busy if I see anyone approach. Shift the dead brown leaves about as if I'm serious about removing them.

A bunch of kids, they must range from six to fifteen,

catch me by surprise. Some have mud on their knees, scratches on their faces, and one has a football under his arm. Another has a foot on my wall. I'd stand amazed if they'd ever blown their noses.

"You the fella who's a boxer?"

The piper stands in the middle of the pack. Others shuffle around him in anticipation. He has a grin which could do with a wipe.

"Yeah."

"Are you the world champion?"

My eyebrows are the slopes on Mount Everest. I scan the housing estate: broken pavements, sheathes of grass poking out from rusted fences and cracks, and not by design. Grey pebbledash, I'm sure all shat on the houses by a pigeon army.

"No."

"What did you win?"

"Who did you beat?"

"Why you living here? You must have been a shit boxer."

Because the boogie man, Jim, won't find me here.

"I bet you were one of the women who held the cards, what do you call them …?"

"Ha, telling us which round it is?"

"Yeah."

They all got involved. The youngest laughed to maintain his position and make sure he got his slice of meat from the kill.

"Were you one of them women? Are you a bird?"

I realise my tongue has slipped between my teeth in time to prevent a chomp. I lick the back of my molars, across every crook. If I kept silent, they'd crow. If I bit, they'd hyena-howl all the way home.

Kieran saves me from such a decision. He's made it in

four minutes, twenty seconds. The lad's a slouch, but he faces these kids down.

"What you all doing?"

"Just talking." The middling kid eyes me without an ounce of fear, despite my size and the pounds I still pack. "Checking out the big lad, here."

Jesus, this kid has some front.

"He's great, isn't he? He's teaching me how to box."

"Who boxes anymore? Everyone's doing MMA now." The fifteen year old has opened his gob for the first time.

I'm sure Kieran's neck hair has just flick-knifed. "Is that what you're doing?"

"No."

"Well, shurrup, then."

The fifteen year old's eyes fill with impotent rage. He wants to clout Kieran in the face, to put in concrete the pecking order round here, but he fears the eleven year old will send him nose first into the wet leaves and windswept sweet packets. I see every cog churn in the teenager's face.

I resist the urge to put a hand on Kieran's shoulder. I feel a bit weak for that feeling, but he saved me from some shit there. From what I might have done. The hyenas move on.

***

Kieran wants to wear the gloves, but they're too big for him. He ducks and weaves, but looks like a fish thrown on a boat's floor, his hands and wrists wrapped in bandages to protect his weak bones. He wears football shorts and fancy Nike trainers which probably cost more than the rent. They're too big and his legs look like golf clubs. I dance around him with my palms out for him to hit. He tries, but he's all aggression and no skill. The air whistles with every throw he aims, until his arms dangle, too heavy for him to hold up. I make light slaps on his cheeks to show him the importance of guarding his face. Once that brain rattles round your skull you'll kiss the canvas.

"This is bollocks."

The outburst stuns me more than any of his punches and I drop my guard. He goes for it and wallops me in the right cheek. I counter, all instinct, and slam him with the back of my hand across the living room floor. He slides until the skirting board blocks further propulsion.

He grits his teeth, holds his head, and makes thin lines of his dot-eyes.

"It's not bollocks. It's art."

He rubs and opens his eyes to me. "It doesn't feel like art."

I nod agreement. "No, not when that crystal-glass-sing cracks across your skull. The art is in avoiding that." I pull him up, surprised he offered his hand. "Come on – outside. Get some fresh air."

The grey clouds merge with the houses so you can't much tell where either begins and ends. His chest is up and down like the throat of one of those toads. His hair is drenched and he stares at the brown grass in my back garden. He might never have pondered life as much as this. Boxing does that for you.

"Why don't you box anymore?"

I scratch at my thoughts and paint a grin. "I'm getting on."

"You're not that old. I mean, you're old, but you're not ancient."

I shrug and fail to avoid running a finger down my crooked nose.

"You got battered in a fight, didn't yer?"

I bobble my head like one of those daft figurines

people put in the back of their cars. Suck at my gums.

"You did, right? Who battered you?"

Ahmed conjures in my head – he pops his gumshield at me, the Alien mouth which makes me crick my neck to hide the nerves.

"It was a long time ago, I can't remember the details."

"You can't remember? He battered you that bad?"

I let my silence divert his questions. He checks out my backyard and the big brick wall at the garden's end which starts the next row of houses.

"Alan says you're a bum. You don't work and just live off the taxpayer."

"I don't need to know what Alan thinks of me."

Now I'm pissed. People talking about me. They'll chip away until they get to the marrow.

"I reckon mum'll dump him soon. They argue all the time. Mostly about me. He is an arsehole. I hope she does dump him, but I'm scared of who she'll get with next."

"She has a lot of boyfriends?"

"Not a ton. That I remember anyway. She's been with burger boy for about two years, I think. He's a slimy bastard."

"They teach you words like that at school?"

"I don't know what they teach at school. It's all shite."

I couldn't take philosophising with an eleven year old. Weariness slides behind my eyes. I go inside and slump on my armchair. I tell the boy to let himself out.

***

My eyelids flutter open at how the water dances through pipes behind the walls. The room is pitch black and my ears feel they are beneath the surface in a swimming pool. The ache behind my eyes shutters them again, and I let the night take me away.

The bangs on the door wash away that drowsy wooze and I stand as I would confront an attacker. I fear for the door's hinges, and I swing it wide open. I lose my grip on the handle and it slams into the wall. Rhiannon looks like a hurricane hit her and pulled her hair to every point of a compass.

"You alright?"

"No. Is Kieran still here? Kieran?"

She's loud enough for neighbours to hear. She sways to see round my shoulder, like I have the lad tied up on the settee.

"I don't think so." I check my shoulder to make sure, but I know he isn't.

"Why are all the lights off?"

"I fell asleep. I told him to let himself out. Come in." I scan the street as she barges past, and close the door on any eyes.

She seems hesitant. She wraps arms round her waist and it makes me nervous. What does she think I am? I switch the lights on and check the rooms. He's not in any of them. I follow her pinched eyes up the stairs and hold my breath. My suitcase.

She's upstairs. I switch the light on for the landing and jog after her. I told him to leave. I try not to check her arse, but I can't help it. She thrusts my bedroom door wide as a TV policeman might and I hold my breath again. What does she suspect? She rushes past me to the next room. I swear she resists the urge to kick the door open. She shoulders it ajar, instead, and covers her mouth.

"Kieran …"

I tower over her to see. He's face down on the carpet, his arms by his side. I flick the light switch and scowl. She kneels by his side and turns her head to me. I feel the silent accusation and it makes my skin pop sweat. I don't know how to react, apart from tremble and fail to form words. The kid's chest is up and down, and the odd sigh makes a mockery of his mum's panic.

She nudges him with a hand and he stirs. Sits up, rubs his eyes. I half-expect a bunch of Disney birds to land on his shoulder and twitter, he looks that innocent. He plants his palms on the floor and gathers a sense of where he is. Blinks at his mum, then me.

"Love, you alright?

"I'm fine. What's up?"

"I told you to make your own way out. You came up here?"

"I didn't think you'd mind."

"Come on, love, let's make our way home."

He stands like he's had a few, plants a hand on the cupboard, his fingers inches from my small fortune.

"Is Alan home?"

"Yes, he is. He'll be wondering where we are." She looks up at me, all sheepish, and serves me an apologetic smile.

"I'd rather sleep here."

"That's not going to happen."

"Why not?"

"Because … It's not appropriate is it? Fred, here, hardly knows you."

"Alan hardly fucking knows me, and he sleeps under the same roof as me."

"Kieran – language. Please."

She cringes like she'd been caught out training the boy to parrot her foul tongue. I didn't give a monkey's. I just wanted him out. I'd allowed people to know me. It should never have happened.

***

I make it deep into the woods, deeper than fag packets and empty beer bottles could penetrate. A silvery carpet stretches ahead through trees bearing Christmas card glitter which the early morning moon enhances. I nearly punch Rhiannon in the face as she jogs in line with me.

"What the …?"

"Ah behave, big man."

I suck on my teeth and let her stay by my shoulder.

***

Rhiannon sits on the arm of my armchair. I focus on objects around her to avoid a dip down her cleavage – a rollercoaster ride I couldn't prepare for after all this time. Kieran dances around me. Jabs at my palms as I encourage him with praise mixed with little stabs at his ego when he gets cocky. His mum oohs and aahs at her son, which eggs him on to stupid combinations which I end with a quick slap to a cheek.

"Do you need to do that?" She's all concern for her little petal, but I side-eye her into silence.

Kieran gets into mode, makes clean contact with my right palm, then my left and follows it with a right hook that just might take an opponent out of consciousness in a real fight.

"Whoo." His mum claps and rocks on the arm. The furniture squeaks and I fear a night in front of the telly sat on the numb-inducing kitchen chair.

She makes little touches on my arm during breaks. Runs a hand through her lush brunette locks, and twirls some round a finger. I've been out of the game so long that her little brushes make my skin tingle and vibrate to my crotch, which shifts like a mole readying to poke up out of the earth.

"Your arms are really thick." She pokes at my biceps

and I move away. I'm uncomfortable. I'm sure her son paints images behind those blank eyes - and her man is only four doors away, unless he's showing underpaid staff how to flip burgers tonight.

Last night she thought me the Child Catcher. Today she makes eyes at me. I don't know what to think. My old man always told me to watch out for the fast ones. They always wanted something - and would fuck it out of you if you let your guard down.

"I work out."

"I bet you do."

Kieran screws eyes at his mum as if her chit-chat churned his stomach. We check each other for answers at the loud knock on the door. I plant my feet in concrete. Nobody ever knocks for me. That's how I want it. Rhiannon rocks off the arm and answers it for me. My nerves shred at her fella's voice.

"Alright, love, what's the story?"

"Kieran's connecting his punches correctly - according to Fred."

"Is he now? I'll be the judge of that."

The dishrag now sits on my armchair's arm, and though Alan must weigh the same as a bag of Walker's crisps, my furniture moans anyway. He nods, expects me to return that melon-lip smile. My lips won't allow such a thing. They feel dry and cracked, and no amount of lube from his words will change that.

Kieran's demeanour changes. His loose feet have become tree roots, his punches droop and hit like blancmange. He mutters and scratches his nose. I'm not sure if he wants to distract me so he can smash a flurry across my hands.

"What are you doing, lad?" Alan ghost-punches, an attempt to make Kieran shadow him. Words of wisdom spout out the man's mouth like an overflowing toilet –

Feint left, smash right.

Wobble your head a bit, drop your shoulder.

Jab left, jab again. Uppercut, quick.

Rhiannon has shrunk into herself, and her eyes hollow and burn out. She offers me coy looks, embarrassed at her man. What does she want from me? To step in and rescue her from a life with him? Nah. That's my dry bones conjuring lust. She glowers at him, though, and gives me sunshine. I shake myself and focus on the boy. Tell him to lift his hands and cut that Prince Naseem shite out. Tell him to work his feet and get off his heels. Alan nods. Tells the boy to listen to me. One more word makes us both drop our arms and turn in his direction.

"Will you piss off?" Kieran thrusts his bandaged palms at Alan. I expect his fingers to wave a 'come on, then' at him.

Alan shrugs his shoulders. He's seen this before. Many times, I can tell. He raises a Roger Moore eyebrow at me. "You know what? You're pretty good at this."

My teeth are tectonic plates.

"We ought to set up a little business. A boxing gym. You can train the little shits round here, instill some discipline and make them ready for work when they leave school."

Rhiannon rolls her eyes. "You've always got an idea rattling round your skull, but you never follow through."

"What are you talking about? I run my own business."

"No, you run a franchise burger joint. You don't control opening times. You don't control prices. You don't control the offers they force on you. And you're losing money. You'll be on the dole queue before you know it."

Her smirk paints his face red. His temple throbs. I check his hands. Fury has made fists of them. I wonder if he hits her. The idea sends my heart round Silverstone, but I calm because I can't see her allowing him to lay a finger on her.

"It could work." He nods at me. "Your boxing expertise, my business nous … that'd be a nice little venture."

My eyebrows hit my hairline. "The kids round here could probably pay, what, a quid a week?"

"Not much." Rhiannon shuffles against the wall. She enjoys his pain. "How many sessions a week, per boxer? The kid might be in five times a week. All for a pound. How many boys round here? Not enough to pay wages and make money."

"Well … doesn't have to be just the boys. Men can come and train, too."

Rhiannon slaps her leg and tries to grab the laugh before it explodes out her mouth. She fails. "The men round here? I've seen less fat on a Netto joint of lamb. You're having yourself on, love."

I enjoy the sarcasm which drips from every letter of that "love."

Alan puts his hands in the air. "I'm just trying to help. I mean, you don't work – as far as I can see. I'm just trying to help get you off the state teat, that's all. Especially as I heard you cocked up a fight a while ago. Lost somebody a lot of money. And yourself, I'm guessing."

I wink at Kieran. "That's enough for tonight. You did well. A bit of polish and you'll be a knockout."

Kieran's mouth slides to the side and his eyes narrow to fill his vision with Alan. I'm sure he weighs up whether he can use his new skills on the man.

"It was a pleasure having you all over, but I must get on with stuff."

Alan smiles and I read his words before he opens his gob. "Hard work watching telly all night, right?"

"Always." I usher them all to the door, like relatives I barely know who overstayed their welcome. Alan's grin remains plastered. Rhiannon follows him out and mouths an apology to me. Her eyes seem like an invitation. To what, I don't know. Kieran keeps his head down and his shoulders slumped at the prospect of a night spent with this man.

I shut the door and curl my arm over my head. Rest my forehead against the wood. My frame tightens around my lungs and I have to drag air into them with the deepest breath. I turn and stare at my armchair, the only comfort in my life. I tramp upstairs and open the suitcase. I flick the wads and wonder what life might have held if I'd not bet on myself losing.

I tramp the streets once it's late enough to step outside without the need to force a smile and expend breath at passing neighbours. The moon's a lazy eye, half-closed, as if it knows my presence but acknowledges my mood. On my way back I see Rhiannon in my peripheral vision through her window. She's in a deep kiss with Alan, who has his hands in her hair. I stare between them and my feet, and will myself towards my front door. My flesh shrinks to my bones so tight I think it crushes my spirit.

***

I'm exhausted this morning. I dreamt of music and friends. Beers in the pub. The rip of my zip jolted me from sleep five, six, seven times. I let out the longest sighs every time I realised Rhiannon's hand down my jeans had happened only in my head. I slap at my cheeks to wake up.

I bleed out the annoyance at Alan's suggestion from yesterday, because it's his suggestion, but there might be a way to get a council grant. I don't know how it works, but the treasure trove in the case will sink with the weight of utility bills in the not too distant future.

My morning run makes my eyes flit around bird-like for

predators. I hear footsteps behind, but see nothing when I swivel my head. I hear ghost-laughs, whispers on the wind, mixed in with the rustle and sway of branches. I run harder until I'm way over the usual pace and my heart demands I stop. Jim's monkey grin seems carved in that tree.

Now I see them. Not a man behind an oak with a shotgun aimed at my belly, but some of those little bastards who caused me such grief the other day.

"What do you lot want?"

The eldest steps ahead of the four other boys as they approach me, his face spotted with rain like the rest. Steam billows from the little dragon. I reckon he's thirteen and his spots are two.

"We heard you're doing boxing lessons."

I flick my tongue behind teeth. He takes my silence as confirmation. "We all want to learn."

I don't think the youngest does. He's just social. Teaching these kids seems the same as arming ISIS with nuclear weapons.

"I'm thinking about it. It depends …"

"On what?"

"Whether it's viable."

Their little faces screw up goblin-like. "What's that mean?" The younger one said it like I'd accused him of some crime even he couldn't contemplate.

"So you won't do it?" This kid looks like someone stuck a pump needle in his ear and worked that arm until his face ballooned.

"If you say it like that, no."

"You're just training Kieran, then?" The eldest wants the last word. "You want to cum up his bum? Is that what you're after?"

I'm lost for words. I try to grip some as they run up and down my tongue, but they slip away like melted snow at the edge instead of shooting off to smash around their ears. They detect weakness in me. They know I won't hit them. They know I don't have allies. Alan doesn't count and they're not scared of him or Rhiannon. I get on with my jog. Their taunts push me on like a high wind. I fill my head with Rhiannon, but all I can see are Alan's hands in her hair like the heads of venomous snakes.

***

"You're gonna listen to that twat and train everyone around here?"

I'm all out of breath to realise who's at my door. I stare at him until Kieran forms in my vision. I snort the foggy air up my nose like sedative and scowl at the footprint he's left on my door as he pushes away.

"Those arseholes just want to copy me. They'll treat it all like some joke after a bit, and ruin it."

I shifted my attention from the footprint to the boy. Those accusations the little bastards aimed my way force me to check my shoulder. I feel ashamed, as if a grown man shouldn't talk to a kid like this, though we're in daylight, on our own street. Little runty bastards.

I bolster myself and sit on the wall I shampoo-bottled him from that short time ago. "Ruin what? What do you want?"

"Something … I dunno … something more. I don't know. My teachers say I have potential – if I apply meself. But apply to what? I don't get what they teach. I don't see how it'll help."

"Everyone needs an education these days, lad."

"Alan's got an education. Mum says he's got a degree. From university. And he runs a fucking burger joint. He borrows money to look like he's living like a businessman, but he's as skint as a badger's arse."

He kicks a stone and it rattles out my gate and pings off the neighbour's blue Mazda.

"Oi, what are you doing?"

He shrugs his shoulders. "Who cares?"

"The owner will care."

"Why do you fucking care? I didn't even know you lived on this street. I thought your house was empty, if I ever thought about it at all. You haven't been out and about with anyone. Who are you?"

There's a question. I've hidden so long that outside makes me itchy and exposed.

"You don't even work. How do you live? On benefits?"

"I live, and that's all you need to know."

"Well … mum likes you. She talks about you in the morning."

I hold his eye. I want him to tell me more, but I can't ask what she says because it draws me in to other lives. I've gone from anonymity to kids tracking my steps first thing in the morning. A mum who jibber-jabs with her son is only the tip of a tentacle which might crawl from this estate and wiggle a "follow me" finger to someone I don't need back in my life.

Kieran's eyes are wide open. An invite to peer into his depths for lies he defies me to find. "I don't mind. Anyone's better than Alan."

"Where's your dad?"

"Ran off to Cardiff with a Welsh bird when I was four. Fuck him."

"You don't need to swear so much, lad."

"Will you fuck off with the 'lad?' I want to get my right hook down."

"School?"

"It's Saturday, you prick."

"Jesus, your tongue."

"I didn't take you for a vicar. Are you going to teach me or what?"

"Does your mum know where you are?" I grind my teeth at the check over my shoulder. It's becoming a habit.

"Course she does. She encourages me. I reckon you'll be in her knickers by the end of the week."

"Get in there and bandage your wrists." I follow him in after I unlock the door, my cheeks full of bewildered, Puritan breath.

***

I'm putty. A typical fella who can't think straight once the loins have stirred. I'm against the counter-top. My eyes are all over the place. Rhiannon's scent floats around the inside of my nose and seeps into my mind. Frazzles thoughts. Can't say anything other than "bhhhh", or something. She changes hands and that little moment almost brings me back to my senses. I almost let my wonder at Kieran's long toilet break make me limp. Alan's hands in her hair last night almost makes me point to the floor. But I'm so close I shut the world out. And then ... and then ... well, there you go. She leans in to kiss my cheek, all breathy and sensual.

"Thank you for helping my boy. You deserve this."

It's almost as if he knew when to pop his head round the bend and enter the kitchen. I've re-buckled my belt and Rhiannon has run her hand under the tap. I'm on the bare floor with a cloth for the mess. Her sheen matches mine. I snatch a quick in-the-know smile from her which lights a lot of damp coals in my chest. Mum and son share a glance. He smirks and shakes his head in a way I could mistake for just the bob you make as you walk.

"I have to go. We have to go." They rush away. Maybe Alan is on his way home. They both appear all flustered.

Can't blame them. I think the lad knows what his mum just did. I'm a little embarrassed for him. It doesn't last long, because I bask in a glow I haven't felt for some time.

***

The next day I watch Rhiannon head down the street. She pads across the road from one neighbour to another. They don't look best pleased. This woman, like the man before, starts all sunshine, as if happy Rhiannon has acknowledged their existence, but again, the woman's forehead crumples like a crisp packet from a flame's touch. Shakes her head, purses her lips. Looks towards my house, then tuts her way home. Her look my way must have been the nearest focal point, or maybe Rhiannon had told her about the hand job she had given me. Nooooo way.

Rhiannon controls my movement. I'm light on my feet. I feel strong. I eye my home and project home improvement schemes on the walls and empty spaces. I wonder if I should buy her a gift. That money has to last as long as possible. I run upstairs, each step a cloud I bounce off. Pull the suitcase and stare at the dosh. Buy her what? Jewellery is cheesy. I hardly know her. A hand-job doesn't constitute diamonds and gold. Still, posh nosh would paint over my grey life.

A knock on the door jolts me from wild fancy. The woman's son. Kieran's boxing lesson. He's early, but there you go. I'm ready to use all this energy. It bubbles and pops under my skin. I'm all Fred Astaire in the way I walk. I heel the suitcase beneath the bed and miss half the steps on my way to the door.

"In you come, lad, let's get on it."

"Alright, calm down, old man."

He pushes past me as if all this is still a chore. He wraps his hands and we start. He's loose. He connects his punches and I'm impressed at the sting from clean hits to my palms. He's good. Which means I'm a good trainer. Could I make a go of this? Become a new Brendan Ingle? Mould all the little shits round here into boxing gold? Aggghh, I'd become known outside this estate if I did that. Then someone would run me through with a spit and roast me on a fire.

I put the idea down a disused well and make Kieran skip. He cranes his neck to see out the window.

"Concentrate on the rope, Kieran, or you'll break your neck."

I'm fond of the lad, despite his sewer mouth. He works and learns quick. In six months I could have him inside ropes. His jabs are sharp - his hooks are quick and clean. He transitions to defence fast. He avoids my counter slaps most of the time.

His eyes wander to the window again. And again. That's a lot of people. The net curtain makes them look like an army of the dead, but they're more animated than that. They gather outside my house like crows on a telephone line, their beaks wet at the prey below.

My walls are damp from the work Kieran puts in. I close the curtains to avert his distraction, and the chatter outside roars to the clouds. I'm sure the windows rattle as sometimes they do during heavy thunder.

The roar lowers and settles into a hummmm. I'm distracted. What is going on out there?

"Keep skipping."

Kieran wavers between emotions - his face seems to blister and expand at some internal fire. There's fear, a smirk, some voodoo in his eyes as he sees something beyond what lies in front of him. Which, when you look at my living room, isn't much at all.

"Go on. Keep at it."

He skips faster, enough to carve a bowl into my floor,

as I peer through the curtains. I ought to duck, but I don't quite believe the brick exists, though it arcs in the air and falls at just the right time to smash through my window. Glass shards hit my face and scatter across the floor like diamonds. I squeeze my eyes, though I know they're safe. I pat at my face and wince at the pain. I stare at the blood on my fingers and check on Kieran. He stares at me with eyes that see some fruition, though he carries on skipping, as I told him. The rope catches his foot and he falls, though it seems incredible he could fall in such a ragdoll fashion from such light contact. His face hits the corner of my armchair as he goes down, and he emits a scream I ought to have loosed on the world from the stabs in my face.

My front door shakes and rattles. It won't take much more before it rolls from its hinges. I hear distinct words emerge from the hum - Scum. Wanker. Sick bastard. Pervert. Paedo.

Paedo.

Paedo.

I taste copper in my mouth. Kieran writhes on the floor. I should help him, but I'm rooted to the spot, as if Jim has my feet ready in concrete. Their accusation drowns Kieran's wails. The door finally gives and I shift into a boxing stance. The first few pile in, eyes undead-wide and in search of flesh. My flesh.

"Jesus."

A man deepens his presence into my home, every step as if on a tightrope. They're all men and every one glares at me and this boy on the floor. His bandages are off and his wrists are red. His eyes plead to them. I'm all fucking dazed and confused and words come out all consonants or all vowels.

People flood my front room and hallway. "Paedo" and "poor lad" fills the hot, rancid air. They shuffle Kieran to the back, who's all tears and wild glances.

"What the …" I say the same thing five, six, a dozen times. No one listens. Two big men make it to the front with iron bars in their hands, held like rifles. They stand guard. The kids who followed me this morning bang on the windows. The house shakes. Low voices of expectation whirr. I put a palm out and tell them I have no idea what all this means. The gesture triggers a reaction. I sidestep the iron bar and shake at the swish. I know what contact would have done to my head. The other man joins in and the crowd sways back to give room. The second man swings and I arc my upper body to avoid catastrophe. The first strikes again. The iron bar's end snags my t-shirt. The man falls into his swing and almost sprawls across the surface. His fingers are splayed on the floor. I stamp my boots on them like I would on a spider. He screams. I don't have time to stare at his perfect circle of a bald spot. The second man strikes down and the iron bar would have split my head in two if he'd connected. As the bar hits my floor I hit him with a flurry of jabs. He wobbles and I right hook him to the floor. He's out and he's lost teeth.

Sweat stings my eyes. Nobody looks at the men, not even at the one who simpers with his bad hand beneath an armpit. "I don't know what the fuck you think I've done, but you're all wrong. Get out."

"Fire."

A woman's voice. I can smell the burn. Rhiannon's in the hallway comforting her boy. Black smoke filters into the hallway. Yells and blind screams could peel the paint from the walls before the fire licked it away.

"Don't panic." I relax as I shift into help mode. Rhiannon's by my side, here to assist. I'm confused, until fire rockets shoot from my fingertips at the sight of Alan in a trot down my stairs with the red suitcase. I don't have time to take a step. My head rings at the blow. I'm convinced my brain has caved in, but I'm having this thought … I'm on the floor, a place where I vowed never to fall again. I'm gone.

***

My headaches come and go. When one arrives it's a runaway train that smashes into the barrier at the back of my head. It crushes memory into dust and I sometimes see only shades of black.

"What do you want?" I rest the brush against the ropes surrounding my ring.

Kieran plants the suitcase by my feet and looks up at me. "I've wanted to say sorry for years."

He's fourteen now, maybe fifteen. He smells like he's interested in girls. I glance at the suitcase and touch its red fake leather.

"Anything inside?"

"Nothing. They spent it all."

"With your help, I suppose."

"I saw you fight those men. You looked so cool. Made me feel guilty."

"And you come only when the bag is empty."

"I was eleven. I … I didn't know any better. I was a little bastard. I've had this urge to come for a long time." I can tell he wants to stare at his feet, but I give him credit, he keeps eye contact now. "You never came after us? My mum put your stuff, after that hand job she gave you, all over my jeans and told everyone you tried to rape me." His eyes catch fire. "I never got over that one."

I fix on a point beyond his shoulder. Makes him check behind, all nerves. "I'm not that kind of man, Kieran. I just wanted to help you. You were on the road to a shit life, and I just wanted to … help."

His forehead wrinkles sorrow and he can't help

touching his lips as he stares at the knife-grin Jim finally cut into my face. He gestures sympathy and walks away, his shoulders hunched. He glances back and offers a regretful smile. It quashes my urge to put him in the suitcase. The boy had come good after all.

Free Fall

By Bill Baber

Dedication: *To my mother Betty who fought the brave fight and went down swinging. Miss you mom.*

When you are broke and the cold spring wind is blowing down Virginia Street with teeth that bite as deep and jagged as a shark, Reno is a lonely damn place to be. I wasn't broke but sure had been on a number of occasions so I knew the feeling as well as my name. I was looking for someone who didn't have a dime and perhaps not much time. Trying to find him was depressing- but looking for a lost soul in a town that is littered with them is enough to give anyone the blues.

There were only two things Fast Eddie Morrow did quickly. Drink and lose money. Maybe there was a third. When he combined the first two, he had a tendency to piss people off in pretty short order. I met him when he first moved to town. I was tending bar at the Cal- Neva sports book which may have been the most colorful place in town. The drinks were cheap and everyone from the cream of the high rollers to the lowest down and outers rubbed shoulders there, sharing stories of the bets they won and excuses for the ones they didn't. I'm not certain what spawned our connection. He certainly wasn't a very likable guy so maybe I just felt sorry for him. Maybe his pathetic life made the deficiencies in mine look pretty damn good. But at some level, maybe I saw the past that I had escaped in him. He was surly at best and could be a real prick when he was losing, which was most of the time. And, he was a cheap bastard. Even when Eddie was flush he never tipped. Not bartenders, dealers or even waitresses.

No one knows what he was trying to find in Reno. Conversely, he may have been trying to lose himself. Maybe he wanted to live out some self fulfilling prophecy that proved he was a loser. I don't know that it had to be that way for Eddie but it sure seemed to be beyond his control. Perhaps some of us are born with a self destructive gene that lies dormant until a chain of events or destiny ignites a slow burning fuse that simmers until the final implosion. Even if he was a loser, there was something about watching Eddie come unwound that was disturbing – even to a jaded observer like me. Most tapped out bums illicit no sympathy from me. I had seen it too many times and knew that when you lived on the edge it could be a fast, hard fall that resulted in a painful, rough landing. Eddie's descent was quicker than most. A fool would hit the bottom; Eddie just went right on through. For him, there seemed to be no bottom. But for some still unknown reason, his situation affected me.

He had been in Reno for a few months when he told me his story. It was unlike any I had heard. He was 43, had married his high school sweetheart who left him after fifteen years for his best friend. Eddie had once held a decent job with the post office. He had security and a good pension, owned his own home, and was living that increasingly elusive American Dream- then he threw it all away for this nightmare.

His father had been a farmer and owned sixty acres just outside Santa Rosa where he raised prunes and hops. Eddie told me picking either of them was like hell for the living. Hot, dusty, and to hear him tell it, the monotony is what almost did him in. Fill a bucket; dump it in a bin, do it again and again. All day, all week, until every stinking tree or bush or whatever the hell they were growing on was picked clean. He thought Sisyphus got off easy pushing a ball up a damned hill over and over. His mother died when he was a kid and the old man worked him and his older brother Albert pretty hard. Albert went on to become a successful electrical contractor and Eddie ended up here in Reno. I got the feeling Eddie didn't care for labor of any sort and that he wasn't too fond of his brother either. It seemed there was more than a little Cain and Abel to their relationship. Albert was the favorite; Eddie never seemed to measure up. I often thought he was the kind of mailman that could easily go postal. Sometimes you could see smoke from a smoldering fire behind his eyes. It wouldn't have surprised me to hear that he'd shot a casino up. Anyway, the old man died and left the farm to his two sons. Based on an appraisal, Eddie sold his half to Albert for a million and a half.

Two years after he sold his interest in the farm, the city of Santa Rosa extended its urban growth boundary. The building boom of the late 90's was in full swing. Albert sold the land for nineteen million. That was another bet Eddie lost. After selling his house and cashing out his pension, he hit Reno with a little over two million dollars. It was destined to not last long.

For a while, he lived in a comped room at the Sundowner where he dropped a couple of grand on a nightly basis. But not all business is good business and they soon tired of the drunken rampages that followed his losing streaks and 86'd him. That became a pattern and it wasn't long before the only clubs he could still get into were the Cal-Neva, which had the reputation of being something of a dive, and Fitzgerald's where they never seemed to bounce anyone. It wasn't long before he was living at The Riverside, a decrepit old dump that had once housed a casino but now rented rooms monthly to pensioners, daily to derelicts or even by the hour for actions and acts that were on the wrong side of the law.

Luck is something a gambler either has or he doesn't.

It's something you are born with. It can't be created. Maybe luck was another gene that poor Eddie was genetically short changed on. I have known gamblers who knew all the angles, the odds, the systems. What they didn't have was luck. If they could, they would have gone to Oz looking for a wizard to supply it. Those guys are all broke. Without a doubt, Eddie was the unluckiest guy I ever knew. And he had no clue as to what he was doing at the tables. He was just born to lose.

I used to watch him play. One night at Fitz's, he dropped forty grand in two hours at a blackjack table. He was betting a thousand a pop and had started the session by losing ten hands in a row. He wasn't doing himself any favors either. He was splitting face cards and hitting 15 and 16 when the dealer showed breaking hands. It was like Zeus was sitting at God's right hand hurling lightning bolts at him. He would have 19, bam, the dealer had 20. Or he would hit sixteen and draw a three or a four, then bam, the dealer would hit 12 and draw a 9. It was as if he was giving his dough away or they were stealing it from him, it was hard to tell which.

The next day, he might play the slots, pulling the handle on a dollar machine a thousand times and getting stiffed. Didn't matter what he did, he just lost. He knew nothing about the ponies but I would give him a tip once in a while since I heard things around the bar. He never bet any of them and when a horse I gave him won, Eddie offered some lame excuse as to why he put his money on something else in the race.

Eddie wasn't much to look at. He was about 5'7" and balding with thick features and an expanding gut. He dressed like a real square. Sans- a -belt slacks, polyester shirts and loafers. But hey, in this town, you start throwing money around the way Eddie did; you're going to attract women the way a pasture draws flies. For a while he dated a dancer from the MGM but once she determined Eddie wasn't giving anything away she dumped him. Then it was a dealer from Sparks. Same thing, when it became clear there were no diamonds or fancy cars in it for her, she was gone. Toward the end it was a crack head that had once worked out at Mustang Ranch and lived a floor below him at the Riverside. Eddie wasn't about to keep her high so she split. He didn't care; all he wanted to do with his money was lose it.

As his stake dwindled, he started hitting the booze pretty good. At first, Eddie drank bottles of Heineken to chase shots of Crown Royal, but when the money was running out, he started downing well bourbon as if he were trying to drown in it.

It was the dead of winter and he was down to his last few hundred bucks. Behind on his rent, he looked like crap. Hadn't had a haircut in months and his clothes were filthy. He rarely shaved and smelled bad. Lost his last dollar at the craps table betting crazy propositions and vanished.

I didn't see him for a couple of months and didn't really miss him much. One day, another degenerate who got some kind of a disability check around the first of every month and had it blown by the 10th, told me Eddie had been hanging around the rescue mission where they would feed you as long as you were sober. When they wouldn't let him in one night because he was gassed to the eyeballs, he took a swing at the guy who ran the place and got thirty days in the slam.

A few weeks later, on a bitter cold, late March afternoon I took a walk down that way. It was spitting snow and the winds bite was nastier than usual. Maybe I wanted an up close and personal view of the bottom, just to remind me where I had come from. If that was the case, I certainly got an eyeful. It took some searching before I found Eddie huddled in a doorway reeking of vomit and piss on the corner of 10th and Virginia - a few blocks south of the clubs -

wrapped in a thin, dirty blanket. I swear I saw the angels of death hovering over him like buzzards in the desert. Through chattering teeth, he asked what the hell I wanted- then said he hadn't eaten in days, but had bummed enough change to buy a bottle of white port earlier that morning.

I gave him a fin and told him to get something to eat. Without a word, he cast aside the blanket, like a snake shedding its skin and headed north on Virginia. I hustled around the corner and paralleled him on 9th. I went two blocks before cutting back over to Virginia. I was a block behind him and fully expected him to head for the cheap drinks at the Cal- Neva. Instead, he ducked into Fitzgerald's.

You might have heard about what happened next. It was in all the papers, all over the news. He walked up to the huge slot machine they have by the front door of all the casinos, a progressive machine with a jackpot of 2.5 million. He fed it the five and pulled the handle. Bells rang, lights flashed and suckers stared. Four sevens on the center line, Eddie was rich, again.

Most rational people would see the situation for what it was, a chance at redemption, and an opportunity to have lived an adventure along with a wakeup call to rejoin the squares in the real world. They would believe that for once, fate was left handed and threw them a fat one. Not Fast Eddie, he must have still had something to prove to someone. Or maybe it was just that with every dollar he lost, Eddie wanted to scream at that real world, "Screw You! I'm doing exactly what I want and don't give a fuck what you think."

That's all been a while ago. Eddie just disappeared. I heard he went to Vegas. Maybe he thought some different scenery would change his luck. But luck is a lady you can't seduce no matter where you are, no matter how much dough you have. She was just another fickle dame who continually thumbed her nose at Eddie. That money wouldn't last any longer there than it had here. See, that's the thing about gambling. No matter who you are or how much you think you know- the casinos, card rooms and race tracks slowly grind every last dime out of you. One day you are riding high, the next you are broke and wondering how the hell it could have happened. But you know, gamblers always know - they just won't admit it. Maybe that's what I liked about Eddie; he had no expectations about winning.

Spring will arrive soon and he has one thing going for him, he will most likely be broke again but at least spring is a hell of a lot warmer in Sin City than it is here. That you can bet on.

Strangers In Vegas

By Aidan Thorn

Dedication: *For Simon, you fought and taught me so much about living life at such a young age. I'm richer for having known you, even if only for a short while.*

On first sight of the grotesque and bloated Manhattan skyline from his hotel window Alan Simmons knew that Las Vegas was not for him. He'd probably known it before standing at the floor to ceiling window and looking, but the view had confirmed it. Further along the infamous strip Paris and Italy had been bastardised, that sat more comfortably with Simmons - he wasn't a fan of either place. But, he had fallen in love with New York just four days before when he'd crossed the Atlantic for the first time. Now, as he knelt on his balcony with his hands cable tied behind his back and mouth wrapped in a gag, his heart sank. He realised a mockery of the Empire State Building and the rest of New York's mesmerising skyline with a roller coaster wrapped around it was going to be one of the last things he saw.

He closed his eyes and tried to remember the majesty of the real thing, but it was hard to concentrate with a gun pressed into the back of his swollen right ear. It felt as if there was a rhythm to the gun pressed into his head. In reality, his head was throbbing from a beating received sometime earlier. Exactly how long ago Simmons had no way of knowing. He'd blacked out after the first dozen or so blows. When he had been slapped back to consciousness he found himself bound, his two attackers stood over him. One of the men was built like the trunk of a 200-year-old Oak and was nearly as tall. His face the sort of blank that suggested he wasn't one of life's great thinkers. The other man had a more natural build but was unnaturally ugly. He was dressed sharp but his face spoiled the look.

They'd dragged Simmons out into the stifling Las Vegas heat. They were on his balcony. Sweat ran from his pores and merged with the blood on his shirt. The metallic taste in his throat told Simmons he'd be coughing up more blood soon.

When he stepped off the plane in Nevada the first thing that hit Alan Simmons was that desert heat; it was like standing next to an open oven on a hot day. The heat right now was just as intense only it didn't bother him as much as the pain searing through every bone, organ and welting across his skin. He coughed deep, his ribs strained painfully and the blood came. The attackers took a step back to avoid the splatter.

"I guess if you could go back and make some different choices you probably would, hey?" asked the smaller of the two attackers. He was the sort of ugly that could turn even the freshest milk. Despite his action, as he stood over a broken Simmons his tone was almost friendly - sympathetic even.

Simmons might have agreed, if he had any idea what these men were doing here. He had been knocked out from behind in the hotel corridor as he'd swiped his key card in the door to his room. He'd seen the two men walking towards him, as he'd approached his door, but hadn't expected what followed, why would he? He'd even nodded a hello at them.

His attackers had dragged him into the room and brought him around, a glass of cold water thrown in his face, before dishing out a vicious beating. There had been no words, just a few grunts of exertion. Alan Simmons hoped, at least, that before he died he would be told why. Until the man in front of him had spoken just now on the balcony,

Simmons assumed that this was a robbery and they weren't going to risk leaving a witness. In the moments before he blacked out for a second time Simmons had not recognised either of the men that had forced their way into his hotel room. But then, he'd only been here a few days - he wasn't exactly Mr Vegas, he didn't know anyone here.

It appeared Simmons was at least going to get his wish of knowing why he was about to die. His attacker did not wait for Simmons to try mumbling an answer through his gag. The question had been rhetorical.

"Yeah, you'd keep your pudgy little nose out of my business if you could get a do over," the attacker continued, still keeping the tone light, there was even an indication of a smile at the edges of his mouth. "But, I can't act on what you would have done had you known the consequences. I sort of wish I could, I don't like this part of things, really I don't. But, the thing is you can't undo what you've done, as much as I'm sure you want to right now, right? No, the damage is done and so I've got to put you down. I just hope my little whore was worth giving your life for. Of course, she might have promised to stay with you once you'd whisked her away, but I think we both know that's a fantasy too far, right?" he lifted his foot and tapped Simmons sizeable belly, it wobbled with the gentlest of impact.

As his flabby gut moved and the words left the mouth of the attacker with the ugliest face he'd had the misfortune to look upon Alan Simmons understood why he was either about to be shot or thrown off of the balcony of, the most comfortable and palatial room he'd ever laid his head. If it weren't going to hurt so much he'd have laughed.

Five Days Earlier...

The American Airlines flight had left New York's JFK airport as dusk settled over the city. Office blocks still buzzed with activity, and bar staff readied themselves for the onslaught of after-work socials and pre-theatre diners. Tourists stared skywards despite themselves, wowed by the scale of the surrounding buildings. Simmons had looked out of the plane's tiny window and watched as the Big Apple went about its business. And, as he bid farewell to the city that never slept he felt his eyes go heavy and settled back into his cramped seat. He drifted off before the seatbelt signs died back into darkness.

After five hours in the air the plane touched down on tarmac in Nevada. Alan Simmons hadn't set his watch to Nevada time and had trouble working out what time it should be. He was tired and that was adding to his confusion. He had intended to sleep for the duration of the flight but his economy class seat had not been built with the comfort of a man of his size in mind. As heavy as his eyes had gotten, he'd been unable to sleep for more than a few minutes at a time without waking up in discomfort. He'd been sleeping well on this trip; better than he ever could at home. But, he'd never been able to sleep properly on a plane.

He had an excellent view of the glowing neon Las Vegas strip from his window seat as the plane taxied a glaring contrast to the pitch black of the desert night. The plane came to a halt and he waited as passengers in a hurry shoved through the narrow walkway to disembark. He let the rush die down - he was here for a few days and was not inclined to hurry. This trip to the States was his retirement treat to himself. Something he'd never had time for during a life dedicated to the job. A job that had taken far more from him than 30 years – it had taken everything. Last week he had been clearing his desk of personal belongings and paying for drinks for well-wishers he barely knew outside of work as he said goodbye to those thirty years in law enforcement. The label of Detective Chief Inspector that he had worn proudly in front of his name for the past decade and a half would be used no more.

Las Vegas was the second stop of a three-city tour. He'd already enjoyed sightseeing in New York and was looking forward to relaxing in San Diego, but Vegas was the real deal, this was the important one. It was here he intended to sink into the one vice he indulged that didn't involve stuffing his face. He wasn't interested in burlesque shows, Elvis impersonators, trips to the Grand Canyon or rollercoasters. He wanted to spend four days on an air-conditioned casino floor without windows or clocks and lose himself throwing good money after bad. As he made his way through the airport passing the rows of glowing fruit machines he knew he was in the right place. Clearly some of his fellow travellers had the bug worse than he did, they were already filling the machines with money. Simmons could wait; he wanted to do his gambling on the strip, that's why he'd come.

Bags collected and sitting in a taxi, Simmons watched as the price on the meter turned as quickly as the wheels on the car. It was clear he'd left New York where taxis carpeted the roads yellow, provided the city with a soundtrack of horns and screeching tyres, and cost next to nothing.

"Where d'ya come in from my man?" The driver asked, another fifty cents adding to the total in the time it took for the question to come out.

"New York."

"New York? But your accent ain't no American that I ever heard."

"I'm from Southampton in England. I just flew in from New York."

"Nice, I got family over on that coast, brother and his wife live in Philadelphia. You like New York?"

"It was great, wish I'd had longer."

"Well you're in Vegas now, boy. I hope you enjoy that even more." The car pulled in under a monster of a building the size of a small Hampshire village and the driver turned to face Simmons. "This is your hotel. I'll grab your bags from the trunk and one of these fine gentlemen will help you to the lobby to get you checked in."

Before the car came to a stop a smartly dressed young man was next to the back door ready to open it and help him out. Perhaps the price of a taxi ride in the USA was directly related to the level of customer service received - in New York he'd barely raised a grunt from a single driver until it came time to pay the fare.

If the service from the airport to the hotel was impressive, the hotel itself went another step beyond. The lobby was palatial and after stepping into a lift, or 'elevator' as the young lady behind reception had called it, that was bigger than his kitchen. Arriving at his room that was as large as his house back in England, and orders of magnitude more luxurious. He could get used to this. With greater energy than he had exerted in more years than he cared to remember he leapt onto the giant bed. He rolled over three times before reaching the edge – impressive for a normal sized man, even more impressive for Simmons. There were walk in wardrobes that lit up when he opened the doors, two large televisions, a bath he could swim in and the whole room could be controlled through the TV remote – he could even order room service through it. For a place that made its money 22 floors below keeping people hooked to machines and gaming tables it seemed counter-productive that they would make the rooms so beautiful that you'd never want to leave, but he wasn't complaining. He kicked off his shoes, laid back and started an interactive tour of the hotel through one of the TV screens. He was a little more than a minute into the tour when it struck him that the all of the restaurants, bars and casino facilities that flashed before his eyes were in the same building as he was. He hit the off button on the remote and headed back to the elevator.

He walked up to a fruit machine and tried feeding it money, and, suddenly, his illusion was robbed of its romance. He'd always dreamt of standing before a machine as it noisily chugged out coin after coin, but now he saw they neither took or paid out real money. He'd have to load his 'members' card with credit if he wanted to play, somehow a little receipt with your winnings printed on didn't hold the same appeal to the ex-Detective. It didn't stop him heading off to the cashier booth and loading up with credit though.

He looked longingly at the games tables as he made his way back from the booth. He'd had a long day, starting over on the east coast and the flight had been as tiring as it was uncomfortable. As much as he wanted to play the tables, he knew he needed a clear mind before he sat down in that area. Tonight he'd stick to the machines. He could get an early start on the tables tomorrow morning, refreshed and ready.

The casino floor was bustling with tourists, like six-year-olds on a bowl full of sugar they buzzed with excitement. Vegas appeared to be the place that Americans came to let their hair down and act like kids again. There were parties of people in their 40s and 50s drinking cocktails from yard glasses and acting like first year students newly arrived in their new town. In Chicago, San Francisco and Washington these people were probably accountants, doctors and architects but in Vegas they were free of the daily grind. Surrounded by so many people, high on life, Simmons felt truly lonely for the first time since arriving in America. He found an area of machines that was unoccupied and sat. He wanted some space and his own company only as he worked. He was not a very social animal. One of the things he had enjoyed most in New York was that as he walked the streets and avenues of crowds he got a feeling that everyone was alone. He felt like he belonged there. He didn't need anyone else in New York, he didn't receive strange looks when he sat down alone in the evening for dinner or sat at a bar for a beer. He would never have felt comfortable walking into a pub back in England and sitting by himself and so he rarely went in them. Back home he'd feel judged and mocked by those around him, feel eyes watching him, wondering what the weirdo sat in the corner was doing there. In New York, he'd been able to relax and enjoy the company of the city's parks and towering architecture. Las Vegas on the other hand was a revellers paradise. The good thing about the part of the casino he had found was that the few people around appeared completely focused on their particular game, hypnotised by the lights and lure of a potential win. Again, he could be alone and comfortable with that.

"Evening sir, can I offer you a bud or bud light compliments of the casino?"

Simmons hadn't seen the young woman approach. She was dressed in a feminine version of the bellboy's uniform. She held a tray of bottled beer and smiled all the time she spoke. Simmons looked up from his game and straight into her smiling face. She was immaculate and very beautiful although the bland hotel uniform and understated make-up was clearly designed to keep her from being a distraction from the games.

"Thank-you, that would be great."

"So what's it to be, regular or light?" she asked pointing to one of each type on the tray she carried.

Simmons had never even heard of light beer until he'd arrived in the U.S a few days before, he certainly didn't understand it.

"Regular please," he responded. He'd never ordered

'regular' food or drinks before but over here they didn't seem to understand 'medium' or 'normal'.

"A man after my own heart," the waitress handed over his bottle and gave him a wink. She was young enough for that to still be true, but if she was going to maintain the figure that was hidden beneath her uniform she'd be moving to the light beer or cutting it out altogether soon, Simmons thought.

He thanked the waitress but she lingered at his side, he quickly realised that she was expecting a tip. He had nothing smaller than a twenty-dollar bill, that seemed a lot for a complimentary drink but this was America, a tip was expected. He pulled the note from his pocket and wondered if he could ask for change. The waitress's smile broadened as she glimpsed the money and before Simmons could make an arse of himself she had solved his dilemma for him.

"Thank you sir, how about we say the rest of the night the beers really are on the house," she turned, flashing another smile, and left him to his game.

Simmons hadn't been planning on drinking twenty dollars' worth of beer this evening but he liked to get value for money so he would. He continued with his game and despite small victories found himself seventy dollars down very quickly. He put his luck down to flight fatigue affecting his concentration but couldn't make himself walk away despite wanting to. His addiction meant he always had to take just one last spin of the wheels. And when that one was done, there would always be just one more. The waitress returned at regular intervals to pick up an empty bottle and replace it with a fresh one sweating beads of cool moisture. She was as good as her word and didn't linger long enough for Simmons to have time to tip again. On the occasions that he was quick enough to look up and thank her she just winked and replied 'No problem, Sugar' as she walked away. At a hundred and ten dollars down and with five Buds sunk, Simmons considered calling it a night. He looked at his watch and discovered that it was a little after two in the morning. Where had the time gone?

He gave himself ten more minutes. Another Bud arrived.

At 2.40am he'd had a winning forty minutes and was back to just seventy dollars down. A young woman in tight denim hot pants cut high on her ass and a tight white vest top that just about kept her decent put herself on the stool at the machine next to Simmons. He carried on playing but it was difficult not to look to the side after every few presses of the buttons. He wasn't distracted by the women's looks, although he couldn't deny the girl was pretty, if a little too heavily made up, no she was obviously losing bad and wasn't doing so quietly.

"Oh shucks I really shouldn't play these things," she said glancing coyly in Simmons' direction. She caught him looking back. He gave a brief smile that probably looked creepier than his intended supportive. He made to turn back to his machine but she seized on the brief eye contact and used it to try to strike up a conversation that he wasn't all that interested in engaging in. A beautiful smile flashed across her face and he eyes shone with welcoming kindness.

"Hi there, how are you making out?"

"Better than I was an hour ago but not as good as I was before I left my room," Simmons replied trying to keep his eyes on his machine. Not an easy task as his neighbour had bounced off of her stool leaving her own game and was now leaning against the machine he was playing.

"It's always the way right?" she beamed at Simmons.

Her outfit, or lack of it, attracted attention, as it was designed to, and Simmons was pulled in. Her perfect smooth tanned skin was taut over an athletically muscular and yet feminine body – a body that was draped over his machine seductively.

He hit glowing buttons trying not to appear the dirty old man that he felt, his mind imprinted what his eyes had taken in.

He lost.

"Oh honey, too bad," the girl said as her attention flicked from the machine to Simmons. "Maybe we should both call it a night. Why don't you come and join me for a drink."

Simmons gave her a look that said, what's wrong with you? It wasn't that he didn't want to take her up on her offer he just couldn't understand why she was interested in him.

"Come on honey," she said, walking her fingers up Simmons arm and resting a hand softly on his shoulder. "What d'ya say we get a couple of drinks, head to your room and you could put that money to better use?"

Feeling embarrassed that the penny hadn't dropped sooner Simmons let out a laugh of resignation, "Oh I get it you're a whore," he said dismissively.

The prostitute tried to maintain a smile but it had turned from warm to awkward. She pulled her hand away and stepped back slightly from the machine.

"Don't like what you see?"

She shook her hair and gestured towards her figure, highlighting it in all the right places. It was a little self-preservation on her part. The way she shook her hair and held her arms out pointing to herself was a gesture that she didn't look comfortable making.

He pressed a couple of buttons and lost again. His embarrassment at not realising he'd been sitting with a working girl combined with his frustration at another loss came out in an angry outburst.

"Go on, love, fuck off and bother someone else. I'm not interested in your disease riddled…" He looked at her crotch unable to say the word in front of a lady - even if she was a whore. "Look, I'm just not interested and anyway, I don't pay for it, alright?"

The prostitute looked hard at Simmons. She was trying to disguise her upset as anger but she wouldn't have fooled a blind man. She looked him up and down before turning away, shouting back over her shoulder. "If you don't pay for it, I guess you've never had it then!"

***

There was a carpet on Simmons' tongue and pressure behind his eyes when he woke up. He'd drunk far more than he'd intended and was going to pay in more than just a 20 dollar tip and his losses at the fruit machine. A look at his watch told him that despite getting to bed well after 3am he had woken up before seven. His body clock, dragged between the time zones of the UK, New York and Nevada, was all over the place. He pulled himself from the gigantic bed, stepping onto lush carpet he lumbered to the bathroom. Every footstep jarred and made his head pound.

There were two tiny heavy bottomed glasses by the sink. He filled both with water, drank one straight down and carried the other to the balcony doors. The automated curtains fought against him as he tried to pull them back; hands weren't supposed to open them. He wished he hadn't bothered as the gap revealed the fake Manhattan of the New York, New York hotel. His nausea got worse. He looked along the strip, it was a deserted soulless vision in the early hours of the morning. Very different to the vibrant place that he'd arrived at the previous evening.

He needed fresh air. He opened the glass door to step onto the balcony but found his need unsatisfied as the stifling dry heat hit his clammy face. It felt as though something was squeezing his eyes out of his skull from behind; the cloudless sky was too bright. He stepped back inside and pulled the doors shut. He was thankful for the tinting on the glass and air-conditioning that chilled the room. A growling and empty ache from low in his stomach told Simmons that he had an appetite for food, which left him with a problem because he had no appetite to go outside into the heat. The thought of the hotel's bars and eateries bought back too many memories of a night he'd rather forget. He found himself crouched next to the open door of the mini bar refrigerator. The cold air from inside was welcome, even if the bright light was not. Every item inside was fun size in everything but price. He could never understand where the fun was in eating barely enough food to taste it, especially when it was costing more than the full sized version. Simmons could probably just about satisfy his hunger by emptying the entire fridge but it would cost him almost as much as he'd lost the previous evening. The chilled air from within the open refrigerator door ate away the beads of perspiration on his face and Simmons resolved to head onto the strip and seek out a seek out a place that served breakfast, just as soon as his knees allowed him to stand.

***

Breakfast had been large. Even at his girth, and with an appetite that would have forced a small café in England to close its doors, Simmons had struggled to finish the entire plate. He had found a faux biker bar serving breakfast across from his hotel on the strip. The only customer, Simmons had placed a well-thumbed paperback copy of Lawrence Block's *Hope to Die* on the table whilst he ate. He didn't read whilst he sat there. The book was a prop – it was supposed to tell people *I'm a cool guy, comfortable in my own company.* A glimpse of himself in a mirrored pillar told him he wasn't pulling off the desired look. He was a retired, overweight gambling addict with a hangover and no amount of books on a table and drinking espresso from a tiny cup was going to help him look like anything else.

Feeling better for having eaten, Simmons decided against heading straight back to the hotel. He took the opportunity of quiet pavements to look around the famous Las Vegas strip. Walking had always been something Simmons had done slowly. Those first few years on the force had involved a lot of beat walking which meant slow steps as he'd scanned his eyes across his surroundings looking for wrongdoers. He'd never broken the habit of a slow walk and age and size had slowed his pace further. He shared the streets with early morning joggers, taut with athletic muscle and a few drunks that hadn't quite made it back to their hotels.

He also noticed a number of drunks that hadn't slept under a roof of any kind for some time. Surrounded by more extravagance than should rightfully be crammed into one city sat these men with nothing. Their cardboard signs communicated witty and imaginative begging messages that might have tempted Simmons to part with some cash had the people sat behind them not been chemically enhanced. Before he could feel guilty for walking past these poor empty souls he saw something that struck him with shame and embarrassment.

She was walking towards him, head down and determined – the girl from the casino a few hours ago. Sunglasses now covered the eyes that couldn't smile when her face had but there was no mistaking that perfect figure still barely covered by tight denim shorts and a flimsy white vest. She paid him no attention as she passed him. He stood frozen with shame at how he'd reacted to her approaches just hours before. He hadn't been angry at her, more at his luck at the slots and the fact that he, a 30-year veteran of the police force, hadn't worked her out. He knew she hadn't been there by choice and that it must have been a pretty shitty set of circumstances that had led a girl that looked like her to be propositioning a man like him for sex.

"I'm sorry about last night," Simmons found himself involuntarily calling after her as he thought on his lack of decency. He surprised himself but not as much as he surprised the woman he called after.

Initially she threw a look over her shoulder, apparently more to look for where the voice had come from than because she'd thought that it was aimed at her. She took a step or two before stopping and taking a second look as she realised that Simmons was talking to her.

"Me?" she asked, gesturing to herself. She didn't appear to recognise Simmons and this saddened him deeply. Not because he wanted her to remember their altercation, but because if their exchange hadn't stayed long in the memory it probably hadn't been the worst thing that had happened to her in the past few hours. As she stepped tentatively towards him, he saw a red puffiness around the edges of her sunglasses.

"Sorry, yes, um we met briefly in the casino last night." Simmons stumbled awkwardly over his words. "I was having a bad night at the slots and I took it out on you. I just wanted you to know I'm sorry."

"Oh yeah I remember, hey don't sweat it," she said with a resignation in her tone that suggested she expected to be treated badly. She turned to walk on.

Simmons couldn't let go, "Is everything ok?" He called to her back.

She stopped and her shoulders dropped in that way a teenager does when challenged by a teacher.

"Everything is wonderful honey," she responded sarcastically without turning around.

She didn't move and he took this as an invitation to approach. As he did she turned to face him, tears had started to fall over the patchy redness around her eyes.

Simmons felt uncomfortable at the thought of her walking off upset and alone.

"You're probably hungry. Can I buy you something to eat?"

"I'm off duty for the night honey. You had your chance last night, oh and just a tip you don't have to buy a girl like me dinner we're sure things."

Her harsh self-deprivation was a clear attempt to detract from the obvious emotions she wore on her face.

"I'm not interested in any of that I just thought maybe you'd appreciate a good feed and the listening ear of a stranger."

She tilted her head in a bewildered way that said, is this guy for real, before her emotions got the better of her and she sobbed. She nodded her head and tried for a thankful smile.

***

Her name was Natalie, she'd told him after he'd introduced himself as Alan on the way back to the faux biker bar that he had left less than an hour before. After returning from the bathroom freshened up from her tears, she had ordered the same gut-busting breakfast through which Simmons had struggled. She sipped from a large glass of fresh orange juice whilst she waited for its arrival. Simmons had considered ordering more food but stuck with coffee.

"Where you from, Alan?" Natalie asked breaking the silence after the waiter had delivered their drinks. She was clearly deflecting the conversation away from her obvious problems before Simmons got a chance to ask her what was bothering her.

"England."

"Well I kind of figured that," she said "I meant whereabouts in England."

"Originally Southampton, but I spent most of my working life in and around London."

"And what is it you do in London?"

"I was a Detective."

"Well whoops!" Natalie said mockingly putting her hands out in front of her as if to offer them for cuffs, "Why, was?" she asked.

"Because I'm retired," he replied. "This trip is the first thing I've done since. I was on a plane to New York a couple of days after my last day on the job."

"New York?" Natalie was puzzled.

"Yeah I spent a few days there first."

The waiter interrupted the small talk. He brought Natalie's food and ran his gaze over her body before offering Simmons a look that was at once envious and accusatory, as though he wanted to say, you dirty, lucky bastard.

Natalie stopped asking questions as she greedily shovelled her greasy breakfast into her mouth. Simmons watched in astonishment as her appetite appeared to outstrip his and yet she maintained a figure that couldn't spare an ounce of fat.

As she ate Natalie's pace slowed, she looked at Simmons and blew out her cheeks signalling that she was nearly beat. As her mouthfuls became less frequent Simmons seized the opportunity to try to find out what had been troubling Natalie when they'd met on the strip.

"So Natalie, you were clearly upset when we met this morning what was that all about?"

She forked another mouthful of bacon into her mouth and chewed it for longer than was needed to delay her response.

"The short answer is that I'm a prostitute, Alan."

She'd replied in a way that made Simmons feel cold for having asked such an obvious and painful question. Simmons wore his regret at her situation on his face. Natalie read that regret and in an attempt to make it disappear, she quickly flipped the subject back to small talk.

"This breakfast is good, thanks for doing this for me."

He nodded and tried to smile, but it couldn't quite form. Natalie could see she'd made him uncomfortable.

"Don't sweat it, Al. It is what it is. A girl's got to eat right? And, it's not every day a guy stops her in the street and offers to buy her breakfast." She spoke in the third person distancing herself from what she did for money. She was also trying to make light of the unusual and uncomfortable position that they both now found themselves in.

Simmons had spent a lot of time interviewing people, victims, witnesses and criminals. He had a sense for when someone wanted to talk but wasn't quite ready. He was getting that feeling from Natalie. She'd been deflecting and avoiding, she wasn't just going to throw everything out there. She wanted Simmons to work for it, pretend she didn't really want to say anything, but she'd be disappointed if he didn't continue with his interest. Simmons had faith in his theory but decided to test it.

"Well it's been good meeting you Natalie. Again, I'm sorry for how I treated you last night but I'd better get on with my day so I'd better get the bill."

Her expression gave her away before she spoke.

"I don't mean to take advantage, but I could use a coffee before you get that check, or bill as you say," she said bill in a mock English accent.

He'd been right, she wanted someone to talk to and talk she did.

***

Simmons listened as Natalie described her life in perfect and depressing detail. From falling in love with the Las Vegas showgirls, she'd seen on TV as a child and dedicating her whole life to dance with the dream of becoming one, to stepping off a Greyhound bus in Las Vegas, having travelled from Detroit, to follow that dream.

Natalie had been at the front of the queue when the bus opened its doors. She'd stepped into the Nevada sun heaving a suitcase in one hand and clutching a letter tightly in the other. She hadn't let the letter out of her sight since she'd received it two weeks before. It was a letter telling her that she'd been successful in an audition and she was now a member of a Las Vegas dance company.

As an eight-year-old girl, she had been mesmerised by the outfits and flawless beauty of the girls as they'd effortlessly breezed through stunning routines on her TV. She had trained night and day in various disciplines of dance and gymnastics. Her parents had been supportive of her enthusiasm for something that would keep her healthy and out of trouble. Their support dwindled quickly when they realised that her early inspiration was not going away and she intended to follow her dream of becoming a Las Vegas showgirl. Natalie was a bright girl and her parents felt her capable of achieving anything she put her mind to. Unfortunately, for them she was strong willed with a single focus. As she got older nearly every conversation, Natalie had with her parents ended in an argument. They tried to convince her that her dream was pointless, that competition was high and that she would be unlikely to achieve her goal, perhaps she should focus on something more worthwhile. Her relationship with her parents fell apart. But, that letter clutched tightly in her hand was validation of her determination. She had been right - her parents would have to live with that.

But, it hadn't worked out. Natalie was good, but the standard was higher than even she could cope with and the choreographer that ran the dance company didn't like her. Natalie told Simmons how within six weeks of arriving to fulfil her dreams she found herself without a job.

***

"I was staying with a girl, Sarah, who'd put an ad in the paper. I didn't know her too well, but she seemed friendly enough." The coffee that Natalie had asked for before starting her story had sat untouched and cold. "She found me sobbing in my room, she was kind to me – she listened."

Simmons had spent more days than he cared to count in interrogation rooms. Experience had taught him that a person introduced as 'seeming friendly', was usually far from it.

Natalie continued, "Sarah suggested I go out with her that evening to cheer myself up. I wasn't keen, but she kept on, 'come on kid, just come for one drink, I guarantee you a good time,' so I went."

It was obvious Natalie was heading somewhere she wasn't comfortable talking about. She stopped and sipped coffee without reacting to the fact that it was now cold. Simmons sat silently. He knew it was best to let someone speak in his or her own time. She had offered her story; she'd get there eventually.

"Sarah introduced me to a guy, Gino. He was a funny looking little man, but he was saying all the right things and with my confidence on the floor, I guess I was just happy to hear a compliment or two. I let him buy me a few drinks, he asked for my number, I wasn't keen but he knew Sarah so I couldn't give him a fake one.

"Long story, short, turns out Sarah and Gino were more than friends, they were business partners. I'd been played. Rent day came around and with no work I couldn't pay. Sarah kicked up a stink, told me I'd have to get out if I couldn't pay; she wasn't running a charity home. Within an hour of that exchange, my phone rings and it's Gino offering me a 'business opportunity'. The timing seemed odd, but I didn't think on it for too long. I agreed to meet him and discuss it."

Natalie told Simmons a familiar story, he'd come into contact with plenty of prostitutes in his time on the force. None of them had longed to go into that profession from an early age, they'd all been trapped by drug addiction or circumstance – Natalie was no different. She'd faced such a hard time from her family over the pursuit of her dream. She didn't feel she could return home and face them. Better she kept up the pretence, sent then letters postmarked Nevada and let them think she was a success – even if it meant she walked the deserted early morning Strip in tears most days.

***

"You couldn't find another dancing job somewhere in Las Vegas?"

The question sounded tinged with judgement, he hadn't intended it to.

"They call Reno the biggest little city in the world. If that's true of Reno the opposite is true of Vegas. It's a big place, but everyone's in the hospitality and entertainment game, and everyone knows each other. Once I was sacked from that first job I had no hope of finding another. I turned up for auditions, most of the time they wouldn't even see me."

"And you couldn't go dance somewhere else?"

"I could, but every time I thought about doing that I just heard my parents' voices in my head saying, I told you so. I know it's crazy, I know I'm living a lie but if I can send home the odd letter postmarked Las Vegas, upload a photo or two to Facebook of me stood in front of the Bellagio fountains and pretend everything is OK, it feels like they don't get to win. They'd been awful to me about my dream to come here and became a Showgirl. When I got the job here, they finally admitted that they were proud of me, told me that it was my determination that got me where I wanted to be. I got here in spite of them, there's no way I can leave here yet… one day, but not yet."

Simmons shook his head with resignation.

"You think I'm stupid, don't you?" Natalie asked. "Don't worry; I know I'm stupid, I know there's nothing rational about how I'm living. But you didn't grow up with my parents."

"I don't think you're stupid, I just wish I could shake you kids sometimes."

Simmons banged a fist on the table, his face had reddened and the corners of his eyes had moistened. His reaction shocked Natalie. The waiter had been making his way over to refill spent coffee cups, he checked his step and headed back to his counter.

"What the fuck, Al? Why so angry, you don't even know me. This time next week you'll be back in England and I'll be long forgotten. I'm sorry I unloaded my shit on you, but it's not your problem. You've got a holiday to enjoy."

"I'm sorry, your story just hits a little too close to home. Your relationship with your parents reminds me of mine with my son."

Natalie tried to take some tension out of the atmosphere. She joked, "I suppose he's a hooker too."

"No, he's dead."

***

Coffee cups were refilled a couple of times as Simmons told Natalie about his son. In so many ways, Natalie's situation was nothing like the one that Alan Simmons described, but in one, it was the same. Natalie had allowed her poor relationship with her parents to drive her into the hands of people that wanted to exploit her, regardless of how much it was hurting her. His son, Ian, had done similar.

Bullied as a child, because his father was a policeman, Ian had turned to drugs at a young age. He'd wanted to fit in with his peers and rebel against his dad. His habit ultimately landed him in prison and got his throat cut. Simmons blamed himself for Ian's death and knew that if Natalie's parents were aware of how she was making a living, and why, they would feel equally culpable.

"I've never spoken to a stranger about that before."

He looked more than a little embarrassed to have exposed something so personal.

Natalie recognised his discomfort.

"I'm sorry, what happened to your boy, that was terrible."

Simmons nodded and silence hung in the air for a while. They were no longer the only customers in the restaurant - neither of them had noticed other diners arriving. After an uncomfortable amount of time, Natalie broke the silence.

"As sad as I am for you, Alan, and really I am, I have to say I don't do drugs. I can't really see how what happened to

Ian is relevant to me."

"You don't? It's not about the drugs. You don't see that your toxic relationship with your parents is what drove you into this life? You don't see that in keeping up this façade that you're a successful Las Vegas showgirl and not a prostitute just to prove your parents wrong the only real loser is you? Ian hated me; he rebelled against me so strongly that he ended up dead. You've put yourself in a very dangerous position. You could equally end up dead - and for what? So you can pretend to them that they were wrong and you were right? I've only been in your company for an hour and I already know you're better than that."

Natalie felt awkward. She knew that this man sat opposite her, despite not knowing her, had summarised her problem perfectly. She flushed red with embarrassment and tears soon followed.

"I don't know what to do."

She wasn't looking for an answer but Simmons gave her one.

"Leave here. You cannot be a success here, but you can anywhere else in the world. You're only here because your parents didn't think you couldn't make it here. I'm sorry but you can't, not now – you've said as much. Get out, go somewhere else, you don't have to go home, New York, LA, London, Paris, it doesn't matter, just don't do this anymore."

Natalie dried her eyes and shook herself proud – or tried. He could see right through the *façade*.

"I'm sorry for what's happened to you, really I am. Thank you for the breakfast, but you don't even fucking know me."

It was hard to tell whether the anger in Natalie's tone was directed at Simmons, or whether she was simply frustrated by the situation. She stood and Simmons watched as her perfect dancer's figure strutted away. He wanted to follow her – to shake her until she listened. He just sat and watched - another damaged soul that couldn't be fixed. It wasn't his place to fix Natalie, but it wouldn't stop him caring.

***

He spent the days that followed as he'd intended, attached to gaming tables. He won and lost by the hour, trying, and failing, not to get attached to the money that fleetingly moved through his possession. The design of the chips was intended to detach them from the reality of their relationship to money; they were brightly coloured playthings to throw around on a whim, a hunch, a feeling. Simmons had never been able to fall for the trick though, he only ever saw the cash – but he was an addict, he couldn't stop.

A Shrink would probably tell Simmons that somewhere, deep in his roots, he wanted to lose – needed to even. They'd say he was using the anger and frustration at the loss of money to mask the things he was really angry about. The wife that left him bringing up their son on his own, the career that he'd given everything to and the son whose death he blamed himself for. A shrink would probably tell Simmons all of that, but he'd never find out because he'd never visit one.

He only left the tables to answer the calls of restrooms, his bed and his stomach. The tables were good for something; Simmons only ate when he had to and found he was probably only really eating twice during the day. He never slept well, but a combination of confusion around time zones and the timeless environment of the casinos played havoc with his rest. He went to bed in the small hours and woke again in the only slightly bigger ones.

Each morning whilst most of Vegas slept, and some of

it hadn't been to bed, he walked the strip. He convinced himself that he was looking for a different place to try the breakfast offering. In reality, he was hoping to see Natalie. He didn't want to speak to her, unless she approached him, he just wanted to see her and hoped there weren't tears in her eyes. Four mornings Simmons walked sections of the strip and each time he returned with a full belly but unsatisfied, he hadn't seen her.

At the door to his room Simmons, was trying to get his mind off the girl he could do nothing about and back on the gaming tables. He'd take a shower, brush his teeth, go down, and put in the hours chasing the house.

He felt the whack on the back of his head. There was a spark of white light. He didn't feel his face hit the door. His legs went soft. The world went black.

***

Back where we began...

Beaten and about to be killed, it wasn't easy for Alan Simmons to collect his thoughts. But, he could still add two to two and work out that ugly was Gino, Natalie's scumbag pimp. A number of thoughts flooded through his head, they were no longer about his situations, but Natalie's.

Clearly, Natalie had disappeared. Maybe their conversation had knocked something lose in her head and she'd decided to get away from Gino, away from Las Vegas and start afresh someplace else. He hoped that was the case, but Simmons had been conditioned to pessimism. Natalie had been upset when she'd walked out of that diner days before. What if he'd gone too far in telling her she couldn't be a success in Las Vegas, something she'd worked toward her whole life? She knew it herself, but having a stranger say it to her, maybe it had been enough to tip her over the edge. Maybe she hadn't run away, maybe she was lying somewhere undiscovered with a litre of vodka and a bottle of pills in her stomach.

Simmons didn't want to die not knowing. He started to laugh underneath his gag. It was unnatural and hurt him almost as much as if he was taking the beating again. He exaggerated the laugh, it was designed to tell Gino that Simmons knew something he didn't and that Simmons couldn't believe how stupid the pimp was. He was gambling that he'd pique Gino's interest enough to remove the gag and get a conversation going. He'd been gambling all week, what harm would one more roll of the dice do?

"Can you believe this fucking guy?"

Gino spoke to his larger accomplice who shrugged blankly, in that one action it became clear to Simmons that the big lad was here for size and size alone.

"What the fuck do you have to laugh about, fat man?" Gino said.

The falsely friendly tone had been dropped. Simmons had annoyed his attacker, but he could also see that he'd achieved his aim. Gino's eyes told Simmons he wanted to know what it was that Simmons was finding so funny. Gino turned to his Muscle.

"Get that fucking gag off of him."

Bingo!

The big lump wretched the gag away and Simmons took a big gasp of the still Vegas air.

"So fat man, what's so funny?"

"I take it we're talking about Natalie?"

"Ha! She really went hard on you didn't she, you schmuck. Told you her real name and everything, I guess she told you she loved you too?"

Simmons ignored any attempt to belittle him and

pushed on.

"I take it she's gone walk about then?"

"You fucking know she has, fat man. But guess what there's no happy ending for you, because firstly, whatever she's promised you she isn't waiting for you in some hotel somewhere and secondly, my friend Tommy and I are about to throw you off of this balcony."

"OK, but before you do that, tell me a couple of things…"

Simmons was trying to sound calm, detached from everything that was happening. It was a technique he'd picked up as a detective, pretend the situation isn't really that important to you, you've got something else you'd rather be doing, but you'll listen if you really have to. It worked more often than not, the subject was usually so irritated by this attitude it loosened their tongue. They couldn't bear not being the most complete focus of attention. And, it was just about to work with Gino.

"What?"

"Well first, if Natalie is missing, why do you think I had anything to do with it and if I did why would I still be here? Secondly, how do you know she's run off and hasn't been kidnapped or is lying in a ditch somewhere? I don't know if you know this but she's a prostitute, she could have met a right wrong'un.

The last comment was an exercise in sarcasm that was lost on Gino and probably the big lump with him, it was difficult to tell with the lump though, he was blank behind the eyes.

"I know what she is, she fucking works for me, stupid!" Gino responded proving sarcasm could sail above his head even on the 22nd floor. "And I know she ain't been kidnapped because she lives at my girl's place. She's cleared all her stuff out and scrawled 'fuck you' in foot high lipstick letters on the bedroom wall."

Simmons felt relief rush over him. His pessimism had been unwarranted. All the evidence pointed to Natalie deciding enough was enough and making a break for it. He allowed himself to smile inwardly at the thought that he might have helped influence that decision.

Gino was still answering Simmons questions.

"As to how I know you were involved. I know people in this city. When Natalie went missing four days ago, I started putting feelers out. One of the waiters at the grill over the road from this hotel said he'd seen her the day before, taking breakfast with a fat man. Said, Natalie and the fat man appeared to be having some sort of deep and meaningful conversation. Then it all ended in a bit of a shouting match. That was the last time anyone saw her. Strange that she should go missing right after that meeting, right?

"Do you know what I think happened? I think she convinced you to help her get away, got you to give her some getting around money and promised she'd wait for you somewhere – which she won't be by the way. She then told you that she'd stage a shouting match, so it would look like you weren't friendly and when she disappeared no one would come looking for you. You went along with it all because you were thinking with your dick."

It was a complicated theory, Gino clearly watched too many prime time TV cop shows but he'd convinced himself of its validity.

"Anyway this morning when that same waiter saw you walking past his place he was a good little boy and he gave me a call. I promised him a bit of cash, but we'll see."

Alan hung his head in mock defeat.

"You know what, that's pretty much spot on," he lied. "OK so a few details are wrong, I suggested the staged argument, but otherwise, you've got us bang to rights.

Problem is this; I'm not going to tell you anything. I know you'll think I'm a crazy old fool, but I'm in love with Natalie and I don't care what you do to me."

Simmons knew his lies would only end one way but he was at peace with that. He hadn't been able to save his son, but he'd helped a young girl back onto a better path, he had nothing left to give. If his death would satisfy Gino's desire for retribution over Natalie's defection, and mean Gino wasn't going to keep looking for the needle in the haystack, that was OK by Simmons.

"You're a fucking fool, but I thought as much. So, now we have to throw you off this balcony, make you look like another suicide loser that couldn't handle the losses at the tables."

"Suicides tend to go silently; I'm going to scream your name out as many times as I can before I hit the ground."

Gino's Big Lump of muscle didn't need Gino to instruct him, he roughly fixed the gag back in place so Simmons couldn't scream. Gino bent in close.

"I know, I know, suicides don't tend to gag themselves either. That's why my buddy Damien is waiting down there to remove that when you hit the floor." Gino nodded over the balcony.

Simmons had to admire Gino's planning.

The Lump and Gino hoisted Simmons up onto the balcony's barrier, a considerable effort. Underneath the gag, a smile spread across Simmons face. He closed his eyes and as his attackers let his weight drop over the edge of the hotel he didn't see the fake Manhattan, he pictured Natalie, dancing and happy.

Regarding Henri

By Darren Sant

Dedication: *To Joanne who took all life had to throw at her with unwavering dignity.*

Chapter 1: Murder in Mind

The whole office is alight. A golden flame engulfs the room as Craig stares down from the third floor window. He shields his eyes from the setting sun and his frown deepens with the fading of the day. He straightens his tie habitually and admires Moira's slender legs in the car park below as she walks briskly to her BMW, her buttocks rising and falling hypnotically beneath her knee length skirt. He imagines that he can hear the tip tap of her stilettos from up here. He thinks once more his wife, Trisha. The cheating bitch. He imagines a blade in his hand and suddenly its crimson, dripping with her blood, her lover already lying dead beside her. Craig sighs. He could never do it, but maybe if he is clever he could get himself some solid evidence for a quick divorce.

He'd never forget that night, a week before. She was out for her regular squash game with Suzie. Craig had been rooting around for his spare phone charger and struggling to find it, then at the back of a drawer he'd found it. An iPhone; an unfamiliariPhone. He'd turned it on and found it had nearly a full charge. It was keylocked, of course. He'd tried her usual password - her car registration. She loved that little Fiat 500 more than she loved him, he was certain of that now.

The phone, like a drunken lover, soon spilled its

secrets. Reams of texts from her to a man called Chuck. Filthy texts, describing what they'd do to each other when they next met. Then came the photos. Her in all of her fucking Victoria Secret splendour, licking her red lipstick smeared lips, her large breasts spilling out of undersize cups. He felt physically sick when he saw the cock pictures that were sent in return.

Craig's heart hammered in his chest and he felt faint for a moment. They were supposed to be trying for a baby next year, for God's sake. He'd held up the phone the cause of all of his misery and drew back his arm. A small voice in his head said, no, be smarter than this. You can get your revenge. With an effort of supreme will he controlled his breathing and lowered the phone. He went back to check the texts, then the contacts. He'd soon found e-mails between them too. Modern phones love tracking your location in apps and he soon had a few clues where to look for Chuck. He switched it off and carefully replaced it where he'd found it. There would be a reckoning.

Chapter 2: Henri

Henri sighed and scrubbed at the tiles until her hands were red and sore. If he saw mould on them again he'd beat her, that had been the threat. Keegan's threats were never idle when it came to violence.

She had that nagging voice of her dead Mother in her head again. I told you that boy was no good, but you didn't listen. Of course, the trouble was, no boy had ever been good enough to meet with HER approval. Keegan had come along on his Harley clad in tight leather and she'd stuck the finger up to her Mother and her own future. Now, here she was, stuck with that fucking brute in a hick town without friends or allies. She could pack up and leave but where would she go?

She straightened up and held her hand to the painful spot on her lower back. She winced once in pain and then in disgust as she checked her reflection in the bathroom mirror. Her wavy brown hair was starting to grey. The beginnings of crow's feet were encroaching the corners of her eyes. She looked tired and exhausted.

She decided to have a shower. That would put some colour in her cheeks. She slipped off her grubby blouse and reached around to unhook her bra. Suddenly a leering voice assaulted her ears.

"Don't stop on my account, darling."

Marvin the landlord was stood in the doorway chuckling, his piggy eyes were glued to her breasts and he was almost slobbering into his filthy matted grey beard.

Henri gasped and crossed her arms over her modesty. "Get out of my house you dirty old bastard."

His humour turned to anger as he jabbed a finger at her. "MY house and don't forget it. The rent is a week late. Get that drunken bum of a husband of yours to pay up or there will be trouble."

He turned as if to stride away, but stopped suddenly and spun back on his heel.

"Unless you want to come to an arrangement..."

He looked her up and down and touched his crotch for effect.

"Fuck off! Or I'll call the police."

He slouched off laughing. "I'll be back if he doesn't pay, bitch!"

Henri sat on the bath and sobbed.

Chapter 3: The Watcher

Chuck was six foot three and all of it muscle. His tightly wound dreadlocks whipped around as he turned sharply eyeballing the door of the bar. A workman bounced in suddenly finding energy after a day of slacking. He made eye contact briefly with Chuck, but then, knowing what was good for him, he looked away. When the guy had bought a beer and taken a seat near the jukebox Chuck said to Nick, the barman, "That him?"

"Naw, that ain't Keegan."

"You sure he'll be in?"

"Usually is by now."

"I swear Nick if you've fucking tipped him off..."

Nick held up his hands in a placatory gesture.

"I know better than that. What's he done anyway?" Nick drew in a breath, he'd overstepped the line in being nosy. First, rule of being a barman: don't ask. They'll soon tell. Surprisingly he got an answer and not a smack in the mouth.

"He likes to gamble, does Keegan. I bought his debt. Five large, I intend to collect and soon."

Nick nodded and wiped down the bar top, it was usually money related when Chuck got so personally involved.

In a quiet corner of the bar Craig pecked away at his phone with a stylus pretending to be busy but looked up now and then to check that Chuck was still at the bar. He could see the appeal. He was a big good-looking bastard, but he had a psychopath's gleam in his eye. Trisha always did get off on a bit of danger.

She was always pushing him to be rougher with her during sex, but Craig just didn't get off on it. Well that big bastard at the bar probably enjoyed that sort of thing.

Craig lifted his phone, zoomed in and took a quick photo of Chuck at the bar. He'd need evidence. Too late, he realised his mistake. Bright light burst out from the phone. He'd left the damn flash on.

Chuck saw the flash and ran over. "What the fuck do you think you're doing?"

Craig stumbled over his words.

"Answer me. Are you a cop?"

Chuck had his fists clenched as he stared at the frightened looking man.

Craig put his phone slowly on the table and then looked up.

"No, I'm not a cop. What I am is a man with a FAULTY FUCKING PHONE."

When Craig yelled the last few words even Chuck took a step back, such was the violence and venom in his voice. Craig pressed his advantage. "And if I don't get this report in by tomorrow I'll lose my FUCKING job. My wife is a nagging bitch and all I wanted was a quiet place to finish my report and EVERY fucking time I try to send this god damn PDF it takes a cunting photo instead."

Chuck breathed out and suddenly burst out laughing. "You are one uptight dude. Nick bring this man a beer on me." He yelled to the barman.

"Thanks," mumbled Craig.

"Get another job, man," said Chuck as he strutted back to the bar.

Craig knew that if he hadn't focused his anger that way he'd have launched himself at the arrogant gangster. He'd get his punishment and that right soon.

Chapter 4: Keegan's Fury

Keegan punched the button and the virtual reels spun again. Four muted dings as the reels stopped and he was another five dollars down the drain. He bashed a button in frustration. The cashier behind her screen gave him a warning glance as his reward. It was pay day and already half of his wages were gone.

An hour later and he left the bookmakers, a measly hundred bucks left of his pay. He had no choice but to head home, no bar tonight. Damn, this unlucky streak had to end soon.

***

Henri heard the front door slam and flinched. He was home early. This was rarely a good thing. She put down her coffee and stood up to greet him.

His face was like thunder and his once attractive green eyes sparkled with malevolence as he entered the living room.

"What the fuck? I go to work all day just so you can sit here and drink coffee."

Henri watched his anger rise the way a rabbit would a fox: terrified but unable to move. He had a small vein in his forehead that inflamed when he shouted and it was engorged now.

"But hun..."

"Don't hun me, you useless cunt."

He stepped forward and raised his hand, but for once there was no accompanying slap.

"You're not worth the damned effort. I'm going out."

He stormed out. Henri looked at her watch. Three minutes is all he could stand to be with her. She collapsed back into the chair and for the second time that day sobbed her heart out.

Chapter 5: Nick's Warning

Keegan stormed into the bar and breathed in the familiar stale beery smell. He felt his anger abate a little. A couple of beers and he'd be able to cope better with his rage.

He slapped his hundred bucks on the bar top.

"Nick. A beer, burger and fries, and tell me when that runs out."

The barman stopped wiping the bar top and regarded Keegan with almost scientific interest.

"Keegan, you amaze me."

Keegan shrugged, "Sometimes I amaze myself."

"If you'd come in fifteen minutes ago you'd be picking your teeth up from the parking lot."

Keegan frowned, "What are you talking about, Nick?"

"Chuck-knuckles-Van-Cleef is looking for you."

"The fuck?"

"He's bought your gambling debt and he wants your ass on a silver platter."

Keegan went pale, "Better make that a Jack Daniels. A double."

"I'm under orders to let him know if I see you and since I'm not a total bastard I'm going to give you ten minutes head start."

Nick plonked a large Jack Daniels on the bar.

"This is on the house. Drink it, take your cash, go away and sort your life. The clock is ticking."

The barman pointedly looked at his watch.

Keegan gulped down his bourbon with one long swallow, grasped his cash and made for the door with not a word of thanks.

Two seats down the bar Craig had heard every word and now he had a plan. He quickly followed Keegan.

Chapter 6: The Man with the Plan

Craig saw him scurrying across the parking lot, almost at a run. He'd be out of sight any moment. Damn! That man was fast. He shouted. "Hey, Keegan. Wait up!"

It was lucky that he'd heard the barman use the guy's name. At the far end of the lot he saw Keegan stop and hesitate.

"Hey man, just wait there a moment, I just want a quick word."

Craig strode confidently across the parking lot, taking advantage of the Keegan's hesitation. He reached into his pocket and withdrew four fifty-dollar bills from his wallet. He held them out to the fearful gambler.

"Two-hundred bucks to buy thirty minutes of your time. We have an enemy in common and we can both solve that mutual problem if you just give me some time."

Keegan looked fearful but he eyed the money greedily.

"If this is a trick?"

"I just want a chat. You get to keep the two hundred bucks regardless."

Keegan stepped forward ready to grab and run but Craig drew back his arm.

"Let's get the fuck out of here before our mutual friend arrives, eh?"

Craig pointed to his BMW parked in the corner of the lot. He walked towards it, after a brief hesitation Keegan followed.

Twenty minutes later, Craig parked up on a high bluff overlooking the lights of the town. Keegan had two hundred bucks in his pocket and Craig had stopped at a drive through for burger and fries for them both on the way. Things are looking up thought Keegan. However, he didn't like the remote location.

"You're not a fag, are you?" he eyed Craig with suspicion.

Craig burst out laughing. "No man, I'm not a fag."

Keegan eyed him for a long moment then took another huge bite of his burger. He opened the car window and threw out the wrapper.

Craig looked vexed, "Fuck's sake, there's a garbage can just there."

Keegan shrugged, "Get over it, Mary. Now what do you want? And how do you know Chuck Knuckles?"

"They really call him Chuck Knuckles? It sounds like Chuckles."

Keegan grinned and shrugged, "You wouldn't say that to his fucking face."

"Fair point. Now, I need your help to put that bastard away."

"You don't strike me as a cop."

"I'm not."

"Then what's your interest?"

Craig thought for a moment wondering how much he could trust this man. He decided, not a lot.

"We have a score to settle, is all you need to know. If you help me set him up then he can't bother you from jail, can he?"

Keegan thought this over. It would certainly buy him time but he'd never been a grass.

"If I help you I want five-thousand bucks, too."

Craig shrugged, he earned in excess of a hundred thousand a year. Five grand was a drop in the bucket, but he couldn't show that to a man like Keegan, so he decided to play the game.

"You're fucking joking. This ain't my BMW, it's the company's. I can't afford five-thousand. Make it three."

Keegan made as if to open the door, not the best bluff,

since they were miles from town.

"Four."

Craig feigned relief, "Deal."

They shook on it.

"Now I'm going to need some information from you. I deal with sharks every day at work. Well, I do give financial advice to lawyers. Like lawyers, criminals can be single-minded bastards and your friend Chuck will do what any good lawyer will do and follow the money. We need to act fast to press our advantage. Here's what we do…"

Craig outlined his hastily formed plan at length as the full moon shone down upon them.

Chapter 7: A Feisty One

Henri waited until eleven thirty, but still he didn't come home. She made her way to bed and slipped between thin sheets. She was tired from sobbing and from being angry and at the damned injustice of just about everything in her life at the moment. Fuck him, fuck the landlord, she wouldn't take much more of this. She'd blow this damn one horse town and find somewhere decent.

As she drifted into an uneasy sleep a loud thundering crash awoke her. She sat up in bed blinking. Had she dreamt it? Then another shuddering crash filled her ears. Someone was breaking into the house. She reached behind the headboard and drew out the little Ruger 9mm she kept for home defence, or secretly, for Keegan if he ever got too out of hand. He didn't know she had it or he would have sold it for liquor or gambling long ago.

She got out of bed and hid behind the bedroom door. She flicked off the safety and tried to quiet her pounding heart. She heard bangs and crashes throughout the house for a few moments before the bedroom light was flicked on and a large black man flew into the room holding a metal clad baseball bat. He slammed the bat down upon the bed then yelled in anger as he noticed there was no one there. Unfortunately for Henri his violent entry had caused the lightweight door to move, exposing her hiding place.

It was now or never! Henri kicked the door and it hit his thigh harmlessly. She raised the pistol and squeezed, but he'd turned in time and raised the bat. The bullet ricocheted off the metal surface and thudded harmlessly into the wall on the other side of the room. The man looked amazed, but his surprise didn't stop him for long. He lunged forward and grabbed her, wrestling the gun away. He threw her onto the bed. She grunted and used the momentum to throw out a kick which smashed into his chin, throwing him against the wall. The gun flew from his hand and skittered across the floor.

Henri crawled across the bed reaching for the gun but he was too quick in recovering and grasped her from behind. Two hard punches to the head had her subdued and dizzy. A third put her lights out.

When she awoke she was secured to the bed using several pairs of her best nylons. A rough square of gaffer tape covered her mouth. Her eyes widened as she saw the man sat across from the bed smirking at her. He had impressive dreadlocks and a swelling where she'd caught him a glancing blow with her foot. Despite her predicament she felt energised. The adrenaline was pumping and she never realised that she could fight so well.

"You're a feisty bitch, aren't you? How does a little runt of a drunk like Keegan handle you?"

She did her best to say fuck you behind the gaffer tape.

"Now listen and listen carefully. Nod once if you're going to be a good girl."

She thought for a moment and nodded, at the same time she tested the bonds that held her outstretched arms to the headboard.

"I have no quarrel at all with you, but your husband owes me money and I intend to collect, tonight. I'm not going to hurt you or rape you. It's him I want. Now, I'm going to remove the tape and I want some answers. Scream and I swear I'll knock your fucking teeth down your throat."

With a swift movement he yanked off the gaffer tape. Henri grunted briefly but showed no other sign that it had hurt.

"What's your name?"

"Minnie fucking Mouse."

He laughed, "I don't suppose it really matters. Where is

he?"

"He never came home tonight."

"Are you lying to me, Mrs Mouse?"

He stood to full height and loomed over her. Jesus, she thought, he's huge.

"I'm not lying. I haven't seen him tonight."

"I can't say I'm surprised. That coward probably knows I'm after him by now if that loose lipped idiot at the bar has seen him."

He sighed and ran a hand through his hair.

On the nightstand Henri's phone rang. The deadly serious silence was punctuated by Thunder by AC/DC.

Chuck waited a few moments before answering.

"Ah, good evening Keegan. Chuck here. You owe me five-thousand fucking dollars."

"I know."

Chuck muttered something about a barman under his breath.

"I'm just keeping your little girly company. My, but doesn't she bite!"

"Fuck you, Chuck."

The gangster laughed.

"Every time you piss me off, Keegan, you little shit, I add five-hundred bucks to your debt. I might just take out my anger on your little woman her."

Henri glared at Chuck who winked at her and pressed a finger to his lips.

She yanked at her bonds in frustration.

"How did a loser like you get such a fine piece of ass anyway?"

Chuck waited for the angry response. Instead he heard, sincerity and fear. The momentary bravado had gone.

"Leave her out of this, okay? I have your goddamn money. That's why I haven't been home yet. I was sorting it out."

"And you have the money now?"

Chuck heard him hesitate.

"Y-yes."

"If you're messing me about I swear I'll-"

"I'm not Chuck.

"Then get your ass back here with it."

"There's a small problem."

Chuck bellowed down the phone, "WHAT?"

"The rich fuck that owes it isn't playing ball and…"

"And what?"

"I swear he came away from the casino with ten grand or more. Chuck, he's in a little motel and alone. Ripe for the taking with all that money. I just need a little help."

Chuck thought about it. A little extra effort and he could double his payout. Maybe more, but was it worth the risk? Was it a trap or trick of some kind. He dismissed that. Keegan didn't have balls.

"Alright you useless fuck. Where are you?"

Keegan told him and then hung up. His heart pounding in his chest.

Chapter 8: The Briefcase

Keegan turned to Craig.

"I hope you know what you're doing because if we fuck up we're dead. This guy doesn't mess about."

Craig sat with his feet on the bed idly messing with his phone. The one flaw in their trap was that perhaps the motel room they'd chosen was a little too low rent for the story they'd spun Chuck. Still, the location was perfect. It would have to do. He looked up and winked at Keegan.

"You're a worrier. Is he on his way?"

Keegan nodded.

"Good." Craig launched himself off the bed and letting in the cold night air, he walked outside to where the car was parked. He could hear sirens in the distance and the sound of gunfire. Damn, this was a crazy place for a hick town. He opened the trunk of the car and withdrew a briefcase. He'd had this ready almost since the first day he'd found out that Trisha was cheating. A little package of revenge just waiting for the right time. That time was now. He felt no fear for what he had to do just a cold icy confidence that scared him more than anything else.

Back in the room he heard Keegan taking a noisy shit in the bathroom. He sounded like a bear giving birth. Disgusting bastard that he was.

***

On the highway Chuck turned up the volume of the stereo. The Rolling Stones sang about sympathy for the devil and Chuck sang along. In the trunk his insurance policy bound and gagged kicked and tried to yell behind the gaffer tape that covered her mouth. Her eyes blazed with anger and she knew that she'd never kowtow to another man again if she got out of this alive.

***

Keegan emerged from the bathroom with an awful smell accompanying him. Craig wrinkled his nose.

"Get outside and be ready. They'll be here soon enough, you disgusting prick."

Keegan gave him the finger, but did as he was told and closed the door behind him.

He went over to the briefcase and clicked open the brass locks. He pocketed a small tube and laid out some other pieces of equipment carefully on the bed. Then he sat and waited whistling idly.

***

Keegan stood by the car his teeth chattering. He wondered if it was too late to run. But he knew there was nowhere to go, Chuck would find him and kill him for messing him about and Craig, he didn't know what to make of him. He seemed calm, far too calm. He eyed the room and wondered if he should go to the bathroom again.

***

Chuck flipped off the lights when he was a few hundred yards from the Motel's car lot. There was no point in taking chances. The bass drum of Henri's struggle still struck up a steady rhythm against the trunk of the car: an amazing woman; very persistent. He swung the car onto the parking lot and saw Keegan dancing from toe to toe in the cold right underneath a light, the damned idiot.

He pulled up close and leapt out of the car. He quickly

swung a hard right at Keegan who went down like a sack of potatoes. When the skinny man got to his feet, Chuck bellowed into his face causing the skinny man to cower away, "That's for fucking me around, you little shit!"

He shot a hand out, grabbed Keegan by the ear and dragged him to the back of the car. With his free hand he clicked the trunk release and the lid of the trunk popped up with the force of Henri's latest kick.

Henri glared up at both of them. Her anger far from abated she swung a foot up causing Chuck to step back quickly and slam the trunk shut.

"You trick me Keegan, you weasel, and I swear she's a dead woman."

He shoved Keegan for good measure and drew out a small pistol which he pointed at the gambler.

"Show me where our rich friend is, let's get this over with."

Keegan spat out a large gob of blood and wiped his nose. He nodded dejectedly and slowly shambled to the room where Craig lay in wait. He pointed so that Chuck could see which room he was headed to.

"Now knock on the door."

Keegan knocked. They waited. No answer.

"Knock louder."

He knocked again, louder. No answer.

"Turn the handle."

The wife beater did as he was asked. The door slowly creaked open. Chuck wrinkled his nose and laughed.

"It stinks like shit, he's on the fucking John. Walk in, slowly."

Craig saw Keegan walk into the room and heard Chuck's barked orders. He was crouched to one side of the doorframe. He waited a moment for Chuck to cross the threshold behind Keegan and he burst forward and sprayed the can of pepper spray right into his face. Again and again he depressed the little button in quick succession. The gangster immediately fired a quick round and Craig heard a grunt followed by a thud.

Chuck dropped the gun clawed at his eyes yelling in pain. Craig wasted no time. He launched a kick right between Chuck's legs. He struck home and Chuck fell as if he'd been axed from behind. Craig laid the boot in on his prone opponent until he stopped moving.

Chapter 9: Consequences

Craig looked for Keegan and saw him in a puddle of blood on the floor.

"Fuck!"

He leaned over and saw that the random bullet had struck Keegan's throat. Even with such a small calibre weapon it was game over for Keegan as his arterial spray already covered the walls of the room.

***

Chuck groaned as he awoke. His eyes were on fire, he reached to rub them and found his hands were stuck. He felt handcuffs restraining him to a bed and his legs were bound with something. After a couple of minutes of agony he managed to open his eyes a slit. His balls throbbed in time with his other pains. He saw a blurry figure in front of him. He looked down at himself, his shirt had been torn off and his torso was a bloody mess.

The blurry figure before him was holding something up. A gun? Perhaps a phone? Chuck heard him speak, but couldn't reply. His mouth was gaffer taped shut.

"Good evening, Trisha. I thought I'd send you a little video. I'm sick of you and your cheating ways. You'll never see me again. I thought I'd brand your latest sex toy for you."

Craig panned the camera down on Chuck. His bloody mess of a chest had the word TRISHA CHEAT carved upon it.

"This will remind you what you are every time you fuck this creep. Oh, and one more thing, you'll have to work harder from now on for your orgasms."

Craig panned the phone to the bloody stump of a cock between Chuck's legs. He laughed. Chuck who had just regained some more of his sight tried to scream behind the gaffer tape and fainted.

Craig strolled from the room to the chill pre dawn parking lot. He breathed in the frigid air and sighed. It was over. He felt for poor Keegan. He was scum, but he'd gotten caught in the crossfire, collateral damage. He cocked his head a moment and listened. He heard a steady thump he looked around for the source and realised it was coming from the car Chuck had pulled up in. He walked to the car and sure enough the sound got louder. He went round the back of it and popped the trunk. An attractive, but angry woman glared at him. He carefully pulled off the gaffer tape from her mouth and used his pocket knife to cut her bonds. He grunted as he helped her out of the trunk. She was stiff from the journey and nearly fell but he supported her.

"Thanks," she mumbled, "Where's Keegan?"

"I'm sorry to tell you that Keegan is dead ma'am."

She paused and sniffed, "Chuck did it?"

"I'm afraid so, a stray bullet hit him in the throat."

"Can I see him?"

"Sure, you want to?"

She nodded.

"Lean on me."

She hobbled stiffly as Craig led her to the room she looked emotionlessly at the body and then with venom at Chuck, who was once again conscious. She stepped forward and reached between his legs and squeezed the ruined slashed thing she found there. He thrashed around but was bound securely and couldn't move far.

"Now who's the feisty one, you bastard?"

Craig had slipped outside and was in his car. He started the engine. Henri wandered outside and stood in the doorway.

"I guess we both lost someone we love one way or

another Miss -"

"Just Henri."

"Craig."

She nodded, "You going my way?"

"I'm leaving this godforsaken hick town forever."

"Good enough for me. Mind if I tag along?"

Craig thought for a moment before opening the passenger door.

She slipped in beside him.

A loud siren started up nearby. It was quickly getting closer and fast.

Henri bit her lip.

"Aww, fuck it. Drive!" She yelled, leaping into the car and slamming the door closed.

Craig floored the accelerator.

Uncle Jim

By Ryan Bracha

Dedication: *Uncle Mick Porter. The hardest bloke I've ever known.*

As he edged toward the bathroom, the scratching shuffle of the soles of his backless slippers rubbing against the threadbare carpet punctuated the sounds of the air whistling through his large nose, broken some years ago by a man he could barely remember. The air around him was cold in the early winter's morning breeze that passed through the rotted window frames with ease. Window frames that might once have been painted with a pale blue gloss, but were now just a quickly diminishing, black-brown accident waiting to happen to some unsuspecting passer-by. Another symbol of this life, doddering toward the grave. Around the window the spores of damp mould released themselves from the blackened patches that grew larger by the day, as the once white, but now yellow painted wallpaper had given up the fight for territory long ago. The spores wandered unseen in the air, clinging to any surface that would allow. His thin grey dressing gown. His cutlery drawer. His lungs. He reached the cold bathroom, and pulled at the lighting cord out of habit, forgetting that the bulb had expired last week. His slippers kissed the lino in a sticky percussion as he stepped toward the toilet with the loose seat. The misting of his light breath danced in the morning's sun that sparked through the cracked and mottled glass of the bathroom window, as he pulled at the tie cord around his waist, the only thing that kept his piss-stained pyjama bottoms still up around his thin body. Loosened, it allowed the worn fabric to drop around his legs with ease, to the floor, and he slowly turned himself and lowered his bony, meat-free backside onto the ice-cold seat of the toilet. He'd long ago given up attempting to stand for the long periods of time that he required to squeeze out the few drops of piss that he could muster. Seated, he rested his elbows on the yellow skin of his knees, closed his eyes, and he pushed. He wasn't certain that he was pushing the right muscles to allow his bladder to relieve itself of the thick, almost brown urine that had been sloshing around inside him as the urge to piss woke him this morning. He reattempted, and felt the droplets edge along his urethra towards their desperate release. As he heard the light tinkle of the urine drip slowly into the water below he exhaled. The tickling relief that washed over the lower half of his body allowed him to afford himself a thin smile, which faded as he watched and frowned as a silverfish danced and traversed the base of his crusted bath. He muttered to it that it could go and fuck itself, but it paid him no mind. Just wandered along its way, another reminder of his diminishing worth on the planet. He pushed again. Another three, four droplets of sticky piss released themselves. It would have to do. He didn't have the energy this early, to attempt any more. He swore at his bladder, and used the cistern of the toilet to assist him in his effort to stand from the loose seat with his left hand, as his right grabbed a handful of the material of his pyjama bottoms. There was no way he'd be able to reach from a standing position to get them. Not anymore. He gasped gruffly as his bones clicked during the effort, and shuffled from the toilet without flushing. He passed the spotted grey mirror that hung over the bathroom sink, a flash of his weathered walking corpse of a body in the corner of his eye that he chose to ignore.

He didn't like what old age was doing to him. The erosion that time had inflicted upon him, that had turned him from a vibrant young man, with the teddy boy quiff and the bright red platform shoes, through middle aged singledom still working the nightclub scene well into his sixties, enough to have the kids who frequented the same haunts dub him *Snakehips*, and then finally to the here and now. His hair that he was losing in clumps every time he took a rare bath. The bones that were losing grip on the shrinking muscles that worked them. The creamy eyes that sunk deeper and deeper into the skin that stretched around his skull on every day that he remained alive. The face, unshaven, save the attack with the trimmers that his care worker, Sandra inflicted upon him on a Tuesday morning. The memories of the things that he'd said and done through his long life fading, like an advertising poster in the window of a long closed shop that faced south. Sometimes the memories were stronger than others, sometimes he only remembered his name, no matter the intensity with which he tried to force his cerebrum into working properly. He ate only when he remembered to, which was once a day if he was lucky. Nothing substantial. A biscuit, or a sandwich. Something easy. Then on a Tuesday morning Sandra would provide him with the only substantial sustenance. Something cooked and on a tray that she fetched with her. When was Tuesday? He didn't know. He may well be welcoming her in the next few hours, she might have just this minute waved cheerio as she moved on to whoever. He didn't care. He didn't think he liked Sandra. She was stealing from him. She'd written herself into his will without his knowledge. She'd once slept with his friend behind his back in the seventies. Sandra was the girl who'd told her lies. He thought. It might not have been her. She might be the loveliest person in the world, but for him she represented the outside. That hour that she spent from her fresh faced arrival to the cheery goodbye, where she'd talk to him about a world he didn't understand anymore, represented that life continued with or without him.

He dressed himself as best he could. Pulled on the stained brown trousers over his bony legs and sagging backside, neglecting the underwear. He huffed at the effort, and opted to leave on only his vest, under the dressing gown. He tossed his pyjama bottoms onto the fabric chair which sat by his wardrobe, and let his eyes try to track the dust that the impact had released, twisting and curling in a merry dance in the slice of sunlight which pierced the darkness of his room through the perennially closed curtains. He barked a cough, and sat himself on top of the pyjamas on the chair. Pulled the packet of cigarettes from the bedside table, along with the brass lighter that he'd acquired… He couldn't remember when. He'd just always had it. He watched the glow of the petrol flame spark into life, and pulled it toward the end of his cigarette. Embraced that first real rush of nicotine of the day crackle into his bloodstream, awakening in him a rush. He smiled a black toothed grin, and blew smoke across the sliver of light in the darkness. Now he remembered. Sandra was the German girl. The one he had. No, that wasn't him. He wasn't there. He just heard the story. He shook his head, and the memory erased itself as quickly as it had puffed into his psyche. Sandra, whoever she was, no longer existed. He smoked the cigarette, and stubbed it out into the mountain of butts that had begun life at some point last year, when he'd last remembered to empty the tray. The pile smouldered in a throat-restricting cloud of burned plastic, and he hoisted himself upright. Telly. He would watch telly. The people who shouted at each other on a stage whilst a man with a microphone shouted at them to be quiet. Maybe they would be there. He collected his lighter and cigarettes and shuffled from the room barefoot. He couldn't remember where his shoes were. He couldn't remember that he needed them, anyway, so it didn't matter. The stinking, smoky bedroom disappeared from memory as he emerged into the landing. He had a pleasant reminiscence when he saw the photographs on the wall. The images of he and his friends dressed up together. He frowned at the lack of glass in them, the paper picture dull and powdery where they were once glossy and reflective. Photo frames needed glass. Where did the glass go? He couldn't remember. He paused, and nodded affectionately to a man he once knew standing beside a younger version of himself. Both were dressed alike, in their suits. They had their arms around one another. Wide grins. They looked alike. Who was it? A brother or a cousin? He couldn't be sure. He didn't have family. Not anymore. He didn't think. He shook his head sadly, and continued along the landing. The frames of the pictures were thick with dust, but he didn't care. What was dust to an old man? Nothing but a yardstick with which to measure the length of time since happiness was commonplace and forgetful loneliness was the prominent feeling. He'd once doubted he'd ever clean the dust from those frames, but just now, he couldn't remember when that was. He approached the top of the stairs, and gazed down upon the lower level of the house. It was in a slightly better state that the upstairs, but he had Sandra to thank or that. Left to him, it would remain a cluttered and dirty extension of the first floor. Beyond the bottom of the stairs was the front door. The three out of four diamond shaped glass panels smashed and boarded up from who knew when, and the fourth which has a long crack that ran from the bottom to the top. The letterbox taped shut from when somebody had poured petrol through it and attempted to burn down his house. That happened. He was sure it had happened. Did it happen? He frowned, and placed a hand on the railing. The screws and Rawlplugs at the top end had come loose, so the railing pulled away from the wall a little as he descended. Wobbling uneasy against the loose fixings, he stepped down again. And again. As his foot lowered to the next step a loud bang startled him. Once, twice, thrice. His hand reached for the railing, but undershot the aim and he ended up grabbing at nothing. The shock of the bangs forced his foot just too far forward of the step, and he slipped as his heel clipped the corner of its intended placing. His knee buckled. His frail hands clawed at nothing as gravity did its job in dragging him ever further toward the ground. His frail body twisted sideways and he bounced from step to step. His face cracked against the wall, snapping the front two of his black tobacco stained teeth. He wailed in agony as his hip shattered against the impact of his body hitting one of the bottom steps, and as he came to rest in a tattered heap at the foot of the stairs, he whimpered and sobbed. He had no idea how he got there. He only knew that he wanted the pain to end.

The bangs came again. Three in quick succession. Then a voice. Jim, it called out. Jim Harris, are you in there? He couldn't speak. Tried to call out, but nothing came. Jim? The voice asked. Can you hear me? The letterbox tapped as fingers tried to force their way through. The shape of a person's head arose from the bottom of the one panel of glass that remained intact. Pushed its face up against the window. A face he recognised. A woman. Older than he remembered. He tried to hold out a hand to make himself known but the pain. It was too much. He wailed in agony. The light faded. Darkness prevailed. Nothing.

It doesn't take much to force the door open, because the wood around the frame has rotted away that much, and I take in the sight. His pathetic and decrepit body folded in two at the foot of the stairs. His shallow breathing. His bleeding face. I close the door behind me and I hurry toward him. Jim? I'm asking as I slap at his face, hard. Can you hear me? I punch at his face. Jim? Wake up, you filthy old cunt. I punch again, but remember myself. I promised myself I wouldn't lower myself to his level. I promised that. He doesn't wake, so I hurry through to the kitchen, and I take a dirty glass from beside the sink and I fill it with water. I leave the glass in his living room, and I go back to Uncle Jim's broken body. He grunts and groans as I drag him along the floor into the living room and out of view of the front door. I drop him onto the stinking shitty carpet and I throw the water onto his face. He gasps awake and his head shakes at the neck as he struggles to focus on me. He moans in pain, and doesn't come round as much as I'd hoped. I say hi, Uncle Jim. His face twists as he tries to recognise me, but it's no use. He's clueless. I ask, do you remember me? He moans in pain some more. Mutters something I don't understand, and then starts up with telling me how much it hurts. Says please. Please, help him. I stand over him, and his hands shake by his face. I sigh. He says he doesn't know what happened. Asks why it hurts so much. I tell him it looks like he fell down the stairs. He says it hurts again. I shake my head. I say that's too bad. I ask if he remembers me again. He says he doesn't remember anything anymore. He asks if he's going to die. I say not if I have anything to do with it. Not yet, anyway.

The agonising electric bolts thrashed at his core as he lay on the carpet. The woman stood over him, before moving to draw the curtains, and then back to the sofa and dropping herself down onto it. She watched him. It was definitely her. He couldn't remember her name, but it was her. He remembered the pigtails, and the pretty red and white chequered dress that she wore. The smattering of freckles that dashed across her nose and cheeks. The curled under fringe. The lovely young breasts. The miniskirt. It was the seventies. She'd been out with her friends in the disco, and had been taken by his moves on the dancefloor. She'd watched with fascination as her feet seemed to move faster that anybody else's in the place. He'd had so much more rhythm than the younger lads in there. That's what she'd said when they'd finally spoken. Him at the bar smoking an Embassy, her coming over to ask him to buy her a drink. They'd spoken for hours after that. Then every night he went out, she'd be there. They'd chat all of the time, and she'd call him Uncle Jim, and then. No, that wasn't him. He didn't do that. No. It was an innocent friendship. They'd lost touch when. When. He couldn't remember. She was older now, obviously. Plumper. Harder of face. Still beautiful, but with a stoniness behind the eyes. She watched him with contempt. Asked him for a third time if he remembered her. He smiled. Said her name. She laughed without humour. Another ripple of agony washed over him. He asked her to help him. She laughed again. He told her that she hadn't changed, to which she retorted that she had most definitely changed. That he'd changed her, in many ways.

Who does he think he is? Does he think that we can just drop into a conversation about the weather? About the fucking old times? He remembers. He definitely remembers. I will him on. Apologise. Just fucking apologise and we can move on with this. You can see out the rest of your filthy days filled with a shame that you clearly don't seem to feel. With remorse. With anything other than this pathetic gaze up at me from your stinking floor. He asks me how I am. He actually asks me how I am! Who the fuck does he think he is? I spit at the floor. I hate spitting, but it just feels right to do it. And the carpet is dirty enough to take the hit. He frowns, and asks me what's wrong. I ask him how Sandra's doing? He looks at me with confusion. I ask him venomously if he's tried to fuck her yet. He doesn't say anything. I say I know he hasn't, but I know he looks at her tits. I know he'd love the faculties left to at least give it a go. I say don't bother. I tell him she's his daughter. I promised myself I wouldn't, but I start to cry.

It didn't make sense. What was she saying? He didn't have children. He'd lived a single life through choice. He didn't want kids. He gasped through the waves of pain that blitzed his nervous system. Told her she'd got the wrong person. She shook her head and said not likely. He'd taken her virginity. He was her first, and because of the way he'd done it he was the last in a very long time. He couldn't make sense of it. Sandra didn't exist. Not anymore. Sandra was a figment of an imagination he'd forgotten how to use. A shadow flickered across the pale light of the front window. Help? He tried to call out but the effort was too much. Just let his head drop to the floor, and allow his eyes to work from where he lay. He watched the woman. She smiled dolefully as the front door opened and closed. Looked up with love to the new addition to the scene. He let his eyes flicker to the body of the new person. Recognition washed over him. Sandra. He did know her. She did exist. She helped him. She was the one face he trusted. He smiled. You, he said, please help me. She gazed down upon him with a sadness that he recognised from every other time she'd been here. She asked the woman what she'd done to him, and was rewarded with the news that he'd fallen down the stairs. He'd broken something. He wanted to say that it was his hip, but couldn't. His eyes filled with scarcely earned tears. She crouched down beside him. Held his head in her hands. Hi dad, she said. She asked if he was sorry for what he'd done. If he regretted his actions at all. He didn't know. He didn't know what he'd done. He told her this. He couldn't remember. She began to cry, and held his head tighter. She smiled sadly, and said, of course you don't. As a tear dropped from her eye and down upon his face, she moved her hands to his neck, and began to squeeze.

The Caller

By Cal Marcius

Dedication: *For Nicole and Henri and everyone battling cancer. In memory of my Aunt Giesela.*

Time works differently in a place without light. You have to rely on your other senses, your hearing and touch, your smell. The walls are colder at night, and feel damp. And it's quiet upstairs.

There are no heavy footsteps now, no work boots marching over the polished wooden floor. It's just me and the chain around my ankle, never letting me forget where I am every time I move. The skin around my ankle is chafed, sore to the touch. I tried pushing my trousers through the gap, to stop it from hurting, but it comes out so easily, I stopped trying.

I can't sleep tonight. He hasn't been back for a long time, which means he's on the hunt again, and I dread hearing the screams from next door. Dread the moment he opens my door and tells me it's time to talk on the phone.

I think about my family, my brother, wonder if he's okay. And I think about how all this began.

***

I could see Scott through the window, sitting in one of the big armchairs every coffee shop seemed to have these days. I hated sinking into the soft leather, wondering if I'd hit the floor with my arse at any second. I preferred something solid like a wooden chair. Something I could get up from without the assistance of another human being.

Scott looked like he'd been waiting a while. Empty cups and plates on the table. He was reading the paper, the supplements carelessly thrown on the floor next to him.

"You're late," he said, without looking up.

"Actually," I said, pointing to my watch, "I'm ten minutes early."

"Would've been if you'd turned up an hour ago."

"You said eleven."

"Clocks went forward this morning."

Scott closed the paper and looked at me, a stupid grin on his face.

"I knew you'd forget," he said. "Seriously, every single time?"

I shrugged. I mean, what was the point in turning the clocks back and forward? You couldn't outsmart the seasons. One way or another you had to deal with the darkness.

I pointed at the paper. "Anything happening?"

Scott shook his head. "Nah, same old shit. Corrupt governments, people dying and wannabe celebrities. But it passes the time."

"You want another one?" I said, pointing at his empty cup.

"Large cappuccino and a biscotti."

I was back a few minutes later with the orders and put everything in front of him.

"They found the guy that went missing," Scott said, after I sat down.

"Good."

"He's dead."

"Fuck."

I was hoping he'd be okay. I'd seen his picture plastered all over the news a few months ago. Distraught family members making a public appeal for their son and brother to come home. We knew what it felt like to lose someone. Mum died in a car crash when I was twelve. Dad two years later from a broken heart. People said that it was the asthma and his bad heart, but we'd seen what her death had done to him. He'd lost his will to live, and one morning he didn't get up, and never would again. Now it was just the two of us.

"Did they say how he died?"

"Just that he was found in a shallow grave," Scott said. "Poor bastard."

We headed to the cinema after the coffee shop, watched some French art film that showed more tits and swinging dicks than a nudist beach.

"You coming home tonight?" Scott asked after.

I shook my head. "I wanted to talk to you 'bout that. I'm thinking of moving in with Mike."

It wasn't hard telling my brother I was gay after what we'd been through. Before he got married he hadn't exactly led the celibate lifestyle. With commitment issues and the constant hope of finding the perfect woman he'd slept his way through the city. Though telling him I was moving out felt like an insult to the years he'd sacrificed looking after me.

"Finally," he said.

Not the reaction I expected.

"What d'you mean, *finally*?"

"No offence, but I don't wanna share the house with my little brother for the rest of my life. I've got a family, Nick, another baby on the way."

"I thought you liked having me around. Free babysitter and all," I said, a little too aggressively, but Scott just smiled.

"You're hardly ever home," he said.

"You could've said something."

"I couldn't throw you out. Who d'you think I am? You're my brother. I was hoping you'd figure it out yourself. Just took a little longer than I thought."

"I feel such an idiot," I said.

"Don't. I'm coming across like one more than you. Sorry."

Two days later I moved in with Mike, Scott driving the hired van.

***

I was still lying in bed when my phone rang. I could hear Mike downstairs in the kitchen. It sounded like he was wrecking the place. I was tempted to ignore the phone, but I got up and answered nonetheless.

"Scott with you?" my sister-in-law said.

"Nora? Hold on, I'll check."

I looked out the window to see if Scott's motorbike was parked on the drive. Nothing.

I walked downstairs, phone in hand, and asked Mike if he'd seen my brother. The fridge door was open. Yoghurt dripped from a shelf onto the tiled floor.

Mike just said, "Don't ask," and I walked back upstairs.

"Sorry, Nora, he isn't here. Tried work?"

"I did, but . . ." She started to cry. "He isn't there either. He said he had a meeting. What if he's having—"

"An affair? Scott? No way. He wouldn't do that to you guys. Especially not when you're pregnant."

"Where is he then?" I could hear the accusation in her voice. That fiery Italian temperament coming through.

"I don't know, Nora. I bet he'll be calling you any minute. I wouldn't worry. Why you looking for him anyway?"

"I just wanted to talk to him, that's all."

"Don't worry, okay. I know Scott. He wouldn't cheat on you."

"You're right. I'm sorry. I think it's the hormones. I hate that part of pregnancy. You get so emotional about everything. I'll let you go."

I put the phone on the nightstand and went back to bed. I'd been working all night at the club. I wasn't worried about Scott. He loved Nora, was looking forward to the baby. Couldn't wait to hold it in his arms. He'd become the image of our father, loved the domestic life, kids. He was adamant none of his would ever grow up without their parents. It was great seeing him like this.

The next time I woke up it was dark outside and my phone was ringing again. I checked the display. Nora's name sent a shiver down my spine.

"Nora?"

I wanted to say something else, but all I could hear was her crying.

"Nora, you alright?"

"Something's wrong, Nick. Something's wrong."

I waited for her to elaborate, but nothing came. "What d'you mean?"

She spoke between sobs. "Scott called . . . he was crying . . . and then . . . then he screamed, like he was in terrible pain . . . and the line went dead. Oh God, Nick, what's happening?"

I was up in seconds.

"I'll be there as quick as I can, Nora. Stay put."

I tried to call Scott's phone. I hit the redial button over and over again, but the line was dead. I dressed hurriedly and ran down the stairs, slipped and banged my knee into the banister.

"Fuck."

Mike came out of the living room. "What you shouting about?"

I grabbed the car key. "It's Scott," I said, and slammed the door shut behind me.

***

There were flashing blue lights in front of Scott's house. They questioned all of us, even Mike. A day passed, then another. Not a word from Scott. Then they told us there'd been others. Young men, dark haired and blue eyed. Same as Scott. Same as me. A serial killer, they said. They even had a name for him. The Caller.

He would torture his victims, then put them on the phone to a loved one, make them scream and then disconnect the call. It was the last their family would ever hear from them.

Seven victims in five years and the cops had nothing. No fingerprints, no fibres, just a pile of dead bodies. They couldn't even trace the calls.

"So, you're saying my brother is as good as dead?" I said to one of the detectives.

"I'm sorry."

I shook my head. "I can't accept this. I can't just sit here and do nothing."

"We'll make a public appeal. Ask him to let your brother go," he said.

"And if he doesn't?"

"We'll keep searching. I promise you, we'll do everything we can to find your brother."

"How soon can we do the appeal?"

"A few hours."

And that's what we did. In a room full of reporters and camera crews, flanked by detectives and liaison officers, I directed my message to The Caller.

***

"Do you think he saw it?" I said to Mike that evening, holding back tears.

Mike was quiet. I could see him thinking it over, before shaking his head.

"Why did you say all those things? That he could take you in exchange for your brother. Why?"

"I don't know. I thought I could draw him out. Make a mistake, reveal himself. Don't these psychos like to bask in their glory?"

"You're nuts, you know that. You've given this guy an open invitation to kidnap you. What the fuck, Nick."

Mike got up and stormed out of the room.

We didn't speak for the rest of the night. I let him cool off, while he gave me time to think about what he'd said. The implications hit me at last. There had been no consideration for anybody. Not for Mike, not for myself. I'd wanted my brother back and declared open season on myself.

Mike was in bed. I climbed in beside him and edged my way towards him.

"I'm sorry," I whispered, but he didn't reply, and I fell asleep with my arm wrapped around his waist.

***

We waited. Days. A week. Two weeks. I couldn't sleep. Couldn't eat. Couldn't bring myself to go to work. Nora's family came to look after her and my niece. I went to see them, but most of the time Nora was resting or inconsolable. They were worried with all the stress that she'd lose the baby.

Mike took time off work. He accompanied me on every trip to the police station, every trip to the shops or the club. He suggested I dye my hair or shave it off. Told me not to draw attention to myself. We argued. I cried. We made up. Friends came to visit, asking for news I couldn't give. My boss turned up, telling me to take as much time off as I needed. Saul wasn't just my boss, but also a friend. He said just the right words to make me believe we could save my brother. And I believed him. I had to.

Week three the doorbell rang and one of the detectives handling the case stood in front of me.

"Your brother's alive," he said, and I broke down.

Luck, that was all it had come down to. A man walking his German Shepherd in the woods. The man, Frank Thompson, was a handler. The Shepherd a search and rescue dog.

My brother had been buried alive. A snorkel covered with a piece of mosquito netting taped to his mouth.

We waited at the hospital for hours. Scott was in surgery. Before they wheeled him out they took us to another room and told us he was in a coma. The doctor couldn't say if he'd survive, but he said to prepare ourselves, that The Caller had done unspeakable things to Scott. Nora couldn't handle the stress and her family took her back to the house.

I stayed. I slept in a chair next to my brother's bed, holding one of his bandaged hands. His face was the colour of a ripe plum, swollen to almost double its size. There were tubes coming in and out of his body, machines whirring in the background. I couldn't take my eyes off him, worried that if I did he'd slip away from me unnoticed.

***

Mike told me point blank that I looked like shit, and I should go home, get some rest.

"I'll stay," he said.

I had been at Scott's bedside for five days, only left if I had to use the bathroom or go to the cafeteria. I couldn't just walk away. What if he came to and I wasn't there? What if he thought I didn't care? What if the machine came alive announcing the end of his struggles? What fucking if . . .?

"You're gonna run yourself into the ground," Mike said. "Listen. Go home. Get some rest. Anything changes, I'll call."

Reluctantly I agreed. I took my jacket off the chair and left.

It was still light outside and I left the car parked in the garage, desperate for some fresh air and a walk. I didn't go home like I'd promised Mike, instead went to the club to see Saul.

The club was busy. Life had continued without me. The people who recognised me smiled uncomfortably, not knowing how to approach me. You could see it in their faces, they all wanted to ask, but they all let me be.

Saul was behind the bar, serving customers, doing my job. Any other day he'd be sitting in his office, or taking turns with the other DJ's. Considering he owned the club, he worked as much as any of us.

I bought a shot of tequila and a beer and sat down at the bar.

"Any change?" he said.

I shook my head. "Still in a coma."

"He'll get through it, Nick. He's a fighter, and he's fit. That helps a lot."

I signalled for him to give me another tequila. "Make it a double."

"I don't think that's a great idea."

"Don't, okay. The last thing I need right now is a lecture."

Saul shrugged. "I'm just saying." He poured me a double and pushed it across. I knocked it down in one go. I could feel the heat spreading through my body, my brain comfortably starting to swim. It felt good.

"Thanks for doing my shifts," I said.

"Take as long as you need. The job's always gonna be

yours."

I got another tequila, then found a table in the back of the club, away from prying eyes.

From time to time, someone bought me a drink. I talked to strangers, people who didn't know who I was, until all memory failed and I sank into unconsciousness.

***

I woke up with a tremendous headache. I was lying on the floor, drooling, my arms twisted behind me, pins and needles running painfully through them. I didn't feel like opening my eyes, my head was hurting too much. I kept them shut, wishing I hadn't drank so much. I tried to reposition my arms, but I couldn't move them. I tried to wriggle my fingers, get some feeling back into my hands, but it just made everything worse.

Someone whispered softly into my ear.

"I've come to collect. Take your time though, we're not in a hurry."

Collect? Collect what? Confused, I opened my eyes. I had to open and close them a few times before I managed to focus on the man kneeling in front of me.

Saul was smiling. Dressed in jeans and a workman's shirt, he patted my face. "You've been sleeping for fourteen hours. Hung over?"

I nodded. I had no recollection of having gone back to his place or spoken to him after I'd retreated to my table. Fourteen hours. Mike. I'd completely forgotten about Mike. I had to call him. Tell him I was sorry. That I just wanted to drown Scott's image for one night.

I made a move to get up. But Saul pushed me gently back down again. "I need to make a call," I said.

Saul smiled. "It can wait."

"Mike's at the hospital. He thinks I've gone home."

"Nick, the only one calling from your phone will be me. Remember, I'm collecting on your promise."

"What are you talking about?" And that's when I realised why I couldn't move my arms. They were cuffed behind my back. In a sudden panic, I pushed myself backwards and into a wall.

"I let your brother live. You said yourself, I could take you. Millions of people saw the broadcast."

"Not you," I said, choking back tears. "Not you."

Saul stood up, arms spread like Jesus, and turned until he was facing me again.

"*Me*," he said. "All these years. Who would've thought. You know, Nick, I actually like you. You're a nice guy, good worker, but your brother ... The attitude. D'you know he came to me once? Threatening me. *Me*. He thought I had a thing for you. Remember. When I let you sleep at the house after work."

He laughed. "Should've seen his face when I brought him here."

"You tortured him."

"He fucking deserved it."

"He was just protecting me. Like he's always done."

"He had no right."

"So you tortured him?"

"Yes."

Saul looked confused, as if he'd expected me to understand why he'd done it.

"Just let me go," I said. "I won't tell anyone. I just wanna go back to the hospital."

"You shouldn't make a promise you can't keep."

"You haven't kept yours. My brother's in a coma," I shouted. "That's not life."

"Neither is it death."

"You tortured him. Buried him alive. What kind of life does he have now? Even if he does live, what kind of life is that?"

Saul looked at me, one hand below his chin, mockingly. "Why don't we ask *my* brother?" He walked past me, towards a chair covered with a blanket. I hadn't even noticed it. He pulled the blanket off, revealing a frightened man. A frightened man with silent tears running down his face.

"Eight years I've been looking for him," Saul said, removing the duct tape from the man's mouth, "and he walks into the club asking for reconciliation. Fucking joke." Saul slapped him across the face, knocking his brother's head back.

"Jason, meet Nick." Saul pointed at me. "Nick. Jason. Dad's favourite son." He grabbed Jason by the hair and turned his head towards me. "Tell Nick what you and the old man did to me. Tell him," he shouted. "I wasn't a killer. *They* made me into one.

"Years of abuse. Locked in the dark. Beaten because I didn't look like them. Being told your mother's a whore. Told I didn't deserve better. I'd never have killed all the others, but then you meet boys at the club like Scott and you, and they all remind you of him. So you take them and think of Jason. You do all the things you really want to do to him. You're satisfied for a while, but Jason's still out there, somewhere, living."

He slapped his brother again. Jason whimpered, drooled.

"Jas, how about it?" Saul said. "Did I turn out alright? Answer Nick's questions. Is his brother gonna be okay?"

His voice came as a whisper. "You would've killed them anyway, whatever happened to me."

Another slap, even harder. "That wasn't Nick's question, Jas."

Jason looked at me for the first time. His left eye was

swollen shut. The upper lip cut, dried blood clinging to it.

"I'm sorry. I'm so sorry."

Saul walked over to me and kicked me in the stomach. I rolled onto my side, desperate for air, and he kicked me again. This time connecting with my ribcage. The pain was unbearable. I started to cough. At last oxygen filled my lungs.

"You going to listen to me now, Jas?" Saul said.

I couldn't hear his answer. Maybe he just nodded. Saul spoke again. "You do what I say, and he'll live a little longer. Now, answer him."

"What d'you want me to say?" Jason cried. "I don't know if he'll be okay. I'm sorry for what I did to you. I am. That's why I came here. I'm the one who let you go."

"You think that makes it okay?" Saul said. "I haven't forgotten how you held my head under the water. How you broke my fingers one by one. And I haven't forgotten how you buried her in the ground, screaming. Dad threatening to put me in beside her if I didn't shut up. I can't sleep at night. Every time I close my eyes I see mum, pleading with you to let us go."

"I know what I did," Jason said. "You have me. Let him go. He's got nothing to do with it."

Saul punched Jason in the face, breaking his nose, blood spurting all over Jason's shirt. I wanted to cry. I'd never been so scared. Here I lay, knowing that my time was running out. Knowing that I'd die at the hands of someone who took pleasure in torturing people. I had Scott's image in my mind again. The cops telling me that he'd been burned and his legs and arms broken. As desperately as I tried, I couldn't hold my tears back and I started to cry.

Saul laughed. "Nick, Nick, Nick. Even your brother had more dignity than you."

"My brother didn't know what you're capable of. He didn't have the image of him lying in a hospital bed in his mind," I said.

Saul looked at me, bemused.

"You came to my house. Pretending you cared. And all this time you had him tied up and beaten, or was he already buried?"

"I'm a bit sketchy on the details, Nick. Sorry," Saul said, and laughed.

"I hope they get you. I hope they put a fucking bullet in your head. You fucking cunt," I shouted.

Saul's expression changed. He wasn't laughing anymore. When he walked towards me, I kicked out at him, at his legs, and he almost tripped. He managed to grab hold of me, and I spat in his face. He slammed my head into the floor and started punching me. I could feel a couple of my teeth break loose, the sharp edges cutting my tongue.

He grabbed hold of my hair and got up, dragging me to the other side of the room. He took an old broomstick and started beating me with it. With each blow I fought back less, then stopped resisting altogether. By the time he was done, I was a whimpering, bleeding mess on the floor.

He left. Came back hours later. He came over and dragged me into another room. I'd stopped crying by then, just lay there feeling the pain. I didn't resist when he grabbed my legs and pulled me along the floor into a room with a chain attached to the wall. He stopped in front of it and attached the chain to my left ankle.

"Saul?"

He looked at me. "I'll stay with you if you let me live."

He put his hand on my face, wiped his thumb over my wet cheek, then got up and walked out of the room.

"Please," I said. "Please, don't kill me."

***

Minutes later I could hear screams from the other room. I could only imagine what he was doing to his brother. I felt sick, terrified. I couldn't move. All I wanted was to run away, escape. Be with my brother again, and Mike. Just be safe.

The next time I heard his brother scream, I could smell burned flesh. And after a while the screams died away and with it, I knew, his brother. I lost all control over my body. I threw up, and felt the warmth of my piss spreading down the legs of my trousers. I felt ashamed, but I couldn't help it.

Saul didn't come to see me for a very long time. I was just lying there covered in blood and piss, hoping for some kind of miracle. I thought about Scott in his hospital bed. Thought about Nora and the kids and Mike. I knew they'd be worrying about me. Mike would be blaming himself for my disappearance, for not having stayed by my side and protected me.

I was shivering, and not just with the cold. I didn't want to think what Saul was going to do to me when he returned. I drifted in and out of sleep. Every noise woke me, but he didn't come back.

I don't know how many hours had passed. I heard footsteps in the next room, rustling, then silence, and I fell back asleep.

When I woke up Saul was kneeling beside me. I jumped, scrambled backwards.

"Get up," he said.

I looked at him, but didn't move.

"Get up," he shouted.

I stood and took a few tentative steps, realised Saul had taken off the chain. I wondered if this was it. If he'd force me to make my last call.

"Walk."

I walked ahead of him, a million thoughts going through my head — run, talk, plead.

I did nothing.

"To your left," he said.

I followed his instruction, opened a door to my left and walked into a bathroom. On a wooden chair lay a pile of clothes and a towel.

"Clean up," he said. "I've got a job for you."

I looked at him. I didn't know what to think. He was calm, almost relaxed. As if nothing had ever happened. He'd become my boss again, the killer gone.

He closed the door behind me, leaving me on my own. I heard the key turning in the lock, and footsteps walking away. There was no mirror in the room, just the small cubicle shower and the chair. I opened the glass door, switched on the shower and stood back, waited for the jet of water to shoot out. When it came, I was surprised. I don't know what I'd expected, poisonous gas or a chemical that would melt my skin. I couldn't say.

I took off my clothes, threw them on the tiled floor, and stepped into the shower. I watched the dirt and blood rinse off and disappear down the plughole, but the heat, though it stung my skin, was comforting.

A knock on the door. "You done?"

"Almost."

"Five minutes," he said.

I savoured every minute, but didn't want to anger him, afraid of what he would do.

When I opened the door, he stood in front of me, looking me up and down.

"Not a bad fit," he said, pointing at the t-shirt and trousers he'd given me. "Get your stuff. Washing machine's over there." He pointed toward another room. I grabbed my old clothes, and followed.

He showed me how to work the washing machine, then took me into the room I had last shared with his brother. I could see bloodstains, remnants of burnt clothes. There was a smell I couldn't describe, but I knew it was one of pain and death.

"Clean this shit up, then paint the room. Everything you need is in the corner."

Next to an old wooden chest of drawers stood a bucket of white paint and a set of rollers.

"Will you let me leave?" I said. "When I'm done?"

He slapped me across my face with the back of his hand quicker than I could blink. He grabbed me by the throat and pushed me against the wall.

"You fucking lying to me? Huh? Are you?" he hissed. "Remember what you said?"

I was struggling to breathe. With every question he squeezed harder. I had my hands on top of his, and was desperately trying to free myself from his grip. I could see little pinpricks of colour dancing in front of my eyes. Feel myself getting weaker. My struggles becoming pathetic strokes of intimacy.

Saul let go and I fell to the floor.

"You stay, or die," he said. "You choose."

I was coughing, trying to get back my breath. My hands were shaking as I pushed myself up.

"I'll stay," I said. "I'll stay."

"Then get to fucking work."

***

I did my best to please him, showed him I was serious about staying. If I could earn his trust, wait it out, maybe there was a chance of getting out of this alive.

Weeks passed. A month. Saul chained me up in the room every time he left the house, and made me do odd jobs when he was in. Then one day he threw a newspaper at me and said, "Front page."

There was a picture of Scott leaving hospital, flanked by plain clothed police. By his side, Nora cradling their newborn, and my niece, holding on to my brother's wheelchair. The headline read, *"Caller's Last Known Victim Leaves Hospital."* There was a follow-up a few pages on. A picture of me, smiling for the camera at Mike's last birthday party. *"Brother Still Missing."*

"I kept my promise," Saul said, and walked out of the room.

I couldn't bring myself to read the articles, but I kept the paper next to my pillow. Just knowing my brother was safe gave me some sort of peace. My sacrifice hadn't been for nothing. His children would grow up knowing their father.

As time went by Saul gave me more and more responsibilities — designing flyers for the club, new drinks menus. I started cooking most of the meals, baked bread. One thing I was actually good at. As a child I had spent hours in my father's bakery, helping him make bread and bread rolls at three in the morning, just so my mother could make sandwiches for the first customers at six o'clock.

But Saul was careful. He didn't eat unless I ate first. He served me, making sure I hadn't tampered with the food. He'd swap plates and glasses and cutlery, beat me if it wasn't to his satisfaction. I could never be sure how he'd react.

I learned very quickly how to prioritise. Work for the club always came first, then any other work he wanted done. As for food, I had a list of meals I could prepare in less than fifteen minutes. Omelettes, salads, sandwiches, stir fries, leftovers from the day before. I could tell by the look on his face if I'd fucked up, and I'd watch him leave without a word and come back with the stick.

I could handle the beatings, but he didn't always need an excuse, just the drink and his memories of a childhood he couldn't forget.

I feared mornings, his return from the club. Wondering how much he'd had to drink. Listening to his footsteps, if they were heavy or if he was dragging his feet. On those days he'd turn into his father, a sadistic piece of shit that took pleasure in the hurt he could inflict on people. He'd call me boy or bastard. Call my mother a two-timing whore. It could last hours, sometimes the whole day.

After a while he let me have a small TV. The basement I occupied was on constant lockdown, secured by strong doors and locks and soundproof walls. The only sunshine I saw was in the movies and documentaries that he let me watch. I longed to breathe the fresh air, touch the grass again or smell a flower. I wanted to lie next to Mike. Meet Scott for coffee. Get a hug from my niece.

I wanted a miracle.

***

In late August Saul didn't come home for almost a week. I was slowly running out of food and I slept most of the time, worrying that he'd left me to die. The TV ran in the background all the time. I couldn't stand the quiet. I'd convinced myself that if I'd switched it off it would mean the end to everything.

It took a while for me to realise that the screaming didn't come from the TV, the crying and pleading for mercy. I didn't want to hear these sounds, not again, but the moment the screams quietened down I was terrified that Saul was coming for me.

I could hear him talk. His voice sounded different somehow, muffled. Or maybe it was just because of the door between us. The screams started off again. They were longer and more persistent this time, then they died away completely. It stayed quiet for a long time. No sounds, not even footsteps, as if everything had frozen in time.

Hours later he made me clean up the blood, let me eat, and locked me up again. He didn't say much, just that I was lucky. A few months later the same thing happened again.

The days leading up to Christmas, everything I did was wrong. The flyers weren't the right size or were too crowded with information. I misspelled one of the cocktails on the drinks menu. The food wasn't hot enough. The basement too dusty.

Christmas Eve Saul came into the basement, stinking of drink, a bottle of Beluga Gold Line in his hand.

"Drink," he said, handing me the bottle.

I had a few sips, and handed it back to him.

"All of it."

I looked at the bottle. He'd had most of it himself already. I took it back and drank some more, but I wasn't fast enough for him. He grabbed my jaw and pushed the bottle further into my mouth, pouring it down my throat. I choked and coughed, and he hit me for wasting expensive vodka.

"You think you're clever, boy? Do you?" He threw the bottle over his shoulder and I could hear it shatter in the next room.

He spat in my face, pulled a lighter from his pocket, and lit it. I tried to scramble away from him, but the chain around my ankle tightened.

"Cry and I'll break your legs," he said, bending down, bringing the flame to my face. I could feel it licking my skin and I pulled away, but Saul wasn't satisfied. He grabbed the back of my head, put the flame to my hair. I could hear it sizzle, feel it burn.

I punched him. A right hook straight to his temple. He was stunned for a moment, his eyes glassy from the drink.

"Fucker," he shouted, and got up. He stormed out of

the room, came back a minute later with handcuffs.

"Turn over," he ordered. "Give me your arms."

I put my hands behind my back, felt the cold metal snapping shut around my wrists, felt his weight against my legs.

I turned and looked at him, watched as he took a pack of cigarettes from his shirt pocket, and shook one out. He lit it, puffed on it until the end glowed orange, then blew the ash off. He pressed the cigarette against the inside of my arm, but I didn't cry out. I squeezed my eyes shut, and pressed my face into the pillow. Praying for it to be over.

***

My hair is slowly growing back. The burn marks are fading. Life outside is continuing without me. I work hard, take punishment without complaint. Saul's coming up with new rules on a weekly basis. There are times when I have to wash and iron all his clothes but not fold them. I'm not allowed to make a sound when he beats me. I have to eat from a bowl under the table like a dog. Have only one meal a day.

I think about taking my own life but I'm afraid of fucking it up and the consequences of that. I'm scared of hearing him return, scared of smelling the drink on him.

The thing I fear most, though, is hearing the screams from the next room, and knowing another man has fallen into his trap. When it happens I pull the covers over my head and pray the door between us stays shut. I feel my heart thumping in my chest, the sweat working its way to the surface of my skin.

***

And now I can hear him walk past the door, stop, and turn

back. I hear the key in the lock and the door open. I hear him walking towards me and grabbing the chain around my ankle.

"Get up," he says.

He unlocks the chain and I push off my covers. He's holding a knife, smeared with blood.

"Finish him off," he says.

I look past him, into the next room. I look at the bloodied figure slumped in the chair, his hands tied behind his back, his feet bound to the chair.

"Please don't make me do this," I say, shaking my head.

Saul slaps me across the face. Hard.

"Finish him off or the next guy I bring back is your brother."

I take the knife out of his hand, and he steps back, keeping his distance.

I walk up to the man in the chair. I can feel the knife in my hand shaking. I don't want him to suffer any more than he already has, and I wonder what the quickest way would be to put him out of his misery. I lift my arm, hesitate, and lower it.

"Do it," Saul says. "For Scott."

I look back at Saul and know if I don't kill this guy Scott will be back, and this time Saul will make me watch when he tortures him. I raise the knife, close my eyes and stab him in the neck.

"That's my boy," Saul says, smiling.

I pull out the knife, expecting a torrent of blood to squirt from the man's neck, but there's only a trickle, and Saul starts to laugh.

"He was already dead," he says. "Jesus, you should see your face. Priceless."

***

Saul laughs so hard he doesn't realise the mistake he's made. Crossing the invisible line between us. Misjudging my reach. He looks down at his stomach, at the knife, and at the blood seeping through his shirt. I stab him again and Saul cries out. His survival instinct kicks in and he punches me so hard I almost pass out.

I stumble and fall, lose the knife, and he throws himself on top of me, punching me again and again in my face. I try to reach the knife, but he swipes my hand out of the way, tries to grab it himself, and I push my thumb into the cut in his stomach. Saul screams, and rolls off me. I finally manage to grab the knife and sit up. I stab him in the back, two three times. And I run.

Along the corridor, past two more rooms, I can see the black metal door that will lead to freedom. When I turn the handle I realise it is locked. There's no key. I look around, hoping I won't have to go back, but the key isn't there.

Saul's still where I left him, on the floor, groaning. I look through his pockets, find a bundle of keys in his jeans. He tries to stop me, grabs me and whispers in my ear. His movements are slow and weak. And for the first time in all these months I'm not afraid of him. I see him for what he really is, just another human being. He's not immortal. He bleeds. He has weaknesses like the rest of us.

I take the keys, run back to the door. In my haste to find the right one I almost snap one in the lock. It's not quite the right fit and when I try to pull it back out it bends. My hands are sweating. It takes five attempts to find the right one. I climb the stairs, have to unlock another door at the top. This one I find straight away. The door leads into a hall and the entrance. I can see trees, snow, and I run outside. I don't look back.

I run until I can't run anymore. I just want to get as much distance between us as I can. I'm not sure where I'm going. I'm in the middle of nowhere. I follow the lone country road, past bare fields and woods. I walk for almost a mile before a car approaches. I step into the road, spread out my arms, waving them frantically.

The car stops. Inside, a middle aged couple. The man gets out of the car, asks if I'm okay, and it all comes out, and I say, "Help me. My name's Nick Foster, I've been kidnapped."

I can't feel the cold on my bare feet, not until I sit in the car, and they ask if I want the heating turned up.

I shake my head, and wipe away the tears that stream down my face.

***

He's still out there, somewhere. They found nothing but a pool of blood. The club has been shut down. His house boarded up. They promise us that they will get him, but I'm not so sure. Officially Saul doesn't even exist. There's no birth certificate, no paper trail, nothing.

I'm at the airport with Mike, saying goodbye to my brother and his family. They're moving to Italy, closer to my sister-in-law's family. A new beginning.

Scott can't remember what happened to him. He read the articles in the paper. Bears the scars. But his mind erased all trace of everything. Doctors say he might never regain his memory, and Scott hopes it stays that way. I wish I was that lucky.

I remember everything. Every day of the ten months I was locked up in the basement. Most of all I remember The Caller's last words to me, whispered into my ear.

"You're a dead man."

Deathsmell

By Linda Angel

Dedication: *to my brother, Graham Crowder*

They say there's a smell, and they're right. It's apparent in three forms: as a before, a during, and an aftersmell, like some fucked-up scenty version of the past, present, and future. It's the aroma of the persistent imminence of death.

It's been noted in hospitals, in nursing homes, and in all of those other obvious places where drain-circlers tend to dwell. But it's also – quite curiously - been recorded immediately preceding the occasional accident or six; events involving hitherto healthy - and unsmelly - people.

First, there's the oft-reported sickly-sweetness, quite unfamiliar to the common nose and pretty much indescribable. This can manifest itself a week or two before a person's demise, and is quite common in the elderly. Then comes stage two: the *during* pong - this one can take many forms depending upon the manner of death and whether or not there is any soilage as the person loses all control. Afterwards, stage three: the whole gamut of *after*stink as the corpse goes through the various stages of decay.

It's the first one that's the most baffling; usually, you have to have the right sort of nose to detect that kind of thing. As other smells can mask it, so your nose has to be *listening*. In order to intervene and impede (or indeed entirely prevent) stage two, your nose *must* be listening.

Sniff up: can you hear it?

***

This was a small day. Rank, backed-up drainshit meant that the city was particularly malodourous and maladministered, and its inhabitants no fresher - speakers reeked as they exhaled mucky breaths into noses that begged to be pegged. Indoors, amidst a veil of cloudy disharmony, there brewed a storm of an altogether different arrangement.

A fucked bedside clock told Victor the Author that he was already ten hours into the day; this was not particularly welcome news. Unless he could be saved, this day would probably be his last – and he probably knew it. There were no more words to write, no more stories to be written – just the ending to his. A familiar feeling, that. He'd had so many final days, each of which he'd sniffed info his life – and out again - like slightly whiffy friends.

To further blacken the cloud already hovering over his bonce, the gobshite in the flat next door was at it again. Music -if it could even be *called* that- blasted through the dividing wall, its thumpy resonance causing Victor's bits to jiggle and forcing him to throw open a window or two to let out the shitty songs and let *in* the outdoor noise. If music be the food of love, this was emotional vindaloo for the hungry deaf.

Probably a woman, that – or a gay fella, based on the glittery sound of the ridiculously happy jollystuff feeding into his ears. He was more into the PROPER sort of music himself – music that had a soul, tunes you could taste. Thrash was his thing - the really fast and heavy stuff was music he could *smell*.

With the openness of our man's bedroom window he observed – not for the first time - that the place known as Outside had the particularly distinct whiff of a disused ol' factory. As the fragranced few passed by the street-dwelling trampy types, the pong hovered somewhere between affluence and effluence.

You could ask anyone – they'd all say the same thing. Even the tramps – and they're the ones who honked the worst, being absolutely fucking rank 'n' all. Especially the skinny beardy dude who was made dead the night before. He used to smell of old stale piss but now it was more like a fresh concoction of stewed apples in stinkwater- for whilst he was yet inexplicably deceased and covered with garbage, pissplebs urinated on him as they stumbled home after a few jars. Ah – the local boozer: that thinkless, thoughtless drink tank. And this: even fresh piss goes stale.

The dead dude, due to his lifestyle choices – or, more accurately, the choiceless existence that'd been thrust upon him - was of indeterminate age. He could've been in his twenties, thirties, anything up to sixty-odd. The beard either aged him, acting as an apparent life-speeder-upper, or it reflected a long and hairy existence - apropos with a hairy death.

Turns out he'd met a shitsack scumbag pantshitter who'd been so afraid for his *own* life that he'd taken someone else's. The dead life of a bum who'd been in his way as he'd legged it from a gaggle of chavs. A quick push, and he was over. On the way to overness, his head'd hit the wrong bit of concrete floor in a wrong and concrete way.

And either nobody cared, or everybody didn't; for there, amidst the shitrats and ratshit, his remains would – well, do just that. Just another piece of garbage to ooze and rot, to smell until it could smell no more, and to eventually become part of the street like masticated gum.

The interior of the pub was all smashed glass and hash - that REALLY stinky shit. It stunk and stank of really feety cheese that'd been wrapped in old stale cabbage leaves and then smooshed into steaming dog shite. Considering the greenshit was usually set alight – when it wasn't baked into a cake - it made for one minging barbeque: smoke it and face death, nose-on.

The bar itself was fuckder-than-fucked: its comb-over carpets had seen better days before many a vicious beerfest had been spewed upon its threads.

Around the corner, there was the local Chinese – the place was on its third owner in as many years. The previous one had been closed down for serving hound chow mein and bullshitting customers that it was beef. Yeah, alright, mate. Beef doesn't fucking bark. Beef doesn't hang from a fucking washing line stripped of both dignity and skin and marinating in the halitosis-air. Dog smog, it was.

Despite labelling a brand of human AND a species of food, if you were to say the word "Chinese" to anyone from this neck of the scumwoods, you'd see their eyes widen as they threw up in their gob a little. Vulgarity knew no racism here: the black folk reeked of struggle, the essence of Eastern (and indeed *all*) Europeans could be tasted on a garlicky tongue, and the flatulent habits of the Irish drifted along like a perpetual swarm of very honky locusts. But the Brit-bouquet was one of the worst; natives with their white, wet-dog and stale biscuit essence flocked together and rejoiced in their bigotty hideousness like pigs in satin shit.

***

Back inside. If you could be a wall-fly you'd have seen Victor for the useless twat that he was, lying in bed wearing 50 years on his decades-unshaven face and a scruffball cat on his scrawny London body. The mog was flopped across a Victor-shaped, sheet-covered lump, nestled into a concave, malnutritioned stomach - having just rubbed a shitty arse in a human face and having licked the bedsheets clean of last night's equally shitty dinner. The pair now lay in their own and each other's filth, exhaling their distinct brands of crudded-up breath into the already-indecent air.

Aside from necessary (and often, futile) toilet-dashes, the man had hardly prised himself out of that bed in a fortnight: V stands for Velcro-arse.

The apartment honked of deadstuff. With V's incessant desire for something's flesh, the fridge held nothing but stinky meat: reeking bacon, foetid pork chops, and an old chicken carcass that was so far gone it was green and furry and smelled like arse. Two more days and that thing'd be up and about.

"*I suppose you need feeding.*" Victor said to a cat that wasn't listening.

Mismatched dishes filled the sink – each piece caked with dried-on bits of crap. The floors, along with stinkily unwashed clobber, displayed an equal share of the apartment's dinner-splats, retaining anything that had ever splotted or dropped.

A small nodule of erupted spleen caused V a moment of agonising pain, and a little bit of throbbing gristle made his throat cough up gobby bits of crap and crappy bits of gob.

"*Pfhaaaackkkkk*" he said, with an equal amount of self-hatred and phlegm.

Whilst Victor was hacking, and whilst he was grubby and stuck in the past, and what with his already smelling dead 'n' all, his headvoice continued along its poetically desperate path. He was dying anyway for certain- but there lay stuff and crap and things in his path yet. But those were just bits. Those bits of stuff and crap and things. Logistics.

As hard as the satellite crap was, the crap floating around orbiting this whole thing, this new aspiration of his was just deathly *right*, so any living logistics could go and get fucked – just like his clock. And as he fucked logistics off, so his headvoice became silently angry at the noise coming from his neighbour: *turn the music DOWN, for fuck's sake!*

***

In the apartment next door – which was a universe away – sat a once-despicable person of ignoble rank and title who - unless she could save someone today - would remain undignified and potent. It was right there, in Dustycunt's place, that she pondered and hypothesised, postulated and mused about the fact that she could fucking well do with a cuntduster.

It'd been a while;ladylessness apparently being the cause of her dry spell. According to the most meaningless people (she chose her friends well but was lumbered with unpickable family), she was an unladylike cunt, for thirty times a day, her father would tell her so. ***Mary Isobel!***He'd full-name her each time she swore, even though he cussed like a motherfucker himfuckingself.

She shouldn't speak with such vulgarity, he said. She should DRESS like a lady, he said – and save swearing for sailors and pants for workmen.

The fuck? Was this the eighteen hundreds? Did they still even HAVE sailors any more? They sure as shit didn't have ports - and any docks round their way had long since been filled in and had had shitty prefabs built on 'em after that. And from fuck knows where, there seemed to be an endless supply of equally shitty prefabricated people to move into them. Just like that rank twat next door.

She'd never even seen him in the flesh – the fucker spent all day holed up in a shit-smelling hovel, whose stench seeped out onto and into her turf via the underdoor. Convinced that the fella was somehow finding his pongsome way over to her apartment atom-by-atom, or by some weird and stinky form of seepy osmosis right through bricks and mortar, she shoved a draught excludery- snakey-thingy up against the bottom of her door. Her imagination imagined long-hairedturdy-arsed cats and honking dogs – although the only barking she'd ever noticed was courtesy of her neighbour's hacking cough.

"*Pfhaaaackkkkk*" she heard, as she turned up her music to out-drown him. Disgusting.

Similar sick-making scummery was to be had right around the city; there were definitely no ladies there, where smoky people coughed up their guts along with their existence. And in that classless town, every fucker was orange - daily trips to the Electric Beach had made sure of that.

By the age of thirty, most women weren't visibly female any more but rather resembled leather handbags without the straps. And just like handbags, they were full of unnecessary shit.

Everyone around there was a scumfuck. It's not so much that they were poorly educated; more that they weren't educated *at all*. And what with Dusty being a bit of a gobby loudmouth, she found herself correcting the uncultured and grammarless as part of her community duties.

Despite her own experiences of being shoddily-upbrought by her twat of a dad, and notwithstanding her early school-eluding, lessonless life, she'd not done too badly at the ol' English lit. A bit of Pygmalion here and there, and a smattering of Clockworky classics had taught her how to speak properly improper, like. But droogishness aside, and wordy inventiveness apart, she had a plethora of other abilities making for an oddly classy sort of classlessness.

The chavtastic parents in that particular woodsneck were wholly and exclusively responsible for keeping the local shitty food joints in business. Babies' prams were freckled with sausage roll crumbs; prams whose plastic rain covers bore the holey scars of clumsy fag burns from dozy-arse parents. Toddlers toddled along at fag-end-height, McSomething's tots promising to behave so that they'd be happily rewarded with Unhappy Meals.

Dusty no longer bothered speaking her mind about fast-food injuries; the poor kids in her area were probably too far gone with their chicken nugget and fatty pasty addictions. Processed shite for under-processed minds, that's how she saw it.

Whilst parents fucked with their kids' health and put the DIE into DIET, Dusty worked a day-job as a ledge-talker-downer. That was the only way she could really improve this place, since educating herself with literal literature hadn't done a thing. There were various shifts, with various sorts of customers – if you could call them that. Some of them didn't mind *what* you called them, what with being at their tethers' end 'n' all. But there was a thing, and the thing was this: she had to fuck the swearing off. And there was another thing: she had to use her real name.

This job – this new altruistic existence - came about as a result of contemplation: perhaps she could atone by proxy for others' fuckuppery by perhaps saving a life. Not her own – it was too late for that. And no atonement would be had by breeding- she was an unmother of the highest degree. Plus, didn't you have to ugly-bump for that shit to happen in the first place?

Despite a sewn-up encrusted decade or so, Dusty's last fella had still fucked her hard for their entire relationship. He hadn't shown any interest in her *that* way (bonkingly speaking) for years – not that she'd have noticed in any case, what with his pathetically tiny fingerdick being what it was. Or wasn't.

The last whiff she'd experienced of *that* sort of thing had been a forced threesome a few months back, which had failed to re-ignite the flames.

UGH – she recoiled and recalled the tete-a-tete-a-tete.

*VILE.*Chickbits did nothing for her.

Fingerdick could speak for himself. He could fuck for himself too, he remembered, and ended up bending the wannabe quazi-lesboslut over the kitchen counter to finish the job.

So then there was the split. And after they'd splat, Dusty was free in all the ways he was not. And despite her being a cynical bint of the highest order, tainted by a planetful of twats, today she would prove to be uncontaminated.

***

The entire population, without exception, were so fucking peopley as far as Victor was concerned – and he was fucked if he was going to continue breathing their air. Even his own parents, who hadn't listened to nature and had kept on trying to reproduce despite a dozen pre-V miscarriages, were pigshit-thick and entirely unworthy of this place.

How'd they not realised they weren't destined to be parents? He was *not* meant to have been. Twelve babies hadn't birthed – could his mother not have taken the fucking hint and either had something stitched up or refrained from fuckery altogether?

Both Ma and Pa had even personally recommended upon occasion that it might be an idea if he were to *just fuckingdrop dead*, and here he was now, forty-odd years later, pondering the possible hows. *More* and *further* possiblehows, that was, having already tried and failed a dozen times. Twelve not even terribly imaginative methods. Twenty pills here, two bottles of vodka there, a rope that broke, an unsharp knife that hadn't sliced, those sorts of things. Lame ass typical things – just like him.

"Just go and hang yourself, Vic, ya smelly bastard," his

father'd said. No bones about it. "Have done with it. Save yagettin' a bath." Comments like that were the norm, regardless of pertinence. His mother was just as bad; Victor'd say something entirely schoolboyish from an eleven or twelve year-old mouth, and she'd pipe up with "if you don't like it, you can always top yerself." Big help, she was. If only she'd piped down now and again.

If only.

He reached into his RAM and retrieved a twenty-year old memory. Something Novembery and wintery...something to do with homework. Whatever it was, it was quickly followed by the recollection of Ma suggesting he use said homework as bog roll. And after he'd gone and wiped his arse with it, it was then highly recommended that he should chuck it on the bonfire along with his sorry self.

Self-harm was only around the corner from puberty, and once *that* had set in, his arms'd had fun with knives. They weren't even sharp; that was the thing. Sharp would have been quick and far too easy; and although he would have liked to cut out the pain with one edge, his uncuttable-butter arms were the only ones that reminded him he was alive. Hugs, shmugs. His best mate was a stainless steel blade.

Now, they *do* say that suicidal tendencies reflect a lack of self-worth and a sentimental feeling that the world would be better off without the suicidee. This was not true of V: he told himself that he was too fucking *good* for this place, despite the insights of his sperm donor and womb lender. He was superior in intelligence and wit – if not so much in aesthetics – and 24/7, he would contemplate the uncontemplateable and think the hitherto altogether unthunken thoughts.

According to his inner monologue, if everyone were to think like V, there wouldn't be half as many problems on this fuckforsaken planet. But still, without someone to save him, he went to work on removing himself from it.

***

He was either mad because he was a writer, or a writer because he was mad. And before he could look up the expiration time involved with various forms of Victorcide, he'd already decided that swinging was a tad ropey and that he'd be aiming in the wrong direction with the gun idea.

"*What if I were to survive?*" he asked his cat. "*What if I were to end up cabbaged with a broken neck and an unfixable spine?*"

"Miaow".

Like most writers, Victor's interwebular search history might bring to the mind's ear a certain Bernard Herrmann score – yet, none of the repulsive search results were bad enough (where bad means *good*, of course). He had to be certain. Plus, the last time he'd tried the hanging thing, the rope'd let him down (quite possibly because it was a tad wispy and string-like, not unlike his chickenshit self).

"*How about jumping?*" He paused before veering off in the direction of no.fucking.way.

"*…I could land on someone…I don't want to take anybody out with me*".

Bless him: he had a conscience.

And whilst he contemplated the things he might have to do, he simultaneously supposed that he *could* get somebody *else* to do it. But that would be a fuckload to ask a friend – and if he were to ask one of his more unsavoury associates, he'd have to pay money he didn't have. Fuck! Was he stuck in this world?

Only he could answer that. He needed to be in the right frame of mind, perhaps – or rather, an even wronger one. He wasn't quite depressed enough, maybe. Yes – that might be it. That was it. Depression: that's the thing that had been shaping his life and would soon be shaping his death.

As for how they'd tell his story once he'd snuffed it, Victor didn't give a shit, really. History, he thought, isn't even history anyway. It's just a bunch of folks' *opinions* on history. The yawning volumes of yore were packed with mere impressions of what actually happened – the stuff people wanted you to believe.

F'rinstance, everybody knew that Christopher Columbus was basically a murdering cunt with a penchant for genocide, unlike his depiction in cute little bookie-wooks. How the fuck can you discover somewhere that's already been discovered? Inhabited? And yet, the brainwashery persisted in schools and books. Gandhi was clearly a terrorist - just like Mandela, and Kennedy was nothing if not over-rated (handsome bastard that he was).

Victor, exhausted from overthought, drank a drink and slept a sleep. But not before he asked his cat, "is she even *out* there, puss? Does she exist?" He didn't even know why he used the feminine gender – the person for whom he was seeking might well have been a bloke. It didn't matter to him; he just had a feeling. Maybe he thought he could smell her on the horizon.

"This isn't about love, puss". This had *never* been about love. Or even about soul-matery or any of those sorts of things. Romance had nothing to do with anything. When Victor spoke, thought, or dreamed of The One - his One, none of those things had ever once entered into the equation.

It would have been a *lot* simpler had he tried embryonically harder not to exist. His entire self, his entire *being*, had been one whole miscarriage of justice.

The cat had nothing to say.

***

Imagine knowing you were never wanted, certainly not loved, always despised. How would that FEEL to a child? It was fucked-up that with her fucked little life and an underfucked little body, Dusty felt rather fucking fucked. How she'd survived seven months of gestation in a stoned womb, a coke-absorbing vessel into which bad news and booze were poured was a perplexingly odd boggle; one she didn't care to overthink.

That said, she always hoped there'd be a spirit of the kindred variety – one who'd get her. Perhaps one who'd been there himself...although she certainly hadn't found him yet. Not even close.

Dusty shouldn't have been. And had her parents ceased to fuck, her deathly life would have been prevented. But there was a thing, and the thing was this: Dusty's past, still addled with drugs and life, didn't matter - whilst she was born clean and alive, she didn't want to die dirty. Worse still: the idea of living mucky and unloved. Blood transfusions at birth were inherently miraculous considering the hens' teeth nature of AB Rhesus negative.

"Who's the biggest fuck-up of 'em all, eh?" Dusty asked the bathroom mirror.

She considered her decayed decade and tried to back-mind all the shitc; all the things for which she blamed herself, all the crap things she'd done, and the good things she hadn't. But at the forefront, she believed herself utterly culpable. She was the common denominator after all – if he'd been happy – if she'd have*made* him happy, then surely he'd have treated her right, right?

The mirror told her yes.

And then she went to work on going to work. A quick brush of the hair, which smelled a little greasy and could probably do with a shampoo, and a cat's lick of the face. A dash of mascara and she was ready for her job: a helpline of sorts, for the OUT of sorts. Sometimes she succeeded, sometimes she didn't. And oftentimes, outcomes escaped her. Today would be different. Very. She'd be escaping herself.

***

Victor uncatted his bed, uncluttered himself, and shuffled to the bathroom. For the first time in 20, maybe 25 years, he had a shave. Of course, he had a scissorin' first, being that the razor wouldn't otherwise've been able to encounter his face. It was rather surprising to see what was under there – moles with which to reacquaint himself, a dimple he'd forgotten, and a jawline you could slice yourself on. As he introduced himself to the universe of his own visage, so he said his farewells.

"I can't say I'll miss, you, old chap."

None of this small bigday was planned, of course, as far as timing was concerned. It's not like he had his alarm clock set. But he knew – he'd always known - that he would *know* when the time was right. He knew that when the moment was right, he'd be leaving the apartment for the last time.

Catface ended up in a carrier, complete with dry crunchy food and water. A note was placed on her collar, in one of those cute little locket-type-things, upon which was scrawled unimaginatively: LOOK AFTER ME. I WANT TO LIVE. It was so generically lame that three seconds later, V'd forgotten what it was he'd written. That's when it was time to leave.

Victor yanked on the door handle, allowing in the stench of the corridor. His face lit up like the Hindenburg the moment he did the opening. Except his blimp wasn't falling – it was rising. This would be the day. He didn't know how he knew – he just did. Maybe he could smell it.

He left the cat out in the hall, and as he walked away, blew a kiss to kitty.

Victor reckoned that his bits'd last twenty-four hours – after he'd snuffed it, there'd be a small but distinct window of opportunity to save a life. Of course, this would be left to science, as he wouldn't be there to tangibly hand out lungs 'n' shit. He'd have to trust. Something he'd never done in his life.

Victor ended up at an internet café fifty feet from his apartment. Sure, it was as scummy as the rest of the town, and was about as much a café as the recycling plant down the road. Stank the same, too. It honked of its stinking, soggy offerings: floppy eggs, rubber bacon, and curled-up crusty butties.

Victor ordered what turned out to be zombie coffee: it'd clearly been warmed up and had come back *not.quite.right.*

Graiiiiins.

He grabbed a mug, and chose a spot right in the corner – the most private position he could find. Once he'd settled into said posish, he needed to determine the answers to his questions – but he knew that first, he must establish what those questions were.

Opening an on-line chat would be easier – and infinitely more private – than a 'phone call. He was shite at actual speaky conversation in any case, not knowing what to do with dead air, not knowing what to say at any given juncture, and generally not knowing much of anything at all.

Typing in the words *Suicide Help* he found a friendly-looking website that offered that for which he'd been looking.

~Good morning. My name is Mary Isobel. Can I take your name please?

-It's not important.

True – it wasn't.

~If you give me your name I might be able to help

you on a more personal level.

-Really. It's fine.

~That's not a problem. What shall I call you? Sir, or Madam?

-It doesn't matter.

~I could assign you a name. Shall I call you Cheryl?

-I'm a bloke.

~John. Shall I call you John?

-Jesus.

Jesus.

~You want me to call you Jesus? Are you Latino? Is it HEY-Sooce?

-Can we get to it? You can call me V. Is that better?

~That's fine. Hi, V.

She was in. With a pure dose of dusty cynicism, she was in. V took a swig of the caffeinated brownshit - noticing it had a peculiar pungency about it - and continued to type.

-OK. I need some help.

~That's what I'm here for. I just need to tell you first that everything that goes between us STAYS between us, ok? We're bound by the Data Protection Act.

-OK. I know.

~What can I do to help?

-Well...

He paused for a wee while.

~Are you still there, V?

-I'm here.

~What is it I can help you with today, V?

-I have a few questions. And things to say. I have things to say. I'm just going to come out and say it, OK?

~Please do. I'm listening.

He came out and said it:

-I'm going to kill myself today. And before you say don't, please just listen.

~I'm listening. Go ahead.

-Don't try and talk me out of it, it's a done deal.

~I won't.

-You won't? Isn't that your job?

~Yes it is – but no. I won't. And do you know why? Because I was thinking the same thing only today. And I thought to myself "what if someone tried to talk me out of it?" and knew that nobody could. If I was that determined, nobody could.

-What the fuck?

~I'm sorry. This isn't about me, it's about you. Please continue.

He wasn't sure that he *could*, now, after that. What the ACTUAL? Did she just…? How could she…? That's if she even *was* a she, that is. Maybe they feminised *all* their workers, regardless of the existence of tackle, because women were supposed to be easier to talk to?

-I'm not sure I can, now. Sounds like you need a bit of help yourself.

~I'll be fine. I'm not actually going to do it. It was just a thought.

-That's not a normal thought to have, Mary Isobel.

He was in.

~Maybe so, V, but it's only empathy, you know. It's the way I am. I do this day in day out, and I can't help employing a little introspection. Puts me in the shoes of the caller. Well, I say "caller", you know what I mean.

Of course he did. He wasn't stupid. He was a WRITER.

-Are you sure you're OK to continue? I don't want to cause you any problems if you're not at your best.

~V, I'm fine. I just wanted you to know that I understand what you're going through. Also it kinda makes it obvious I'm not a robot. So many of these on-line chat things have automated responses at the ready and I wanted to reassure you with something a little – well, human.

-OK. That's true.

~So go on. Tell me your story.

-I want my story to end.

~Really?

-Yes. And please know this is not about anyone else.

~How do you mean, exactly?

-It's not because people will be better off without me. Because I know that's a thing. With a lot of people, that's a thing.

~That's true, V. So why have YOU made this decision?

-Well, I'm ready to see what else there is. I'm fed up of this place.

~Aren't we all?

-Maybe so. But there are those who are quite happy to stay here.

~Meaning?

-Well, ya know. Kids and stuff. People I could help.

~What do you mean, V?

-I'm an organ donor.

~I see. Me too.

-Exactly. You GET IT! Finally, someone who gets it.

~I do, V. I do. What's the point in existing, miserably, when you could be put to good use?

She paused to extract her bra's underwire from her

armpit, whose aroma screamed "WASH ME!"

~So, V. What do you think the other side is like?

*-Should you even be asking me this stuff? I mean –
aren't you supposed to talk me out of it?*

~You said not to.

-I did, yes. But-

She typed back before he could finish his sentence.

*~I'm just interested in you, V. And you sound like
somebody I can talk with. I don't get to have very many
deep conversations, you know. In this line of work, I
mean.*

-I bet you don't, right?

~Nope. Not once.

He believed her. But he had a question. It was a dark
one, but it was on his mind; therefore it needed to be off.
Speaking of off – that's what the cream in his coffee
probably was. Phew. That stuff was rank. He carried on
sipping the vile concoction as he continued with his thought-
train:

*-Has anyone ever – done it whilst you were talking
to them?*

~Once.

-What happened?

*~Well, I can't discuss individual cases due to
confidentiality. It was hard, though.*

-Wow. That must've been though.

He corrected his typo:

t o u g h

*~It was. But only the police are entitled to see the
details. I can't discuss it.*

*-I know. But still. I'm sorry you had to deal with
that.*

*~It's ok. I couldn't save him. He was always going
to do it.*

-Like me.

~Yes, I DO like you, V.

-That's not what I meant.

~I know. I'm just saying.

-Saying? Like…you like me?

~Of course I do.

-What's to like?

~What's not to? How about your youness, V? Everything. You came on here and opened up. Not a lot of people do that. You talked to me like a person. You cared about me when I mentioned dark thoughts.

-Of course I cared. I do care.

~You're good people, V.

He was. So was she.

-Me? Nah.

~You are. You cared, you asked if I was ok, you came on here and said you were going to donate your organs-

-I mean it though. I want to help people. I've tried many times, and I'm useless.

~I bet you're not. Tell me something you've done. Something you've acheived.

achieved - sorry, V. There's no spellchecker on here.

-It really doesn't matter. Not now. Nothing matters.

~Everything matters, V. Tell me something good you've done. Go on.

-I can't. I'm no good at that. I can't big myself up.

~Come on.

-I don't know.

Victor paused and thought and thunk and paused a bit longer and stopped and scratched his arse. Whilst he scratched his arse he recalled how his cat would scratch at the wheels of the computer chair upon which his lazy arse usually sat. This gave him an idea; a lame one but the only one he had:

-I got my cat from a rescue centre.

~Why did you do that?

-Well, because there are enough things out there that need rescuing. Without going to breeders and stuff.

~You're right. So tell me what else you've done.

-Like helping old women across the road and stuff?

~Anything.

-Ok.

He paused for breath as his breathing skipped a beat and his heart gasped for oxygen. He was going to have to big himself up here – something to which he wasn't accustomed. Nobody'd ever asked about him. Nobody'd ever cared enough before to ask about his interests or the things he'd done.

-I took another cat in.

~ You mean like a stray?

-I don't know. I don't know if she was a stray, feral, or what. It might have been a bad move – it could have been someone's pet. But she seemed sad. Looked up at me like she wanted to come home with me. So I took her in.

~That can only be a good thing.

-I guess so. And I never saw any missing cat posters, so maybe.

~Yes! You went with your instinct, and helped someone in need.

She pressed RETURN too soon.

~Well, something.

She had it right the first time:

~Actually – no. Someone.

-I agree. I don't see cats as anything less than people.

~That's because you're a good man, V. Ok – what else?

Victor's headvoice said ERM on repeat whilst he thought about what to type.

-I donate blood. I give blood each time there's a local campaign.

~Of course you do – because you were talking about organs earlier, right?

-Right. I don't see the point in wasting anything – let alone something that can give LIFE to the unliving.

~I'm the same. I donated last month – I'm a rare blood type so they need to stock up on mine.

-Me too. I'm AB Rhesus Negative.

~Well, V – it's a small world.

-Really? You too?

~Yep!

-Blood buddies! Who would have thought? And here you are, talking to me.

~We have more in common than you might think, V. Most people do, in fact. You take any two people and get them talking long enough, they'll discover all kinds of coincidences.

-Coincidences? Is that all this is? You don't think it's anything deeper?

~Do you?

-I don't know – maybe? Like kismet or serendipity maybe? I don't know.

~I'm not really a fatalist, V, I'm sort of a skeptic. But I guess on some level, well – I don't know.

Victor went quiet. He ceased hammering the keyboard whilst Dusty hammered some more.

~Are you there?

V?

Are you there V?

V?

Are you still there?

He was. He was still there.

-I'm still going to do it, you know.

~Well, if there is nothing I can do to stop you – like, talking with you hasn't helped, then maybe we can talk about how and why you're going to do it.

-Ok.

Ok was something he clearly wasn't. Victor felt this line of questioning was a little – well, *off* – and barely professional.Not that he was particularly arsed from a consumer perspective – but he did find himself worrying about *her*. What if the conversation was audited? What if, after he'd done the deed, this stuff was monitored? Taken away for evidence? Surely this Mary Isobel chick would be paddleless up a very stinky creek?

Dusty knew she was taking a risk – and a major one. She knew that if he DID go through with it, this whole conversation could and would be used as evidence. But somehow, for some reason of inexplicability, she didn't care, even though today may well be his deathday.

~Come on, V. Speak to me. I'm a good listener.

He gave her stuff to hear.

-Well. I was thinking later tonight.

~Why at night?

-Well, it's quieter. Fewer people about.

~Ok. That makes sense. How?

-I haven't quite decided. Pills, maybe.

~Ok, can I just say something?

-Course.

~Don't poison your system. If you take too much of the wrong stuff, they might not be able to harvest as

many organs.

    -Oh. I hadn't thought of that.

No shit, Sherfuck. Victor's headvoice What-The-Fucked itself.

    ~It's true, V. You pump all kinds of crap through there -then you might not be any good to anyone else.

Shit. She was thinking about all the things he hadn't. Being a writer, you'd have thought that in order for his story to have the desirable ending, he'd have already done his research. He'd have to look it up.

    ~Of course, the good thing with pills is...

There was a GOOD thing? The fuck?

    ~...the paramedics will work on you for a while in case you're saveable. Accidental overdose.

    -How's that a good thing?

    ~It means if, when they find you, you're already circling the plughole, they'll keep your organs ticking over so they can at least be used for someone else. And they can tell whether you're gonna make it.

    -I'm not sure what your saying.

    -*You're*

    ~Ok, let's suppose it's apparently intentional. Clearly intended.

    -What?

    ~Well, if it looks like a deliberate suicide – you know, like if you were found hanged, say, they'd treat it as a crime scene. They'd have to process the scene, inch by inch. You'd be left therefor hours, possibly. Maybe even a day.

At best, she was guessing. Worst? Utterly bullshitting.

    ~They only have so long to take your bits, V. After a few hours, you'd be useless.

He hadn't thought of that. Bollocks.

    ~Whereas, if it looks like you intended *to be*

saved, even if you're already shaking scythes with death, the paramedics will work on you and you won't have to worry about them keeping you there too long. They'll get you in an ambulance. And then, once you pass away, you'll already be in hospital. One thing, though: make sure your donor card is clearly visible. Or easily findable.

-How long do I have?

~Four hours, V. Four hours until everything dies.

She thought it was closer to twenty-four – or maybe even longer - but she was IN. She was in, and *in* she would stay.

-So I'd have no way of raising the alarm. How would I call for help to get the ambulance there?

~Well, there's the obvious one, V.

-If I call 999, they might get here too soon and save me. I don't want that. I might end up fucking cabbaged or something.

~You have to consider all that, yes.

-Well, I could rely on someone to ring 999 say, two hours after the event.

~They'd be a really shit friend, V.

-Or a really good one.

~I suppose.

-Seriously. I mean it – If I got the right person...they could help.

~V – listen. Please. With your blood type. With OUR blood type – you need to be careful. You go doing stuff without having your bits taken care of, well, they could go to waste. You know what I'm saying.

He did.

~You ok, V? You still there?

He was.

-Yes. I'm here.

~So come on, why do you want out? Are things THAT bad?

-It's not so much that – more like I want to see what else there is. I'm bored here. Restless. There's nothing for me any more.

~What about – ethics? Do you have any beliefs?

-No. I'm agnostic. Erring on the side of atheism.

~Me too. But V – what if we're wrong?

-What?

~What if everything they say is true? What if we end up in some sort of purgatory for our sins? What if you go through with this and end up being eternally damned?

-Don't be ridiculous.

~It's something to think about, that's all. You said agnostic before you said atheist, so you're not sure, right?

-Well, no. How can you be sure of anything unless you SEE it?

~My point exactly, V.

He took a look at the corner he'd backed himself into.

-But don't forget – I could save a life. I could save SEVERAL. Surely any deity would weigh all that up before punishing me?

~It doesn't matter. Ten, twenty lives, V – your one life is equally as important. Even if you're not a believer, you have to see that. You HAVE to.

-I don't know. I'm not convinced.

~One life is the same as many. It's what a person DOES with their life that can make themthirty, forty people.

- Wow.

Yeah. Wow.

~One thing I do know, though – doing this job – is

that suicide is anything but selfish. That's what they say – the people who think they know it all but don't know ANYTHING. It's anything BUT selfish. Like you – you want to help people. You're thinking straight – despite the topic, the whole reason you're here.

No reply. She continued:

~Why ARE you here, V? Specifically here, I mean - why did you come to this website?

-All the things we discussed, I guess. I wanted to know someone cared, I guess, before I went. Well…before I go.

~Of course I care! And if I do, I can guarantee there will be plenty of others who would, too.

-I know.

~Listen, V. I know you said not to talk you out of it, ok? And I know I can't convince you because I can never convince someone whose mind is made up – but I just want you to do it right. I want you to be happy when you go, and you will only be happy if you know your bits are being taken care of.

-Yes?

~Yes. You know what I'm saying.

That he did.

For her plan and his to be realised, ego disposability needed to become a thing. He needed to sniff up and listen. For once in his self-sorry existence, he needed to listen.

The conversation darkened – or lightened, perspective-dependent. Plans were made. Pauses were had to enable tea-making and coffee drinking (and to permit visits to horrible-smelling bogs).

Victor stumbled away from the conversation and back into his apartment along with the cat carrier he'd left in the hall not two hours before. He hadn't expected this. Instead, he'd anticipated a barrage of *don't do its*. But no – here he was, awaiting a visit from Mary Isobel. And he wondered if the door would ever be knocked.

Women had let him down all his life – his mother, his lovers, his sisters who'd died before they'd ever lived, cheap cheerleaders and garbage girls, unhelpful shop assistants, female writers who'd never touched him...the list was...well, endful. Because it ended here. It ended with Mary Isobel. She was and would be the only ever She.

She just had this WAY about her – a way of looking at things from a brand new vantage point – no matter the situation. Even on-line – this girl he'd never met. Those babies who'd failed to be – making him think that *he* shouldn't have been either...well, she'd done the undoable and convinced him of the opposite. *You weren't meant to die then*, she told him. *You fought – from the womb, you were a fighter*, she'd explained. And he believed her. He believed that if he were the ONLY one out of a whole bunch who'd made it, then surely he was *destined* to survive.

His purpose was apparent: he'd been destined to survive life – to survive THEN so that he could die NOW.

***

Once Dusty's day was over, she realised it'd been a good one. Better than usual. She felt better about herself now - despite the smell she could detect from her underarms. She'd taken a little risk back there – and she reckoned it'd pay off. That dude was gonna wait for her. She'd be there soon – and FUCK, was she excited: this was the first time she'd done this. The first time she'd urged herself up from her fat arse, instead of paying lip service and sticking to dull and meaningless call scripts.

I'll help you do it, she'd said. *I'll make sure it's painless. And I'll make sure you get to hospital asap.*

This act – unusual though it may be – would be her true calling. She'd been doing it wrong all along – trying to save lives that didn't want saving. Offering the wrong sort of help.

She'd obtained his address, and she was going there. And at the same time, she was going home. Perhaps this was the serendipity of which they'd spoken – what were the chances of living in the same apartment block as some bloke who'd messaged you in your professional capacity? Her head flooded itself with numbers.

There were around 9 million people in London, she reckoned – and in the UK, total? That was something like 65,000,000 to-one. And living next door? This guy had to be special. He *had* to be. He was, at the very outside, special enough to have earned her trust, as she'd earned his. P'rhaps the universe had sent him to her – to make it easy, y'know – to ease her into this new line of work. Made sure she didn't have to travel far. Picked a guy for her – THE guy. The Guy Next Door.

She hadn't let on when he'd provided his address. He might've found that a little creepy to say the least – and creeping him out was the last thing she wanted him to do. He couldn't hear the gasp she'd given, nor could he see the chicken bumps on her goosies.

In addition to sharing rareness – such as the blood thing, and the address thing – they shared so much more; in the last few screen-pages of conversation they'd learned as much as two people ever *could* learn about each other. Tales of the past that made their present what it was, unborn siblings, future hopes whose outcome would only be determined by current events, gods and science and magick and all those loudly hitherto unspoken things.

A ten minute bus ride, that's how close she was to saving a life - so close in so many ways. And his was the one worth saving in the oddest of ways. By letting him go…by letting him let HIMSELF go…she knew – she just KNEW – that she wouldn't have a job tomorrow. She knew that the risks she'd taken were non-transferable, just like her bus ticket. In no way would the boss overlook the intimacy of the conversation she'd had with V. *Remain impartial, and keep cool.* Those were the rules, and she'd broken them. She'd broken them maybe sixty times in one conversation.

But it was worth it – and despite the dodginess of the situation, she'd find a way to do it again. This just felt right – again: like her calling. She could help numerous people this way – the way they *needed.*She would be the enabler.

Fuckgivelessness was a virtue, along with the absence of shitgivery. Not once did she have a re-think; not even fleetingly. He was worth it – he just was. He was and would be the only ever He: for he would be her first.

Dusty imagined how he'd look when he opened the door – not that she cared. He could be fat, scrawny, hairy, baldy, black, white or anything in between – and he'd be V. Just V. And she wanted to help – she MUST. The mustness clearly came from an empathic place; knowing how much he wanted to do this. Knowing how many people he could help – save – after he'd gone…this would mean that she'd get to save them too. To be part of it.

She also knew that this was different. She wasn't going to talk him down from a ledge, as she'd done so many times. She wasn't going to cut the rope before he jumped. She was going to hand him the gun. She was going to administer the pills. This wasn't like you see in the movies – some big dramatic stand-off where the good guy – usually a cop - saves the sick guy before he offs himself. This was the exact opposite. V had to die; it was his destiny. London needed his parts.

If she didn't get there, he might never go through with

it. She'd made an early promise not to talk him out of it – and now she had to talk him IN.

Head in the clouds of mist and altruism, Dusty crossed over to catch the bus back. Overcome by an abrupt stench as she walked, her nose tried to pin down the notes: a bit of vanilla...essence of cloves, maybe? Nice things. But nice things that were surrounded by the smell of sewers. Like when someone goes for a crap and sprays air-freshener – and all you end up smelling are flowers that smell like shit.

S...c...r...e...e...c...h.

Her concentration and timing must have been a little off, along with the timing of the bus to nowhere that took her on an immediate and final journey.

***

She never came. Not that he was surprised, of course, but he was in the very least disappointed that she never came. She was supposed to be *the one* to get him through this – she was supposed to be **The One**. **The one** for whom he'd waited – perhaps not for all his life but certainly for all of his living death. **The one** to help him DO IT. **The one** to give him the courage, **the one** to allow him to pass calmly to the next plane of existence.

He loved her and hated her at once. This one platonic love – no ties –indeed utterly tieless. **The one** who GOT HIM. Who would understand the place from which he came and why he needed to go back there. **The one** who got away.

She was supposed to make sure his remains helped others to remain in a state of being, and she'd let him down. She'd let *them* down too, by default.

He couldn't do it without her. Unless he found another Her – which he knew he wouldn't. He was only happy when he was miserable, and the extent of his current misery made him happier than ever.

Outside, the clouds pursed their lips and blew; tumultuous cumuli that dripped and dropped rainful tears of tearful rain. The roof slates chattered their applause for the wind's performance with their ovational clicks and clacks. And on this small day, whether or not the weather was angry out there, it was far more tempestuous inside.

This would be the perfect suicide: long and painful, and a fitting end for a man who was only happy when he was unhappy. Victor DeConstantine was going to live to death. There was a warm and imminently catful bed waiting for him; he knew that once he let her out of the carrier, the bed'd be the first place she'd jump. And he was right, too. She jumped, she pissed, and she conquered.

For once, Victor stripped the bed straight away. He'd had enough stinkiness. Time to smell nice for once. As he bundled the sheets into the washing machine, he walked around inside his head and planned a relaxing evening. He might go and grab a book. Grab a snack. Have a nap. He just needed this sudden... tightening... chest... of... his... to... hurry... up... and... untighten. Piss the fuck OFF, pain!

His already-overloaded brain crammed in a few more thoughts of life before death before his neurons got a little busier and made his right arm reach for the telephone. At least he'd be able to hear the operator – for once, next door didn't have the music blasting. He did have Mary Isobel's number but... only... had... the... strength... to... dial... three... digits...

***

In a London hospital somewhere, somewhen, appeared those involved with a Road Traffic Accident of the Most Unfortunate Variety – one traumatised driver, thirty-seven dazed passengers, and one fresh DB. She'd just stepped out from nowhere, she had. She wasn't looking, they said.

She had ID – always taking her passport along for the same reason she always wore matching underwear: Just. In. Case. Perhaps she had a feeling this was always on the cards for her; or at least a feeling of its possibility. Maybe she'd *smelled* it coming. Not a sixth sense thing, more of a literal, tangibly nasal and utterly scientific one.

As she'd been discussing with somebody earlier, she also had a donor card. Being of the rarest blood group, she'd done the noblest thing. There were at least three people already on the waiting list who would benefit from bits of Miss Mary Isobel O'Brien.

And one more, a bloke who'd just arrived. Complete heart failure. He'd had the strength and the presence of mind to call it in; and as the crew rushed into his apartment, a cat tried to rush out. One of the crew had caught the mog mid-dash, stopping to search its collar for a name-tag. There wasn't one. Just this - a note, scrumpled up in one of those little locket-type-things: LOOK AFTER ME. I WANT TO LIVE.

The air in Victor's apartment smelled daisy-fresh.

Pass The Parcel

By Robert Cowan

Dedication: *to my Uncle Robert Crichton and Aunt May Burns, whom I would have loved to have known better.*

Danny McKay took a long, slow breath, dragging the sea air deep down into his lungs, soothing the cravings he still felt three years, four months, two days and…nearly twelve hours after his last five minutes to midnight Marlboro. He gazed wearily out to sea, lost in his own thoughts, knowing how lost he was as he searched for somewhere to rest his soul, somewhere pure, elemental, painless. But seagull shit splattering the handrail a few inches to his left brought him back to Fuckland. He also had a job to do. He glanced at his watch, a cheap garage bought Casio digital he replaced when the battery died. Ten fifty five am. He looked behind to 'Gerry's Café'. No sign of Tom's car. As he turned his attention back to the sea, a ladybird landed on the back of his hand, resting from its struggle against the breeze. With his left thumb Danny pressed down slowly, feeling its shell crunch, rubbing the debris off his thumb onto the handrail, wiping the back of his hand against his trousers.

"Messy little fucker."

Ten minutes and another aerial near miss later he heard the first sound of the 67 Mustang. It was another sixty seconds before it came into sight. Stealth technology it was not, but Tom McLaren was not a stealthy guy. He didn't need to be. He had fear…and he had Danny. He strolled over as the driver got out.

"Greenpeace not blown that thing up yet?"

"Funny cunt. It's still cleaner than a Volkswagen."

Danny smiled and entered the Café, empty aside from a couple of old ladies chatting over scones, as Tom led the way to their usual table in the back corner.

"We eating?" asked Danny, scratching his grey flecked stubble.

"Somewhere to be?"

"Not really."

"Good, cos I'm starving. Couldn't get near the Cornflakes this morning for that little bitch Stacey. Christ, does she like to fuck."

"Bless."

"Seriously, all fucking night we-"

"I get the picture. Please, have it back."

"Ha. Anyways, what you having? Full English?"

"Yeah, go on, and a pot of tea. The coffee in here tastes like something scraped from your underpants."

Tom gave Danny the finger, got up and strolled over to the counter. The mousy young girl eyed him nervously. Even though they'd gone through this little ritual many times, his appearance, shaved head, tattoos and thug physicality still made her uneasy despite the friendly banter and tips. Danny didn't mind that one bit. Order placed, he sat back down, ready to get to business. "So like I said on the phone, I have a job for you. Or rather two."

"Two?"

"Well, more of a double."

The waitress appeared with the tea, sitting the pot down shakily in the middle of the table, then left.

"I'll be mum," said Tom, pouring. He looked disdainfully at the weak brew. "Maybe leave it for a bit. As I was saying, a double.Two guys, same place, same time. I need them both done."

"Fine, but does it need to be together?"

"Yeah, if you do one on his own, the other will

disappear as soon as he hears. It needs to be together."

"That's going to be tricky mate," said Danny, adding another crease to his many-furrowed brow. "It's going to take a lot of planning, surveillance, time. And time is money."

"I've got solid info that they'll be together on Wednesday night, but let's start at the beginning eh, after-" Tom nodded at the approaching waitress who put the grease laden plates in front of them. It was Danny's turn to play mum as his associate reached inside his jacket, pulling out a brown envelope. From it he removed two photographs, each of a middle-aged man, snapped unknowingly as they went about their business.

Danny's fork stopped an inch from his mouth, some unrecognisable meat product hovering, awaiting its fate. "Isn't that…"

"Yeah."

"Isn't he…"

"Yeah, problem?"

Danny's breakfast got a reprieve as he sat the fork on his plate. Danny didn't reply straight away, staring at the photo, letting the initial shock dissipate. "Emmm…guess not."

"I don't need guesses. I need to know."

"No. No problem. What's he done?"

"Does it matter?"

"Not really, just curious."

"You know what they say."

"Who's the other joker and what's the connection."

"Just another posh boy who thinks he's entitled to take without paying. Who thinks the rules don't apply. Well our man thinks differently."

"But…the shits really going to hit…This is going to cost, you know that don't you. Plenty. You sure about this?"

"They were useful at first, had good contacts but now

the pricks are just taking the piss, not taking calls. Like I say, our man wants it done. End of fucking story.

"I'll need to disappear for a long while after this, so-"

"Don't worry; you'll be given a new identity, set up somewhere a long way away. Somewhere sunny. You'll be looked after, don't worry. You'll get the double fee for the hits and the same again as a bonus. Like I say, looked after."

Danny thought for a moment, before looking Tom in the eye. "How do I know I won't just disappear for good once I've done the job?"

Tom didn't blink. "You don't."

***

As they exited, Tom took out a packet of cigarettes, smiling at Danny's sigh. "Want one?" he laughed.

"No thanks."

"How longs it been."

"A fucking long time. I'll let you get back to melting the ice aps. I'll call you when it's done."

"Cool beans, Popeye."

"I have no idea what that means."

"Me neither. My son says it…But he's a twat."

***

Back amidst the squalor he called home, Danny sipped some own brand instant coffee as he waited for his far from instant laptop to power up. He picked up the brown envelope Tom had given him and emptied the contents, spreading them on the scarred wooden tabletop till all was in sight. As he studied the photos once more, regret made an unwelcome appearance but was quickly shown the door. Second thoughts were not an option. He took another sip and shuddered.

Note to self, the pension fund would have to take the hit for decent coffee. Danny picked up the photo he hadn't recognised, glancing down at the name. "So, who the fuck are you then, 'Simon Philips'?" With the laptop finally operational, he Googled the name. "Well, you're not the 'top session drummer' Simon Philips, that I do know. Be a shame to pop a drummer…well, maybe Phil Collins," he muttered to himself. A minute later Danny had his man and his face had a smile. The words 'hedge fund manager' made his heart sing. Shooting an Eton educated fuck whohoovered coke he hadn't paid for while he played share price roulette with pensioners cash…well, that was a clear public service. The other guy? Those were muddier waters, but only for said public. Danny's task was clear, so he punched in the familiar sounding address included in his 'information pack' and Google maps did the rest. Now he had three days. Three days to plan, survey, find a way in and a way out. This was one job he could not fuck up.

***

Danny parked as close as he could to the location, got out and opened up the hatchback. The Jack Russell cross looked up at him, its tail wagging frantically. "Out we get then Stan." Danny lifted him out, picked up the lead and attached it to the dog's collar before setting off at a leisurely pace. Danny had acquired him on another assignment; collateral damage in the making after his previous owner had got too greedy, but Danny had immediately taken a shine to the friendly little fella. Some undemanding company in what was a necessarily lonely life. Since then the dog had proved useful many times, allowing Danny to stop whenever required without raising suspicion, and the fact he rarely barked helped him remain unnoticed. He soon reached the red-bricked apartment blocks and within a couple of minutes had identified the entrance door to the address Tom had given him. He stopped and watched as Stan watered the plants. Danny had been in apartments like these before and though the security guards were usually a joke, more interested in watching TV and porn, he knew a card was needed to access the lift. On a previous job, he'd simply approached a returning resident, stuck a gun in his ribs and walked in. This time his limited time window made that too risky. He had to have a card in advance. That was when Stan unexpectedly proved his worth again. As Danny stood watching the door, a lady, and she probably was, exited and stopped beside him.

"Well, aren't you cute," she said, stroking Stan's head. "I just love Jack Russell's. I have two myself, well at mummy's. They don't allow pets here you see. Stupid people."

Danny smiled and nodded at the lady then, as her attention returned to her new four-legged friend, opened her handbag.

"What's…" She glanced down at the dogs undercarriage, "his name?" she asked, without looking up.

"Stan."

"Well you're a lovely boy, aren't you Stan? Yes you are."

Danny quickly removed the purse and with its owner's attention still fully on Stan; he found what he was after and returned it.

"Well it was lovely to meet you Stan, but I must be off. Cheerio," and with barely a glance at Danny, off she went.

Danny waited until she was well on her way, before heading back the way they'd came. Ideally he'd have liked to carry out a dummy run, but the no pet's rule had screwed that up. Still, Danny was happy enough that he had what he needed. "Good job Stan. You've earned some of the good grub tonight."

***

As the sunlight began to fade, Danny looked at his watch. It was time. He finished his cup of freshly ground Columbian, took a leak, fed Stan and pushed the oiled and silenced Glock into the shoulder holster. Putting on his jacket, he checked himself in the bedroom mirror. Smart enough to blend in, but not stand out. He yearned for a cigarette.

Forty minutes later he pulled up in a stolen BMW 520d, a skill he'd honed many times since learning the basics in the University of Prison. He only hoped there were no other graduates roaming this particular street on this particular evening. It was a crisp night, the low temperature adding to the adrenaline shake, but the ten-minute walk worked it off. Or it did till he got to the entrance and the fear said 'Hi'. Danny hated it, the burning in his stomach, but knew it helped him stay sharp. It was just a matter of control. As he entered, he knelt down with his back to the security desk, pretending to tie his shoelace as he scanned for the lift. Finding it, he stood up and, like a resident, walked straight to it. He felt the guard's attention on him as he pushed the floor number, waiting, waiting, then a familiar voice, a female voice. The elevator door opened and Danny got in, quickly jabbing the third floor button as the sound of high heels on marble got closer and closer, their click clack speeding up as the door began to close, as Danny held his breath…until the elevator rose.

By the time he'd reached the third, Danny was composed, blocking out any emotional or nervous distractions, controlling his breathing to maintain calmness. It was a job, nothing more, so get it done. Exiting into a long empty corridor, he checked door numbers to find his way, quickly working out his door was to the right on the left hand side. All was quiet. No thrash metal crack dens here. Twenty-seven steps and he was outside. He clenched and unclenched his fists before removing his tools and studying the locks, shaking his head with a smile. 'Piece of cake,' he thought to himself, before putting his ear to the door, checking for sounds of life on the other side. Thirty seconds and he was in. Home security? If only people knew. Danny was amazed at the length of the tastefully decorated entrance hall, counting eight doors leading off it to…well that was what he had to find out, and quickly. He listened at the first on the right, and hearing nothing, opened it and went in, closing the door behind. Switching on the light he found himself in a kitchen, a kitchen through which he was sure no baked bean or Pot Noodle had ever passed. Pristine white and bigger than Danny's entire flat with top of the line everything. But before envy could grip him, the sound of a door opening shocked him back. He moved silently beside the door as footsteps approached, resting his hand on the Glock. The footsteps stopped and a door opened, across the hall by the sounds of it. Danny decided to wait. A couple of minutes later, the door opened with the sound of a toilet flushing and the departing footsteps. This time Danny counted them. Waiting momentarily, he opened the kitchen door and took seven steps, which narrowed it down to two options. He chose the one on the right. Bingo. From the other side of the door he heard voices, but muffled. These were rich bastard doors he thought to himself as he pressed his ear hard against it. Listening intently he heard a man's voice, and maybe another…but then something about 'Pass the parcel', before his heart sank as he heard a child's voice, then music. "Fuck," he whispered to himself, realising things had just become far more complicated. A fucking children's party. Tom, you fucking arsehole! Danny stepped back, mind reeling, trying to figure out his next step. He couldn't just stroll in and shoot them in front of a kid, and no way was he 'leaving no witnesses'…but he'd taken the job and the man upstairs would accept no excuses. How could they have fucked this up so badly? Or had they known and just expected him to do it? Probably. But Danny was no child killer. He decided he had to make sure, know what he was dealing with, but if there was a kid on the other side of the door, he was out of there.

Danny took a breath and slowly cracked open the door. With it open a few inches, he could see no people, just hear music and voices from the other side of the room, still obscured by the door. He decided it was too risky to go further…and then he saw the mirror and the mirror revealed all, searing it into Danny's soul forever. Six men, naked, sitting in a circle, grinning feverishly as they passed the 'parcel', a parcel in the shape of a boy, naked, four, maybe five years old, crying when the music stopped and his young body was torn at by grasping, groping hands until the music started again and…Danny knew he had to postpone…Fuck that. He flung the door open, fuelled by revulsion and rage.

"Leave him alone you fucking degenerates!"

The men turned sharply to face their accuser, faces suddenly drained white with shock, eyes bewildered and fearful. They all froze, even Danny, knowing the enormity of the moment, unsure of his next move until the boys frightened, despairing wail shattered the silence.

"It's okay son, no one's going to hurt you."

As the boy continued to sob, Danny tried to sooth him, speaking gently. "What's your name son?...My names Danny, what's yours-"

"Who the hell are you?" asked one of the men, covering himself, more from embarrassment than shame.

Ignoring him, Danny continued. "Don't worry about him kiddo, I won't let anyone hurt you."

"Seriously? You appear to be a bit outnumbered in case you hadn't noticed," said another voice, with a hint of bravado.

Danny looked into the boy's eyes. "Look son, I know you probably don't feel like trusting anyone right now, but I need you to trust me…just a little bit, okay? I need you to close your eyes for me, and keep them closed 'til I say, no matter what you hear, okay?"

The boy nodded, warily closing his tear filled eyes.

"Good lad."

"Look, this has gone on long enough. You've obviously broken in to rob the place, but you can see that's not going to happen now is it," said the second photo.

"And you've no doubt recognised me," said the first photo arrogantly, "but I wouldn't get any ideas about blackmail. It's six of us against you. And we are all -"

"Fucking perverts?" spat Danny.

"Know your place, damn you!"

Pop, splat, thud.

"Oop's, sorry your Royal Highness. Bit of a twitch there. You were saying?"

The royal and the four others looked open mouthed at the body and the brain spatter, the room as silenced as the Glock now smoking in Danny's hand.

"I..I..I didn't mean you wouldn't be compensated. W..we could make-"

Pop, splat, thump.

"Fuck, there I go again. What am I like?"

"Christ, stop shooting people! What do you want?"

"What's the boy's name?"

"The boy? ...I..I don't-"

Pop, splat, thump.

"It's…Barry…no wait…Gary. It's Gary! It's Gary!"

"And where are his clothes."

"In the room across the hall."

Danny turned to the boy and kneeled beside him. The boy winced.

"It's okay Gary, it's okay," said Danny softly, putting his hand on the boys trembling shoulder. "Nearly there mate, nearly there. I just want you to go into the other room and get dressed, just don't look to your left, okay?"

"The boy nodded and slowly shuffled towards the door."

"You can open your eyes Gary mate, just don't look left. Get dressed, but stay there. I'll come get you."

When the boy had left, Danny closed the door. "Where did you get him," Danny asked the remaining three. Danny's two assignments just shrugged, looking over at the third who answered reluctantly, staring at the carpet. "We just…had him delivered."

"What? Like a fucking pizza?"

That thought brought a smirk to the man's face, quickly followed by a bullet.

Danny looked at the two remaining faces, now weeping in front of him. The faces in the photographs.

"Who are you? Why are you here?"

Danny said nothing, he just looked at them, trying to understand, to grasp how anyone could become…this. But what did that even matter. "Tom sent me. Says you haven't been paying your bills."

"You mean this has all been about money? I have money. I'll pay you a fortune if y-"

"Shut the fuck up you twisted, inbred, self-serving piece of shit. The only words coming out of your mouth should be an apology to that little boy you've…Christ knows what you've done to him. But any apology would just be a lie to get your skins off the hook. You should be grateful to him though, because if he wasn't here, well, this would be a *lot* fucking slower." As their heads slumped, Danny looked at his watch. "Fuck it." He then walked over and turned the music up. "I'm sure we've got a few minutes, eh?" With that he put the first bullet through the royal knee. "Well, well. Red, just like the rest of us then eh. Who'd have guessed?"

When the apartment had fallen silent, Danny crossed the hall and knocked softly on the door. "Time to go Gary."

The door opened slowly and the boy emerged. A boy used to obeying. Danny led the way and Gary followed slowly behind, eyes down, both silent as they walked. They got into the lift and as it descended, Danny bent down. "Up you come," said Danny, lifting the boy gently as the doors opened, positioning him between his face and the guard as they both made their escape. Out on the street, Danny lowered the boy down onto the pavement, smiling as he felt a small hand take his as they left Dolphin Square behind.

***

Danny parked the BMW in an alley just around the corner from his flat, away from prying eyes and cameras. "You sit in the back mate, I'll just be outside." He took out the burner phone Tom had given him and dialled the pre-programmed number, ringing four times before Toms voice answered.

"Is it done?"

"Did you know?"

"Know what?"

"Did you fucking know?"

"What's happened? Are they dead?"

"Did you know what they were up to…with the kids?"

"Oh that…I'd heard rumours. You know what those public school types are like. But that's not our problem, so I'll ask you for the last fucking time. Is it done?"

"Yes, it's done. But…"

"But what?"

"There were six of them."

"Six? Fuck! That prick didn't say anything about that. Just that they'd be together. Him and our two friends. I'll kill that fucker when I see him!"

"I wouldn't worry about that."

"How'd you mean?" Tom was silent for a moment, processing. "What the fuck's happened?"

"They're all dead, all six of them…and I'm going to need another passpo-"

"What!? Six of them!? Holy fuck Danny! Holy fucking fuck! Two was risky. I knew that. But six? That's a fucking massacre. You've opened the gates of hell on us Danny. The gates of fucking Hell!" The line went silent again, until Tom spoke again in more measured tones. "I suppose you did what you had to. No witnesses. No loose ends. Makes sense."

"Yeah?"

More silence. "Hey, look, it is what it is, but we need to get you off the streets Danny boy. Tell me where you are and I'll come get you. And what was that about another passport?"

"Passport?...Oh yeah, for…Stan, one of those dog passports things."

"Sure thing Danny. Whatever you need. We can sort this out. Just tell me where you are?….Danny?...Dan-"

Danny put the phone in his pocket and leaned into the car. "I'll be right back kiddo, just stay here okay?"

Gary nodded without looking up. Danny closed the door and walked to the corner. Slowly he looked round it, checking for any unfamiliar cars or faces, but all was as it should be. Maybe Tom had meant it after all. Big bucks, safe haven…before. But now he knew he had little time.

***

Ten minutes later Danny put whatever he could carry into the boot, apart from one thing.

"You like dogs Gary?" A smile was all the answer Danny needed. "Gary meet Stan. Stan…Gary. We're all going on holiday, okay mate?"

"Okay," smiled Gary.

"Good man." Danny turned the key and the car pulled away to…

***

Six months later

Danny yawned as he sat slumpd in the garden chair, soaking up the sun as the radio played quietly in the background. He looked out across green fields, peppered with sheep shepherded by mountain peaks and shimmering streams. Not a human in sight. He'd rented the cottage for three months now and it finally felt like home. He pushed himself up straight, ready to…well, at least think about doing something. He reached over and turned the radio off, and sighed contentedly. Then he heard it…a rustle, movement behind him. He tensed, a reflex built up over years in 'the business'. As he started to slowly turn around, his heart stopped as he felt the cold metal press against the back of his head. Danny had no doubt as to what it was. He waited for a word…or oblivion. When nothing came he continued turning until…

"Gary son, what have I told you about playing with guns?" Danny nervously took the gun from the boy's hand, knowing it to be loaded albeit with the safety on. "I'll buy you a toy one to play with okay?"

"Okay dad. Sorry."

"It's okay son, no harm done. Where's Stan?"

"In his bed."

"Lazy sod, bring him out, it's a beautiful day."

As Gary disappeared into the cottage, Danny slumped back in the chair with a sigh "Jesus H Christ." A moment later he felt a tickle on his hand. He looked down at the ladybird basking in the sunshine, smiled and closed his eyes.

Then Tommy Came Home

By Craig Furchtenicht

Dedication: *This story is dedicated to my beautiful wife, Henrietta. Her strength and determination never cease to amaze me. She is my hero, my source of inspiration and my muse.*

Tommy was nearly two years older than me on the morning he up and vanished. That might not seem like much now, but at the time that vast difference in our ages seemed like an eternity. He waved his firstborn status over me like a banner, my brother. Indian burns to the forearms and expertly administered titty twisters came aplenty back then, whenever I'd lose sight of my lowly station in the fraternal pecking order. Those angry red welts were ever present on my bare chest. Like that of a Bindi on the forehead of a Hindu. A constant symbol of my lowborn ranking.

Yet not a day goes by that I haven't longed for just one more playful jab to the arm, that familiar reminder of who was actually boss. I can shut my eyes and almost smell the artificial grape sweetness of that ridiculously oversized glob of Bubble Yum wedged between his back teeth. Some sad part of me actually misses the way he chomped on it while he affectionately pressed the side of my face into the driveway outside our bucket of rust mobile home. Forever ingrained in my memory is that purple tinted grin hovering over my shoulder as he demanded a submissive cry of "Uncle!" from the side of my gravel-chafed mouth.

I never knew my father, our father. He up and vanished, too. Only his departure wasn't quite so dramatic. A month or so after I was born he took a notion that the whole fathering thing just wasn't his deal anymore, so one morning he packed his suitcase and hightailed it out the front door. They used to say that Tommy looked just like him, the ones from the neighborhood that knew him before he skipped out on us. "Spitting image of your old man," they would tell him. "You, not so much," they'd say to me. Sometimes I wonder if that's the real reason he left. Either way, it never bothered me much. I never knew what he looked like. Mother had destroyed every photograph, every trace of him long before I was old enough to realize that I even had a dad. Hard to miss somebody when you don't remember what their face ever looked like.

I doubt that I'll ever forget the face of my big brother though. Not the twelve year old version of it anyway. The one that filled my waking hours with a mixture of glee and terror. At least up until that morning he went and disappeared on us. The day I became an only child. I see him looking back at me each time I bother to open the refrigerator door. Top shelf on the right, nestled in between last night's leftovers and whatever condiments happen to frequent the narrow glass ledge at any given time.Just below the bare bulb that flickers an uninviting amber sheen on every morsel, every crumb of nutriment that I put into my body. There is always my Tommy, staring up at me without a worry in the world. An image frozen in time.Or at least chilled to the recommended 36 degrees Fahrenheit.

When was that picture taken? Nine maybe ten years ago? Jesus, had it been that long since the morning he sped away on his Schwinn Manta Ray to deliver the morning edition of the Register? Before he vanished without so much as a trace, leaving me to fend for myself. The more I think about it, I'm pretty certain it's been more than ten years. I know for sure that it's been at least five since they stopped selling milk in those cardboard containers.

We only kept the one in the fridge because of Tommy's picture being on the front of it and all. Mother wouldn't have it any other way. For the last decade, every gallon of milk hauled home from the grocery store got transferred directly into that same tattered waxy box with my brother's fifth grade class picture printed on the front. The same photo most of the newspapers printed alongside the articles covering his disappearance. They all used the same one, the news people. Especially the Register, on account of it being their paper he was delivering on the morning he went missing.

A handful of the big name dairy companies jumped on board not long after my brother vanished. They pasted the photos of missing kids right on the front of their cartons in hopes that folks across the country, who otherwise may have never heard about kids like Tommy, might recognize their waxy likenesses and feel compelled to alert the proper authorities. At least after those same authorities finally quit figuring them for runaways that would eventually find their way back home, hungry and full of shame for the way they scared their folks half to death with worry.

Those slightly dimpled, tragically innocent faces that graced the business end of the cartons also served as a scare tactic for some of the more assertive parents. A cruel device to warn... no, threaten their children about the dire consequences of talking to strangers. Plop the grinning image of an abducted twelve year old on the table next to your kid's favorite cereal and ramble all through breakfast about how the Johnson girl down the street narrowly escaped being pulled into the backseat of a Cadillac just last week, and now you've got their attention.

"You wanna wind up on the front of the milk like that there Martin boy, son? Keep dicking around on the corner with your friends after dark and that's exactly what'll happen. Then where will you be? Sitting in some stranger's kitchen somewhere with a sore ass, eating your Fruit Loops and wishing you'd listen to your old man."

Yeah, even Toucan Sam himself starts to look a bit like Stranger Danger after those prophetic pearls of wisdom. Sad thing was, none of those well-meaning parents felt even remotely compelled to burden the psyches of their impressionable young offspring with the awkward reality of what would actually happen to them after their impending kidnapping. Just that they would achieve semi-celebrity status and never have to endure another early morning lecture at the breakfast table. Talk about mixed signals.

Mother once boasted that Tommy's picture was the very first one they used for the milk carton campaign. She stated that little fact with a beam of absolute pride in her otherwise vacant eyes. Always striving to be the first and best at everything, her Tommy was. Even in his absence my brother managed to be the brightest star in her tilted galaxy. I don't know about any of the other carton kids, but nobody ever bothered to call the number printed along with Tommy's name and the date he was last seen. I guess that whoever took him must have driven him so far away that they didn't sell those brands of milk in their stores.

That never squelched Mother's steadfast belief that her eldest boy would someday return from wherever it was that he went. I've tried to explain to her a thousand times that it probably didn't work that way, but she wouldn't hear it. She kept his side of the bedroom we once shared exactly how he left it that morning a decade ago. School clothes he must have outgrown years ago were stowed neatly inside the battered chest of drawers opposite our bunk beds. His Chicago Cubs bed cover turned down to half-mast as if Tommy were about to tuck himself in for the night at any minute. A partially assembled model of a '69 Chevelle, random plastic car parts peppered in a decade of untouched dust, still stakes claim to every available square inch of the desktop in the corner.

"When Tommy comes home," Mother would say. It was always *when* and not *if* he would return. "He'll see that we haven't forgotten about him and simply moved on with our lives."

One look around any cluttered room in our cramped abode and the truth of that fact was painfully obvious. To this day, there is not a single wall in the trailer that doesn't bear at least a photograph or random memento of my brother. From school report cards to his faded Little League jersey each splintered sheet of panelling is adorned with something to keep the memory of him fresh in our minds. Even the inside of the bathroom holds a picture of him, carefully framed and facing the toilet. No words can describe the uneasy feeling that comes with having your brother and the rest of his first communion class watching over you while taking a shit.

It's like living inside of a museum, this fucking place. Come one, come all. Step right up to the ne'er celebrated repository for all things Tommy. Careful what you touch, though. The curator is known to be unstable at best.

The first artifact for Mother's collection came after the police returned my brother's Schwinn from where they'd found it abandoned on the curb a few doors down from the start of his paper route. When they brought it back the choice fire engine red finish was still mottled with a powdery black residue from the stuff they use to check things for fingerprints. Finding none other than Tommy's, the sheriff came to the determination that it served no real value to the investigation and ordered it released from the county vault and to be delivered to our door. He saw no reason why a grieving mother shouldn't have at least something tangible to remember her boy by. Apparently rules pertaining to chain of evidence hadn't quite yet caught on with the rural law enforcement community back in the early 80's. Sheriff Hill had no way of knowing that his well-intentioned judgment call would set the tone for a lifelong obsession spurred by a mother's grief.

To this day the bike leans against a wall in our living room like a garish monument. Gathering mites and earwigs, the yellowing copies of the Register Tommy never had the chance to deliver remain inside the wire basket between the handlebars, just how he'd left them that morning. It's parked there beside the television set, which is somewhat inconvenient seeing as how we live in a trailer home and all. But Mother just didn't have it in her heart to leave her lost boy's most prized possession exposed to the elements, so there it stayed. Throw in ten years of unopened Christmas and birthday presents and there is hardly enough room to walk let alone sit and watch TV.

The very presence of that blasted contrivance of sprockets and wheels hung over my heart like a mechanical albatross. I can't go anywhere in the front half of the trailer without seeing that goddamn bicycle looming in the corner, taunting me. No matter which way I turned my head, there it is Gnawing at the edges of my peripheral like a pestering migraine. A nagging reminder of the day my brother sacrificed himself to save me from monsters that I'd never get a chance to meet. Tommy was always the brave one, our mother always said. I was the clever one. If she would have been there that fateful morning she could have seen first-hand how truly spot on that assessment of her two boys really was. She would understand why I was still here and Tommy was... well, who knows where Tommy went.

I rode it once after he up and disappeared, Tommy's

bike. I woke before the sun one morning with the idea in my head to collect the fees owed to my brother from his paper deliveries. It was the least I could do to contribute, being the newly appointed man of the house by way of default. A hundred times I must have jogged along behind him on that route. I knew it by heart, the names and house numbers of each customer. My intention was to surprise Mother if and when she ever decided to get out of bed. To show her that even without Tommy we could still get by – that I could earn money to help with the bills.

I quietly rolled the tires across the living room carpet and down the steps to avoid waking her. It wasn't until the porch light Mother kept burning around the clock was nothing more than a white pinhole in the darkness behind me that I dared to mount the seat and pedal away. Within minutes I was halfway across town and traversing the hill of the first block on Tommy's route. For a fleeting moment I was just another kid with a shiny red bicycle, basking in the liberating triumph of my youth. At that very second I too had not a worry in the world.

It wasn't until I knocked on the first door with no response that I realized the one key flaw in my ill-devised plan. At that hour I must have been the only human being awake in the entire county. By the time I approached the fourth unanswered door my heart settled back into the pit of my stomach. The prospect of being the sole breadwinner of my dwindling household quickly dissolved into grim apprehension and the serenity of the predawn stillness morphed into sheer paranoia. Shadows played tricks with my head as I began to ask myself, what if they were to come back? The monsters in the navy blue van, the one with the dark tinted windows.For me this time. There was no doubt in my mind that it was me that they were after the first time. It was only because of Tommy that they'd missed their mark.

This time I was all alone without anyone to offer themselves up in my place. No older brother would save me from the boogiemen this time.

A thousand tortured thoughts raced through my fearful young mind as I sat down on the curb beside the bike and fought back the urge to cry. Each gust of wind that shifted through the treetops was the sound of slowly approaching tires. Every distant yap of a restless neighborhood mutt the metallic screeching of brakes. Instinct begged for me to jump back on the bike and pedal away, never stopping until I reached the inner sanctuary of my tiny trailer home some eight long blocks away, but my legs were too paralyzed with fear. Just as I was beginning to accept my inevitable fate a porch light washed away the darkness.

Just before daybreak a kind-hearted gentleman named Alvin Bayer dropped me off at home. Mother was waiting at the bottom of the front step, concealing her anger only long enough to thank the kind man for bringing me back safely. The brisk morning wind couldn't mask the white-hot rage simmering beneath the billowing fabric of her nightgown. Oblivious to the mounting tension, Mr. Bayer whistled a cheery tune as he unloaded my brother's bicycle and leaned it against the railing. He climbed back into his pickup truck and bid us farewell as he went off on his Good Samaritan way.

She'd only ventured outside the trailer three times since Tommy's disappearance. Once to file a missing persons report and then back to the courthouse to threaten Sheriff Larson with a lawsuit if he didn't get off his lazy ass and get busy finding her son. The latter occurred exactly forty-eight hours after the first, which at the time was the standard waiting period before a reported child was actually deemed to be officially missing in the eyes of the law. The last time she ever set foot outside was the morning she dragged her only remaining son through the doorway by the hair while the brake lights on Alvin Bayer's pickup faded out of view. She had put her hands on me for the first and last time that day. To put it more accurately, she beat me within an inch of my life. Now I have the bike beside the TV and a right ass cheek full of scar tissue as a constant reminder of how fucked our lives had become after Tommy up and vanished.

After that Mother sank into a deep depression, splitting her time between hibernating for days on end in bed and binging on the casseroles and relish plates sent over from sympathetic neighbors and the local church groups. When the fleeting moment of empathy from the outside world dwindled from our refrigerator, I began making weekly trips to the grocery store to replenish her new source of false comfort. Despite my young age, it was left up to me to fix the meals and maintain our rundown tin can of a home the best I could. For all intents and purposes I suddenly found myself the unwilling caretaker of my grief-stricken parent. What little sanity my mother had left inside of her had evaporated just as Tommy had seemed to do on that early Fall morning. Both never to be seen again.

By the time the first anniversary of my brother's disappearance had come and gone Mother had packed enough pounds onto her five foot two frame that she could barely walk unassisted. By year three she was unable to get out of bed at all. I remember one early morning, trying to hoist her swollen body up from the mattress long enough to use the bathroom. I was a teenager by then and just beginning to grow into my own, but my new found strength was no match for her steady increase in size. The row of framed photos of Tommy loitering on the wall above her bed were no help. They just leered down at us with that same stupid grin on their faces.

In that moment, with my porpoise of a mother half in and half out of the bed, I found myself hating my long lost brother for the very first time. I've since read that there are five stages of grief one goes through when dealing with loss. Mother had never made it past the initial stage of denial. She spent the days before being confined to the bed waiting for Tommy to return home at any minute. Eventually her deluded mind adopted the notion that he was safe and sound in his own bed, sipping his glass of warm milk like a good boy. I settled for the next stage in the progression, anger.

Sometimes I would hide in my room and pretend like she didn't exist at all. I would stare up at the slats beneath the empty mattress overhead and wish with all my might for the chance to be truly alone in this world. I often wished that it would have been me in the back of that van, going someplace far away. Other times I would sneak to the edge of the hallway and press my ear against her bedroom door, listening to the long gurgling sound of her breath against the noisy CPAP contraption she wore at night. I would strain and listen; just knowing that each gasping exhale might be her last. I would hold my own breath until my lungs protested for mercy. Only then would I release the spent dead air and wait in silence. I was always keenly aware that just one watery swallow down the wrong pipe, one irregular heartbeat and I would finally be free from the both of them.

Most kids grew up wanting to be rock stars or pro athletes, the usual stuff. All I ever dreamed of was being rid of my obese, delusional mother and the ghost of a brother she pined for. Tommy was long gone and basically so was she. Only she didn't know it yet.

You can only imagine my surprise when he turned up out of the clear blue the other night. Ten long years without so much as a phone call or a clue to his whereabouts and suddenly he was standing there at our front door alongside a grimy wisp of a girl, who couldn't have been more than a year or more into her early teens. First he was gone, vanished without a trace. Then, surprise! There he was looking up at me from the bottom step, one arm holding the semi-conscious girl upright, as though he'd only been gone an hour rather than half our damned lives. His other hand held tightly to a case of beer that hung down past his hip.

In the harsh glare of the porch lamp his face was tempered by a network of fine lines and scruff, but it was undeniably the face of my long lost brother. He was the last person I ever expected to see when I'd answered that door. My first instinct, although I didn't actually act on it, was to jab him on the shoulder with the tip of my finger to make sure he wasn't a ghost or maybe some other figment of my imagination. Anything to convince my reeling mind that he was in fact actually real.

"Tommy?"

"Well," he said before draining the last swallows from the beer in his hand and tossing the spent can over his shoulder. He let out a long, watery belch and craned his neck to get a glimpse of the living room behind me. "Are you just gonna fucking stand there and stare at me all night or are you gonna let me in?"

I guess the question was of the rhetorical persuasion, because they were already pushing their way past me before my awestricken brain could begin to articulate any kind of response. Along with the beer on his breath I picked up the unmistakable odour of pot smoke emanating from the both of them as they squeezed on by. I'm not sure if he was what you'd call drunk or stoned yet, but he was well on his way. The girl, on the other hand, was undoubtedly thoroughly wasted.

Again, just like he hadn't been AWOL for over a decade, he plopped down on the middle cushion of the couch next to his drooling lady friend and wasted no time making himself comfortable. "Love what Mom's done with the place," he remarked with one elbow jacked up on the partly empty case of Pabst Blue Ribbon. His eyes surveyed the living room, taking in the various artefacts from his past. I found it somewhat disturbing how foreign he looked surrounded by the hodgepodge shrine dedicated entirely to him. Like the only knockoff in a gallery full of masterpieces, he looked perfectly out of place.

"Yeah, she's had a rough time dealing with your, uh..." I paused, searching for a less abrasive substitute for the word, ABDUCTION. If there was one, it sure as hell wasn't coming to me fast enough. "I mean, since you've been gone."

"No doubt. I saw her on the TV a couple of times, raising holy hell with the cops and all."

"No kidding?" I asked, sounding much more surprised than I'd actually intended to. "You saw her on TV?"

Between generous gulps of foamy beer the brother I used to know snarled, "Yeah, they let me watch it every now and again... when I wasn't busy getting tagged in the ass by rednecks for money." The grin reappeared once again, only this time much darker than before. "You know, while I was gone and all."

Unsure of how to respond, I stared sheepishly at the floor beneath my feet and found myself wishing for the ability to disappear beneath it. The one silver lining in that grey cloud of awkwardness was that at least the elephant lurking in the room had been properly introduced. No further need to ask him what he'd been up to for the past ten years.

He fished two fresh cans from his cardboard armrest and tipped one my way. His crooked grin softened into an equally lopsided frown as I declined with a curt shake of my head. Tilting the can back and studying it against the lamplight, he seemed to be searching for that one good reason why any red-blooded American would turn down a perfectly good can of PBR. After finding none, he shrugged and cracked it open for himself. His attention then shifted to the pile of unwrapped presents on the floor next to him. He culled out the most sizable of the bunch, held it up to his ear and gave it a good shake.

The girl had all but melted into the cushion beside him, but when that festive holiday paper rattled between Tommy's palms she became instantly reanimated. It left me wondering exactly what the hell kind of drugs she was on. She repositioned her body to face him, hands drumming excitedly against the bony thighs folded Indian style in front of her. The more I looked at her, the younger she was starting to appear.

"What is it, baby?"

"Dunno," Tommy replied. "Shut up for a second and we'll both find out, won't we?"

I watched as he laid waste to the wrapping on the box marked:

X-MAS '83
To: THOMAS
From: SANTA.

I couldn't see the tag from where I stood, but then again I didn't need to. I'd lived with the steadily growing pile for most of my life. As the shreds of discarded ribbon and paper settled at his feet, I couldn't help but share her enthusiasm. If my memory served me correctly, the only thing I'd gotten for Christmas that year was a Star Wars puzzle book.

"What is it?" the girl repeated, leaning forward to get a closer look at the unwrapped box that Tommy held at arms length in front of him. "Something expensive?"

"It's a fucking Atari, Holly. A goddamn antique. Worth maybe ten bucks in a pawn shop if we're lucky." Tommy snarled his nose before casting the package aside and blindly pulling the next gift onto his lap. The loose wrapping did little to conceal the tell-tale form of the baseball bat he was supposed to have gotten for his thirteenth birthday. Less than ten seconds later it found itself sharing real estate on the carpet next to the video game. The process repeated itself for the next twenty minutes with the same result. Gift after unappreciated gift became revealed only to be tossed aside. Each one, a gift that I would have killed for as a child.

"Baby, I'm bored," Holly finally spoke up. "This place is lame. Can't we just go back up to the gas station and hitch a ride with one of the truckers. Find a straight one this time so you won't have to..." The back of Tommy's hand stopped her words cold.

"You shut your mouth, talking like that." Tommy snatched the girl by the back of the neck and pulled her face into his. A thin trail of blood trickled from the corner of her lip as she strained to break free of his grip. "Ain't neither of us doing any of that sick shit anymore. That's the reason we left in the first place, remember? We're in control now. If anyone's going down on somebody now, then that somebody's gonna be me."

Holly's eyes began to well up as Tommy eased his hold on her neck. They harbored no anger or fear, only a dopey, lovesick stare that made me pity her and disgusted me all at the same time. "I'm sorry, baby," she whispered.

"Yeah?" Tommy asked as he cleaned her lip with the back of the same hand that had split it in the first place. "Show me how much?"

She leaned forward and planted her damaged mouth firmly onto his, hand wandering southward until it was burrowed wrist deep inside the denim covering his crotch. Tommy pulled her close and greedily returned the favor. He sat his unfinished beer on the end table and climbed on top of her. They went at each other like animals in rut with no semblance of shame and appeared completely oblivious to the fact that I was still standing there.

I felt the hot rush of embarrassment rise to my face as I watched, a captive audience to my twenty-something brother dry humping his tween girlfriend on the very spot where I normally ate my dinner and watched my favorite shows. Only I'm not exactly sure why I was the one feeling ashamed, but the floor beneath my feet suddenly became quite inviting again. For a lack of anything better to do I backpedalled into the kitchen and opened the refrigerator door. Anything to avoid watching the depravity unfolding on the couch.

"Uh, can I get you guys something to eat?" I asked, finally thinking of something fitting to say. "We don't have much, but you're more than welcome..."

"Nah," Tommy replied, coming up for air. "I've got enough crank in me right now to fuel a rocket. Couldn't eat right now if I wanted to. And Holly's fat enough as it is, ain't that right babe?"

"Yeah, I'm watching my figure," Holly said, pulling away from his face long enough to nod in agreement. The girl couldn't have weighed more than eighty pounds, soaking wet.

I looked into the fridge at the fresh-faced twelve year old, top shelf on the right, and blinked. That comforting image would be forever tainted by the sight of the wasted burnout sprawled across my couch. Too preoccupied with the jail bait moaning beneath him, he paid no mind to me standing in the middle of the kitchen, staring him down like a rabid animal that had just wandered too close to the yard. I let the fridge door ease shut and felt the hairs on my forearms stand at attention. Gooseflesh spread over my body like wildfire as the scales of my conscience teetered between pity and repulsion, love and logic. *Christ, Tommy. What the hell have they done to you?*

Lights from a vehicle passed through the window over

the sink, casting a shadow of myself that orbited the span of the kitchen. The car slowed as it traversed a series of speed bumps that served sentry to the trailer court entrance/exit, then sped up again. I didn't even hear Tommy get off the couch until he was pushing me aside to peer through the blinds. He ducked low until it passed, squinting through the opening until the brake lights faded out of view. It was then that I first noticed the dark splotches of dried blood that covered the sleeve of his jacket. It covered his hands as well, at least the one that hadn't been rooted between Holly's thighs. Call it a hunch, but I doubted that any of it had come from either one of them.

"Tommy, I think it would best if you left now." The words fell from my mouth as if someone else had put them there and then forced them to come out with a slap on the back. "I'm sorry, but I just..."

Tommy held up a hand before I could finish. It was the Holly hand, not the bloody one. Not that it should have mattered, but it did. "Yeah, I was just thinking the same thing myself. But I'd like to see her before I go. Just to tell her... you know, just to let her know."

"Yeah," I said softly, struggling to maintain eye contact. This time it was me letting him off the hook. Some things you just can't put into words. Not ones that make any kind of sense and still come out sounding anything like you meant for them to sound. "I know, Tommy. I know."

"Maybe she could help me out. See, I'm in kind of a pinch and need to borrow a little cash to lay low for a while. I done some things, fucked up things. I just need a little coin to get my shit squared away first. Got me a little business arrangement brewing in Chicago." He tipped his chin in Holly's direction and gave me a sly wink that sent a chill down the back of my spine. "Then I'll be good to go, you know?"

"Okay, Tommy. I'll tell her you're here," I lied, lifting a glass from the strainer by the sink and filling it with the refrigerator door only halfway opened. The last thing I wanted was for him to see his own picture on the carton as I poured from it. No sense in strolling down memory lane that late in the game. Showing him what he was before turning into the same kind of monster as the ones that took him, the ones that turned him into one of them. It was the least I could do for him. After all, it was me they were after that morning, a lifetime ago. Tommy had saved me from them, and now it was up to me to save him from himself.

Before I had even made it past the living room, my brother and his blushing victim of circumstance were back at it on the couch. First I heard Holly giggle with delight. Then I heard her cry out in pain. The sounds of tearing fabric and flesh being slapped followed me all the way down the hallway.

As I opened Mother's bedroom door it took everything in me not to change my mind. It would have been so easy to simply turn around and walk back out. If she had been sleeping, I probably would have done just that. If she hadn't been waiting with her head propped up on a stack of pillows, wearing that same look of disappointment she greeted me with every night when she realized it was me and not her Tommy. Things might have turned out very differently that night.

"Did you leave the light on for your brother?" Mother asked between her labored wheezing and hungry gulps of milk. Most of the air behind her words failed to make it past her lips and was diverted back down the length of the straw resting against the multitude of folds that formed her chin.

"Yes, Mother. Porch light's on." I nodded my head and pretended that the rising head of aerated skim didn't play hell on my already fragile gag reflexes. The sight of the frothy backwash nauseated me almost as much as the sour stench her room had taken on. An empty lasagne pan crowded her nightstand, adding yet another layer to the potpourri of odors. The home health nurse that stopped by twice a day spoon fed whatever she asked for. Judging from the container's dimensions it was intended to feed a family of four. There was nothing left to show for it except dried sauce caked to the wrinkled aluminum edges and a greasy tablespoon welded to the bottom.

I winced as the slurping noise from the end of the straw signaled an empty glass and quickly pulled both away from her face. Her greedy mouth followed my hand movement until her massive girth prevented her from rising any further. "And a glass of milk on his dresser?" She closed her eyes and conceded to the effects of gravity that forced her rotund head back into the pillow. "Tommy loves his milk before bedtime, you know."

*Tommy never liked his milk any time of the day,*is what I wanted to say to her. "Sure, on his nightstand," is what came out of my mouth.

Head still nodding false assurances, I scraped the tip of the straw against the bottom of the glass. The handful of pills I'd ground into the drink were almost all gone. The massive dose of the same medicine given to her by the nurse just hours earlier was nothing more than an opaque ring of chalky silt coating the bottom. Enough to do the trick anyway. Enough to keep her out long enough for me to make things right.

With a crumpled hand towel I found beside the evidence of her caregiver assisted gluttony I gently swiped away the lactose goatee running down her chin. She was already snoring as I slipped the straps of her CPAP mask over her ears, the hollow mechanical drone of the breathing apparatus drowning out the increasing sounds coming from the living room. As sleep took hold a flaccid arm fell from the rising swell of her bosom, revealing a tattered photograph secreted in her relaxed palm. The smirking likeness of my brother peeked up at me from between her meaty digits, taunting me. I snatched the picture from her hand and crumpled it into a tight little ball before dropping it into the dirty lasagne pan. I wished Mother sweet dreams and quietly close her bedroom door behind me.

I had never loved my brother more than I did in the few seconds that it took to walk back into the living room. My mind barely registered the sight of him mounting his underage girlfriend. No more than his ears heard the scrape of the bat as I snatched it from the gift-wrap and loot piled on the floor. Holly's muffled cries were merely white noise in the background, muted by the pounding of my own heartbeat as it flooded my temples. There was no malice behind that first looping swing from the hip. Only brotherly love.

Tommy cried out in shock as the tip of the bat grazed his scalp. He rolled sideways, peeling himself free from the bruised flesh between Holly's thighs and landing on the carpet below. With his fingers still intertwined in stringy blond locks, he was slow to defend himself from the onslaught. This allowed for the second swing to connect full on. That one was for our Mother and her stolen sanity.

Holly screamed and crab walked on the back of her hands and feet until she ran out of couch cushion. She fell headlong onto the Schwinn, which showered her in yellowed copies of the Gazette as it toppled over. Her screaming never let up as she brushed away the crumbling sheets of newspaper that had likely been printed well before she was even old enough to walk. With her jeans still balled up around one ankle she scooped up what was left of the beer and bolted half-naked from the trailer. It would have been easy to run her down, tackle her before she made it past the front door.

But then what kind of person would that have made me? A monster, no better than the bastards that took our Tommy.

So I went back to work with the bat instead. Furiously swinging for those very same monsters that had robbed us of our Tommy. And for the ones that had a hand in making them who they were as well. I swung for the milk carton kids and all of the families divided in their absence. For the unsung siblings, forever in existing in the shadows of their ghosts. I swung until the tape on the bat grip became too slick to handle and my arms had grown numb. I didn't stop until the back of my brother's skull blended into the carpet underneath him.

Utterly exhausted, I let the bat slip from my fingers and collapsed on the couch that was still warm from the coital exchange that I had so violently interrupted. My eyes wandered from wall to wall, where a dozen images of my brother met my gaze. For the first time in my life I found myself finally at peace with those crooked smiles, each without a worry in the world.

I smiled right back of them and said, "Welcome home, Tommy."

The Burned Earth

By Gareth Spark

Dedication: *I dedicate my story to my cousin, Beth Spark*

One

A storm was coming. In the distance, above the abandoned city, the sky had started to bruise; thunder cracked as though the air was breaking and it started to rain, softly at first, then with an increased force, droplets the weight of coins hammered into the dust. Two figures, dressed in dark Magistrates uniforms rode tired horses along the trail. The first, a tall man, of around forty pushed the broad hat back from his head and glanced behind. It was not regulation wear, but Mason Lee found regulations did not hold up against the Waste. His horse, a cloud-white mare, was mud splashed. It pushed forward, head down, as its long lashes beat away dust rising from its matted fur. Lee sighed and looked over his shoulder at his new deputy. Casey, fresh from the Academy; raised in the affluent Glass Borough of Trinity, never drawn a weapon in anger, never been as much as a league into the Waste. She'd been brought up behind walls, like most of her generation.Her hair was a fashionable black and blonde, brushed back and she wore the black uniform of the Magistrates. "Goddamn it," he heard her say quietly, as she tried turning her recalcitrant bay horse on the wet mud.

"Problem?" Lee asked, with a sly grin. He looked younger than his years, everywhere but around the eyes. Those never changed, no matter his expression, remaining always a hard flint grey.

"I am not yet used to horses," she replied. Thunder

cracked against the range and a rising wind screamed through the long grass.

"Then you'd better get used to them," he said, kicking his own animal forward, "you'll learn same as we all learn, that in the Waste a horse can mean the difference between being a good 'strate and a dead one."

"I don't see why we didn't bring the whole squad; ride them down, like in the old days," she said.

Lee laughed. Lightning flashed across the steppe and when he spoke, it was with a shout, above the weather. "It'll only take the two of us, no sense bringing 30 men and women out into this nothing.There are the big towns, those are rare, and mostly eastward; you had a tutor, know there's nothing west of here 'cept a few mines and cattlemen, maybe some backward tintowns, then the mountains, then the poisoned lands and a whole lot of nothing. That's why these bastards head west and not east; they head away from men."

"Lord knows why, no home for folk out here."

"They ain't folk."

"Sir, but they are, men and women, same as we."

"No they aren't."

Thunder cracked again and Lee pointed north to the ruins of a highway of the Old World; a shattered bridge spanning a weed broken highway and rows and rows of broken cars, left from the last day of that time, generations back. "Well take our shelter. Don't want you thunderstruck your first night on the plain."

He lit a fire beneath the shelter of the bridge. There was a space above them where a section had fallen and the stones were like fangs against the grey sky. Rain fell through it like a torrent. Casey looked across the flames as the horses skittered and complained off to one side. "You think about them?" She asked. "All those people fleeing through here that day?Just like blowing out a candle they say."

"Can't say I ever do."

"But why?"

"Because they're gone and that's that; I never knew a soul of 'em.I find thinking of the dead won't ever change a thing."

"I don't know," she said. "Suppose it happened again.'

"If it does, it does."

Thunder growled above them and she reached for the water. The leather flask was rough, shapeless, and the water was warm as spit. She rubbed her eyes. "How far have we gone?"

"A few leagues maybe; no way we're going to catch that old fraud tonight, not with this weather turning on us, so may as well set up here a while. Wait for morning."

"Then what?"

"Then we'll take him back for justice to deal with."

"You can still trail him," she asked, gazing nervously at the air as another tear of lightning shone across the endless line of ruined cars and bones, each testifying to a lost life, an army of ghosts pulled up like a bulwark against peace. "Through all of this?"

"I don't need to trail him; only one place for him to go out there."

***

They came not long after darkness had fallen, drawn by the fire, a pack of them. Casey had been unable to sleep and she heard them first, a broken howl echoing through the rain. She glanced over at Lee, wondered if she should wake him. His hat was low over his eyes. The horses began to complain softly. She drew the bolt pistol her father had bought anddropped it in her haste. "Damn,' she said. She glanced over the flames. Dark shapes darted between the wrecks.

"Sir," she said, quietly.

"I hear 'em," Lee said. "They won't come close to the fire. Don't know what it is."

"Are you certain?"

"Of course I'm damn certain."

"They said you were a strange one..." She started. Yellow eyes glanced at her from the shadows, and then disappeared.

"I'm not the one brought a toy gun into the Waste, girl, and I don't care who your father is, but doubt me again and I'll take you straight back to the academy."

"They're surrounding us!" She gasped.

He sat upright and spat into the grey dust; his eyes flashed angrily at her and his loose black hair hung forward over his brow. "You scared? Good, you should be, without this fire these dusthounds'd rip your throat out like it was nothing and eat every last bit of you to your fingers and feet, but they ain'tgonna, not tonight. That feeling you have. Get used to it. There's worse things out there than a handful of starved dogs."

He lay back down. "Besides, I got this." He lifted his pistol. It was old, unspeakably old, but as well cared for as a beloved child.

"That antique even work?"

"Work and shoot, girl." He smiled and pulled the hat back over his eyes. Two Dusthounds snapped at each other, snarling from the shadows. "Now get some sleep; we have a long ways to go tomorrow."

***

They rose before the sun. The sky was pale over the wasted city to the east. Broken towers rose like the fingers of a dying hand against the first pale touch of the sun. Lee drank water from a dented pewter flask, wiped his mouth with dusty fingers then looked over at Casey, still sleeping. She had requested the transfer from the City Watch, and when he'd refused, preferring to work alone, the Captain started leaning on him. Seems her father owned the drinking water running into Trinity from the big muddy, which made him someone with a powerful voice. He even had a seat on the council, reporting directly to the Senate, so for the first time in many years, Lee had company. Her hair had fallen forward over her face and she snored lightly. He watched her, then turned and spat in the dirt. A Dusthoundlaid dead on the sun-cracked mud, stomach torn open and innards scattered by its brothers. Lee nudged its tan fur with the toe of his boot. Over the last ten years, he'd noticed every critter west of Trinity was changing, mutating, and becoming bigger, faster, and meaner. Maybe it was in the order of things. He heard Casey mumble his name and turned. His overlong black hair was greasy and he pushed it away from his face as he spoke. "Morning, girl."

"Can we have less of the 'girl' stuff? I'm a Magistrate, same as you."

"They ain't no Magistrates same as me."

"You don't know how true that is."

He laughed. "Maybe they were once, when the world was pulling itself out of the dark, when the cities were just an idea and men were looking for some sort of governance. No need of men like me in the East, in Trinity, back there I'm out of place. Here?" He laughed. "Wait until you see places like The Barrows."

"So what'd the plan, sir?"

"First off, don't 'Sir' me, secondly, we're headed down this road for a place called Bitter Water, bout fifty miles north and west of here, means a hell of a lot of riding."

"Suits me fine," She said, standing. Her new range

uniform was already starting to show signs of fatigue from the Waste. She fastened back her hair as Lee picked a candy cane from his shirt pocket and popped it between his lips. It drooped from his mouth like a pipe stem as he walked. "That really is a bad habit, you know?"

"I've had worse."

"Candy rots your teeth."

Lee started to saddle his horse. "Well thanks for the concern regarding my dental well-being. If you have to know, it stops me smoking 'bacco. Only thing ever worked for me.'

"How do you know Ling's in Bitter Water?"

"It's the current hideout of Karl Brady, calls himself Redteeth. He runs a gang outta that town, attacks caravans, Guild convoys, travelers. His ol' buddy Ling used to bring 'em the best Trinity 'shine, occasionally girls."

"Hookers?"

Lee mounted his horse and smiled down at Casey. The broad brim of his hat cast a shadow over his eyes. "He'd drug 'em in his bar, sneak 'em out through the pipes under the city walls, a half dozen at a time, and sell 'em to assholes like Redteeth. We couldn't ever prove it, and you know how it is in the City 'strates these days, you have to prove ever' damn thing before you can hang a man. Me? I'm just hoping Ling comes out shooting. I'm taking him off this world, one way or another, afore that sun goes down.'

"You think those girls might still...I don't know... be OK?"

Lee crunched the candy cane between his teeth. "Why do you think they call him Redteeth?"

"I...I don't know."

The sun broke over the hills and lit the earth a dusty scarlet. Lee checked the chamber of his pistol and said, "Because he eats 'em when he's through."

***

Bitter Water stood at the place where the Montenegro River split in two. The forks of the river protected it on three sides, deep black water thick as sludge. The Magistrates had left the horses a half mile behind and walked up through the late afternoon light. The sun was behind them as they settled on a ridge overlooking the town. Casey lay in the grey dirt beside Lee, peering through the long, dry grass that was their momentary shelter at the shanties and rusted steel walls of the settlement below. Bitter Water had been a regular town, and a few of the Old Earth buildings stood empty along what had been Main Street. Casey read the signs for a barber's, a drugstore and a garage, but that was where any resemblance to civilization ended. A defensive wall surrounded the town, old steel, mainly, salvaged from the countless automobiles that lay rusting on the endless, empty highways of the Waste. She saw doors and hoods, sheets of corrugated steel, plastic crates and wooden pallets. She saw immediately it wouldn't defend the town adequately, that it was more of a statement than anything practical. Lee looked through a pair of glasses at the town. She could smell the sweat of his body and the dirty leather of his jacket and heard him sigh. "Shit."

"Trouble?"

He glanced at her, said nothing, and then handed her the glasses. "Take a look yourself, kid."

She frowned at the 'kid', but said nothing. The rubber casing of the field glasses was warm where he'd held it and she adjusted the spacing and looked. They had buggies; she heard the engines revving, and could smell the gasoline, but they were unlike anything she'd ever seen. Painted black as pitch and armored, roll bars mounted with heavy weaponry, tricked out with iron spikes, and sharpened metal. Men worked on the engines; they were dressed in rags more or less: ancient clothes salvaged from ghost towns; blood stained jeans taken from victims; sunglasses, one lens shattered by a bullet. They drank a clear spirit from medicine jars, and yelled and hollered as the light thickened. "Looks like they're going hunting," she said.

"Looks like."

"Where d'they get the gas for those things?"

"Same way they get ever 'thing," he said, "they steal it; kill whoever gets in their way."

She handed him back the glasses. There was a pain in her stomach like a punch, gnawing at her, a thousand stabs of ice that she realized was fear, a fear unlike anything she'd ever experienced. He saw it in her wide eyes and reached over, took hold of her hand. "If they're going, that means Ling'll be in there with the old and the sick. I'll walk in and take him and we'll be a hundred miles away before anyone knows a damn thing."

"Why ain't anything ever been done about them? They're here, large as life, why haven't we taken them down?"

Lee looked at her. A wind blew through the grass, the sound had a dry, dead air, and she felt suddenly the pressure of the dead world around her and ahead of her. It was a land scarred by the dead, made by the dead, covered with the ruins of their cities and lives, their hopes and fears She wondered how anybody could live in the Waste surrounded by so much loss, drowning in a silence that could only ever mock their efforts at a world. Her heart beat quickly against the dry earth, drumming through her ribs as if something trapped behind a wall.

Lee recognized the panic and though a part of him was glad that she was finding out too late the enormity of her position, just what she'd cajoled and threatened and bribed to attain, another part of him saw the frightened young woman and wanted to protect her, to keep her safe. "Just take it easy,

Magistrate," he said, quietly. "We've got a job to do here." A woman's scream rang out from Bitter Water into the heavy dusk, followed by the laughter of several men, and then there was silence. "We'll go in after dark."

***

Night in the Waste, black beyond black and silence broken only by the plaintive sigh of the prairie wind. Dust lifted and blew against her sleeve as Casey followed Lee very slowly, towards the river. He waved for her to be still and they crouched in the reeds growing in the dark mud at the riverbank. A man stood on the far shore, pissing into the river. His gray, matted hair blew stiffly around his face and he giggled to himself drunkenly as he fastened his fly. Lee handed Casey his hat and boots and whispered, "Anything happens to me, you git yourself gone."

"Like what?"

"I ain'tgoin' in there for a tea party, girl, these are not nice men. Blood's gonna get spilled and I'm gonna try and make certain it ain't mine, but if it goes the other way, you don't want to be around here.'

She thought of Redteeth and shuddered. "I can hold my own." She whispered, aware of the hollow timbre of her voice braking against the night's immensity.

Lee smiled and pulled a bone-handled Bowie knife from his belt. Its blade was as long as her forearm. "You just make sure your Ray Gun is charged." With a final derisory laugh, he slipped into the black water and started to swim. The current was strong and he forced his way against it, kicking his bare feet. The cold was harsh after the warmth of the night and it stole the breath from his chest. He fought the urge to struggle, focusing instead on the far shore, sighting a place to head towards and ignoring everything else. The water tasted of spilled diesel and mud and he coughed a little before taking hold of a skeletal branch jutting from the opposing shore. The drunken Raider was sleeping and Lee, crouching, sneaked his way past him, through the opening in the wall and into Bitter Water.

***

There was blood in the wind; he caught the scent of it immediately upon rounding the corner. Torches burning unrefined oil were stuck in the dust along the main street, giving off a dark greasy smoke that clogged his lungs and made his eyes sting. The town was deserted. He kept to the shadows and made his way quietly towards the largest building, where he presumed Ling would be hiding. Human skulls tied up with old rope, hung in threes from the ancient streetlights. They knocked together in the wind as Lee passed. Somewhere, a man laughed. A pool of human effluence streamed from an alley to the side and Lee stepped over it, headed for an old jailhouse at the end of the street. Rusted bars crossed glassless windows and he rushed across the open ground and glanced in. There were bodies in the corner, white, naked, leaking blood across the dry concrete. They had chained Ling to the wall. His face was a mess of broken bone and bruised flesh and he hung from the chains around his wrists like a ragdoll at the end of its use. At the far end of the room a skinny weasel of a man, dressed in a cracked leather vest and jeans, his arms scarred and heavily tattooed, sang an old song and drank 'shine from a jar. He laughed to himself and splashed a little of the liquid at Ling. "Hey," he said, "wake up." Then he laughed again. He was still laughing when Lee cut his throat.

Lee pushed his body forward from the old kitchen chair then stepped through into the jail cell. The floor was gritty beneath the bare soles of his feet and the river's mud had stained his undershirt. He crouched in front of Ling and sighed, cleaning the broad blade of his knife on the cotton of the other man's shirt. "What you got yourself into, huh?"

Ling opened his one good eye, he was dazed at first, then focused and when he saw who sat before him he laughed, and swore in Mandarin. Then he said, "I never thought you'd be my knight in shining armor, Magistrate."

Lee smiled. He sat on a chair opposite Ling. He motioned to the bodies, he could now see all belonged to men. "Ol' Redteeth still knows how to welcome honored guests I see."

"That son of a bitch," Ling spat blood on the floor. "Last load of 'shine I brung him blinded three of his boys. Had to put 'em down and he thinks it my fault. Those unfortunates..." he coughed in pain and spat again...."Mercs I hired to watch my back."

"You should hire better," Lee said. "Well, I was going to bring you in, take you to Justice, but it seems justice done found you already, so I reckon I'll be on my merry. Hope you're still alive when Redteeth tucks in."

He stood and Ling started to protest. "You can't leave me here, Lee, not like this, not like this, pal, come on! I know shit; I know a ton of shit you'd kill to know."

Lee smiled. "There ain't nothing you could tell me that'd please me more than leaving you with these cannibalistic bastards." He started to walk toward the door. "Here I was expecting to see you in luxury too, well, goodbye Ling."

"I know where she is!" Ling yelled with his last reserve of strength.

Lee paused in the doorway. Finally, he said, "Now that is of interest to me."

"Unchain me, come on."

"Tell me first."

"You think I was born dumb?"

Lee sighed. Then he turned and marched across the room. "Keys?"

"That guy you killed."

Lee found the keys on a chain around the dead man's neck. They were sticky with blood. He unfastened the manacles and caught Ling's weight. "So where is she, huh?" Lee said, half carrying and half dragging the wounded man to the doorway. "Where is my wayward wife?"

"She's..."

Ling's head disappeared in an explosion of blood and bone. Time seemed to slow for Lee as the body fell to the floor. He looked forwards, his face spattered with scarlet. A dozen men were in the street, all armed.

Redteeth was sliding another two shells into an old-fashioned breech-loading shotgun. His dirty black beard hung down over a large, beer-swollen stomach that was naked beneath a leather vest. He smiled and Lee saw that his teeth were indeed red. "I never did like that man,"Redteeth said, walking forward, "but I like the so-called law even less." He turned to his men and yelled, "Boys! Supper's here!" Then he slammed the stock of his weapon into Lee's face and the latter slumped to the ground, unconscious.

Two

Casey watched through the glasses, now set to Night Vision, as the buggies wheeled back through the darkness towards Bitter Water. The lenses lit the landscape an eerie green; she adjusted the tone and made out five or six vehicles raising clouds of dust as they tore down what had once been a road. "Damn," she said, feeling a sickness of fear thrill through her, "God damn." She scanned the few sections of the town she could see as the raiders climbed from their spluttering, night dark vehicles. There was no sign of the Magistrate. Then she heard a gunshot followed by triumphant yelling and screaming, and lay flat in the dirt, looking up at the stars, breath stampeding from her lungs in little panicked gasps. OK, she thought, OK.

She slid sideways across the dirt until she was away from the lip of the bank, and then sat up and stared straight ahead towards the horses, tethered to the sun-blasted remains of a tree. The animals were calm, nuzzling in the patches of sweet grass growing in the shelter afforded by the trunk. Lee's long rifle hung along the flank of his horse in an antique leather holster. Something like a plan started to form, and she smiled.

There were voices coming from the town, raised, hoarse with yelling and she looked back over and saw the prostrate figure of the magistrate being dragged through dust that spilled petroleum had rendered to a black mud. He kicked his bare heels and she saw he was coming round. She skittered through the dust, slid the long bolt-action rifle from the embossed leather scabbard just as the first crack of lightning lit the air to the west. The smell of an approaching storm filled the air and for the first time the horses started to kick. "Shush, girl," she said to her own animal. The rifle was heavy in her arms and she carried it halfway along a dirt track towards the north, running parallel with the fork of the river. She glanced across and saw Lee illuminated in the glow cast from a series of torches lining the main road out of town. The path brought her closer to the riverbank and she was aware of how fast the water there was flowing, just how dark it was beneath the smoking, endless blackness of the night's work. She heard the fat man's voice clear over the hollers of his man, and judged by the habitual tone of command it carried that this was Redteeth. He was talking to his men, promising things, women, meat, drink, taking the time now and then to kick at the struggling Magistrate. She was dangerously close and fell down to take cover in grass that stank of smoke and storm. There was a lone, lightning blasted tree on a small hillock outside the town, littered with skulls. She saw bleached bone light up in the far away thunder glow of the coming storm and heard Redteeth say, "This here is our killin' place, Mason Lee; it's where such as we, driven out here to the end of man's justice institute a law of our own." He laughed. His voice, beneath the growl and wind-scoured tone of the Waste carried an inflection of learning; there was something of the preacher to his rhetoric. It was so at odds with his primeval aspect, it almost made her laugh. She sighted down the barrel of the rifle at the nearest man, 20 yards distant, on the far side of the water. He wore dark leather and primitive tattoos covered his naked scalp. She trained the rifle on the back of his head.

Three men forced Lee to the summit of the mound and forced his bleeding head over the rusting engine block of an ancient car. He struggled and they struck him again as Redteeth indicated with a nod of his head towards a tall man who stepped forward. A primitive mask of tree bark and leather hid his face and he was naked save for the coal black tattoos covering his emaciated body. He carried a machete, with a rust spattered blade.

"So," Redteeth said. "You come for the Chinaman, did you? Knew where we were the whole time, but you never come for us. You know why, boys, we are too strong for 'em, too goddamn mighty. The old God grew tired of this world and left it in the hands of devils that carried away its men and women and left only the truly wicked behind, to make over this world as a new Hell. You hear that, 'strate? Who y'all think you are fooling with your cities, tech, and 'progress'? Ain't no such thing, and they know it boys, this world belongs to dogs like us, to blade and bullet and blood."

"To blade and bullet and blood," the men intoned, bowing their heads slightly.

Lee raised his head as thunder growled, closer this time. Casey felt it shake in the earth around her. She switched aim onto the figure with the machete. His teeth glittered in the dry lightning flooding through the sky like a flash of white flame. She guessed they were metal of some kind. "Redteeth," she heard Lee say, though his voice was faint, "you're one crazy bastard."

One of the men holding him struck the Magistrate and she saw blood run forward from his face. She clicked the safety off the rifle and held her breath.

"You got guts, Lee," Redteeth crouched in the dirt close to the engine block. His back was to the river, so Casey struggled to hear what he said, "guts ain'tgonna save your soul. Do you see that? That storm is the voice of poisoned lands, the place y'all forgot when you turned your backs on the Waste and hid behind your walls." He stood and looked up at the gore-dappled tree. "I wish you knew just what waits, out there, where the sun goes to die. I wish I could keep you alive for the final judgment, but, you know, the boys is hungry."

There was laughter and Casey squeezed the trigger - click. She tried again - click. "Shit."

That was when she heard the first shot.

Three

Blood sprayed above Lee's head and fell like black rain across the white bone scattered before him. At first, he thought it was his own, and then he heard the machete clank to the earth beside him and saw the butcher's rangy figure thud against the tree. Lightning flashed. He looked up and saw Redteeth's eyes wide as another of his men fell dead, shot through the chest. They couldn't see the shooter that much was obvious. Lee felt the grip holding him loosen and then he fought to his feet. The raiders fired into the darkness wildly, their dark faces stamped with bone-tight fear, lit by the dual bursts of muzzle flash and lightning.

Lee reached down, gripped the sweat-slick handle of the machete and swung for one of the men who'd held him tight over the makeshift butcher's block. The blade cut through the man's neck with a heavy crunch and caught in the gristle of his spine, and he fell, dead as beef. Lee reached down and fought with the raider's buttoned holster for the pistol, an old-fashioned thumb-buster. He aimed it at Redteeth and fired. The shot was wide.

The raiders started to run back towards the fortified town, but the shooter was good and they fell, limbs flailing in the roadside ditch. Lee followed and each step he took with his naked, lacerated feet left trails of blood in the sand. He fired again and yelled, "Redteeth!" The latter turned and in that instant Lee saw the shooter, sky-lined on the bluffs to the west, a tall, lingering darkness shaped against the storm-shocked air. A rifle in their arms, raised and aimed, spat death.

Redteeth's plump face disappeared in an explosion of blood and shattered bone, and then he was gone. The last of the raiders dashed inside Bitter Water and the gates of scrap and waste closed after them.

Lee wiped the blood from his face and squinted back

towards the bluffs. The figure, whoever it had been, was gone. Thunder rumbled against the stars.

***

He and Casey rode a league or two before Lee pulled his white horse up by the side of the trail. "Hold up," he hollered to the deputy as she carried on ahead of him. She pulled tight on the reins of her horse and turned on the path. The storm had long passed but there was still the sense of it in the air, electric, dull, as though something in the sky had broken and was now crackling out of control. The first touches of dawn grayed the sky to the east ahead and the early morning heaviness of dew on the dust was sweet on the range. "They might be following," she yelled.

"They ain't," he rubbed his chest; sure a rib or two had cracked.

"How can you be certain?"

"Girl, I can tell you right now Bitter Water'll be empty by noon. These Waste Rats are superstitious bastards, and they'll be figuring the place is cursed by now. In a sense they'd be right." He coughed and spat into the dirt. "First thing I intend to do is head up to the Guild battalion, get them to send a Century of their best head-stompers down here, just in case."

"Thought you didn't hold with the Guild?"

"Like everything in this wicked world, they have their uses," He started climbing down from the horse with a groan, still dressed in a mud-stained union suit and bootless. "Now let me try and get some of my dignity back by clothing my ass."

He pulled his black Magistrate's uniform from the saddlebag and dressed slowly, each movement and action punctuated with groans and complaints of pain. Casey studied the scars marked over his chest. He looked young for his age, and as with most men of his background, a malnourished childhood had left him slightly built, small, but still a sense of contained power came from him, of endurance, as if something created from cheap but durable steel. He caught her looking and she glanced away to the light patch of sky that would soon be dawn. Her hair flickered in the chill breeze. "You nearly died," she said, softly.

"I surely did."

"How can you be so calm about it?"

"Well," he said, "I've nearly died a heap of times; you kind of get bored with it after a while." He grinned. Blood stained his teeth. "No man knows the day or the time, says that in the good book they all had in the old days, I expect had that shooter not appeared my head would be decorating the gates of that town right now, and these old bones of mine'd be swimming at the bottom of a chili pot." He laughed and reached for a candy cane at the bottom of his saddlebag. The horse skittered and he calmed it as he mounted the animal and kicked his heels. The soles of his boots were sore against the lesions on his feet and he winced as he kicked at the flanks of the animal with his heels.

"Who do you think that shooter was?"

"You see them?"

"I saw them through the glasses, but the lightning blinded me, by the time I got my sight back they'd gone."

"Could have been just about anyone," Lee said, crunching candy between his teeth. "A rival gang, some woman's vengeful bedfellow, maybe even Ling had a fella watchin' over him, who went monkeyshit soon as he died." He laughed. "Maybe it was my guardian angel, shit, whoever it was, I owe them every day I have coming, that's for sure." He nodded to the sun, breaking in an explosion of gold and rose over the desert ahead, making the rocky bluffs and broken down trees burn against the immensity of the sky as if the earth had raised all its colors to protest against such emptiness.

There was howling in the distance, carried by the breeze, and she could not tell whether it came from the throats of dogs or men. "I never knew it would be like this."

"Welcome to the burned Earth," he growled. "C'mon, we got hell's own amount of riding to do." He spurred the horse and was soon far ahead, wrapped up in a cloud of dust so thick, it was as if the earth itself had reached up to claim him.

Take My Pain

By Matt Mattila

Dedication: *Olkkobuppani, jaJoonakäinenmyös.* *For my grandfather, and Little John, too*

I knew the girl wouldn't have nothin on her so I didn't try nothin. I stayed in my alley and let her pass. I kinda wanted to chase after her. Girl was fine as hell. Soft face, brown hair, not too tall, good curve under the designer clothes. Maybe if I had more teeth I could get a good lookin girl like that. Maybe I'd need more clothes. More money for sure. I was full of shit. What kinda cutesy chick like that wants to mess around with a hobo for God's sake?

I coulda used her money. I ain't the kinda cat who robs people. I ain't big enough for it. I ain't tough enough. I'd feel bad. I ain't never been friends with none of em.

None of em came on my sidewalk. They knew it's mine. They stayed the hell out of here. All the civvies knew it too. That's why they all passed by here. They thought they'd be left alone to walk all by themselves.

That's why I came down here.

I was lucky enough to be here. This is a walking city. Nobody got cars. Well nobody 'ccept cabbies but they don't count. Traffic ain't too heavy down this way. Never non-stop. Always enough time to scurry down our alleys when some snitch catches us hustling and run off and come back when it's all cleared up and quiet again.

I know I ain't got much but I got a plan.

Five minutes. That's the rule this time of night. Hang back in my shadows till something soft and smart lookin pops by. Pop out and don't show my teeth too much. My smile's still kinda charming regardless. Tell em they dropped something. Ask em for directions. They got any drugs on em? Not good to be carrying that kinda thing around here. Do something, anything, and get em talking. Ease into it if they don't get scared quick. Never be upfront.

Never beg without a reason. It ain't gotta be real. It just gotta make sense.

The wait could last a long ass time. Five minutes feels like forever round here. I go back to my stool inside the dark and sit on it and stay quiet and start restin light.

It wuhn't rainin yet but the clouds said they wanna. Street's empty. I gotta watch that's a couple years old but it keeps time all the same. I don't look at it tonight. I didn't even know how long I'd been sittin in that empty and silent dark.

I couldn't see from all the way back here. I could still listen. A rumble of truck tires going too damn fast. Wind blowin through buildings blastin the chill I know's killin me. A party boomin a couple blocks over. The buzz of the highway high above and far away.

I sit. I wait. I'm one with my mind and that's when the trouble always starts.

Hollow clompin. Light taps. Jingle keys. Nervous steps going by snail like.

I looked up. Guy seemed the givin type. Good suit, winter hat over his ears matchin his jacket, shiny brown oxfords on his feet, leather bag big as a computer over his shoulder. A techie. A grown up hipster. These guys always help poor hobos like me.

Couldn't've leaped out at him when he's going right past. Give him a sec. Old tie-bag of bottle caps at my foot and I tossed it out. Makes a good noise. Loud enough anyone can hear it, I know it. He was five steps away from my alley and looked back.

I was already there, back to him, picking the chip up.

"Hi, sir, sorry," I say to him, embarrassed smile there, hands at my side, takin it slow. "Think you mighta dropped something back there."

Guy gives me a one sided grin and laughs under his breath soft.

"Nice fucking try with that. I think I'd know if I dropped something in this neighborhood. What you expecting, a reward for saving my ass or some shit?"

He came off too strong. No point in dodgin my way outta this. No way I'd get out by keep sayin it's actually his. Pretendin it was his wallet, his phone, his keys. Time to fess up and hope he don't snitch.

"Nah, nah, nah, nothin like that."

Guys like this never give me a last line.

"So why don't you just go to the goddamn shelter like the rest of em, huh? Why doncha?

Hands up and bag of cap's on the ground. Back up slow. Soft smile. A wincing face. *You caught me, man.*

Good exit. I could always fake him out.

This guy saw right through it. He laughed again at me and shook his head and his smile dropped.

"Why the fuck you gotta do this anyway?" he said. "You do know there's a shelter three blocks over right?"

Course I did. We all did here. Most had gone there and fucked up and gotten kicked out. Most here heard the stories and never went. The place took your freedom, they said. It was like living in church. The food was shit. The beds were all stuck in one room and they expected you to sleep and clean and shit and live in there.

At least on these streets you're somethin close to free.

"I gotta make money somehow, man. 'N I ain't no robber."

"You really think you can make money here?"

I started saying something and he put his hand up. I stopped.

"Say what you want about your personal freedom and all that bullshit. You can still have it. You can make actual money and not worry about stove burns or nothin'. You can buy yourself a fucking blanket and sleep on a bed with a pillow and never have to feel the chill again."

Stove burns. The wet chill. This guy got our words down and everything.

"How the hell would you know?" I spat back at him.

He stopped in his tracks, kept shaking his head, gave that small smile again.

"Easy, man. I hustled here for two years."

"Get the fuck outta here."

"Go down Harrison and ask em about Stick if you don't believe me. Why the hell else would I be walking down here this time o' night? I got a TV and a couple kids and a missus waiting for me at home. This is my memory lane."

He got all quiet all a sudden and looked up and turned his head lookin down the dark, dark street.

"This is the only memory I got in this city," I said. "All I got."

The teary-eyed look left him and he looked back up at me.

"Then go to the Brick House and make your own. Tell em at the door that I sent you."

"What if I ain't ready?"

"Then I'll find you when I work and drag you in with me."

He glared straight at me. Never blinked once. His eyes didn't blink. They commanded.

"They're open. They're three streets over. Go. I'll see you there on Wednesday."

I shrugged.

"Know what, fine. I will. I'll try it."

He stuck his hand out.

"Wednesday."

"Wednesday."

I grabbed it. His leather gloves felt warm. He let go first. Stick turned on his heel and walked off, hands in pockets, white breathtrailin him till I couldn't see him no more.

I sat there a long time. Wondered if I shoulda told him to get the fuck off my street. He probably didn't even hustle. Motherfucker musta been lyin through his teeth. No way he ever did. Cat was too soft.

Thought about stayin here keepsavin up. Thought about what'd happen if I stopped hustlin.

For the first time I thought about doing something else to get myself outta here.

The place knew people, they'd said. Landlords. Building owners. People who needed roommates.Hirin places run by the state.

He went home to a wife and kids, he'd said. A house. He had a steady job and ate dinner every night in front of a TV in a room filled with smiling people.

I want that.

I finally said it. I wanted all of that.

It wasn't hard to throw away two years of this. I knew it wouldn't be the day I'd stepped up. This was my corner. This was my home. This place wouldn't ever leave me. After all I'd gone through here this block would always be a part of me.

I sighed, heavy, and followed my breath with my eyes.

Time to leave. Don't look back. Don't you fuckin dare sit down here.

I got out and away fast as I could. Never looked down and never looked back like I'd told myself. The alleys I walked cut through the three blocks. I stepped over boxes and walked around smoldering abandoned dumpsters and defeated gamblers and stacks of leaves hugging the walls and the old drunks who called my name. I never said nothing back. They let me pass. They knew I was taking the Big Walk.

It was on a street like any other around here. Darkness filled with flickering yellow light. Broken gray sidewalks. Dust covering melted piles of snow. Convenience marts and failed pottery shops and bike stores.

Only one place open. It wasn't much. Red mortar two floors high. No alley space around it. A little white light above a steel door.

"A home between homes," the sign said.

I admitted it that night. This'd be my first in so long. I tried not to turn back. The streets were still calling me. I wanted to turn back to the life I'd made myself.

Four steps up and I hit the buzzer.

I had nothing else to live for.

The old man with tired eyes came to the door. Saw me and smiled, instant.

I walked through that door and never looked back.

***

I stayed outta that part of town for years. The Brick House made me, with the seven p.m. curfew and all of that. There were times my first couple of days where I'd roll back on my elbows on my bed and look out the window. The streets were out there. They were still callin me. I'd always try not to sigh and scoot forward on the mattress and lay down. When I didn't have work I slept. I ain't ever been the type who gets bored easy.

I didn't get my first job through the Draft, when some suit'd burst in the room at dinner and announce that his company needed workers. We all pretended to be happy for the chance. The real desperate sunsabitches took it quick. I took their papers, sure, to look good, but I never signed up.

I'm a stubborn boy. Always been. I found it on my own. Went to the library a couple streets over every day. Sat on one of those computers for the first time in years. Took me a while to get used to it. Really, it still does, even now that I own one in my own place. I still gotta look at my fingers when I'm typin. Guess I just ain't used to it yet.

This was a clean start, the suit had said. You can go anywhere now and do anything.

I started in construction. It wasn't easy work. It wasn't amazinmoney like they promised. It went gig by gig. Lots of cuttin and measurin and liftin in places from regular houses to the tops of goddamn skyscrapers that scared the living shit outta me to under the ground in the pipes. Manual labor, at its lowest. My old man back got a twinge one day that never went away. I quit two weeks later.

Something easier that I'd last more than a goddamn month at.

Security, daytime, six hours a night, six days a week. The parking lot gate was easy to learn. The uniform was sharp. I didn't have to talk much with anybody. It was business. It was very easy money.

Enough that the Brick House found me a room in a big house halfway across the city, only a couple blocks from the security gig. Rent was decent, and they'd help me with the first month and down deposit. A bed and a TV and nightstand came with it. The kitchen was shared between all six of us. Two bathrooms on two floors, three people each. It'd be tight there, sure, and the lady in charge was strict about everything. But it was something to start from.

Didn't matter how many people I lived with. I was alone. I worked and got out at two in the morning and I slept.

Never any free time on my hands. A day off a week didn't mean shit. I slept and did my laundry then.

I tried to keep it busy. Free time has always been dangerous for me.

I stayed there close to three years. Never switched jobs. Never even switched rooms in that place. I outlasted half the veterans who'd been there when I'd moved in. Life mighta been sad sometimes, and lonely, but this was the closest I'd ever been to normal. There was nothing I would do now to take that away.

One long night I took a shortcut home. One old familiar street.

It's bare these days. The ones I'd left behind never recognize me. They stay in their own spots with their fires burning light. They look up at me and say nothing. They know there's no point in trying to hustle this time of night.

There was a new cat there last night.

When I walked by he was shufflin in the alley. My old pad.

A clink behind me. He dropped it too far. He ran up. I'd already turned around. His black beard was too dirty. He was too fidgety. His little brown bead eyes darted around. I didn't believe his shit and he knew it. I tried not to smile.

"Scuse me sir," he said, "I think you dropped sumthin back there."

Inevitable

By Graham Wynd

Dedication: *To the indefatigable Debi, quietly strong, ever enthusiastic.*

"What do you mean, mum?" Sarah frowned. It was a warmish sort of late autumn day but suddenly she felt a chill in the neat little red and white kitchen.

"I don't want to make a fuss." Her mother waved her hand as if to shoo away a fly, then picked up the teapot again. It was white, covered with little red hearts, as if it had escaped from a Wonderland tea party. "Can I top you up?"

"No, I'm fine. But which neighbour is this?"

Her mum held up the plate of biscuits, most of which were broken. Probably recycled from the church stock. She always left the best ones for Sundays. "Won't you have another? I'm not going to eat them, you know. Such a waste really."

"But which neighbours?" Sarah persisted. It was no good losing her temper. It wasn't her mother she was angry with, after all. She didn't have time for this right now though. "On that side?"

"Oh, no! The Singhs are so sweet. They always ask if there's something they can bring me when they go out to the big Asda or if I want to come along." A smile flickered across her careworn face, lipstick carefully applied 'just in case' someone might knock at the door. She never wanted to be caught without her face on.

"Then the people behind? I thought they were alright?" Sarah racked her brains to remember the family that lived there. A vague picture of chaotic homeliness swam into view.

"New people. Different. Not our kind." Her mother looked down quickly, as if she had been caught admitting something embarrassing.

"Not our kind? What do you mean?"

"Now, don't be like that. It's not like that."

"Like what?"

"It's not prejudice." Her mother made a face. "I have nothing against white people. How could I?" She reached out to take Sarah's hand. "I loved your dad so very much. But these people, they're not nice. You know, they're like those people on that programme, the comedy one."

Sarah thought of listing all the comedy series she could think of from the beginning of time, but that could take a very long time. "Could you be more specific?"

"They're dirty and eat pizza and whatnot and they were on that show with the fellah I don't much like but he wasn't on it all the time. Nice but dim."

The penny dropped. "Harry Enfield. Wayne and Waynetta. The Slobs."

"That's the one. Very dirty. Eat a lot of pizza." Her eyes strayed to the window. "Most days they have takeaway containers or pizza boxes littered all around. No pride at all. And then the dog gets into them."

Sarah looked at her phone. Time was ticking. She'd need to get moving if she wanted to get the shopping in before it was time to run to the school. So much for a day off. "So, you want them to make less mess?"

"Well, of course, I think we'd all like that. But..." Her voice trailed off and she looked to the window again as if she were frightened somehow of something she might see there.

This afternoon her mother looked older than she had just at the weekend. That was worrying. "But what?" Sarah had a strange chill tickle the back of her neck in that way that always made her feel like something bad was going to happen even though she knew that was silly and illogical. Yet she trusted that feeling more and more since her dad had died. He had been the calm even keel in both their lives for so long. It wasn't right her mum being on her own here. That wasn't how it was supposed to be. "Is there something else?"

"Sometimes, they deliberately throw things in the yard." The words came out as a rush of sounds, her hands flailing a little as if to stop them. "On purpose, I mean. It's not an accident."

"Well, that is what deliberate means." Sarah tried to laugh but the pained expression on her mother's face unsettled her. "Is it just because they're animals or because they're trying to provoke you?" The lateness of the hour was poking at her but this was disturbing to hear. Problems with neighbours were so stressful. She remembered the Mortons, who had put up with the loud parties next door for nigh on three years before at last, blessedly, the family picked up and moved to Leeds.

"I don't think they much like anyone. I don't think it's just me. I don't really know the people on the other side of them, but I expect they're not any happier." They both looked out the kitchen window toward the back garden. All was quiet now. Between the slats of the fence, Sarah could see a couple of dogs wandering around restlessly. A number of pizza boxes had been stacked on top of the bin, either because they didn't fit inside or because they couldn't be arsed to stuff them in.

"Maybe you need a better fence back there. Or I know: we could put some shrubbery along the back that would screen them from view. You know what the man said about good fences making good neighbours." It was a bit of a weaseling move, but she could probably cajole Derek into working this weekend and they could put in some easy care evergreens that would improve the view in an hour or two.

Maybe if the kids helped, it would go pretty fast and they could still all go to a film or something, too.

"I think they might deal drugs," her mother said quietly.

Sarah's heart sank. "Then we need to call the police."

"But I can't prove it." Her mum frowned and stirred her cold tea. "I mean, I'm not positive."

"That's the police's job anyway. You let them do their job." Jesus, Mary and Joseph, that's all she needed—scary drug dealers in this nice neighbourhood and all the mess that went along with it. Nowhere was safe these days, eh? "Have you seen suspicious things over there?"

"They have a lot of visitors who just pop by for a minute. They have a lot of flash things like that car but they don't half look like a jumble shop."

Sarah laughed. "It's not illegal to be tasteless, but I know what you mean."

"Will you call?"

"Of course." But it was a bit tricky after all; turns out the police don't really like anonymous tips unless it's a big crime, so she found herself talking to a very nice sergeant, Sarah realised that a small time drug dealer apparently wasn't that big of a deal.

"We can keep an eye on things, of course," the officer said with a sigh. "But we're trying to focus on the big dealers, distributors really. That's how we get a bunch in one fell swoop. Cut 'em all off at the knees, you know?" It made a kind of administrative sense, but it rather left people out in the cold. But looking at the wealth of paperwork on the sergeant's desk, she could understand how it might be a bit overwhelming dealing with every little part-time drug kingpin.

Sarah worried over it during the week, looking forward to Saturday's gardening time, but the rain came and it wasn't until Sunday that they got in. Derek was grumpy and the children complained that their weekend was wasted as they dug the holes and threw mud at one another until Danni cried and Derek separated them on either side. Sarah looked up from the work at one point to see 'Wayne' peering out at them from the kitchen window. He was just as repulsive as her mother had portrayed him, down to the shiny tracksuit. At least they wouldn't have to pay much attention to him soon, which would be a relief. There was something dead in his look. Maybe it was just stupidity, but chilled her a little and she dropped her eyes to the hole she was digging once more.

Her mum called them all in at midday. There were soups all round while her brown face glowed like the sun. It cheered Sarah to see her so happy again. She tried not to look out into the garden when some movement caught her eye, but she couldn't see anything but their tools and the wet gaps in the turf.

When they returned to get the evergreens in, Danni was the first to notice the change. Or rather she stepped in it. "Oh mum! Dog poo!" Sarah exchanged glances with Derek. It had to have come from the neighbours. But for now it would be best to let it go. "Wipe your foot off as well as you can on the edge of the hole."

"Oh, there's more here," Desmond said, his face contorted. "Ugh!"

"Put it in the holes. That's fertilizer, that is." Grumbling they did so, Danni spending more time wiping her shoe repeatedly than shoveling. Sarah and Derek eased the evergreens into place and they all threw the muddy slop around the trunks until they looked more or less settled. Sarah looked over at her husband and saw the anger clenched in his jaw. He caught her looking and gave a quick shake of his head. She knew the look.

Not in front of the children.

With one thing and another, they didn't talk about it until that evening after the kids were in their bed fighting sleep. Derek was cruising through the listings on catch up to find something to watch. "They're passive-aggressive shits, aren't they?"

Sarah looked up from her book. It took her a moment to realise what he referred to by that, but then she frowned too. "I'm a bit worried. The police said they would keep an eye on things, but that's only for the drugs—if there really are drugs. I don't think they were convinced that there were."

"Is your mum upset?" Derek reached over to take her hand.

"Yes, but maybe the hedges will help. Out of sight, out of mind, eh?"

But when she dropped by later in the week, Sarah was shocked by the poor state of the evergreens. One was completely brown, the others looked a bit yellow. Maybe the roots had got too wet. It was always chancy putting them in this late in the year. "Have they not taken root well?" Sarah asked as she got the mugs from the cupboard while her mother filled the teapot.

"Oh, I don't know. I think not." But her face looked clouded and Sarah felt a flash of anger on her behalf.

"Did those people do something?"

"I—I don't know. I didn't see anything for sure. They were out there and they're never outside, but I thought they were just playing with the dogs. Now, don't take it amiss," she added hastily as Sarah walked to the back door.

"I'm just going to take a look." She walked out across the small garden, a jumble of cutesy gnomes, bird feeders and planters now deadheaded and brown. Up close the shrubs looked even more pathetic. The brown one wasn't done for but it was not at all well. Sarah frowned. She heard a noise and saw 'Waynetta' come out the door with two dogs, an electric cigarette clenched in her teeth. "Afternoon."

The woman stared at her a moment then minced over with tiny delicate steps that belied her large size. The two dogs wheezed heavily as if they suffered from asthma or something. "Those shrubs are too tall," she said without any preamble. "They block our view. And the dogs." She made a scratchy sawing sound that Sarah eventually realised was meant to be laughter.

"Purebreds are they?" Sarah didn't really know how to be rude exactly. It just wasn't the way she was raised. A sort of oblique sarcasm was the best she could do, but her guts clenched impotently as she stared at the dogs.

"Yeah, a breeding pair. Burmese Mountain Dogs, very rare."

Sarah did her best to hold back a laugh. "I think you mean Bernese. From Switzerland they are. Alps, you know."

"Nah, they're from Burma. I ought to know." The woman pouted then sucked in more vapour and blew it out toward Sarah, though it evaporated before it reached her, no doubt disappointing its sender. "Expensive."

"Well, there you are." No arguing with blind ignorance. "Shouldn't they have more space to run around though? Bit small this garden."

"You threatening my dogs?"

"What?" In what way could her words be a threat? "No, I'm just saying big dogs, they need room to move around. Mountain dogs need mountains."

"You stay away from my dogs."

"Gladly." Sarah filled the single word with as much ice as she could manage and turned on her heel. Anger filled her like lava, but she tamped it back down. "Just ignore them," she told her mother as they sipped their tea and turned their backs on the garden. "Maybe they'll go away." Her mother smiled wanly at hearing her own advice to daughter repeated back to her. It didn't help when Leeyanne bullied her in school all those years ago and it didn't help now. But maybe they would move away. She would make another call to the police.

Before she got around to it though, Sarah got another call from her mother. "Can you come? The dog's dead!"

Sarah waved off her boss and stepped out into the corridor. "What dog?"

"Their dog. Wayne and Waynetta." The fear in her voice rang down the line clearer than anything else.

"Well, good riddance then. Maybe they'll bugger off now."

"Language!" Even at a moment like this, her mother was still her mother. "No, the police are here. Please come." And with that she rang off leaving Sarah open mouthed.

"I have to run to check on something," she said with a queasy smile to her boss. Adele was a sweetie but they were having a real push at the moment, deadlines imminent. "I'll be back as soon as I can and promise I'll get to everything as quick as I can."

"Check on your mum," the boss said. Her worried look made Sarah feel even more uneasy. She drove too fast and nearly rear-ended a Fiat who had failed to take off when the light changed. She hopped out of the car when she got to her mum's and ran into the house without ringing the bell.

They were all out in the garden. Wayne and Waynetta were howling louder than the remaining dog. The other lay still under a blanket—one of her mother's, Sarah could see, its worn green tartan a familiar sight since she was wee. "What happened here?" Sarah put an arm around her mother but addressed her remarks to the officer who stood there looking uncomfortable.

"The dog was discovered this morning. Killed by a person or persons unknown. Inquiries are being conducted."

"That is the most passive recitation of facts I have ever heard," Sarah said, fuming even as she tried to hold her anger in check. "These sick people are terrorising my mother."

"Your mother killed my dog," Waynetta squalled. "The evil bitch!"

"Don't you talk to my mother that way." Sarah felt herself go rigid with fury. If her eyes could have shot out lasers the woman would be dead. She settled for sarcasm. "My tiny little mum, who's afraid of your *Burmese* Mountain Dogs," Sarah threw a look over at the copper but his head was bent over his pad again, as if he were recording the ongoing conversation or else hoping they would all go away. The remark was lost on him.

"It's coz she's afraid, she never liked them! At least we'll have the puppies to remember him by." Wayne seemed pleased with himself.

"Did he even have a name?" Sarah taunted.

"He was Ralph," Waynetta said unconvincingly.

"Really, I would have thought his name was Stupid Fucking Dog because that's what you always called him."

"Now can we all just calm down for a moment," the officer said in what was clearly the manner they were all trained to do at the academy. Sarah resented the leveling of them all together, as if her mother was as unreasonable as these two, the improbably named Smiths as it turned out in the written report. Before long tempers were rising again after Wayne and Waynetta accused her mother of dealing drugs while she stared at them in disbelief and the officer finally threatened to bring them all down to the station.

"Are we done here? Come inside, mum. I'll make you a cuppa." Sarah looked at the officer. "Is someone going to remove that? If you have more questions for us, we'll be inside." And she marched her mother back to the house and set about making a pot of tea with her jaws clenched.

"It was just the shock of it," her mother said apologetically as she dabbed at her eyes with a hankie. "The poor thing. You know I don't much like dogs but to see it there with its throat cut like that." She shook her head then tried to smile bravely. "Worse things happen in Syria every day, I guess."

"But they shouldn't happen on our road." Not that it was her road anymore but there was something about your childhood home, Sarah supposed. It would always be your fort, the place you defended, the hole where you could hide.

"Well, at least I didn't say anything about the rat." Her mum busied herself pouring out the tea.

"What!"

"It might have died of natural causes," her mum said apologetically. "I couldn't really be sure. Here, have a biscuit. This one's almost whole."

"Where was it?"

She blanched. "On the step in back. I put it in the bin."

"You didn't touch it did you? When was this?" Turns out it was just the day before. At this rate they were going to be chucking dead bodies through the front door next. "Did you call the police?"

"I couldn't be sure, not really. Nor about the window."

"What window?"

"The car. It was covered you know. They were so kind and it was changed in a jiffy, you know."

Sarah tried to get her temper under control. This was madness. After making her mother promise to call for any little thing, she stopped in to see the sergeant again that afternoon but she was no more helpful than before. "Our word against theirs? They killed their own dog and threw it in my mum's garden!"

"Maybe she just needs to get out for a while. Let things cool down. I've seen very good neighbours come out of incidents like these, once the misunderstandings were past."

Sarah couldn't believe that. She sat at her desk that afternoon googling various ideas for revenge on bad neighbours. Most were either too criminal or too subtle. An idea struck her that might work, was entirely doable and had little chance of rebounding. She phoned Derek. When she had explained her idea, he sighed.

"Well, theoretically it could work. There are a lot of noxious chemicals that could be time released, but it would be far too easy to trace back to me if I took something from the lab. At the very least we'd get a fine and maybe something more serious. I think you should let it go. Maybe the officer is right, have her come stay with us for a wee while."

"Of course, I'm going to suggest that to her but I hate the thought of just abandoning the field of combat to them, as it were."

"That you're calling it that disturbs me more than I can say, love."

"What do you suggest, a voodoo doll?"

"Let it go. Go get your, mum."

"All right. Prepare to be smothered with broken biscuits and tea for the weekend." Sarah didn't tell him the other part of her plan. She stopped off at the electronics store and then picked up her mum, who tutted and clucked her tongue, but gave in and packed a bag. They picked up the kids from school and then went to the house. Sarah ordered a couple of pizzas and when they arrived she used the moment to pull Derek aside while the kids squabbled over the best pieces and her mother tried to make peace.

"I got a night vision camera. I'm going to install it at mum's tonight and keep an eye on things to see what they're up to."

Derek shook his head. "Don't be mad. You're getting obsessed about this. Let the police sort it out or just leave it, even better. You can't tell with nutters like that. They may be dangerous."

"May be! They killed their own dog, Derek. I'm not going to wait until they hurt mum to decide to protect her."

"The best way to protect her is to keep her away from them."

Sarah couldn't leave it at that. When the kids had settled and her mum had brought out her knitting, she kissed Derek and waved to the others. 'Just popping out." On the drive over, she tried to get into stealth mode. Leaving the car down the block, Sarah walked to the door whilst channeling every secret agent movie she had ever seen. Not that they would be likely to see her from the street, but just to be sure she fumbled into the house without turning on the lights, navigating her way by light of her mobile.

It seemed the most logical thing to put the night vision camera in the guest room. The window faced the back garden and from there she might even get a bit of their kitchen in sight. There were two cameras with the recorder. It took a bit of doing but following the instructions step by step, Sarah got everything set up and the cameras pointed so they covered all of the back garden and the sides of the neighbours' house. She left it running and took the instructions with her. She hadn't figured out the way to get the remote set up running but she'd take a look at that where there was more light and get the kids to help. They had a knack for that sort of thing.

For a moment she just sat on the bed. The guest room had once been her bedroom. She could still see the ghosts of her old band posters that had covered the walls then behind the frilly lavender makeover. The thought filled her with that strange mix of happiness and loss that was probably just nostalgia. It lured you in, filled you up, but like fast food, it didn't nourish you at all. You were left hungry and dissatisfied. So you had to go out and find a new home, make a new home—have something to fight for.

Going down to the kitchen, Sarah heard a click and a sudden silence. She froze on the stair. The clock in the foyer had frozen. Power cut, that's what it was. All the whirring electronics that filled every house made so much ambient noise. You never heard it, not really, until it suddenly stopped. Was it something on the block? The winds were a bit wild tonight though not at all like the storms a few weeks back. So maybe somebody had shut off the power.

As if on cue Sarah heard a noise at the back door. The triumph that filled her evaporated when she realised the camera wouldn't be recording anything. She fished the phone from her pocket, then stopped to think. *Would it be better to let them get inside?* They could always prevaricate for reasons to be on the step. Inside, however, illegally so, would make it easy to pin on them.

Sarah reached for the cast iron skillet that always sat on the right back burner of the cooker. Holding it made her feel vaguely like a cartoon character. She wondered if she should keep the phone in the other hand, have it dialed already to 999. There was no time: with a few more clacks the lock turned and the door opened a crack.

It might be someone else.

That thought stayed her hand for the moment. *What if they were armed?* That bothered her, too. It seemed like an eternity passed while nothing at all happened. The door stood ajar and the winds moaned around the house. And then the door creaked open and a shape in the darkness moved. Was it Wayne or Waynetta? Sarah couldn't be sure. Whoever it was they were looking toward the sitting room at the moment.

But they ought not be inside whoever it was!

Sarah brought the pan up, feeling the weight of it multiply as she did so. His head turned toward her at once. It was Wayne. His eyes were white in the darkness. "Bitch!" The word sounded loud in the empty kitchen and unlocked something inside Sarah. She brought the pan down on his head. The impact rang through the kitchen. The pan bounced back and out of her hand, clattering to the tiles. He swore. His body dropped, too.

Then he staggered back up, spewing profanities, holding a hand to his bleeding head, grabbing at her with the other. Sarah wasn't even conscious of screaming as she backed away from him. Her hands flew out, knocking anything off the counters to impede him: bills, bowls, the biscuit tin. But he kept coming at her.

Sarah launched herself across the room. She grabbed at the drawer with the knives, pulling too hard so the whole thing came off its track and smashed to the floor. He grabbed her leg and she screamed again, shaking and pulling away from his right grip. Sarah wriggled around, kicking away at him, feeling her foot hit something, not sure what, pawing through the drawer, not even feeling the blades cut her fingers, not until later when they burned and itched.

And then the big knife was in her hand. She curled up like a cobra and poked it at his hand, willing him to let go, which he did with incoherent shouts. And then he was on her and they were struggling and he was bigger. His breath stank of bad food and halitosis and cigarettes—no vaping for him—and the scent would linger even years later, when she could no longer remember what it was, only feel that unease sneak upon her that made her call the kids and interrupt their days, "No reason really, just calling to see how you are."

His hand reached her neck and somehow that was the moment. Sarah remembered it, how it effaced a childhood memory of being punched in the throat—an accident, but so frightening, so painful, so shocking in its effect. Instantaneous fear from the lack of air: there was something primal about it, animal really. The fear that shuts down everything but that will to live. She shrieked, or meant to. The strangled sound she gave sounded like nothing human. Some nights she would wake up, almost hearing it again, afraid. She would curl up closer to Derek, hoping his warmth would banish the fear that raked her back, almost forgotten.

The knife, miraculously it seemed, was still in her hand and she brought it down even as her legs kicked and her body revolted and then everything slowed and he slowed and then she was kicking free and scrambling across the tiles like a demented toddler and throwing herself against the fridge and bracing for another assault but he lay wheezing on the floor and finally she got the phone out of her pocket, still there, unbroken.

She wiped the sweat from her face but it was red. Her hands were shaking too much. It took both of them to dial the number, tap taptap, just three and then the voice and the words: 'man' and 'broke in' and 'knife' and 'ambulance' and more of them, not sure couldn't remember. Waiting, just waiting and they would get there, they had to do so. Did she remember to tell them to come round the back? Sarah thought it odd that at that moment the only thing she really wanted to do was sleep.

They'd wake her when they got there, surely? And they would get there. He wasn't going to get up, was he? Should she get the knife? If only she wasn't so tired. Maybe just rest for a moment. It would be all right.

Low And Outside

By Christopher Davis

Dedication: *In Memory of Taighler Marie Ray*

"Play ball."

Huh, fucking fat ass umpire. It's not like none of these players are paying the guy any mind, but it's the bottom of the sixth and I think the heat is getting to 'em out here tonight?

That big first baseman there from California has just slid two inches of red Vegas clay soil up and over the plate. I can't really blame the guy for not wanting to work in this heat though.

A postcard perfect summer sun is lowering itself slowly into a dirty western sky over the mountains. The gals are wearing their shortest shorts and showing off summer tans gained from lying around backyard pools since last April.

Me, I'm drinking ice cold beer and just taking it all in, we can call it an alibi of sorts if you will? I've got a good seat, right behind the plate. Fucking A, right where I like it, right where the action is.

The 51's are hosting a team from up north, California, the Fresno Grizzlies. Who the fuck ever heard of a Grizzly in Fresno, huh? If I had my rathers, I'd be at a Dodger game right now and I ain't talking about Los Angeles either. No sir, Brooklyn for me baby.

My partner—well my one-time partner—Tommy Viglierchio, he used to say that I was born fifty years too late. Come to think about it, he was probably right?

"Think about it Sammy," he'd say, "Me and you would have done good running with the big shots, Al Capone and

Lucky Luciano, you know those badass guys that built this country?"

You couldn't argue with my pal Tommy, not when he had his mind made up anyway and he usually did. Fucking cancer was going to get my pal and I knew it, he knew it too and there wasn't anything to do but wait for the pitch.

***

I'd grown up in New Jersey—Cherry Hill—just across the river from Philadelphia. My mom had decided to relocate the family—me and her—when I was twelve. My old man didn't come home one night and she started packing our things in a hurry.

"What are you going to do mom?" I asked in all of my childhood wisdom. My old man worked at the shipyard and I was too young then to know that the mob had put the squeeze on him. Mom did and it scared the hell out of her.

"There's plenty of work for a gal like me Sammy," she said stuffing what she could into the car that she would sell somewhere about Joplin Missouri.

Again I was just too young to understand all of this shit, but old moms knew the game and she played it well. She kept us alive. Fuck, maybe that's how I learned to play. Instinct handed down from my mother?

Anyway, mom looked good for a gal her age. Not that I was looking at her that way you know, but she was a classy looking women. I could see why the old man fell in love with her, long black hair and a smile that would melt the coldest of hearts.

Mom traded our car in Joplin, bought another in Salt Lake before turning south for *sin city*. Like I've said, I think she was pretty smart when it came to playing the game. No one would be looking for Sammy Soriano's old lady and kid to turn up in Vegas.

So I'm about three months into the eighth grade and getting along with the other kids, although the little fucks laugh about the way I talk. "What the fuck," I'd say, "am I not speaking English just like you?" I knew it was the accent, but what the fuck?

This little runt fucker from Atlantic City joins our class right after Christmas. His old man works for some casino that transferred him out west. Thomas Viglierchio was the kids name and we were best friends from the start. Fuck we came from the same state missed tomato pie and even sounded like we learned to talk from the same person, the same fucking person, right?

By our last year of high school, Tommy and I were busting balls for some old dude named D'Angelo. The money was good and it kept us from washing dishes or working the tourist shops that lined the strip like the other kids in town.

All we had to do was wait for the pager to go off and call into the office. That's fucking funny right? A fucking pager, can you believe that? The fucking stone ages I grew up in?

So we'd get this page. Always the same number, the office. Tommy would do the talking most of the time. Fucker reminded me a lot of Joe Pesci now that I think about it. He had that whiny voice you know?

"Who is it Tommy?" I'd ask as to our mark for the night.

Tommy would smile hanging up the phone. His folks were always away somewhere, so we hung out at his place a lot back then.

"Some asshole is talking crap at the Stardust," he'd say, "Mister D'Angelo wants us to have a talk with him."

We'd roll out in a borrowed Mercedes that D'Angelo let Tommy drive. Come on, it wasn't like a businessman could have his muscle showing up on the city bus could he?

It usually didn't take much for me and Tommy to show a drunken vacationer the proper way to behave in our city. We'd listen to this guy's side of the story out behind the building, tell him ours. After he cooled off, he'd apologize and we'd see to it that he got back to his room for the night in one piece.

Once in a while though, we'd get a hard nut to crack and events would escalate in a hurry and I do mean hurry.

"What the fuck do you mean I can no longer play cards here?" This guy asks one night sporting a real bad attitude for a vacationer if you ask me.

Tommy and I have him out back in a service alley between the parking garage and the hotel.

"And just where the fuck, do you think you're going Mister?" Tommy asks in that nasally voice that I told you about. "We're not finished here see?"

"I'm worth ten million dollars," This asshole says becoming quite belligerent now in the dim light cast from twenty sodium lamps nearby, "and no two fucking punks are going to keep me from those tables, got it?"

I got it alright and I think that my pal Tommy did too. This fella needed an honest ass whooping and he was fixing to get one if he didn't settle down. Like I said, most of these guys you could reason with, this guy wasn't having none of it.

"And I'm worth thirty seven dollars and a pack of fucking smokes," I tell him, "It's time for you to leave, *got it?*"

This asshole takes a wild swing and I come right into his ribs under his arm where it hurts. The wind is leaving his sail right about then.

"You little cocksucker," he says starting another of those drunken roundhouse punches, "I'm going to whoop your ass for that boy."

I land a right and a left in his gut and more than the wind is leaving his sail. We give him a minute to clear his stomach of the watered down liquor he's been drinking all night and Tommy grabs this guy's arms to hold them out of the way. I think I broke every finger in my right hand changing this guy's appearance that night?

When I can't hit him anymore, this guy is leaning against the cool brick with his eyes swollen shut and blood running down his face from a broken nose. His split lips are trembling like he wants to say something and he's not breathing too well.

"Now…we're fucking finished," Tommy says giving this guy a good knee to the balls.

We left that dude lying in the alley. We didn't hurt him that bad or we didn't think that we had. He was probably the first real tough guy that we'd had to deal with and maybe just got carried away?

Later that night Tommy and I are talking to these girls in town, me with my hand in a bag of ice and the pager goes off. Tommy has a glance and smiles.

"Gotta go girls," he says and we start for D'Angelo's black import.

Down the block, Tommy's talking on a payphone. I got one of the buckets gamblers use to carry quarters in full of ice and my hand is so fucking swollen that I can't close my fingers.

"Yeah, yeah," I hear Tommy say into the black Bell West handset hanging from a braided steel cord, "Yeah Mister D'Angelo. No Mister D'Angelo. OK," he continues, "Be there in twenty minutes. Yes sir."

Tommy opens the door and gets in behind the wheel. The color is gone from his face and he's just staring at the bright lights of a clear Vegas night.

"What the fuck was that all about Tommy?" I ask trying to read his expression. It didn't sound like another job? I hoped it wasn't another one? I added, "This fucking hand is done for a month, man."

"It's not a job, Sammy," he says still looking at those lights, "Mister D'Angelo wants to see the both of us at his office?"

"Fuck Tommy, did we kill that guy or what? D'Angelo has never wanted anything to do with us other than to have us do the grunt work and be his little bitch nightclub bouncers?"

"I don't know man," Tommy said keying the ignition.

***

Across town, we park the car and walk in through the casino. This big black dude—wearing sunglasses—is walking our way. Me and Tommy are mulling around the machines and figure this cat is going to ask us to leave.

"Sammy Soriano, Tommy Viglierchio," he says nodding over his shoulder, "Come with me."

Other than that this guy doesn't say a thing, not one fucking word? Not in the hall, not in the elevator. I guess when you're that big you don't have to?

At the end of a fourteenth floor hall, our Black Sampson opens a door and allows us in before stepping inside himself. Again, this guy doesn't say a thing?

"Mister Soriano, Mister Viglierchio," A strange voice says from a balcony that looks over most of the southern city, "I'm glad that you could make it on such short notice."

I'd never really talked with the old man. That had always been Tommy's gig. I provided the muscle. And I sure didn't like the idea of hanging out on his balcony this late at night after what we had done to the belligerent fuck behind the casino earlier.

"Mind," Tommy asked walking to the bar.

"Not at all my friends," D'Angelo says smiling, "Not at all, whatever you want. Help yourselves boys."

Tommy fills a clean glass with ice, cracks open a Coke and mixes in a little bourbon. Me I just pour the bourbon over ice, my hand is fucking killing me.

"Come on boys," D'Angelo says leaning back into a plush chair a hundred and sixty feet from the sidewalk below, "Join me for a little business in the fresh air, no?"

Man, that top-shelf whiskey went down smooth and I poured another looking to our host first.

"Go on Sammy," D'Angelo says. He looks up to the black guy by the door and snaps his fingers before nodding at my swollen hand, "Help yourself son, *mi casa is su casa.*"

The black guy has disappeared.

"Boys," he says in a voice gentle enough to remind you of your grandfather, "You're probably wondering why I would call you here to my place this late at night."

The black guy returns with a bucket of ice for my hand and I smile at the old man, he seems like a decent guy.

"Look Mister D'Angelo," Tommy starts, "If it's the guy from the club tonight…"

I interrupted my pal, "Mister D'Angelo, I'm sorry. It's my fault, I don't know what happened? This guy was a real asshole and wouldn't shut up."

"Gentlemen, gentlemen," D'Angelo says raising his hand in a calming gesture, "It's business, nothing more. Sometimes things get a little out of hand, no?"

Man I was glad as fuck to think that maybe I wasn't going to take the quick way down to street level tonight.

"How is he?" Tommy asked sipping his drink. I'd gotten up to pour another. The alcohol was helping with the pain some.

"Ah, Sammy," D'Angelo says, "Let this be the last one tonight huh?"

I nodded agreement, poured another and took my seat next to Tommy. A cool breeze had come up and I wasn't giving much thought to my broken hand, just the cool night air up here. One of those tour helicopters buzzed over with rotor blades thumping the silence and I sipping whiskey.

"The man's OK," D'Angelo said, "Critical condition, but he'll live." The old man smiled, "Until the next time that he blows into town drunk and belligerent anyway? He may not be so lucky the next time?"

We all had a good laugh sitting there. Somewhere below I could hear a car horn and thought of the traffic that must still be plying the streets at this hour.

"You gentlemen have both graduated from high school, no?" he asked.

Both Tommy and I nodded our heads in agreement. Between the ice and the whiskey, I'd almost forgotten my busted hand.

"Twenty-five thousand a year and a car allowance sound good?" he asked somehow looking us both in the eye.

Minimum wage was four bucks an hour then and there weren't any jobs to speak of for recent high school graduates like Tommy and I in Vegas. Neither of us wanted to go on to college, so here we were just taking a few bucks from a casino manager when we got the call to run some asshole out behind the barn.

Neither Tommy nor I said anything. We just sat there adding up the numbers in our heads and smiled.

"Then its settled gentlemen," D'Angelo said, "You'll meet with Alfred here downstairs, Monday night, eight o'clock OK?" He seemed to be asking the black guy more than us.

Alfred nodded his agreement and smiled.

"Alfred will show you around," he continued, "and help with payroll and car allowance and such."

Before we knew it we were in the elevator with Alfred again and stepping out at ground level.

"Keys," Alfred said in a firm voice from behind those polarized aviator glasses. I'd convinced myself that he was blind and somehow knew his way around the place?

"Why dude?" Tommy asked sounding just a little like the belligerent guy we'd beat the shit out of earlier.

"You boys have both been drinking," he said, "and Mister D'Angelo will not tolerate trouble from his employees. I will see to it that you get home tonight and you can see the hotel manager about the keys to the car tomorrow after say…lunch?"

Both D'Angelo and this guy, Alfred, turned out to be pretty cool if you ask me. They'd allowed the two of us a few drinks, but saw to it that we had a safe ride home.

Alfred pointed us to the valet and bid us a good night. Tommy and I are standing there waiting for a ride, a cab maybe? There's no one really coming or going at two o'clock in the morning and the valet's are more or less just dicking around.

This long black limousine rolls to a stop and the window comes down, these two gals—strippers maybe, hookers—stick their heads out. "Hi Sammy, hi Tommy," they say, "You boys look like you could use a lift?"

Man that was one hell of a night and one hell of a ride home. The Viglierchio's are out of town and the four of us kind of had a little party at Tommy's place with the limo waiting out front in the cul-de-sac.

***

So life kind of moved on after we got used to the cars and the money and good clothes, the gals? I don't know if I ever got used to the gals, it seemed that we always had one from the day we started?

Tommy got married at twenty-four and again at twenty-eight and again at thirty-one. The first was a washed up stripper named Misty that was at least ten years older than he was.

"Yeah right," I tell him laughing the night before the wedding, "Like that chick's real name is fucking Misty Streets?"

It didn't matter to Tommy boy, he had a thing for big titties and this gal had a pair of those. They made it just over three years before she lost interest in Tommy and moved on to some old dude visiting from Florida. I hear she's doing well, Misty.

The next one was a hot chick from LA who thought she had a shot in the movies. Tommy bankrolled her endeavors for a year or so until they agreed to disagree for the last time. As far as I know, no one ever found the body?

By thirty, Tommy wasn't looking so good. The color was never good you know. He 'looked sick' my old mother would say when he visited.

From about the time we started working for the organization, we had to carry a piece. It was just protection really. I carried a Colt 1911 in a shoulder holster under my coat. Tommy—and this is funny—Tommy Viglierchio carried a .380 and couldn't fucking shoot worth a shit. One day we're shooting together at an indoor range in town just to stay sharp you know and Tommy blows through ten rounds not hitting the target just twenty-five yards away?

"Hey, fuck Tommy," I say laughing, "You need some glasses brother."

"Yeah," he said, "fuck you and the horse you rode in on."

OK. I loaded and fired my next ten into the silhouette of a man on brown paper.

"Fuck Tommy," I said looking over in my neighbor's lane again, "You couldn't hit that shit with *two* guns?"

By now some of our neighbors were starting to laugh with us.

"Yeah," he said, "Fuck all of you." He made his weapon safe as did I and we stepped back to allow the next shooters a turn. "But I like the name Sammy," he said, "It fits huh?"

From then on, Tommy Viglierchio carried a second .38 strapped to his ankle and called himself *Tommy Two Guns.*

When Tommy Two Guns got married for the third and final time, I knew that he wouldn't make forty-five. Cocaine and hot women would wear anyone down, but Tommy hadn't looked good in years. Three or four packs of Lucky Strikes every day didn't help any come to think of it?

I had been married to the same gal all along, we had a kid and she didn't really know what I did for a living other than I worked as a security consultant for some of the big gaming firms in town. By the time that I tied the knot, I was pulling in a steady fifty G's a year and traded in my company BMW every twelve months.

Vicky—that was my wife of those twenty years—she wanted to finish school when we married and with the money I was bringing down, it wasn't a problem. I figured that her working as an RN at the hospital would provide a life for our daughter if something should happen to me one night like it did my old man. If it came to that, she wouldn't have to work the strip clubs downtown like my mom did to raise me when we first moved out here.

I don't know how many times I wondered if Vicky was working during the night to save the life that I had taken so easily in the dark alleys and roadsides just outside of town. It was my job and it was her job, good and bad?

Vic never was into drugs you know, a good girl, always work, school and work. I tried to stay away from the *coke* as much as I could, but that was hard at times running with Tommy Two Guns the way I did.

After about ten years, I was drinking close to a fifth a night just to get through it. My partner was drinking heavily also and snorting *coke* like it was going out of style plus smoking those cigarettes. Probably would have made it if not for the fucking cigarettes?

We'd done well for ourselves Tommy and I. We each lived in a nice house in the kind of neighborhood that you could be proud of. I had the picture perfect little family and Tommy was chasing whatever blew in on American Airlines that afternoon.

After ten more, Vicky and I were through. She stayed in the house and I moved closer to work in the city.

***

One night Tommy rings my phone, "Dude," he says, "Trouble in 1710. Guy just threw a chair through the window."

Sounded like the guy wanted to jump if you asked me, but I started for the elevator anyway.

I stepped off into a war zone. The whole God damned hall is strewn with shit. Broken glass from lamps knocked off the wall, pictures, upturned furniture?

The next arriving elevator chimes and my pal Tommy steps off. The lights fucked up with the lamps broken, but I can see that he's not doing so well? I had to wonder if the dope alone, wasn't keeping him up now.

"Don't come any closer," this guy is saying as we walk in. The suite makes the rest of the hall look first rate. "You fuck with me and the girl goes over."

The glass—designed to keep washed up gamblers from jumping—was smashed all to fuck. This fucker had tossed a recliner out the window seventeen stories to the street below.

"Let her go dude," Tommy says with that .380 in his hand, "Let the girl go."

"Hey fuck you," this ass wipe says. He's on a bender if anyone ever was. Hoped up on meth maybe and down on his luck, "Did I call for room service you fucking wop?"

I could see the blood boiling up into Tommy's face. Of Italian decent we were, but no one called either of us a *fucking wop* and lived to tell about it. By now Tommy and I had a pretty good routine worked out for getting rid of a body.

"What the fuck did you just call me?" Tommy asked, "What the fuck did he just call me? Did you hear the mouth on this guy Sammy?"

"Let her go man and we can talk about this other shit huh," I said trying not to let it get to me.

"Fuck you wop," he says moving to the broken glass in the window. Dumbass made the mistake of getting himself between me and the girl. As much as I wanted to do it then, I'd have to wait.

Before this fucker knows what hit him, I got the barrel of my Colt pushed up in his ribs real hard.

"What the fuck man," he says, "That hurts dude."

Tommy grabs the girl and starts her off to the door. Me, I march *Asshole* right along behind, through the bombed out hall to the elevator.

"Don't even think about anything stupid, you hear me?" I say in a real low voice so no one nearby can hear. "You and me and my pal there are going to take us a little ride down on the elevator OK?"

This guy was on some shit, but he wasn't going to do anything as long as that cold steel was pushed up in his ribs.

"OK man," he says, "Think you can ease up with that thing?"

I pushed the gun that much harder when I shoved him into the stainless steel of the car's polished interior.

"What the fuck man," he says turning around to meet my fist. The door chimed closed and we start down.

"Need a minute pal," Tommy coughs.

I didn't have the time to look after Tommy right then. "Yeah," I said in a low voice. Tommy fingers the stop button and I pummel this fucker's gut. I wanted more than anything to bust his face up some, give him something to remember me by, but we'd have to walk to the service door when we got to the basement. It wouldn't do to have this guy bleeding.

After about five minutes Tommy starts us down again.

Its seventy-five feet from the elevator to the service door when we stop. Tommy goes after his car. *Asshole* and I take a slow walk with that Colt pressed up in his back.

"Where are you taking me man," he asks and it was a valid question, "The police station? Are you a cop? I'm going to sue you for everything you got man."

"No, no and no," I tell him leaning close so he can hear me, "We're going someplace a lot worse than that pal."

Tommy's got his car at the door when we step out into the night. The back doors open and I shove this guy in to the other side and stick the Colt up in his face so he can see it real good.

"Dry wash west of here OK," Tommy asks hitting the accelerator and merging into light traffic.

"Where the fuck, are you taking me dude?" This guy asks looking at Tommy's eyes in the rearview. "I have rights you know. I want a lawyer."

"Seems that you gave up those rights when you called me and my friend a *wop* pal," Tommy said looking back.

It wasn't ten miles out of town under a silver summer moon when Tommy pulled off the road and continued on a good bit with the headlights off.

"Get the fuck out asshole," I said when the car rolled to a stop.

"Hey man," this guy says, "I want a lawyer man. I want you to drive me to the police station right now."

"So help me God," I tell him, "if you don't get out, I'm going to put a bullet in your fucking head right here."

"OK dude," he says, "I'm getting out. I'm getting out."

Tommy's little .380 fires once, then twice. The dude crumbles to the dirt without another word.

"We going to bury him?" Tommy asks leaning against the car and lighting what must be his sixtieth cigarette of the day.

"No, fuck it," I said walking around to the front of the car, "Let the coyotes have him."

***

Tommy finally did go to the doctor. Whatever they said was between them as Tommy never said anything about it to me. I knew that he was going in for testing now and then, but for what, I didn't know. Cancer or his liver I figured. Like I said, I didn't see Tommy Two Guns celebrating his forty fifth birthday either way?

There's this other guy in town—Vinny the Stick—he's kind of like us. A hit man is what it boils down to really.

This guy from Chicago keeps a woman here in town, just something to fuck when he flies in on business every now and then. Tommy has been tapping his old lady and this guy has warned him a couple of times. Like I said, my pal Tommy knows that the end is near and he doesn't seem to give a fuck anymore?

So this Vinny guy, he pulls up a seat next to me at the bar one night, nods the bartender over.

"Whiskey for me and whatever my friend here is having," he says with smile that I'm sure his own mamma hadn't given him.

"Thanks pal," I say. I know this guy by his reputation, but I've never really talked with him.

"So let's talk about your little friend Tommy Two Guns huh?" He says sipping from his glass, "What do you say?"

I shook my glass and had a sip, "What do you want to know pal?"

"He's been screwing my boss's gal Sammy," he says just like that, "and the boss wants it to stop, got it?"

By now you can probably figure that I didn't like it when people talked to me that way. I mean, I'm forty-five years old and everything that I've got, I worked for it. I ain't nobody's bitch.

"Yeah," I said, "I got it. What do you want me to do about it Vincent?"

I could see the blood boiling in Vinny's face and figured he didn't like to be called by his given name.

"You're going to have a little talk with your friend OK," he says. This guy is a fucking pig if you ask me, a fucking slob. Since when was it acceptable to talk business in a dirty Hawaiian shirt and flip-flops? He reeked of sweat, stale cigarettes and cheap booze.

"If you like," I said doing my best to keep my voice level and not show agitation, "but I don't see what good it would do." I paused to let what I'd said sink in. "Two Guns has a big dick Vinny and your boss's woman seems to need it from time to time?"

"Don't you fucking play with me motherfucker," he says trying to come off tough guy like, "Don't fuck with me Sammy Soriano."

"Look Vinny," I finally say trying to keep the peace, "I'll talk with Tommy, but it won't do any good man and you know it."

"I know it Sammy," he says, "but you can't blame a guy for trying can you?"

"No Vinny," I said looking into the bottom of my glass. "You can't."

So some time goes by. I talk Tommy into using some of his vacation time and a trip to Hawaii.

"It'll do you some good to get away for a while pal," I said, "Chase some island pussy maybe?"

Tommy smiled and shook his head in agreement. I missed the fuck out of that guy. Three months I had to work alone, seven nights a week and every kind of asshole imaginable. Like I said, most of these guys you could reason with. Two or three drove out into the desert during the night, only I drove their car back into town for them.

That guy Vinny the Stick is still hanging around, sticking to me like stink on shit if you really want to know.

"So where's Tommy," he asks one night as I sit at the bar, "He doing OK Sammy?"

Like this guy gave a fuck about Tommy Viglierchio's well-being. Tommy had left a message on my phone a few weeks back. When I returned the call, it was some kind of cancer treatment center?

We did talk in the coming days and Tommy said that he was living the life on the big island, but I knew it was all bullshit. He'd flown to Hawaii and checked himself in for treatment.

"You sure you're doing OK," I asked over a bad long distance connection, "Need me to come over there and see about you? I could probably use a little time off myself?"

"No, no," he said, "and fuck up what I've got going on here pal?" Tommy laughed / coughed, "This little slice of heaven is all mine Sammy. You go find your own huh?"

I agreed and we hung up. I sat there in my car and cried for the better part of an hour. I mean that shit just came out like I had been holding it inside my whole life. You see, Tommy and I had been *whacking* guys for over twenty years, it never bothered me. I figured that someday my turn would come.

Maybe it was the fact that my mom and I had relocated all of the sudden, but Tommy was like family to me, a brother?

I met him at the airport when he flew in. He'd lost a few pounds, but the color was back in his complexion, he seemed happy enough.

"You look good Tommy," I said giving the little guy a hug right there in the concourse. Somehow, I didn't think he'd be coming home you know?

"Yeah, yeah," he says smiling, "Three months of strange pussy and fresh air will do that to you Sammy. You really should think about a vacation yourself?"

"I'll do that pal," I said happy at the thought of running with *Tommy Two Guns* again. I didn't figure it would last, but one more gig to get the blood pumping would be enough for me.

***

So last night, we get the heads up that a couple of guys are up to no good here in town. D'Angelo wants these guys finished before things get out of hand. Sounds like dope, guns, you name it.

Tommy and I roll up to the casino about eleven. Have us a walk through the place just to see what gives.

These guys are running some of the card tables, Mexican nationals up north here to get in on the action. It isn't going to be, but we can't just walk over and tell them that. We like to think of it as international diplomacy?

"Everything going alright gentlemen," Tommy asks walking up to one of the tables. It's funny but Tommy always comes off like some casino manager when he asks the question.

I'm sitting nearby sipping whiskey and keeping an eye on things. No one in the place knows that we're together and we want to keep it that way.

These three Mexicans smile and shake their heads. Tommy snaps his fingers at one of the waitresses and she starts for the bar.

"Enjoy your stay here in Las Vegas gentlemen," he says starting away. I can see Tommy bend and go into a coughing fit across the room. He wipes at his mouth probably hoping that I can't see what's going on?

I start for the service area in the back of the house where Tommy and I can have a little chit-chat.

"Are these the guys," I ask as Tommy walks up. He leans against the wall with one hand and I can see that he's not doing real well. "Hey man," I say, "We can do this tomorrow night Tommy or the next? Let's get you home man or better still to the emergency room?"

"No, no," he insisted, "We've got to do this tonight Sammy."

"OK, how do you want to do it?"

Tommy looked around. I could see a trace of blood starting from the corner of his mouth. "They've got to piss sometime pal," he says, "You walk them to the door and I'll meet you outside huh?"

I agreed and walked back to the bar to keep an eye on these guys. After maybe a half hour, one gets up and starts for a far hall where the nearest bathrooms are located. I follow just to see where he's going.

This guy's standing at the stall with his dick in his hand singing something happy in Spanish. I walk up and stick my Colt in his ribs, "Vamanos mi amigo."

He seems to understand and starts out the door, probably hoping that one of his buddies will see what's going on? They don't and we step out into a warm desert night. Tommy's sitting on a flower planter and leaning against the wall smoking.

Tommy struggles to his feet and walks over to a stolen car he had picked up just for the gig. He pops the trunk and this guy starts talking, Spanish at first.

"No hablaEspanol," I say and he switches to English.

"What the fuck are you doing?" he asks, "Do you know who I am?"

I smack this guy in the mouth still holding the Colt and he goes down. Tommy hands me a big hotel towel which I push against the guy's head before pulling the trigger. In a jerk, his life passes and I bend to push him into the trunk. Tommy closes the door and we both scan the alley. No one out here at this late hour, we usually have to deal with a cook or dishwasher on a smoke break, but not this time.

Tommy manages a weak smile and I go back inside to fish a little more. I'm more worried about my friend than the gig and I'm afraid that for once, I might fuck it up? I've got to keep my head in the game now that it's started and then I'm going to the old man, D'Angelo.

Another of the Mexicans starts away from the table in the same direction. Time is not infinite here in the underworld of Vegas so I intercept him by the hotel desk and help him along to his ride for the night.

Tommy's leaning against the car coughing when the door swings open. He lights a cigarette and smiles.

"That's two down pal," Tommy says holding up two fingers like we did when we played ball back in high school and going into another coughing fit. I'm wondering if we shouldn't just end it right here?

The Mexican is jabbering something and I sock him in the mouth like the last guy. He's a little tougher and requires a few more. Maybe I'm just taking out the frustration that I have for disease that's killing my friend and I work this guy over real good next to the car. He goes down like a cheap prize fighter and I feel the bones in his side crack with every kick of my handmade loafer.

"That's enough Sammy," Tommy says in a coarse voice, "Go get their friend and let's get the fuck out of here?"

I'm down with that. The sooner we can get rid of these fuckers, the sooner I can get Tommy to the hospital and the treatment he desperately needs.

My hand is hurting just like it did when I was kid and Mr.D'Angelo called us up to his office. It didn't matter. I'd see this through and drive my pal to the emergency room or die trying. If this next guy got out of hand, I'd shoot the fucker right there in the casino in front of everyone. I wanted this to be over.

Number three was easy compared to his buddies. He walked along soaking in Tequila talking shit in Spanish.

"No English, no English," he says when we get outside. I figure that he knows the plan by now after his two buddies haven't returned.

Tommy is sitting in the car with a needle in his arm and I just about loose the contents of my stomach. "What the fuck Tommy," I ask holding the Colt to the Mexicans back, "you doing *smack* now pal?"

"Morphine," he says in a low voice, "Get it from some chick at the hospice." He seemed to think over what he'd said some. "It's been helping for the last few months Sammy?"

Fuck, fuck, fuck, there it was out in the open now. Tommy Two Guns had cancer and the shit was eating him alive.

"Can you drive dude?" I asked, "Or do you want me to do this? I can do this alone Tommy."

"No, no," he said sounding more Italian by the minute, "I got this Sammy, get in."

I shove our friend in against his buddy who is breathing erratically after the beat down he got a few minutes earlier.

"No, no, senior," The Mexican says. I can see the terror in his eyes looking at the death in my pal Tommy's in the rearview as we start away from the city.

I wanted to shoot the both of them and park the fucking car anywhere and maybe flag a cab to the hospital. The car was stolen, so the authorities find three dead Mexicans inside? It was nothing new in the desert southwest, right?

Minutes ticked by ever so slowly turning to hours, maybe days. I expected the sun to rise at any moment although I knew it was no later than one in the morning.

Tommy pulls off the road with the headlights off just like he had done so many times before with me holding my Colt to some unfortunate fucks head. We drive a mile or so off the road and down into a dry wash.

I get number three out of the car and pull the trigger. Nothing fancy for this guy, just a bullet. My plate is kind of full at the moment and I just didn't have the time.

"You OK Tommy," I ask sorting this shit out. We've got two now dead and the one guy just clinging to life after I've nearly kicked it out of him in the service alley behind the hotel.

"Yeah," Tommy says tying off his arm again, "I love you man, always have Sammy. Just like brothers huh?"

Fucking tears are running down my cheeks and I'm wiping them away with the back of my hand. I'll get the guy out of the trunk and the one who's still breathing out and put a bullet in his head to spare him the trouble of dying out here in the dark. I can push Tommy over and drive him into town. I can, there's still time.

"Yeah Tommy," I said, "Just like brothers man, always have been right?"

That fucking little .38 goes off in the car as I'm wrestling with the dead Mexican in the trunk.

"*Fuck,*" I scream. I know that Tommy had pulled the trigger.

Tommy Two Guns is no more. The dead Mexican falls back into the trunk and I walk to the front of the car. Tommy's slumped over the wheel with the needle still in his arm. There's a half bottle of Maker's Mark in the seat next to him and blood running down what's left of his face. I reach in and take a good long pull before I sit down in the sand and think of the shit me and Tommy have been through.

My Rolex tells me that it's nearing four. I've been sitting here for three hours thinking back. It doesn't really bother me that I've got four dead men with me for company? I appreciated the silence.

I wished there was some other way, but it had to be. Tommy would have done the same for me if the tables were turned. One more drink from the bottle and I drag the one Mexican back to the car. Fucking guy was stiff from lying on the cold ground.

Tommy had a lighter in his pocket and I snaked it out before splashing the rest of the whiskey on his dead body.

"I'm sorry Tommy," I said, "I wish that I could do more for you pal, but I know that you understand huh?"

Man, it felt like a weight had been lifted and Tommy was smiling down on me there in the dark from the other side?

Flame from the lighter took to his shirt and I closed the door. Stuffing my necktie into the gas tank filler, I did the same and pushed the lighter in after.

I never looked back once I started for the highway. It was a long fucking walk back to town and the sun would be making its presence known shortly. Before long, I hear the rounds in Tommy's guns and those of the Mexican's cooking off. Five minutes later and the gas tank lets go.

***

Like I said, I wish that I could have done more for my pal. He deserved better, but I think that he wanted it that way? He knew this was the last ride into the desert.

It was just like Tommy Viglierchio, always swinging for the fences you know. He never hit a home run, never could, but he was a good guy to have on your team none the less. Tommy could have played the bench over this last year and let me handle things, but he didn't. I could have found someone else to work with until he got himself better, but he wouldn't have it.

Life doesn't throw perfect pitches every time. Sometimes they're just low and outside and you just have to stand there and watch them go by? Tommy knew this better than anyone. I do too now.

Well that's about it. I think the 51's have got this one in the bag. I'm going to take a piss and get another beer. You want one?

Balancing The Scales

By David Jaggers

Dedication: *This work is dedicated to both of my Grandmothers who fought a hard battle with cancer, ultimately losing, but doing so with grace and dignity.*

I have this reoccurring dream where I'm walking through an empty carnival. The stuffed prizes hang in their booths like bodies from a gallows, and their lifeless, black eyes follow me. The place is abandoned, but somehow I know that there's a monster loose on the fairgrounds and everyone has fled. I look around at the silent rides, sitting like giant metal insects in the grassy field. I walk past a trailer with signs that advertise cotton candy and corn dogs. The lights are off, but I can smell the still-warm grease in the fryers. As I reach the entrance, my feet refuse to move any further, it's like they're glued to the ground. I sense the beast lurking somewhere among the quiet machinery behind me. It is a thing of pure evil, driven and unrelenting. Images flash through my mind of the people dropping their food and grabbing their children to run away, fleeing as fast as they can to escape the coming darkness. I turn to look for this monster and catch my reflection in the glass of the ticket booth. Realization hits me like a punch in the stomach. I see myself, bloody and wild eyed. My teeth are bared and my face twisted in absolute rage. I realize that *I* am the monster.

It's true. I am a terrible person. I've spent the better part of my life coming to terms with that fact. I like to hurt people and I've never been good at anything else. Breaking bones and dumping bodies just comes natural to me. It's a talent I guess. I've been fortunate to have found a profession that allows me to channel it. There's always somebody willing to pay to make some prick disappear. Capitalism and a never ending supply of revenge makes for good job security.

I am also a creature of habit. It's important that I keep a measure of control in my life. Predictability keeps me calm and that's a good thing for everyone else. Nobody wants a monster like me going off the deep end one sunny morning. They wouldn't be able to count the bodies. I keep it steady, up early for a run, followed by a workout and breakfast at the little diner at the end of the street, the Over Easy Cafe. With a routine as clockwork as mine, I see a lot of the same people every day. Though we never speak, I feel like I know them. I know that the manager Harvey, a scrawny little guy with a ratty mustache, has it bad for the little blonde waitress that brings me my eggs every morning. I can see it in his eyes. The lust. I can also tell that she would rather get it on with an alligator than spend a minute alone with him.

I see all of this as I sip my black coffee and eat my eggs. A world of chaos and subtext swirling around me and my daily ritual. Being so focused on routine, I notice immediately when something changes. Like the new girl, she started last Sunday. She doesn't make eye contact with anyone including the other girls, and judging by her accuracy with the coffee pot, she's new to this line of work. She's a pale beauty, dark hair, tinted red with cheek bones sharp enough to cut paper. I'm not sure what it is, but I know this girl is broken and she's running from something.

This new addition to my routine makes my brain itch. I can feel the beast stir inside. For years I've been able control it, just let him out as needed. I've always managed to pull him back in. Lately though, I have this nagging feeling that one day the lid just won't close, and the beast will refuse to come back. That's why I need my calm, my predictability and this new girl is fucking with that. She doesn't fit into the tidy, well-oiled machine that hums around me. The diner attracts a certain type of employee, mostly young college girls. I guess it is a combination of the University nearby and the manager's pervy inclinations. The new girl doesn't belong. She's edgy, probably late twenties. She looks to be of European decent, maybe Russian. The other girls pass the time talking to each other about the usual things, boyfriends, classes and spring break. The new girl, doesn't talk at all.

Finally we make eye contact as she refills my cup. Dark brown irises ringed with thick lashes behind black frames. She meets my steady gaze with a slight smile, more a courtesy than a flirt and I see her name tag says Tatyana.

"So you're new here right?" I say.

"Yes, I just started my second full day, does it show?" She says in decent English. Mr.Perv the manager interrupts us before I can say anything else. He's calling her back to the counter to serve two construction workers who just came in before their shift starts. I finish my cup, leave a generous tip and walk out the front door like I do every day.

The girls that work the morning shift all get off around noon and somehow I find myself outside when Tatyana comes out. Normally I would be at the firing range this time of day but here I am, breaking routine, neck deep in the chaos. She doesn't see me so I hang back and watch as she sits down on the bench and waits for the bus. She removes her glasses and wipes tears from her eyes as she sits there huddled against the cold. I walk over and take a seat beside her. She's startled when she recognizes me, but she doesn't get up.

"So, why don't you tell me why you're crying?" I say.

"Excuse me?"

"It's obvious that you have something heavy going on. Maybe I can help. My name is Carter." I hold out a gloved hand. She shakes it lightly.

"What makes you think I need your help?"

I lean back on the bench and take a deep breath of frosty air. "You lie about as well as you pour coffee."

The tears begin to flow down her face. "I know you mean well, but you can't help me Mr. Carter. My life is ruined."

"It's just Carter, and how about I buy you some lunch and you tell me what you mean by that? Nothing creepy, just lunch."

She stares me down through those thick frames for a moment and I wonder if she can see the monster lurking right below the surface, the screaming, wide-eyed demon, straining at the chains to get loose and burn the whole goddamned world down. She's searching, assessing my threat level. After a moment I pass the test and she nods. We get up and walk down the block to Nico's, a little lunch spot I like to frequent. It's part of my routine.

***

Lunch with Tatyana lasts over two hours. Once she gets going she pours out her entire story, stopping only when she can't bear to go on.

"I came over to the states six months ago, a full citizen. It was an arranged marriage set up by my father. Victor, the man I was going to marry works for my uncle in the import business. It was a great opportunity for my family. When I arrived, I learned that Victor would be out of the country for two months for work, so I took a temp job as a nanny while I waited. Victor is a great man Mr. Carter," She says sobbing over her untouched club sandwich.

"My first job was for the family of an attorney here in town. They have two boys, both toddlers. The job was great at first, but the husband… he started flirting, and groping, you know. I made it clear that I was not interested in his advances even if it meant losing the job, but he didn't stop." She breaks down again, this time to the point that the waitress starts shooting me worried looks.

"Go on," I say.

"One morning while the wife was out of town, he slipped something into my orange juice. I…I woke up with my panties around my ankles and my skirt ripped. He told me that if I said anything he would have me deported back to Ukraine."

I sip my coffee and listen quietly. I can see her hands trembling as she lifts the napkin to the corner of her eye, she's on the verge of a full breakdown. The monster inside begins to stir, rattling the bars of the cage.

"I quit immediately, but I didn't say anything, I couldn't disappoint my father. He worked so hard to send me here. Victor came back and we started planning for the wedding. It was so wonderful Mr. Carter." Darkness crosses her face like a shadow as she continues.

"Then, I found out I was pregnant, I had a miscarriage. I tried to explain, but Victor kicked me out. My father and my uncle will not talk to me, they said I've disgraced my family. You see, my life is ruined." The damn finally breaks and Tatyana slumps against the window sobbing. The waitress comes over and asks if everything is alright. Tatyana waves her off and I pay the bill and help her put on her coat.

Out in the cold air, she regains some of her composure. Her pale cheeks are flushed and she looks more beautiful than ever. "A women's group took me in, and I now live with three other girls. The job at the diner is all I have. So you see Mr. Carter, there is nothing you can do to help me."

My gut is screaming to just walk away, this is none of my business, but I don't. Instead I feel a firm resolve growing in my chest. That look in her eyes, the pain of betrayal and dejection makes me want to stay. It hits me that no matter what, I was going down her path now.

"It's just Carter. Listen, this guy can't get away with this. I have a particular skill set. Let's just say I get things done for my employers that may fall outside of conventional methods. If you give me the name of this attorney, I promise he'll pay for what he did to you."

"Are you a police?" she asks.

"Something like that. Here take this for now." I hand her a thick roll of twenties.

"I can't accept this. I don't even know you. Why would you help me?"

"Look, this sleaze bag doesn't deserve to walk around breathing the same air as the rest of us. Fixing things like this is what I do. This isn't charity. I had a sister once; she was a victim just like you. Please take the money."

Tatyana closes her hand around the fold of bills and wipes away a thin trickle of tears from her swollen cheeks. "His name is Richard Fagen."

***

It turns out that dirt bag Fagen was a man of routine as well. Not only did he get home at the same time every day, he had a habit of going for a run around his fancy neighborhood right after dark. I had put in a call to a contact of mine who has a talent for finding things out. According to the temp agency records, this piece of shit had gone through six different nannies in the last two years. All quit for unexplained reasons.

I watch him for couple of days just until I'm certain of the best time to grab him. The monster is fully awake now, hungry for blood. I park a rented car along the curb near a dark patch of sidewalk where the street lights are out. I pop the trunk and leave it ajar and wait in the passenger seat with the Taser readied. When Mr. Dirt bag comes bouncing along in his five hundred dollar track suit, I jump out and put fifty thousand volts to his neck. He convulses and falls into my arms. It's over now, the cage is open and the beast is loose. There is no going back.

***

Fagen opens his eyes and I watch as his pupils dilate with fear. When he realizes he's duct taped to a chair he starts screaming through the gag in his mouth. The room is dark, and cold. I have the windows open and the sound of the barges on the river carries in on the crisp winter air. Fagen's naked, and his skin prickles against the chill. Steam rises from his sweating body. He's staring at me, trying to figure out who I am, why I have him here. He has no idea that the man standing in front of him is not a man at all, Carter Devereux, the lover of routine and order is gone. All that remains is the monster, a beast with no limits and no remorse.

Fagen tries to pull himself loose from his bindings, but only succeeds in tearing his flesh, causing drops of blood to patter on the floor.

"You like to hurt young girls? Put a little something in their drinks. Is that right?" I lean down in front of him and give him a second to take in the emptiness behind my eyes. He doesn't like what he sees and starts crying. "Everything has a cost Mr. Dirt bag. Did you honestly think you wouldn't have to pay?" I walk over to an old toolbox sitting on the concrete floor and pull out a rusty claw hammer. His eyes go wide and he heaves and snorts through his nose as he realizes this isn't a dream.

"You know, the last time I used this hammer I broke a man's jaw and fed him his own teeth one by one. It's amazing what a person will do to stop the pain. What are you willing to do Mr. Dirt bag?"

It's hard to explain what happens to me when I'm working. I feel like I'm somehow at a distance from myself. I'm outside looking in at the torture and cruelty on display before me. The monster does his work, balancing the scales, taking the pound of flesh that is owed. I just watch and wonder if when it's over I'll be able to make it back. Usually, there's an envelope of cash waiting for me at the end, unmarked and sitting in a storage locker across town. This time, things are different. I'm not here on a job. Mr. Dirt bag didn't forget to pay his bookie or try to sneak out of town with a kilo of coke that didn't belong to him. This time, it was somehow personal. This guy took what he wanted from an innocent girl and tossed her to the curb like trash. I thought about my sister, killed herself over this same kind of shit. Somebody had to do something, somebody already damned to hell; a lost cause too far from redemption to matter.

Suddenly I fall back into myself, and that far away feeling leeches right out of me into the cold night air. I'm once again in control and I can feel my hand gripping the hammer. Mr. Dirt bag is staring at me, wondering if this is truly his last moment on earth. Things are crystal now. The shadows in the room stand out in sharp relief, and I can smell the metallic wetness of the river outside. I walk over to the tool box and find a couple of sixteen penny nails.

***

I hold out my cup while Tatyana pours the coffee steady as a rock. She looks better, she still has a sadness about her, but there's a twinkle in her dark eyes when she looks at me now. She told me that she had moved out of the group home and with help from the women's center; she was taking some accounting classes. Victor was gone, but her father had finally broken his silence and they were mending the wounds one day at a time. She never asked me about the details, but she knew what I had done to Fagen. It seems word had gotten around that the police found a local attorney down at the waterfront with his scrotum nailed to a chair, the word rapist scrawled across his forehead in black marker. They're still looking for whoever did it, but Fagen isn't talking. They couldn't even get him to sit with a sketch artist. He said he couldn't stand to see that horrible face again.

***

I still have that reoccurring dream, the one where I'm walking through an empty carnival. The stuffed prizes are still hanging, their black eyes following me. The place is abandoned, and somehow I know that there's a monster loose on the fairgrounds. I walk down the midway, just like every time before, but things are different now. When I reach the entrance, my feet refuse to move, I'm stuck to the ground. I sense the beast lurking somewhere behind me. It's still a thing of pure evil, driven and unrelenting. I turn to look for the monster and catch a reflection in the glass of the ticket booth. I no longer see myself, full of rage. Instead I see all the lowlife scum I ever killed, standing in a group staring back at me. I realize that they will never leave. They are a part of me now. *They* are the monsters and I'm alright with that.

Back In The Day

By Gabriel Valjan

Dedication: *For,*
Warren Larivee 1941-2011
Vincent Tomminelli, 1942-2011

It's an annoying phrase. It really is a bad turn of words that would have you believe the day-to-day living back then was simple, pure, less complicated than today. Anybody with an iota of lived experience would tell you anything that is purported to be simple isn't; anything pure, won't be, and nothing is less than complicated, except dying.

That brings us to the point: dying. This story is about death. Plain and not so simple, complicated and not complicated.

Let's knock the nostalgia stuff out of the way: a murder story needs a *place*. Town was a place to purchase a Pullman ticket. There was usually one bank, one general foods store, and every respectable town had at least one bar or 'Social Club.' In town roads were likely not paved and you could pay a bill with a coin. Couples in town could go somewhere reputable for a bite to eat. A girl was a lady and a woman was a woman and both could teach you a thing or two. A kiss was a kiss and nobody talked about what they did in bedrooms that didn't involve sleeping. In town murder is a cozy affair, about as close and comfortable as kissing your sister, because everybody knew everybody. In town knowing someone meant you knew a name.

Our murder takes place in the city. The city is an altogether different species of living. Nobody will stop you if you want to drink your gin & tonic at 10am. A night can start at 2am and the day can begin at 2pm. There are restaurants, diners, greasy spoons, pubs, and on-the-fly food-stands for your daily eats. There is more than one newspaper with the same story twisted different ways. More than one road gets you in and more than one can get you out. Nobody knows anybody because they're usually from somewhere else, working to get by, and living where they can, often with their own kind.

See, some things don't change about murder. A man has to die sometime, and if left alone he'll die of something. One day. Murder just hurries it along. Women die every day though. They can pick up a magazine and look at the pictures. They die. They can go out to see the pictures, look up at the screen and they die. Beauty kills.

The *why* a man dies is an entirely philosophical matter. We're not talking about the self-ordained kind of death and not the one that the woman upstairs writes on the back of the slip when you're born. I know God is a woman. It explains the humor in this world, like why flamingoes have their kneecaps on backwards. As I was saying about a man and his dying…he could die because he has a cause he believes in, but that really is a lie. What that really means is that a man is willing to put himself in a situation again and again that improves the probability of it happening. Call it possibility and mathematicians will call it probability. Others may call it suicide, and some may call it sacrifice. Dead is dead. Murder is a little more precise than that.

Dying for love? Men may not die for love but they'll kill for it. Let's skip this one for now.

In my city the tough guys are the ones that can afford manicures and the deadly ones get themselves pedicures. In this story the murder is over the most obvious cause – sex. There's your motive.

In this murder there are people: there is a lady, a

mobbed-up mick cop, a Jew, a creative-type brother of the lady just mentioned, and a dead WASP. Oh, and there's me.

I forgot. Back in the day we talked that way. We didn't say Ms., Irish or Italian-American. In my city the Irish were considered equal if not below coloreds. Life was so bad for the Irish that there were signs hung up in the windows everywhere telling them they 'Need Not Apply Here. Irish are Unwelcome' but the mean joke was that the Irish had to see the signs but the coloreds were the ones who could read them. No lie. It took a lot more blood and cracked heads than pulling a pint of Guinness to see an Irishman walking the beat.

Coloreds ran the numbers for the Jews or Italians. Once the Italians either killed off the Jews or the Jews went white-collar and left some version of Shylock to run the neighborhood street corner to feed the anti-Semites there was the rest of us fighting over our daily bread. Nobody wants to talk about these things. Each group had their quarter of the city. The Italians ran their neighborhood like their opera, with a fear of sex, respect for the priest, and every now and then, they put out for display some schlep face down in his bowl of pasta, because he rolled out too much dough that belonged to someone else.

Me? I grew up on the West End with a mongrel mix of Irish, Italian, and some coloreds. Us kids feared the old ladies because every one of them was our Mom and every one of them held authority like the law – more so than the beat cops. Lottie, the colored lady on our block, for example, was one such lady and us kids never called her a shine or a nigger or anything vulgar like that, because if we did there was a gauntlet of apron strings to fear more than Jesus. Today the West End is a place for some nice condos with a hospital facing the river.

Let's get back to the murder. Oh, and one more thing

you need to understand about my city. It's an old city. The rich folks had their mansions all right. The one thing that separated the rich from the poor back then was a zip code. Wealth lived on the top of the hill and poverty at the bottom. Remember that because it is important. Some things never change.

There was Constance but we called her Connie. Sully was the cop. He retired last I heard. There was Ray. He ended up in San Francisco where walking the hills can give you a heart attack. Lest we forget, there is Charles Davenport III. And then there is me.

Always start with the girl. Constance was a constellation in her own right here on earth. She was a genuine Harlow blonde uptown and downtown, half-class and half-trash if there was a glass of champagne in her hand, in and out of a grape-skin dress. That was her dust-jacket presentation to the world. Connie could laugh and play, like a kid in a pile of leaves. I know because she became my Connie.

A girl had to make a living then and Connie was one of the burlesque queens. Stripper isn't the right word because burlesque is a lost art form. There was more suggestion with gloves and boa feathers instead of the bump-and-grind shows around today. Gynecology was something that belonged in a doctor's office and not on a stage or a screen. Burlesque required you use your brain while it worked other parts of you. The end result was it separated you from your money; and on a good night you didn't mind.

If the world enshrined Gypsy Rose Lee for her days at the Addison as the undisputed diva of burlesque then I need to remind you of other legends of tease and taunt, like Little Egypt, and Sally Keith. Connie was what you would call an understudy to Ann Corio, performing at the Howard Athenaeum, the same place where both Booths performed, turning out *Macbeth* and *Hamlet* to sold-out audiences. The

Howard was near the hill where I told you that the moneyed types live. For the time it lasted – and it lasted quite some time – the rich went slumming late at night and the poor climbed out of their boxes and rented out the top drawer, until the politicians razed the Bulfinch Triangle and built those impersonal cheese-grater granite government buildings.

There were no words to describe Connie on the stage. She was a burning angel under the stage lights. She had her name in neon on the marquee. That became a problem and you'll see why soon.

Sully. He was a good guy. We were friends even though we walked opposite sides of the street. His old man worked the docks and his mother schooled him at home about matters back in the Old Country. She was not entirely pleased with the school curriculum those days. She wanted her boy to know that the Irish could write. Sully and I had our differences but a drink and discussing books resolved them quickly. Have to say the Irish know how to write. Sully woke up every morning and crossed himself citing Beckett, Joyce, and O'Brien as the Holy Trinity.

We'll deal with Charles Davenport III later.

Ray. Loved the guy because I had to. He was Connie's brother. He was a well-dressed sight. Ray always wore the soft colors. First time I saw Ray he was wearing these linen slacks that never seemed to wrinkle, a light pink dress shirt and a dead-canary pullover tied off with a polka-dot ascot. He had a slightly pitched voice that turned your head when you heard it. The way he walked I can't describe. Ray was the kid you beat up on the playground until Sis came to his rescue. Ray was a delicate kid, an artistic child, and so sensitive that he could gag on his morning toothbrush. That arrangement with Sis worked fine until Ray miraculously developed a jab-and-right hook combination of his own. Sis got time off and spent it understanding the effect her curves in satin had on the rest of us.

Ray had the habit of visiting Connie after her last performance of the night. She'd sign some courtesy autographs for the men in uniform before she went to her room. Despite what people think, sailors were respectable then and waited like kids staring at the gumball machine to get her sinewy signature; and if they were foolish enough to act improper there was Big Bill, one of the coloreds there to teach them etiquette. Bill was a gentleman and a fine Othello who should have had more in life had people been a little more open-minded.

Ray came in one day. "Connie, I've got the tickets. Bill Tilden against Don Budge."

"That's wonderful, darling," Connie said, as she took off her earrings and worked her way over to the clamshell screen to shimmy her way out of her dress, "When is the match?" her eyes asked over the lacquered wood.

"In two weeks, Saturday afternoon," Ray responded, holding his prized tickets to the tennis match.

"Oh, I don't know, Ray. The girls and I have rehearsals. We have a big show and management is planning to let us know if we have that private show or not. Awfully sweet of you to think of me." Connie had put on a less risqué number and came out from behind the screen.

"Private show? Connie, I really don't like these private shows. I know the money is good, but I worry that things'll get out of hand." Ray looked down at his two tickets and swept them into one, pocketing them.

"Now, your Sis can take care of herself. I took care of you for years and I understand that you're trying to make up for it, but I'll be all right. And besides, I have Big Bill." Connie tilted her feet into a pair of silver heels that made her walk the skyline.

"Big Bill is a good man, but these men have money.

You know that. You also know that if they get hungry they'll want to eat." Ray stood there brotherly.

Mae West hips had nothing on Connie when she walked across the room, not that they would affect Ray. "Now, look here, Ray. I've got my own mind. You're right. They have money and they should have manners, too. If any of those Harvard boys get any funny ideas that Big Bill can't correct himself, I'll just slap the eyebrows off any one of those overgrown brats. It isn't Christmas and nobody is going to undo the wrapping unless I say so. Got it?"

Ray turned a shade. Connie pinched his cheek and kissed it. She took his arm in one hand and her sequin purse in the other. That purse of hers was shiny, small, and held her money clip, lipstick, and a derringer, like the one Booth used.

We met up for breakfast over at Joe &Nemo's over at Cambridge and Stoddard Streets. Breakfast was actually lunch for us but none of us listened to rules, especially Connie. Her one sin a week was one of those famous hot dogs. The place had breakfast and a steak dinner with all the works but Connie always had herself a 'one all around' which is a water-cooked dog on a steamed roll with mustard, relish, onions and horse radish. Joe broke a good egg and I loved his spooning the bacon fat over it to brown the eggs something nice. That was my dish.

Ray told me about Tilden. He had two tickets he reminded me. I knew Ray liked my company but I had to decline. Not a big fan of tennis. He tried Sully later but Sully turned him down because he said being seen seeing Tilden would be bad for his reputation on the force.

Now, Charles Davenport III was, as the name tells you, old money. He lived on the hill and once in a while, when he wasn't making more of it or inheriting it, he came down from his gilded perch to spend it. Charles had a taste for flesh and he used a C note to acquire girls like they were rental properties. Charlie managed to get every girl in the place except Connie.

Connie was no temple virgin nor would you find her in the choir at midnight Saturday Mass, but she was a decent girl. She made her money honestly. The other girls were struggling and they did what they had to do even if that meant the likes of Davenport and his band of bowties.

Charles was a Harvard legacy. His grandfather was a one-dollar-a-year Harvard professor; and rumor had it that if you went rummaging through his closet you might find some Puritans and some floorboards from the Mayflower. He talked proper. He drank tea. He wore his top hat and his bowtie, imported from England. He walked with a cane not because he had a limp but the accessory matched his social status as royalty in the New World. The only thing missing on Charles was that silken handkerchief to pull out from under his sleeve to cover his genteel nose when he passed us poor in the street.

Davenport hired out the hall for the private party. He liked champagne, cigars, and expected with each passing hour that the girls lose their clothing until they had nothing but what God gave them on their first day. Then the real fun would begin behind locked doors and closed windows. Had there been a scream or call for help no cop with the best ears in the city would hear a thing. Big Bill had a full night; and rich, white boys who made in one day several times over what he made all year made him as nervous as a kitten surrounded by unfed German shepherds.

The calendar squares flew off the wall and two weeks later, Saturday appeared. Ray found himself someone to take to that Tilden and Budge match. Him and his friend took the train out of state and had themselves a good time. Sully was at work. I was home balancing the books and planning to read one from Sully's library. I think it was Flann O'Brien. I had tried Beckett but every time I looked up I lost my place in one of his sentences and had to wind back my brain to remember where I was. I gave up. The evening plan was to visit Connie and take her to Joe &Nemo's after the private show.

The phone rang. I don't like phones but my boss insisted I get one. He paid for it so the leash sat on the table. So when it rang I knew it was the Boss on the line. Nobody else called on the exclusive line.

I told the operator, "Put him through."

"What is it, Sap?" I said all polite to the man who paid my bills. Sap was short for Leo Saperstein. He was a professional gambler. I ran his numbers and if I played out like a good ace he might promote me up to the higher rackets. Sap was a New York Jew, had run with Lansky and Siegel, but after his good friend Arnold Rothstein got clipped he left town. He respected Meyer's business-sense but Bugsy Siegel and Charlie Luciano scared him. He told me that Arnold was old business and Meyer Lansky was new business but Bugsy and Charlie were murderous thugs with about as much self-control as drunks staring at a full bottle of Scotch.

"Hey, I think you need to get over to The Howard," he said to me over the phone. We kept our conversations as minimalist as one of those awful canvases in the museums. The cops listened in at times.

"I think there is trouble over there," Leo said calmly.

"How'd you know if there was?" I asked. "And besides, Big Bill is covering the floor. He knows how to fend for himself."

He was about to say something but I could feel worry weighing down his voice. I said to him, "C'mon, Leo, I'm sure it's nothing; and besides, I thought Jews don't touch phones on the Sabbath."

Leo cleared his throat. I knew he was a killer if the push

turned to a shove and the wall was behind him, but only I could get away with ribbing him about his religion. I heard his bristle, "That's Orthodox Jews, numbskull. I'm a reformed Jew."

"All right, all right, Leo. You know I was kidding, right? Keep your yarmulke on, will ya?"

Leo wasn't laughing. "I'm sorry, Leo. What makes you think there's trouble there?"

"My cousin called me and said that Davenport was creeping the girls out, seemed hell-bent on Connie."

"Your cousin?" I asked.

"Yeah, my cousin. He goes to Harvard. He tagged along. He left when things turned sour. I just got off the wire with him." My brain did a swivel and I almost had to ask, Since when did Harvard let in Jews, but Leo was ahead of me by several paragraphs and answered, "Yeah, he's the only Jew in Harvard. Spare me your jokes. We had to change his name a little, but that's another story. If you care about the girl you better get over there pronto. I've seen one crazy Charlie in my life and this Davenport is busting up the place something mean, and I wouldn't put it past him if he'd gut her if he she didn't give him the sugar for his sweet tooth."

I had clammy sweat breaking out on the back of my neck. Leo had his way with words so when he said crazy Charlie I knew he wasn't being poetic comparing Davenport to Luciano. I had asked Leo about Lucky once and the man got as quiet as a nun at high mass. Leo loved his old pal Rothstein and could gab about the man's impeccable brain and clothes, and mock Fitzgerald for his portraying Arnold as the cartoonish Meyer Wolfsheim, but droopy-eyed Luciano gave him the sweats like Davenport was giving me. I mopped the sweat and threw the handkerchief next to the phone. Looking back at it now, I'm sure that kerchief was a modern day Shroud of Turin.

I rang Sully and told him to meet me near the hall. He needled me but all I had to say was that Connie was in trouble. I said Davenport. That was all it took. "Meet you at the Trick & Joke Shop." I knew when I hung up that I could count on Sully bringing his Irish charm.

I snatched some poor Joe out of a cab, sticking a fresh twenty in his hand for my rudeness. My mother would be proud if she were alive. I saw Sully in the dark. He wore his London Fog over his uniform.

"How we get in?" he asked me.

"You're the cop. I thought you guys do this all the time," I replied, unable to get a grin out of him. Sully stingy on smiles meant someone was going to have a bad day.

"Around back, side alley. We can use the door," I directed him. His look asked me how I knew so I told him, "Actors used it to break away from the crowds."

Sully had to ask, "And you use it for your conjugal visits to Connie?" I gave him a cold eye that told him to zip it.

The door gave off a metallic shrill like it hadn't been pulled since John Winthrop came to town. The place was dark. We heard a bottle break but no idea from where the sound came since the theater carried acoustics well.

We found Big Bill on the floor, cold-cocked and dreaming about the big headache that he would have in the morning. Two of the girls appeared out of nowhere running down the curved hall. They were so scared they had no clothes on and we were too surprised to appreciate it. They were terrified. They told us that most of the Harvard boys had left but there were one or two passed out from drinking. When we had asked where Connie was the girls said that Davenport had dragged her off to one of the private balconies.

Sully and I looked at each other. A private balcony was

a sweet view of the stage with plenty of room. The high price also gave the owner for the evening some privacy by providing a door that he could lock from the inside. Unless Sully and I had any ambition to imitate Tarzan the only way up was the velvet curtain and for Connie the only way down was a jump that if she were lucky would break one of her legs like Booth did in DC after he plugged Lincoln behind the ear. There was screaming behind the door. Like an idiot I had to turn the knob to confirm what I already knew. It was locked.

Sully whispered, "I can shoot the knob and we can bust through."

I didn't approve, "And what if he panics and pitches her over the side or takes her with him and uses her to break his fall?" We looked at each other and the idea that Davenport would use her as a flying carpet sickened us.

"Here, take this," Sully said. He handed me a shiv and instructed me to start prying at the wedge and crease where the lock met the wood. I looked at him like his wheel had rolled off his bike and had gone down the street alone. Sully pushed me to my task. "I'll talk to him and buy us time," Sully said. "You have a better idea?" he asked me. I got on my knees next to the door and worked like a quiet termite with one sharp tooth.

"Hey, Davenport!" he pounded on the door. "It's me, Sullivan."

"Which one? Sullivan is a common enough mick name," the snarling voice said from the other side of the nice wooden door. Sully smiled for a second. He looked down and he motioned to me to keep digging away. I did.

Sully used his respectful police persuasion. "The downtown Sullivan, the one you pay fifty a week to overlook your fun and games over in Cambridge. Remember now? Daddy isn't going to be happy about this escapade, Junior, so why don't we call it a wrap and act civil. Let the lady go and

I'll get you a cup of coffee. Nobody will know and everyone will forget. Get me?"

"I paid for her," the man screamed from the other side. We heard Connie's voice saying some unladylike things. Davenport had turned out to be one of those customers who had a broader definition of service on the side.

I was splintering wood with the makeshift knife. The taped handle conformed to my hand nicely. I could tell it had been used but I was afraid to ask, knew I shouldn't. The knife's edge was touching the little metal flap that clicks into place. I just needed to push it and turn the knob just right and we would be in.

"Hey Davenport?" Sully yelled.

"What is it?" rich boy bellowed back. The tone of his voice was telling me I had to get the damn door open soon.

"Why don't you pick yourself another girl? Imagine it, Davenport. The two of you share a nice glass of champagne, an evening out on the town, and when you get back to your place you hold her nice and watch that nice dress of hers drop to the floor. You can read her poetry from Barrett and Browning and treat her to some chocolate and ..." I pulled on Sully's trench and asked him, "What the hell are you doing?" The last thing I expected to hear was the Irish serenade.

His hand turned my head into the door wedge. I got the tip of the knife against the metal and with my other hand grabbed the doorknob. Sully looked down and saw that I was ready. Our eyes met and we agreed that we both would open and charge the room.

The door flung open. I was on the ground crawling and trying to stand up. I didn't see it but a shot went off. I looked up at Sully but there was no smoke from his gun so I spun my neck the other way, looking for Connie. I didn't quite see it the way I should've because it happened so quickly.

It seems Davenport had Connie wedged deep into the seat. When Sully barged in he saw him and the silver tips of her shoes on either side of Davenport's head. As Davenport's eyes met Sully's Connie's long white arm emerged out from the velvet underneath with her derringer. She had put the muzzle up and under Davenport's chin and pulled the trigger.

When I stood up Davenport had already stepped back and was moving backwards to the balcony edge. We heard the thud seconds later. It was an awful sound. Sully and I rushed over to the edge and looked down. Davenport, for all his money, was dead. His body looked like a little contorted puppet down there. He lost a few shirt studs on the way down but the untied bowtie lay nicely on his tipped collar. The coroner man said the bullet hole that let his final thoughts out the top of his head killed him.

The police came and in true city fashion they wanted to haul off Big Bill for killing Davenport. The detectives made a big stink about a colored being bodyguard to a bunch of lily-white burlesque girls. Sully gave Connie his trench coat. I got Leo on the wire.

It all worked out in the end. Big Bill took a bruising at the station but he was let go. Leo knew some judges higher up in the circuit than the ones the Davenports knew. It was nice to see new money beat old money. Leo made all the arrangements. It cost Connie her career in town.

The Davenports weren't an easy tribe to deal with. When Ray came back he did a brave thing. Like Leo's cousin he knew the social scene on the other side of the river and made it known that Davenport was doing his version of a Tilden. See, back in the day gay and queer had a different meaning. It was unfortunate then that when someone used the name Tilden it was like mentioning Chaplin. It was a stand-in for moral degeneracy. When the Davenports heard that Ray was willing to get up on the stand and say that he was one of them and that their boy played in the same pond, it all went away rather nicely in the end.

Me? I owed Leo. He did Connie and me a big favor. The big boys were hammering up a tax evasion charge on Leo. Let's just say that Sully and I looked over the books before the Feds did. With an eraser here and there I made it look like that I had cooked Leo's books and ran off with some of his money. When the bookworms finally took off their green visors and pulled the chain on their banker's lamps they concluded I was liable for Leo's math problem. Since Sully did well with the Davenport case and exhibited his clover charm at every turn, he got bumped up to Detective. I got a nickel upstate but Leo made sure I did only a year.

When I got out Connie was on the other side waiting for me. She was wearing Sully's coat and inside a paper bag she had brought two of her 'one all around' dogs. We were married for fifty-plus years. I'm an old man now but life has been good to me, always been good to me, even back in the day.

Author Biographies

Linda Angel was born in Liverpool where, after a brief dalliance with Radio City, decided that she didn't even have a face for radio. After dabbling in forensics, she finally resigned to fact that she was, apparently, rather good at the ol' writing lark and should probably do more of it. Since then, she's become a produced screenwriter for trafico (filmed in NYC and NJ), and her collection of weird shorts and verse, Stranger Companies, shall be out in 2016, published by Kuboa Press.

Bill Baber has had over two dozen crime stories published and his stories have recently appeared in *Rogue* from *Near to the Knuckle*, *Hardboiled Crime Scene* from *Dead Guns Press* and *Locked & Loaded* from *One Eye Press*. His 2014 short story *Sleepwalk* was nominated for a Derringer Award. He has also had a number of poems published online – one of which is being considered for a Best of the Net Award- and in the occasional literary journal. A book of his poetry, *Where the Wind Comes to Play* was published by *Berberis Press* in 2011. He lives in Tucson with his wife and a spoiled dog and has been known to cross the border for a cold beer. He is working on his first novel.

Jason Beech writes crime fiction and the occasional bit of horror. He learned to write by reading the likes of Ellroy, Iain Banks, and the ton of authors who light up Shotgun Honey and The Flash Fiction Offensive. His books include Bullets, Teeth & Fists, and Triple Zombie (co-authored with James Newman and John Bruni). He has two crime fiction books coming out soon - a novel called Moorlands, and a short story collection, Turn a Blind Eye. You can find him at Messy Business - **jdbeech.wordpress.com**.

Ryan Bracha is the author of the Amazon best selling Strangers Are Just Friends You Haven't Killed Yet, Tomorrow's Chip Paper, Bogies, and other equally messed up tales of love, lust, drugs and grandad porn, and the The Dead Man Trilogy. His latest attack on your sense of taste is his sleazy, supernatural thriller The Switched. **http://ryanbracha.webs.com**

Robert Cowan is the author of novels 'The Search for Ethan' and Daydreams and Devils', with a third, 'For all is Vanity' out in early spring 16. He also appears in Near to the Knuckle's anthology, 'Rogue.' **http://robertcowanbooks.com/**

Christopher Davis is a central California native and grandfather of three rambunctious little ones. When not tending the herd, he writes fiction. Find out more at **www.christopherdaviswrites.com**

Craig Furchtenicht lives in rural Iowa, where many of his stories that span between the realm of drug-fueled crime novels and the absurd take place. His other works include Dimebag Bandits, Behind The Eight Ball and Night Speed Zero. Check out his blog and facebook pages at: **https://www.facebook.com/Fearnotbooks/ http://feartheindie.blogspot.com/**

J. David Jaggers lives in fly over country, where he spends his days in the white collar world of finance and his nights writing about the degenerates and losers dwelling in shadows of our brightly lit society. He has been published in Thuglit, Shotgun Honey, Near to the Knuckle, Pulp Metal, and various other magazines and anthologies. He has a short story collection Down In The Devil Hole available from Gritfiction Ltd. and you can find links to all of his published work at Straightrazorfiction.com

Cal Marciusis a north-east writer who has been published online and in print. You can find Cal at **http://calmarcius.wordpress.com** and on Facebook and Twitter.

Matt Mattila has had his fiction and non-fiction published in numerous magazines, anthologies, and live events online, in print, and in person. You can find his ramblings on both Facebook and eventually on the blog he's in the middle of making.

Keith Nixonhas been writing since he was a child. In fact some of his friends (& his family) say he's never really grown up. Keith is currently gainfully employed in a senior sales role for a UK based high-tech company meaning he gets to use his one skill, talking too much. Keith writes crime and historical fiction novels.
Amazon page:http://www.amazon.co.uk/Keith-Nixon **website: http://www.keithnixon.co.uk/**

Darren Sant is a cynical bloke in his forties. He tries to keep the situations and dialogue in his fiction as realistic as possible but has been known to veer off on crazy tangents. He lives in Hull with his long suffering wife, Julie, and a distainful cat. You can find him on Twitter as @groovydaz39

Gareth Spark's short fiction and poetry appears widely on-line and in the small presses. He reviews poetry for *Fjords Review*, among others. He lives and works in Whitby, Yorkshire, and his latest collection is *Snake Farm* (Electraglade Press).

Aidan Thorn's first short story collection, Criminal Thoughts was released in 2013 and his second, Urban Decay, was published by Grit Fiction in 2015. In September 2015 Number 13 Press published Aidan's first novella, When the Music's Over.
http://aidanthornwriter.weebly.com

Gabriel Valjan lives in Boston, Massachusetts. Winter Goose Publishing is the publisher of his thriller series: Book 1: *Roma, Underground*, 2: *Wasp's Nest*, 3: *Threading the Needle* and 4: *Turning to Stone*. Book 5: *Corporate Citizen* is scheduled for 2016. An historical fiction series about the early days of the intelligence community will appear in 2017. You can visit his web and sample his writing at **www.gabrielvaljan.com**

Graham Wynd A writer of bleakly noirish tales with a bit of grim humour, Graham Wynd can be found in Dundee but would prefer you didn't come looking. An English professor by day, Wynd grinds out darkly noir prose between trips to the local pub, including SATAN'S SORORITY from Number Thirteen Press and EXTRICATE from Fox Spirit Books. See more stories (including free reads!) at **www.GrahamWynd.com**.

Printed in Great Britain
by Amazon